DIVINING the LEAVES

DIVINING the LEAVES

SHVETA THAKRAR

HARPER
An Imprint of HarperCollins*Publishers*

Library of Congress Control Number: 2024945849

ISBN 978-0-06-325526-5

Typography by Corina Lupp

24 25 26 27 28 LBC 5 4 3 2 1

First Edition

For Renee Melton and Angie Richmond, who helped me grow this leafy novel from a vague mental seed into an actual story sprout. This book never would have taken root without the soil and water of your enthusiastic support.

For Annaka Kalton, who brought her gardener self to bear when I needed it most and helped me guide that sprout into a mature tree. What would I have done without you?

And for Lisa Eshkenazi, who swept in with her huge heart and helped me prune the resulting tree into its blossom-bedecked final form. What a generous friend you are.

Go by coombe, by candle light,
by moonlight, starlight, stepping stone,
and step o'er bracken, branches, briars,
and go tonight, and go alone,
go by water, go by willow,
go by ivy, oak and ash,
and rowan berries red as blood,
and breadcrumbs, stones, to mark the path;
find the way by water's whisper,
water rising from a womb
of granite, peat, of summer heat,
to slake your thirst and fill the coombe
and tumble over moss and stone
and feed the roots of ancient trees
and call to you: go, now, tonight,
by water, earth, phyllomancy,
by candle flame, by spirit-name,
by spells, by portents, myth and song,
by drum beat, heart beat, earth pulsing
beneath your feet, calling you home,
calling you back, calling you through
the water, wood, the waste, the wild . . .

—EXCERPTED FROM TERRI WINDLING'S

"THE NIGHT JOURNEY"

On Rama's shady peak where hermits roam,
Mid streams by Sita's bathing sanctified,
   An erring Yaksha made his hapless home,
Doomed by his master humbly to abide,
And spend a long, long year of absence from his bride.

   Some months were gone; the lonely lover's pain
Had loosed his golden bracelet day by day
   Ere he beheld the harbinger of rain,
A cloud that charged the peak in mimic fray,
As an elephant attacks a bank of earth in play.

[. . .]

   Longing to save his darling's life, unblest
With joyous tidings, through the rainy days,
   He plucked fresh blossoms for his cloudy guest,
Such homage as a welcoming comrade pays,
And bravely spoke brave words of greeting and of praise.

[. . .]

   O cloud, the parching spirit stirs thy pity;
My bride is far, through royal wrath and might;
   Bring her my message to the Yaksha city,
Rich-gardened Alaka, where radiance bright
From Shiva's crescent bathes the palaces in light.

[. . .]

Yet hasten, O my brother, till thou see—
Counting the days that bring the lonely smart—
The faithful wife who only lives for me:
A drooping flower is woman's loving heart,
Upheld by the stem of hope when two true lovers part.

—SELECTED VERSES FROM *MEGHADUTA*,
OR *THE CLOUD MESSENGER*, BY KALIDASA
(TRANSLATED FROM THE SANSKRIT
BY ARTHUR W. RYDER)

PART ONE

*O*n the third of the nine nights of Navratri, the celebration honoring goddess Durga, a call as slight as spider silk murmured through the mandir. Most revelers heard nothing, but four-year-old Bhavna eluded her mother's watchful eye long enough to sneak out of the saturated colors and lively music of garba, past a wild pumpkin patch, and into the night-shrouded woods beyond.

A yakshini swayed there, her lithe frame swathed in a sari of fall foliage. Fire gems tumbled from her fingers, ringed her throat, dotted the licorice-dark tresses twirling down her back. She wove about the trees, her skin the color of a peeled cedar and just as smooth.

The trees, clad in leaves of crackling flame, sported the same gemstones in crimsons, oranges, deep yellows, and purples, the fruit dripping from their branches. Those autumn jewels gleamed beneath the black of the midnight sky, ripe with story.

Bhavna recognized them immediately. Hers was a heart shaped by narrative, as dreamers' hearts always are, ever eager for new tales.

"Have you come to trick-or-treat?" the yakshini asked. "It is not yet

1

All Hallows' Eve, and I have no candy for your bucket."

Shivering in the crisp, woodsmoke-tinged air, Bhavna shook her head.

"Have you come to chase away the old year's shadows? It is not yet Deepavali, and I have no oil for your diya."

Again Bhavna refuted her.

"Then why have you come?"

Bhavna had come for adventure, for spells and secrets. For all the things her mother's fables had hinted were real. The deepest part of her heart thirsted for them. She pointed to the grove of gems. "For those."

The yakshini looked wary. *"Autumn jewels are not for foolish mortal creatures. Begone."*

Bhavna stubbornly continued to point.

"I do like your jhanjhar," the yakshini allowed. Bhavna promptly unhooked the silver anklets and extended them in offering.

The yakshini considered, long enough that Bhavna grew antsy. She peered at the glittering landscape behind the yakshini, where witchy daayan cavorted, their long hair swinging freely as they hit their sticks together in dandiya-raas. Though they frightened her, with their eerie cackles and frenzied eyes, she still yearned to go to them, to strike her own dandiya against theirs in the fast-paced dance.

"No," said the yakshini at last. She pointed to the heavens, where even the stars had closed their eyes for the night. *"But you see we lack a moon. Bring me one the daayan will not eat, and you will have your jewels."*

In the years that followed, Bhavna hunted everywhere for such a moon. Even as others went to plays and parties, she perused leather-bound books of myths and lore. She filled journal after journal with curiosities: snippets of furtive nocturnal conversations, pressed moonflower petals, half-finished love songs scribbled on coffee-stained napkins. Each night, the daayan screeched invitations in her dreams, and the autumn jewels crooned promises of magic. Something more, something greater than this.

Five-year-old Bhavna brought the yakshini a small wheel of Brie, which the daayan gobbled so fast, she barely saw it happen. In retrospect, that hadn't been the best decision. Who didn't like cheese?

Ten-year-old Bhavna brought a picture of the moon cut from a magazine. The daayan shredded it to ribbons and scarfed them down, then complained it tasted of newsprint.

"These things have no substance," scolded the yakshini, pushing Bhavna back out. "Bring me a moon with meaning."

Fifteen-year-old Bhavna returned with a lunar lantern, one she liked so much she'd purchased an extra one for herself. This had to be the moon that would illuminate the late-October thicket.

Her heart pounding, she slipped the lamp from its hiding place in the pumpkin patch and hurried toward the trees. Finally she would win the jewels of story and soothe the ache inside.

Yet the clearing was bare. Not a twig rustled, no matter how long she searched; no branch shifted that she didn't brush against.

They had left her. She had failed.

Eventually, knowing she would be missed at the mandir, she left the moon lantern in the dirt. The toy's light shone faintly, lost in the gloom.

Bhavna didn't try again after that, just stayed at the garba each Navratri and gripped her dandiya tightly as she danced, her jhanjhar tinkling about her ankles.

As if the only story that existed was this one.

When the familiar chill stirred her bones in summons once more, twenty-five-year-old Bhavna scarcely dared to believe it.

The forest had faded from brilliant scarlet and pumpkin orange to dried blood and rust, and the leaves had fallen from the trees and crunched beneath her feet. Yet she didn't mind, not when she'd been given one last chance to prove she understood.

The bhootnis whirled that night amid the trees, the vetalis and rakshasis, too. A bone palace rose up around them, the yakshini in its doorway.

"You took too long," the yakshini said, her mouth pinched. "But we still want for a moon."

Bhavna smiled. "I brought you a moon."

She spread her bag's contents over the ground. Unfulfilled wishes in crystal bottles, tiny dreams she'd written down on scraps of paper—both hers and others'—and milky moonstones to bind them, all carefully squirreled away in a wooden chest in the hope that one day, they might be needed.

A moon with meaning—her story for theirs.

The yakshini echoed her smile.

Together Bhavna and the yakshini assembled the shimmering bits of unspoken things into a mosaic, plump and lambent with silver light and longing. Once it had hardened, they mounted the freshly made moon on the shadowed-sapphire sky.

In response, a bevy of monstrous women emerged from the trees: daayan, harpies, faeries, apsaras, naginis, banshees, and more. Their beauty, their ferocity, glowed as each gifted Bhavna one autumn jewel. Story upon story soaked into her skin, quenching her thirst.

Then, led by the yakshini, the circle of women raised their dandiya and spoke:

"Welcome, fellow dreamer, to the Sisterhood of the Moon."

—FROM *THE TALES THAT TREES TELL*,
A COLLECTION FROM ALAKAPURI AND BEYOND

1

The bright green sassafras leaves above Ridhi Kapadia's head whirled in a sinuous dance with the brisk early-March breeze, whispering secrets to those willing to take the time to listen.

Me, thought Ridhi. She paused, the entrance to her woods a few tempting feet away. *I'm willing to listen.*

Any other day, she would have dashed through the slight gap in the trees to write in her journal, maybe embellish the words with purple and white crocuses she'd press between the silver-edged pages, with the hope of channeling those secrets.

Any other day, she'd sit nestled in the dip at the base of her favorite sycamore, the one overlooking the trickle of a stream, and fill her lungs with the fragrance of the forest. Daydreams of that scent would swirl through her, dyed in sun-lacquered grass and clover and textured by wonder tales and poetry, and later, at her desk, Ridhi would strive to reimagine it as a wearable perfume for her online shop.

Any other day. But that day, she had an audition to get to.

As she hurried on, twigs cracked under her shoes, and the spongy moss that carpeted many of the rocks and decaying wood did its best to lure her close. Ridhi could picture a thick clump of it pillowed beneath her head, soft and fluffy, perfect for a nap. She'd been too wound up to sleep the night before, her bharatanatyam routine looping in her mind.

A spot had recently opened up on the elite local team run by the lauded Varsha Reddy, and Mummy had wasted no time wrangling Ridhi an audition. Not only would that look good on her college scholarship applications in the fall, her parents had gushed, but Mummy, a former competitive dancer herself, couldn't wait to see her daughter follow in her stylized footsteps and perform onstage as part of a troupe.

Ordinarily, Ridhi never would have agreed to try out. She had no desire to dance for other people. But one glimpse of Mummy's hope, and all Ridhi's defenses had crumbled. Mummy wanted nothing more than for her lonely daughter to find friends and belong, like she had. How could Ridhi let her down?

Her beloved trees must have sensed her frazzled nerves, reviving her, their presence as reassuring as a river of sunlight. If only she could sink into their comforting embrace.

This particular wild grove half a mile from her house had been Ridhi's sanctuary for as long as she could remember, speaking to her through scattered magic: an acorn hollowed out just enough for a rolled-up clandestine message; a dew-beaded spiderweb shawl an apsara might sling about her shoulders to ward off a chill; even an iridescent blue morpho butterfly that had mysteriously appeared on a bush like a goblin queen's emissary, nowhere near its native habitat. One day, she was certain, her woods, so reminiscent of the stories of the mythical yaksha kingdom and its marvelous capital city of Alakapuri, would lead her there—the sooner, the better.

Right then, the effect was spoiled by the half-crushed juice bottle someone had tossed into a beautyberry bush, directly below a faded "No Littering" sign. Never mind that the recycling bin was a handy two steps away.

With a sigh, she bent and took hold of the grimy bottle's peeling label.

"No fair!" a guy's voice slurred, spooking her. "My turn."

Ahead, half hidden where the dirt path began, a college-aged couple was sloppily making out. The woman held a can of beer out of the guy's reach.

"You can't have it," she taunted.

When he groped for it, the contents sloshed over his hand. The rest of the six-pack lay at their feet, and as Ridhi knew from experience, the cans would soon replace the bottle.

Ever since the convenience store had moved into the adjoining lot, its customers had taken to treating her woods like a dumpster. Not even her trash walks could keep up with the mess.

Ridhi had tried petitioning the city council to designate this copse as a nature preserve. They'd declined on the grounds that Atlanta already had ordinances in place to protect its famous canopy of trees.

It wasn't like she disagreed. The local parks were clean and well cared for, and wandering the leafy streets where she'd spent a good chunk of her seventeen years felt like strolling through an arboretum, rich with crab apples and persimmons and loblolly pines that lent sparkle to the dreariest of gray days.

But *these* were her woods. They always would be.

"Hey!" the guy yelled. "Where's my wallet? Someone stole my wallet!"

The woman shrugged. "Don't look at me."

Tuning them out, Ridhi dropped the discarded bottle into the nearby bin.

Behind her, the boughs rustled once more, shedding leaves as if in thanks.

Her phone beeped. It was Mummy. *You'll be fantastic. Remember to ask after Varsha Auntie's health. She's very traditional.*

I know, I know, Ridhi texted back, laughing. Mummy had given her that same advice that morning. And the day before. Mummy might actually be more anxious about the audition than she was.

Again the urge to stay put tugged at her, but after a last, wistful glance at the trees and the refuge they promised, Ridhi continued along the street.

Unlike her woods, the trees there were waking from their winter sleep. When the wind blew through their mostly bare branches, she shivered and burrowed deeper into her velvet coat. Hints of the numinous soughed in the lessening of its chill, in the tightly coiled buds that would soon unfurl into verdant leaves and chromatic flowers. She wished she could pluck those hints from the first stirring breaths of spring and dab them on her wrists like one of her natural perfumes.

Mummy and video tutorials hadn't been Ridhi's only dance teachers. So had the towering trees, with the graceful arch of their branches, the twist of their trunks, the ripple of leaves like waves of hair blowing back. She battled the impulse to throw down her bag and spin for them, there under the almost-spring sky.

Grasping her pendant of Aranyani Devi, she conjured the picture her mother had painted, of Ridhi astounding a packed auditorium with her skill and poise. It might be a borrowed dream, yet if she angled her outlook just right, she could conform to it, especially as the drive to move, to flow and sway, warmed her like a sample of the enchantment she'd always craved.

The optimism she'd learned long ago to suppress welled up, too, buoyant and so very appealing. Maybe Mummy was right. Maybe when they saw what she could do, Ridhi would find a place among the other dancers. They would take her in, and she would finally be part of something. She'd belong.

That was even worth her dancing for other people.

Reinvigorated, Ridhi sashayed onward.

A glut of cars crowded the curb outside Varsha Auntie's house. Ridhi made her way through them and up the path to the gray brick rancher. Praying to get through the audition, she rang the doorbell.

A woman in her sixties answered. Her white hair was tied up in a bun as firm as her posture, and a vermilion mark at her

11

hairline matched her practice sari. "Ridhi. Your mother didn't come with you?"

"Namaste, Auntieji. No, but she sends her pranaam." Though Ridhi joined her palms and bowed her head as directed, Varsha Auntie didn't seem to register the formality, let alone be gratified by it.

"Hmm." She ushered Ridhi into the entryway, which smelled of smoke mixed with ghee and cardamom, like a perfume gone horribly awry. Maybe Varsha Auntie had been cooking sweets but left them to burn on the stove. Ridhi stifled a snort.

She placed her ballet flats in the overflowing rack by the door, under a pair of sandals, and trailed Varsha Auntie through the house.

No, not a house, Ridhi amended, so much as a shrine to Varsha Auntie's glory days. Dozens of portraits featuring her in thick makeup and gold jewelry, posing with Indian celebrities, covered the walls. Except for her outfits and the celebrities' faces, they might have all been the same image.

There wasn't a plant to be seen, no decorations, no hints of any other hobbies or interests. The furniture in the bland living room was a range of grays and beiges, as if Varsha Auntie's belief in color began and ended with her dancewear. Every blind had been drawn, shutting out the world.

Not the ideal environment, but Ridhi could handle it for five and a half hours of class a week. She wouldn't think about how actual rehearsals topped out at three or four times that number.

"This," Varsha Auntie said, "is a place of dance. We see dance; we think dance; we breathe dance. All other concerns remain outside while you are here."

A tad intense for Ridhi's taste, but for Mummy's sake and the sake of the possible scholarship, she nodded.

Varsha Auntie pointed to a bathroom. "In the future, you will arrive in proper attire and ready to begin."

Ridhi debated mentioning that she'd come straight from school, then decided against it.

In the bathroom, also beige with brown accents, she changed from her purple lace top and rose-embroidered black velvet skirt into a T-shirt and leggings. She quickly wove her loose curls into a braid but balked at removing the rhinestone flower pins; it felt like stripping a tree of its bark.

At least she could keep her golden paayal, she consoled herself. Anklets with tinkling miniature bells were part of any bharatanatyam dancer's repertoire.

Once done, Ridhi dabbed on the solid perfume she'd named Urvashi in Svargalok, letting the blend based on the apsara, one of the celestial dancers in Lord Indra's court, boost her with its radiant, uplifting scents of yuzu, green mandarin, blood orange, fresh ginger, neroli, Indian jasmine, ylang-ylang, lemongrass, and green tea. "Be like Urvashi and her sisters," she instructed her likeness. "You can do this."

She'd scarcely exited the bathroom before Varsha Auntie herded her down the stairs.

Ridhi's heart, already thrumming, did a nosedive at the chatter and laughter coming from the basement. No one else was supposed to be there.

But she didn't have a chance to protest before she was in the studio. It matched the rest of the house, with the exception of the mirrored walls—and the girls in practice saris.

Varsha Auntie's students from the mandir. Worse, their mothers hovered nearby, worrying their daughters' clothes and fussing over their hair. Ridhi was the only one who'd shown up on her own, and the only one in leggings.

Her stomach curled in on itself like a doodlebug. The cars outside, the overstuffed shoe rack, and Varsha Auntie's question. How hadn't Ridhi realized?

The stern lines of Varsha Auntie's mouth eased. "My girls are a team. The audition is for a new teammate, so they must be present."

A team. That made sense, and soon Ridhi would be part of it. Sniffing her wrists again, she did her best to uncurl. She might be inappropriately dressed, she might be alone, but so what?

She'd make Mummy proud and secure a spot on the team.

Her gaze landed on Shreya Prasad.

The flight of fancy crashed. All these years later, it still hurt to remember that she had ever brought Shreya to her woods. That she had stupidly believed Shreya cared.

Sandwiched between two girls on the couch, her mother behind her, Shreya hadn't yet seen Ridhi. But she would. And then she would be watching, threaded eyebrows high with skepticism. Waiting for Ridhi to fail so she could swan on in and take over.

14

Varsha Auntie clapped once, and the surge of conversation ceased. "As you all know, we are hosting auditions to fill out our team today. Please welcome Shreya Prasad and Ridhi Kapadia."

Shreya's head snapped up at that, alarm washing over her before a smirk obfuscated it. She fixed that smirk on Ridhi.

Ridhi scrambled to respond with indifference, but Shreya was already contemplating her fingernails. Like Ridhi was no competition at all.

Her former friend trying out shouldn't have been an issue. Ridhi knew she was the better dancer. Unlike Shreya, she'd trained since she was tiny. She'd rehearsed the routine Varsha Auntie had e-mailed her until it had become as habitual as walking. For Shreya, this audition, this class, was at best a whim, another opportunity to hang out with her friends.

Yet Ridhi's heart refused to still its frenetic drumbeat.

From her position at the front of the room, Varsha Auntie glanced at Shreya, then Ridhi. "Ridhi, why don't you go first?" She played a melody on her phone, the accompaniment to her choreography.

Shreya leaned over and said something to her friend. Both girls giggled.

Ignore them. Ridhi proceeded to the center of the room and raised her arms over her head, stealing seconds to call up the routine on the screen of her mind. From there, she arranged her hips, craned her neck, and pressed her palms together again in anjali mudra, then splayed her fingers in alapadma, or blossomed lotus, mudra. Her bare feet coasted over the floor.

The sunlight from earlier guided her limbs as she melted into the dance.

"What's *she* doing here?" someone stage-whispered, and Ridhi missed a step.

She fought to keep facing forward, but her head swiveled toward the couch anyway.

"I know, right?" Shreya was staring at her with barely veiled contempt, as if Ridhi was the one intruding. "Wasting everybody's time?"

"Relax." Shreya's friend touched her shoulder. "She'll never get it. You will."

It didn't matter how well Ridhi danced or how adept her technique was. They'd already written her off. And, of course, Shreya and her clique all pitched their cutting remarks low enough that Varsha Auntie couldn't hear them over the music.

Ridhi resumed the sequence, but her movements felt stiff, not inspired and fluid. Too many apathetic eyes weighed her down. Too many oblivious voices waited to dismiss her.

The early-March sunbeams in her chest expanded into the scorching white heat of a July afternoon. *This* was how it would go. She'd be trapped in this claustrophobic basement three nights a week with girls who would never accept her. They'd talk around her, exclude her from their jokes and stories, never acknowledge her unless they had to. Even the nicer ones. She might have a spot on the team, but she would never be part of it.

The old epithet echoed in her mind. *Ridhi the weirdo, who talks to plants and thinks they talk back.*

Varsha Auntie frowned. "Is there a problem?"

Yes, Ridhi wanted to say. *There is.* She shouldn't have come. Dance was a language, but she spoke the wrong dialect.

It wasn't too late to salvage the audition. She could still gather herself and show the room what she was capable of. Team morale or not, Varsha Auntie would have no choice but to select her, and Ridhi would learn from an iconic teacher.

Her spirit, however, resisted. Her muscles turned to mud; her fingers, meant to be as dainty as petals, cramped. No, they said, not even for Mummy.

Molding her mouth into a smile, Ridhi completed the sequence, but her performance had as much life as a fallen log, and she knew it. The irony was, she'd still surpassed what Shreya could do.

As if that counted.

"I'm sorry," she rushed to say, staving off the obligatory fake applause, "but I have to go. My mom's expecting me."

Varsha Auntie's forehead wrinkled. "She is?"

Behind Ridhi, the murmurs had begun, and she wasn't about to subject herself to them. "Good luck, Shreya. I'm sure you'll do great."

Snatching up her things, she bolted.

As soon as Ridhi was outside again, her phone rang. She sent it to voice mail. There was only one person it could be, and she was nowhere near ready to have *that* conversation.

How in the world was she going to explain this to Mummy?

The fact was, Ridhi would never fit in, because she didn't

belong with other people. She'd learned that when she was twelve, on a multifamily weekend camping trip. Eager to show off what she knew, Ridhi had led the other kids to a patch of wood sorrel and told them they could eat it. She'd asked the plant for permission to harvest its lemony leaves so she could demonstrate, exactly as Mummy had taught her.

Chetan Gopalkrishnan, who had tagged along, asked why.

Fool that Ridhi was, she'd replied earnestly. *Plants have feelings, too. Wouldn't you want someone to ask you?*

A sneer had spread over Chetan's face like powdery mildew, and his gibes had imprinted themselves on her brain. *Did you hear that? Ridhi Kapadia thinks plants have feelings!* Then his cronies and he had trampled the sorrel. *Oh, no; it's screaming!*

Worse still, the rest of the group had slunk away and left her there. No one had told him off, not even Nilesh Batra, who back then might as well have been a second brother to Ridhi. She would have given anything for the earth to swallow her whole like it had Sita in the *Ramayana*, but she wasn't a queen maligned by her subjects and unjustly exiled by her husband, and this wasn't an ancient epic. She was Ridhi, the resident freak, adrift in the wrong world.

She was fine with that, she thought now, picking up her pace. She had her trees. She had her perfumery business with blends like Sitayana, her current go-to scent retelling the *Ramayana* from Sita's perspective. And soon—Ridhi was sure of it—she would have magic.

By the time Ridhi reached her front yard, the sun was gliding into the golden hour. The familiar sight of light pouring over the wise old oak tree, as thick as glistening honey, soothed her. She wrapped her arms around the oak's ridged bark, feeling its slow pulse, and sank right into her favorite fantasy, the one where the tree's branches settled on her shoulders and stroked her hair. Where it gifted her its wordless guidance.

Where it invited her to leave the mundane realm of human beings behind forever.

With the momentum of the day draining off, Ridhi's eyelids grew heavy. Still hugging her tree, she dozed.

When she awoke, a branch above her head glowed gold in her vision. More than a rainbow's worth of gemstone leaves glimmered along the wood—rubies, carnelians, topaz, emeralds, aquamarines, sapphires, amethysts, rose quartz—each meticulously detailed with veins and stems.

Her mouth dried up. As far as she knew, only the Kalpavriksha, the wish tree of legend, the tree that had anointed Aranyani as the protectress of forests, had foliage like that.

Ridhi blinked, and the branch was gone. Her tree was just her tree again.

Beyond it, however, everything had changed.

Her front yard—no, her neighborhood—had given way to a vast and sweeping forest. Like dancers wearing elaborate headpieces, the voluminous trees and bushes boasted a bounty of vibrant blossoms and enticing fruits. Some existed here on Earth, or as her grand-mother called it, Prithvi.

Others, though, were impossible colors and textures, dreams made reality. Gold- and silver-plumed larks warbled love songs, their feathers shining ornaments against the boughs. On the horizon, majestic blue mountains pierced the sky. No decay, no disease would dare trespass on this place.

The wealth of greenery wasn't anywhere she'd been. It was something else, some*where* else.

Ridhi didn't move, in case she frightened away the vision. Awe lit up her insides, as lush and deep as the golden hour. The yaksha kingdom—could it be?

A breeze redolent with floral essences bore a single leaf toward her. Ridhi opened her palm to receive it. Gradually, inevitably, the cordate leaf came to rest there, striated with the pinks and oranges of sunset and rimmed with gold.

As it made contact with her skin, the forest receded.

Afraid that it, too, would evanesce, Ridhi gingerly rubbed the gleaming leaf between her thumb and finger. Unlike the branch, unlike the forest, it lay there still. Solid. Real.

This had to be the invitation she'd been waiting for. It had to be. And if it was, that meant . . .

Magic, at long last, was coming.

2

Nilesh Batra stretched one arm over his head and braced for the bone-jarring stop as his buddy Amar pulled into the driveway. The ten-year-old beige sedan was a punishment—his parents' hand-me-down after he'd totaled the sporty two-door he'd gotten for his sixteenth birthday—and ran on fumes and duct tape, but Amar still drove like it was a hot rod in a drag race.

"Thanks for the ride, man," Nilesh yelled over the blaring music. No one loved classic grunge more than Amar, who called it the soundtrack to his life. If it wasn't loud enough to make the seats shake and his eardrums rattle, he claimed he wasn't getting the full experience.

"What?" Amar shouted, nodding to the beat.

"I said, 'Thanks for the ride!'"

Amar reached over and punched Nilesh in the shoulder. "Anytime. Now get out. I gotta go."

"All right, all right." Nilesh grabbed his backpack off the floor, which was littered with empty fast-food wrappers and flattened candy boxes. "I'm going." He flung open the passenger-side door, then glanced back. "Tell your mom I said good luck tonight."

With a salute, Amar threw the car in reverse and peeled out, tires squealing. So much for his parents' threat to take it away if he got any more speeding tickets. Oh, well. Not Nilesh's circus, not his monkeys.

Except it was, because then Nilesh would have to cart Amar and crew around everywhere. He pictured the junk in the sedan's back seat and decided he wasn't up for that.

He dug out his phone. It was the usual drama on social media: hard-core fundraising drives for events no one would care about in a month; Katrin Johnson cheating on her boyfriend with another girl; an invitation from Ami Patel to join her physics study group; Chetan Gopalkrishnan ranting that being told not to make raunchy puns in French class infringed on his right to free speech.

Nilesh snickered. *What a tool.*

His feed refreshed itself. Good old Amar had tagged him in some meme about alligator-headed aliens turning up in local tubs. A few girls had sent selfies. Nilesh untagged himself from the meme and replied to the girls with winks and flame emojis: *Hey, how's it going*; *Whoa, nice dress*; and a *Maybe* about the study group. It was all so fake, but everyone felt like they had to play the game. What was the point?

Now he was home, though, and he could clear his head, maybe do another sketch.

Nilesh took a long look at the house where he'd grown up: red brick, slate roof, large windows, wheelchair ramp, four-car garage, and more than enough rooms to host extended family during their visits from India. Add in the arbitrary turret on the second floor, and the house had more character than some of the other manor-style homes in the neighborhood.

How much did houses shape the people who lived in them? Who would he have been if he'd grown up somewhere else?

Still thinking, he went inside and kicked off his shoes.

"In the closet, beta!" Mom sang out from the living room. He could tell from her extra-sweet tone that she was on a call. There was no way she could have seen him, but she always knew.

Nilesh stowed his sneakers in the foyer closet and marched toward the kitchen. "I'm getting a snack," he announced. Their walk-in pantry was always stocked with treats, from Parle-G biscuits to Hot Mix to tubs of peanut M&M's and bags of chips, ready for the visitors who dropped by a few times a week.

"Sunita went shopping today," Mom said, joining him. Sunita, their housekeeper and cook, was, as Mom liked to say every chance she got, the sole reason their household didn't fall apart on a routine basis. "I asked her to get more of that bread you like."

Nilesh dug through the fridge for some pomegranate juice to blend with his lime seltzer. "Awesome. Thanks."

"She made you paratha and green bean aloo sabzi for tonight, hungry-mungry," Mom said. "They're on the top shelf."

"You could've just left money for pizza," Nilesh teased. He ducked when she swatted at him. "Are you nervous?"

Nilesh's and Amar's mothers were both high-powered corporate lawyers at the same firm downtown, and that night they were being honored with awards, some service thing involving lots of speeches and champagne. It sounded pretty stuffy to Nilesh, but it was a big deal for Mom.

Dad, who'd gotten his own share of awards, was an ophthalmologist and part-time professor at Emory University Hospital. His list of accolades rivaled the list of places he'd taken their family on vacation.

Everyone expected Nilesh to keep up with his power-couple parents, and he would. He was going to be an architect. His older sister, Hetal, was majoring in business at Berkeley. Maybe they could found a start-up together.

"Not nervous," Mom corrected. "Just finalizing details for our trip." They were all flying to Hawai'i over spring break. "Think I can pull off a lei?"

"Only if you skip the hula skirt."

Mom laughed. "I think that can be arranged. Oh!" She put her hand to her mouth. "I saw a fox in the backyard about an hour ago. I hope that doesn't mean we're going to start having rodent infestations. Remember when those mice broke in?"

Nilesh slathered a thick layer of hummus over some bread. "Nah, it was probably out hunting for rabbits. When's Dad getting home?"

"Soon." Mom's smile strained at the edges. To her, being anything less than five minutes early was late.

"Did he say anything about scuba lessons?" Nilesh couldn't

24

think of a better place than Hawai'i to have his first dive. And since Hetal had to stick to shallower water, he'd done some research into accessible snorkeling, too.

Mom fluffed his hair. "You'll have to talk to him."

"Come on, Mom. Don't *you* want to see coral and pretty fish?"

But she was like a human fortress. "Go start your homework," she said with a nudge.

"Yeah, yeah, yeah." Sandwich and seltzer in hand, Nilesh jogged up the stairs.

In his room, he loaded his favorite playlist and inhaled his snack before dropping onto the navy-blue duvet with his laptop. He had to draft an essay for world history and knock out some problem sets for calculus. These days, homework had basically turned into school, part two, and he was not a fan.

By the time Mom and Dad appeared in the doorway a couple of hours later, all decked out for the gala, he'd dumped the books and was strumming a few chords on his bass guitar.

Dad wore one of his tailored tuxedos. Mom had gone for a silk sari in black and green and a green bindi, and she was screwing in one of her gold earrings, which matched her kundan necklace and bangles.

"How nice of you to serenade us, beta," joked Dad. "Don't forget us when you're famous."

"Ha, ha." Nilesh plucked another string with his pick, then put down the guitar and texted Hetal. *Okay, go ahead and call.*

Mom came to stand beside him.

"Hey, Dad," he said, grinning evilly, "you know what Mom told

25

me? She's going to try hula dancing while we go surfing."

"I am?" she asked.

"You said you want to wear a lei, didn't you?"

"No surgery or depositions in Hawai'i," Dad said, "so plenty of time for everyone to try a new skill." He paused for dramatic effect. "Especially underwater—I signed us all up for lessons."

"Awesome!" Nilesh did a fist pump. He'd known Dad would come through. "It's going to be so fun."

Looking pleased with himself, Dad wrapped an arm around Mom's waist. "What do you think? Am I snazzy enough to tag along with this lovely lady tonight?"

"I guess," Nilesh allowed. "So corny, Dad." For old people, they looked pretty good. Not that he'd ever say so.

Mom inspected Dad and adjusted his bow tie. "You'll do."

"The only compliment I'll ever need." He planted a big kiss on her cheek, and she giggled like someone from Nilesh's class.

Not cool. Nilesh mimed gagging, then texted Hetal again. *Anytime now.*

When his phone rang, he couldn't accept the video call fast enough. "Good luck tonight, Mom!" his sister chirped, blowing kisses at the screen. "You look fabulous."

"We do, don't we?" Dad said. He turned to Mom. "Come, my love."

Nilesh and his phone went with them to the garage, where Dad's luxury SUV waited. Mom's stiletto heels clacked on the concrete floor. "Behave, all right?"

"No wild shenanigans where you invite the whole neighborhood over," Dad put in. "At least not until the weekend. That goes for you, too, Hetal."

"No promises," Nilesh said, and consented to a hug from each of them before they drove off. Then Hetal and he made faces at each other.

"So, little brother," she told him, "wait until you hear about the guy I went out with last night."

Nilesh settled in for a long conversation. Hetal's misadventures in dating were always good for a laugh. "Where do you find these losers?"

She rolled her eyes. "You think *they* were bad . . ."

Raised voices jolted Nilesh out of his sleep. At first, as he blinked gritty eyes in the dark, he assumed Amar, who had the world's worst handle on time, had texted him. But then he heard doors slamming.

"Will you please calm down?" Dad hissed.

He'd reverted to Hindi instead of the Hinglish they spoke at home. Though Nilesh couldn't really speak it, he understood what Dad was saying just fine.

"We can get past this." A pause, then: "Aruna!"

Something was wrong. Very wrong. Before he fully came to, Nilesh was on his feet and heading toward the noise.

"Get past it? I *saw* her, Dilip." Mom's furious voice sliced through the air. "I saw *you*!"

Nilesh hesitated on the landing. *Saw Dad what?*

"There's no need to make such a fuss," Dad muttered. Keys clattered on the table like he'd flung them.

"Oh, no? Do tell." Mom's laugh was horrible. "I've kept my mouth shut all these years, always looked the other way, but I'm done now."

A chill so intense, it could have come from the Arctic, wormed along Nilesh's spine. Time stretched around him as he shuffled down the stairs.

His parents glared at each other in the yellow hallway light. They were still wearing the same fancy clothes they'd had on earlier, but they looked like strangers. Fun house–mirror versions of themselves. He'd never seen Mom's expression that hard before or Dad that checked out. The scene was straight from the hammy soap operas some aunties they knew binged on Saturday afternoons.

"I always thought at least you'd be discreet," Mom spat. "At my own firm! At an event to celebrate *me*! Do you have no shame?"

Ohhh. Nilesh's sleep-addled brain finally put the pieces together. This *was* one of those inane shows. They'd managed to invade his dreams. His parents didn't talk like that. They loved each other. He just had to pull them out of the studio and into the real world, and the nightmare would end.

"What's going on?" he asked. He'd reached the bottom of the steps but held on to the banister. "You woke me up."

His parents turned to him, wrath on Mom's face, guilt on Dad's. "Your father," Mom informed him in stark, icy English, "has been carrying on with a paralegal at a partner firm. He left *my* awards ceremony to meet her in the hotel lobby."

Carrying on with? Nilesh almost started laughing, too. What was she talking about? Dad would never do that.

28

This dream was getting out of hand.

"Dad?" he prompted, since Dad had missed the cue to dive in and set the record straight.

Dad looked away.

It was then Nilesh knew.

In a dream, the floor wouldn't be hard under his feet. It wouldn't be anything. No, this was real.

He wanted to run to his room and pretend he'd never woken up, but his body had forgotten how to move.

"Your father," Mom went on in that ugly voice that didn't sound anything like her, "has kept his mistress for years now." She glowered at Dad. "We came to an arrangement for the sake of the family, and until tonight, he had the sense to honor it and keep her away from us."

Dad, who could have smoothed things over at any second, kept his mouth shut.

Nilesh, more out of it than ever, tried to reconcile these strangers with the touchy-feely couple who'd left for the ceremony a few hours before. He couldn't. Dad had been cheating on Mom? But why?

It didn't make sense. His parents adored each other, to the point of being revoltingly goopy about it. They always threw big anniversary parties and went on double dates with their friends. They watched movies while cuddling on the couch and sipping glasses of wine.

We came to an arrangement. Nilesh's head threatened to blow up. Not just that, but Mom had known? She'd let it happen?

Did Hetal know? Was he the only one who'd bought into the lie of their happy family?

Something crumbled inside him.

"Did you stop for one minute to think about our children and what this would do to them?" Mom's voice broke. "On my awards night, Dilip. You couldn't even let me have that."

Nilesh did his best to imagine himself anywhere else. Anywhere that wasn't their front hall.

But all he could see was Dad with some strange woman. Kissing her. Pulling back white hotel sheets and laying her down. Nilesh wanted to puke. He wanted to cry.

How could it be true? How?

Dad pinched the bridge of his nose like Mom was giving him a headache. "I don't know what you want me to say, but it's late, and I have a course to teach in the morning. I'm going to sleep."

"Not in my bed, you're not!" Mom snapped. The loathing in that sentence was brutal enough to suffocate Nilesh, and it wasn't even aimed at him. "Not in the guest rooms, either. You can take the sofa."

Dad shook his head. "You're being ridiculous."

It was the stupidest thing, but Nilesh caught himself fixating on the fact that they wouldn't be going to Hawai'i after all. Someone would have to cancel the tickets.

No surfing. No scuba. Never again.

"*I'm* being ridiculous?" Mom spun on her heel. "Go to bed, beta," she called to Nilesh as she climbed the stairs.

The *click* of the bedroom door behind her was so sharp, so final, like an invisible but essential cord had been torn in two.

Suddenly it was Dad and him. Nilesh didn't know where to look.

"Dad?" he ventured, desperate to banish the silence. Willing Dad to make things right.

"You heard your mother. Go to bed." Dad disappeared into the living room, probably to camp out on the couch. The overhead light went off, leaving Nilesh in the dark.

He stood there, alone. How would he ever fall back asleep now?

3

Two weeks later, Ridhi's patience had begun to thin like leaves in winter. She'd carried out every ritual to establish communication she could think of: whispering wishes, lighting aromatic candles, and arranging incense sticks and pressed flowers on her altar to Aranyani Devi. She'd brought offerings to her forest day after day, even during a thunderstorm with gale-force winds, scaring Papa so badly he'd nearly grounded her for a year.

And yet the magic kept her at bay.

As the days passed, Ridhi's certainty that she'd seen the bejeweled branch faded. She'd been out of sorts when she'd dozed off, after all, plus the lore claimed the Kalpavriksha was located up in Lord Indra's heavenly realm of Svargalok. His devatas had laid claim to it on his behalf during Samudra Manthan, the churning of the cosmic Ocean of Milk, or what modern people called the Milky Way, and borne it to his abode among the stars.

The yaksha kingdom, on the other hand, sat entrenched in the earthly Himalayas, on Prithvi but not of it. It was like conflating Korea and Belize.

In fact, if Ridhi didn't have the gleaming leaf, she would have thought she'd dreamed the entire thing.

But she did have the leaf, which hadn't turned up in any of her plant-identification apps or books. No roots had sprouted, either, not when she'd placed it in water and not when she'd tried rooting mix. Unsure what else to do, she'd stored it between the pages of her journal.

Now, seated in the breakfast room with its patterned chairs, curio cabinets laden with potted plants, and walls the gentle blue of flax flowers, Ridhi probed the leaf again. It still hadn't desiccated.

Letting out an aggravated "Arghhh!," she buried her face in her arms. She'd spent her life in limbo, pretending not to care when people denigrated her, shrugging off the world's insistence that wanting more was akin to playing with dolls, a phase to outgrow and cast aside. She was sick of being patient, sick of being scorned for who she was. She didn't just want more; she *needed* it.

That was why, once she'd discovered natural perfumery a couple of years ago, she had saved up her allowance for supplies. Like dance, scent was powerful, spinning a story without words, bordering on mystical in its ability to evoke a mood. Ridhi used it to tell the tales of heroines and monstresses from Hindu folklore and mythology. But she also yearned to star in her own story.

Oh, *why* wouldn't the magic show itself?

She huffed so theatrically that Mummy, off in the kitchen, heard.

"I take it you didn't see the good news?" Mummy called as she lifted a pan off the stove. Like a potable perfume, the base notes of vanilla, raw sugar, and rich cocoa had come together to form a warming, chocolaty foundation with a top note of milky comfort. Mummy stirred in the heart note, a capful of rose water. It smelled like a valentine in a cup. "You got your thirty-first review this morning! Five stars, too."

After selling through her first batch of custom fragrances at a crafts festival, Ridhi had taken the leap and opened an online shop. Hitting thirty-one reviews felt like a milestone, a sign she was moving in the right direction. Strangers liked what she made. But she couldn't enjoy it, not when she knew where this conversation was really going. "I did see, actually."

Mummy set two steaming, unicorn-shaped mugs on the table and sat down beside Ridhi. "That's wonderful! I'm so proud of you."

Ridhi cupped her mug with consternation, suspecting it for the bribe it probably was. She'd half convinced herself that Mummy would forget about the audition results and they could get back to their upcoming project: that Monday's trip to a few local boutiques, where they would try to sell her perfumes on consignment.

Which was silly; wishful thinking was the one type of magic Ridhi *didn't* believe in.

"I got an interesting phone call earlier," Mummy murmured, though her casual tone couldn't disguise how eager she was. "Varsha Auntie. She asked me to tell you again how gifted you are. How the team needs a dancer like you."

As much as Ridhi loved the insinuation that Shreya's audition had flopped, she still wished Varsha Auntie would move on. Stalling, she sipped the velvety reddish-brown liquid. The only flavor she could taste was bitter dread.

Mummy blew on her own rose hot chocolate. "You have something special. We all see it."

"I don't!" Ridhi protested, though that wasn't in the least bit true.

Disappointment seeped into Mummy's next sentence. "She won't hold the spot for you forever. She's already been so patient."

Varsha Auntie really had been incredibly generous, and Ridhi knew it. Yet not even the poison-nullifying horn of her unicorn mug could purify the moment when she'd realized the team would never include her. "Shreya can have it."

"Shreya? Why should she get to control what you do?"

Ridhi muffled a groan. How was she supposed to explain that this wasn't about Shreya? It was about *her*.

Mummy looked more bewildered than ever. "You're a natural, beti! With training, you'll be better than I ever was. Why waste that?"

She would never get it. Everyone had always liked her. When Mummy talked to plants, people found it adorable. When Ridhi did, they found her weird. If Mummy had been auditioning, she would have strutted out with the spot *and* eight brand-new friends, and Shreya would be the one left behind.

"So there's no chance you'll change your mind?" A flame of

hope guttered beneath Mummy's question. "You could dance at the mandir on Holi!"

Holi, the spring festival, was both a time of public celebration and the date of their yearly private mother-daughter ritual. That made what Ridhi had to say hurt even more.

"No." She traced her finger over the chip in the unicorn's horn. "I'm sorry. I know you were excited. So was I."

But I'm not like you. I don't belong here.

"If you're certain," Mummy said, her mouth drooping.

Suddenly Ridhi felt like the worst daughter in the world. All Mummy wanted was to see her happy. How could Ridhi fault her for that?

Sliding her chair over, Ridhi cuddled against her mother's plump softness, breathing in her trademark blend of tuberose and gardenia, which she'd worn every day since Ridhi first made it for her. Mummy rested her chin on Ridhi's shoulder. "My Ridhi pari," she said.

They stayed that way for a couple of minutes before Mummy sat back up. "Your cocoa's getting cold."

Ridhi took another sip. This one tasted like relief. Maybe rose hot chocolate could be a future perfume. Without meaning to, she sighed.

"What's wrong?" Mummy asked.

Ridhi wasn't quite ready to delve into the specifics, but she pointed to the leaf. Mummy loved forests and folklore, too, and she'd been the one to instill Ridhi with respect for plants. "I found this the other day. Do you know what it is?"

"No, but how pretty! Where was it?"

"Near our house."

Mummy squinted at the leaf. "Such an unusual pattern. Like some stationery I once had. But it would be hard to write on a leaf, I'd bet."

"Probably easier to read them." Ridhi touched the leaf, then the page it sat on. "You know, leaves in a book. Ooh, no, like tea leaves!"

"Oh, yes," Mummy mused. "Divination. Hmm. Now you have *me* curious!"

The word *divination* snagged on Ridhi's memories like a thorn on fabric. She'd heard it before—

Her little brother chose that minute to burst through the mudroom door, pursued by Papa, who had picked him up from soccer practice. "Mummmmyyyyy! Ridhiiiiii!" Kartik shouted. "Guess who made goalie today?"

"Slow down," Papa called. "Your shoes!" Two thumps answered him.

The scrap of recollection wiggled out of reach, but how could Ridhi be upset when Kartik's enthusiasm was so infectious? With wide-eyed solemnity, she inquired, "Let me think. You?"

He darted toward the table, hair rumpled, red shirt clinging to him in sweaty creases, high socks streaked with grass and mud, and thrust his overjoyed face in hers. He reeked of eau de soccer player, a scent she would never reproduce. "I kept the other team from scoring *three times*, and Coach was super impressed."

"*I'm* super impressed you remembered to take off your cleats," Mummy teased. "Good job, my goalie."

Ridhi affected a sports announcer's ebullient voice. "Next stop, World Cup!"

Papa touched the small of Mummy's back, then bopped Ridhi on the nose. "What a sight for a Saturday afternoon! My two favorite ladies, beautiful as always."

Mummy beamed up at him, the sort of smile Ridhi rarely saw outside romantic movies, like the person being smiled at contained the sun, moon, *and* every single star. Though they both hailed from New Delhi, her parents had met at graduate school in Atlanta. While Mummy studied computer programming and Papa business administration, they'd twined around each other, as inseparable as ivy on a stone wall. After graduation, they'd returned to India and gotten married.

Seven years after Ridhi was born, they had moved back to America, two kids in tow, to build the next stage of their life together.

The younger of those kids poured himself a bowl of marshmallow cereal and launched into a play-by-play of his triumph. Once he'd guzzled the pink milk, he scraped back his chair. "Come help me with the dungeon, Ridhi."

They were partway through a new video game, and Kartik's character kept dying at the same place. Ridhi bumped his foot with hers. "What if I have other plans?"

The wicked curl of his lip was pure ten-year-old boy. "Then I'll make you drink ant-egg lemonade."

"Ew!" She waited for someone to inform him that no, he was actually going to throw his uniform in the laundry and do his chores before dinner.

Their parents traded a somber glance. "We need to talk to you," Papa said. "Both of you."

Ridhi's stomach twisted, as if the hot chocolate had been spiked with pine cones. That couldn't be good.

"We're going to have a houseguest. Remember Dilip Uncle and Aruna Auntie and their kids?"

What a strange question. The Batras were old family friends. They—well, not Hetal and Nilesh so much anymore—came over regularly, and Mummy and Papa visited them just as often.

"Um, yeah," Kartik scoffed. "They were here last week."

Ridhi's belly knotted itself tighter. "Did something happen?"

"Yes," Papa said. "They're having some . . . difficulties."

Kartik looked bemused. "What does that mean?"

"It doesn't matter." Mummy held up a hand to discourage any arguments. "The point is, Nilesh will be staying with us for a couple of weeks. Aruna Auntie is dropping him off in an hour."

"What?" Ridhi stared at her parents, chagrined. "It's spring break! You can't do that!"

"Ridhi!" Mummy spoke severely. "The Batras need our help. What have we taught you about extending kindness?"

"But he doesn't even talk to me!" Why couldn't Nilesh try extending kindness for once?

"Have *you* tried to talk to *him*?" Papa asked.

"Well, no," Ridhi said, "but—"

"*I* think Nilesh is cool," Kartik put in. "I'm glad he's coming."

You would. Then again, the world at large thought Nilesh was cool. That was probably why he'd dropped Ridhi when everyone else at their mandir had—a fact which Mummy and Papa knew very well.

"Nilesh has been having a hard time." The stern note in Papa's voice warned Ridhi not to contradict him. "He needs a change of scenery, and I know you'll make him feel welcome."

Mummy squeezed Ridhi's hand, and her face was sweet with love, the face of the mother who had always maintained that Ridhi was perfect just as she was. Who had always encouraged her to do what brought her joy. "He needs our help. Can you do that for us?"

Ridhi gave a cautious nod. It wasn't as though she had to befriend Nilesh while he was there. She'd read her books and retreat to her enchanted forest and study her leaf.

And maybe she'd even spot the Kalpavriksha again.

"Hi, Nilesh," Mummy called. "Come in, beta."

Nilesh Batra sauntered into the house, lugging a large suitcase and a backpack. Aruna Auntie stalked in after him, elegant in a mauve raw silk suit and ivory heels. At her urging, he grunted what might have been *hi*.

Ridhi's house—her snug, cheerful house—seemed to shrink with him in it. Her family was comfortable, but his was rich. The sort of rich that bought mansions and set up trust funds for their children and vacationed in swanky European chalets with eye-watering prices. Ridhi and Nilesh didn't attend the same school; she couldn't afford the tuition for his private academy.

Those things hadn't bothered him when they were younger. But this Nilesh wore a petulant sulk, like her house was a one-star motel.

Too bad she couldn't order him to leave. Ridhi moved closer to the bird-of-paradise in the corner, macerating in its tranquil energy, and forged her best imitation of a smile. "Hi, Auntie."

Aruna Auntie's rigid expression lightened. "How are you, beti? You never come to see me anymore."

There's a reason for that, and he's right next to you.

"I'm fine." Ridhi gestured to the kitchen. "Would you like anything to drink? I can make some masala chai."

"Very kind of you. But no, I must get going." When Nilesh made a derisive noise, Aruna Auntie rounded on him. "Thank her! After all the trouble you've caused, you're very lucky that Auntie and Uncle are taking you in."

"Lucky? You didn't even let me bring my car!" Nilesh spluttered.

"I said," she repeated, each word a bar of fresh-forged steel, "thank her. If your car was so important to you, you wouldn't have gotten yourself suspended from school."

Ridhi squelched a gasp. He'd done *what*? Thank the gods Kartik was in the backyard and couldn't hear this.

"Yeah, well," Nilesh said, "if you—"

"Don't blame me for your actions, Nilu." Aruna Auntie ran a hand over her impeccably made-up face. "Why are you behaving like this?"

"Aruna—" Mummy began.

"I don't know, maybe because you and Dad keep making me your little pawn?" Nilesh was almost panting, his glare hot enough to singe his mother where she stood. "Don't blame *me* because you let him cheat on you!"

Aruna Auntie visibly flinched.

Shock and agitation reverberated through Ridhi. *"Some difficulties." Poor Auntie!*

She longed to hug her own, decidedly precious family tight. She especially longed to protect her little brother from the ugliness of the outside world. No matter what, Papa would never cheat on Mummy, not that Mummy would condone it if he did.

Papa took hold of Nilesh's suitcase, breaking the uncomfortable lull. "Let's put this in your room."

Then they were gone, and Aruna Auntie lurched, sobbing, into Mummy's arms. "This is my life now, Meera."

Mummy rubbed her back. "It'll be all right," she soothed.

"Will it?"

Ridhi escaped to the backyard garden, where Kartik knelt in the dirt, hunting new specimens for his ant farm. She sat down on the swing and watched him. Surrounded by trees, grass, and a slew of bushes on the verge of blooming—forsythias, lilacs, clematis, weigela, fritillaria, azaleas—her jittery pulse slowed, and she felt grounded again. She could practically smell the rainbow of flowers and see the wealth of green.

Soon it would officially be spring. Soon Nilesh would be out of her hair.

Oh, why she couldn't live outside until then?

Dinner had been awkward enough, with Nilesh pouting at his plate and muttering one-word responses, that even Kartik had quit trying to engage him. The tentative shoot of Ridhi's sympathy had died off; there he was in her house, eating her mother's cooking, yet he couldn't make an effort to be civil.

Her parents, however, chatted like everything was fine. "Did you know our ancestors practiced tree satyagraha, Nilesh?" Mummy asked. "That's why we honor them with a ritual."

Oh, gods. Ridhi tensed up mid bite. "I don't think he wants a history lesson, Mummy."

"It's okay," Nilesh said, purely to rile her. "I want to hear this."

Of course *that* was what got him talking. Ridhi clenched her spoon to keep from throwing it at him.

"There's no reason to be embarrassed," Mummy said firmly. "In 1730, the Bishnoi Hindu community heard the trees in their village were going to be chopped down to make lumber for a new palace. Some of the women and men protested by wrapping their arms around them. But the foresters cut them down, too. Isn't that awful? The original tree huggers."

"But they didn't die in vain," Papa said. "New rules were passed, safeguarding all Bishnoi forests. Then, in the 1970s, another group of women in the Himalayas followed their example. And more after them, until all their local trees were safe."

That wasn't so bad. Ridhi let go of her spoon and reached for her chapati.

"Ridhi hugs trees, too!" Kartik blabbed. "I've seen her do it."

She shook her head at him, but it was too late.

Nilesh sat straighter, like a plant watered after a long drought. "Oh, yeah? I need details. Lots of them."

Mummy picked up the thread. "Like her foremothers, our Ridhi

43

is very protective of her trees. One time when we went to India, she insisted on visiting every sacred grove we could get to. She said each yakshini needed a special embrace, or she'd feel left out."

"Did you hug all of them?" Nilesh subtly elongated the words. "You can't leave me hanging."

Ridhi wished she'd been sawed down alongside her heroes and heroines. "Can we talk about something else, please?"

She kept to herself for the rest of the meal.

Afterward, while loading the dishwasher, she asked, "Does he *really* have to stay here? It's pretty obvious he doesn't want to."

Papa and Mummy, who'd been packing up the leftover chapati and aloo gobi, turned identical looks of exasperation on her. "His family is falling apart," Papa said. "You can't expect him to be chipper."

"But what about Hetal? Doesn't she have an apartment in Berkeley? I mean, it's not like he's in school or anything."

"Enough, Ridhi," Mummy said, soft and dangerous. "He's staying with us, and you will accept that."

"But—"

"No buts. The Batras would do the same for you if you needed it." Papa stacked the storage containers in the refrigerator. "This hard-heartedness isn't like you."

"I'd never need it, though," Ridhi countered under her breath. "*I* don't get in trouble."

"What was that?" Papa demanded.

She busied herself with starting the cycle. "Nothing."

On her way out of the kitchen, she collided with Nilesh. His little smirk only infuriated her further. "Good night," she bit out, staring ahead.

"Still believe in faeries, huh?"

Ridhi froze.

Nilesh shrugged. "Not my fault your door was open, tree hugger."

Her thoughts shot to her art figurines and mythic accessories, to her faerie and yaksha prints on the walls, to her vine-garlanded shelves and their books on magic. To her perfume organ and her altar. Her private treasures, exposed.

Her own home wasn't safe anymore, and worse, Mummy and Papa didn't care.

Ridhi crossed her arms. "What's your point?"

Nilesh's face twisted in disdain. "The rest of us live in the real world."

It was the cruelest thing he could have said, and he knew it. Right then, Ridhi hated him. "Don't. Go. In. My. Room. Again. Got it?"

She pushed past him and ran upstairs. The moon, Lord Chandra, hung just past her bedroom window, washing her in silvery white.

The nerve of Nilesh. It was so unfair.

Ridhi locked the door, then moved to her desk, which was covered in scent strips, dropper bottles, little beakers, carrier oil, and a dish of coffee grounds.

Immediately above her desk, within easy reach, hung the two shelves that served as her perfume organ, where she stored the bulk of her essential oils, concretes, and absolutes. They glimmered in the faint light from her lotus lamp. The sight of them, the potential they held, calmed her.

Below them sat a cardboard box of samples for consignment. After some research, Ridhi had picked fifteen boutiques around Atlanta to approach and, at Mummy's suggestion, divided them into five groups of three. Then, together with Mummy, who had requested that Monday off from work, she'd planned their initial outing: they would visit the first group on their list, break for lunch, and wrap up with a jaunt around the puppetry museum.

The best part? Nilesh wasn't invited.

Behind the samples was the definition Ridhi had copied out of a book on woodland witchcraft. *Phyllomancy: the tales that trees tell.* The term slotted into place with a green-hued rightness. Phyllomancy, divination by the rustling of leaves. That was what she'd been trying to recall earlier.

The revelation sparked Ridhi's urge to create. Her oils sang to her, eager to be used. She pulled them down—grounding Himalayan and Atlas cedar paired for a base note, layered with Sri Lankan cinnamon for heat, and how could she forget vibrant juniper berry?—and began to blend an invocation to the yakshas and yakshinis, caretakers of the natural world.

The next two hours flew past as Ridhi tested scent strips and combined ingredients. She rejected some and approved others, sniffing at the coffee grounds in between to refresh her sense of smell. Like with any art form, there was a basic structure to the

46

process, but beyond that, she let her intuition guide her.

This formulation, she decided, which now included aromatic, invigorating cardamom and Indian vetiver, would be called Keeper of the Woodlands.

Yawning, her eyes gritty, Ridhi capped the bottle, keen to see how it would bloom. Natural perfumes varied from person to person, their body chemistry playing a large role in the olfactory equation. Wearing one was almost like having your own signature scent, and with this mixture, she might. So far, it was sylvan, herbaceous, and ripe with secrets, exactly like her enchanted forest.

Come to us, that forest hummed in her mind.

Come . . .

Three authoritative caws drew her notice. Gold wood lined with gemstones shimmered at her through the window, dazzling yet dreamlike, each leaf a wish.

The bejeweled branch!

Ridhi bounded to the window, where a pair of obsidian eyes met hers. Like a piece of night given wings, a bird perched on the branch, its purple-glossed feathers limned in silver-white moonbeams. Black from top to talon, its thick, curved bill ended in a fine tip like a hook that made her think of a fountain pen.

The bird was a crow, but not the type of corvid she was used to seeing. This was an Indian jungle crow, a bird that never left the South Asian continent, and in its bill, it bore an ovate brown seed.

Ridhi flung open the window. The crow deposited the seed on the sill, then cawed again.

Before she could thank it, the avian courier was soaring through the sky. The branch, too, vanished in its wake. Yet its delivery, the seed of a shala tree, did not.

Ridhi's nose filled in the blanks. She'd thought the new perfume was done, but she'd been wrong. It needed one more ingredient: shala tree oil. She would incorporate that and let the perfume marinate.

And then she'd bring it to the forest and prove to the yakshas that she belonged there.

4

Nilesh lay in the guest bed, fixated on the familiar yet unfamiliar ceiling. He'd never felt so bruised in his life, not even when Amar and he had taken turns skateboarding off a high ledge and then shoving each other off a bench. They were always pulling asinine stunts, goading each other to stupider and stupider heights, and never bothering with protective gear. Where was the fun in that?

They'd both gotten pretty banged up that day, but only Amar ended up in the emergency room. Nilesh had witnessed all of it: the audible *crack* when Amar landed on his wrist, the hideous purple mottling his brown skin, and the tears leaking out of his eyes. While they waited for help, Nilesh had bombarded Amar with jokes about trying again with a jet pack strapped to the board. The two of them had raved about the high jumps, what it was like to be airborne, what a badass Amar would be in his cast.

Everything but the tears.

Nilesh had been the first person to sign that cast, doodling a skull and crossbones. By that point, Amar showed off his broken wrist like a badge of honor, and Nilesh was glad.

But he'd never really understood how Amar must have felt in that moment of crashing, his wrist fracturing on impact. The realization that the world itself had betrayed him. That maybe he'd cried not just from the pain of his bone breaking but also from the pain of his belief shattering. He'd thought he'd always be safe. Now he knew the truth.

And no matter how many other mindless shenanigans he threw himself into, he could never unknow it.

Amar hadn't lost his taste for thrill-seeking, but he'd quietly started wearing a helmet and elbow pads when skateboarding. Though he drove like a maniac, he made sure everyone in his car fastened their seat belts first.

Nilesh's mouth tasted rank. Where was the seat belt for him?

Getting suspended had been a bonehead move, and no matter what Mom assumed, he knew it. Amar, of all people, had lit into him. *It sucks about your dad. But are you really that surprised? Come on, dude. Everybody's always acting. Everybody.*

Was Nilesh the only person who'd believed otherwise?

He thought back to literature class. Ms. Seifried had been droning on, analyzing some novella about a guy who woke up one day as a man-sized bug. It seemed so utterly, pathetically irrelevant, and Nilesh said as much. Actually, he went on, everything they did in school was a waste of time. They were all just regurgitating lies, when the truth was, everybody was a roach. Especially the people they loved the most. Maybe *that* was the lesson.

Ms. Seifried had told Nilesh that if he held such strong opinions, he could write about them later. So he did.

That afternoon, while she was in the teachers' lounge, he'd gone back to her classroom. Using a black permanent marker, he sketched a giant cockroach on the interactive whiteboard and added a caption: THE REAL ROACHES ARE ALL AROUND YOU.

That, and mouthing off to Ms. Seifried when she'd walked in on him, had earned Nilesh a trip to the principal's office. Refusing to apologize had won him this two-week "vacation" at Ridhi's house—five days' suspension plus a bonus week of spring break prison camp.

But he wasn't sorry. Or if he was, it was because he'd gotten caught. Like Dad.

A bird tweeted right outside the window. Groaning, Nilesh slung his arm over his eyes. He might be able to force another hour or two of sleep before he had to face the day.

Someone knocked at the door. There went that plan. "Yeah?" he called, hoarse.

"My mom says to get up." Ridhi. She came off robotic, like an automated message. "It's a quarter to noon, and we're going to Shivam Bazaar."

Nilesh groaned again and sat up. It was so weird to be back in that room, with its family portraits and desi trinkets and enough plants to start a greenhouse. When they were younger, Hetal and he had spent the night pretty often, and Mom and Dad would come get them in the morning. Kartik had still been a toddler, always running after them.

Gods. So many memories of another lifetime.

Nilesh glanced over at the dresser, where the vial he'd lifted from Ridhi's room sat. He hadn't meant to take it, but it smelled like hope. While sniffing it, he'd thought things could go back to how they'd been before. He'd even seen it in his head.

Then the perfume had faded, and he'd felt worse than ever.

What had he expected? Nothing lasted. He'd wait until she wasn't around and put the vial back.

Ridhi knocked again. Nilesh rolled out of bed and opened the door to send her away. "Are those *mushrooms*?" he asked instead.

She'd paired a long black skirt with the mirror-worked hot-pink tunic from a set of salwar kameez. Her jewelry was a weird combination of antique Indian and eclectic stuff she could have swiped from his school's production of *A Midsummer Night's Dream*—flower earrings, overlapping necklaces, and a bindi. Her typical cheesy *magic is real* kick.

But Nilesh couldn't get past the purple mushrooms sprouting from her hair.

Ridhi moved to touch them before she caught herself. "Barrettes," she said defensively. "They're amethyst deceivers."

Nilesh stared harder. What he knew about mushrooms was limited to pizza toppings and khumb ki sabzi. These were kind of cute—for a kid's Halloween costume. But it wasn't Halloween, and she couldn't walk around town like that. Not if she wanted to get along with other human beings.

With Ridhi, that was debatable.

The line of her mouth dared him to laugh at her.

Well, it would be rude not to deliver. "Fungus," he remarked.

"On your head. Got a hot date with a tree?"

She lifted her chin. "I know you want to ask. So ask."

"About your hot date? I hear those trees are pretty good at small talk. Spruces, especially."

"About my *barrettes*. You want to know why mushrooms."

He made an irritated sound. "Fine, what's the big deal?"

"Because I'm a fun girl." She paused, expectant. "Get it?"

"No."

"Fun guy? Fungi?" Ridhi sighed. "But I'm a girl?"

Nilesh winced. "Don't ever try stand-up comedy. Please."

"Hurry up, beta!" Meera Auntie called from the foot of the stairs. "We're leaving in ten minutes!"

"Coming," he yelled back, then locked himself in the bathroom he shared with Ridhi. He had enough problems without trying to save her from herself. All he had to do was survive the next two weeks, and he could go home.

Nilesh grimaced at his bleary reflection in the mirror. Whatever home was now, anyway.

The Indian grocery store was as congested for a Sunday morning as Nilesh would have predicted, customers wrangling shopping carts, kids, and twenty-pound bags of rice. It wasn't his usual store, so hopefully he wouldn't run into anyone he knew.

When Meera Auntie stopped in the produce section to inspect a pair of long light-green gourds for making dudhi ka halwa, he braced himself and skimmed the mountain of text messages from Hetal.

I'm so sorry you found out like this. You know I am. She'd sent that first one the day after the awards gala. He'd reread it so many times, he'd lost count.

It never hurt any less. She'd known. They'd all known. Everybody but him.

Nilesh scrolled down to the most recent messages.

I know how you feel. I felt that way, too.

Come on. You can't not talk to me. Nilu!

He nearly deleted the rest without reading. But he just couldn't do it.

Don't make me resort to emojis, little brother, not when I helped change your diapers: 😁 👶.

Normally that would have wrung a smile out of him. She'd been two when he was born.

Then he was at the final message. *WHERE ARE YOU? ANSWER ME!*

She'd called him twenty-eight times over the past week alone. He'd sent every attempt to voice mail. They'd have to talk eventually, but not right then. Not while his mind was busy adding up every time Dad had come home late or had a "business dinner." Gone out with friends when Mom had other plans. How much of that had been real?

Mom herself had texted a grand total of once since dropping him off the day before: *We'll get through this, beta. Please behave in the meantime.*

The boiling rage seared his insides again, magnified by the nauseating helplessness. He'd been so naïve.

Nilesh found himself holding a smashed out-of-season mango he didn't remember picking up, let alone crushing. The red-and-green skin bled stringy orange pulp.

Chill, he told himself, and buried the mutilated fruit under the other unripe mangoes.

Across the store, near the cash registers, Ridhi was scooping fresh samosa into a paper bag.

Seeing her, Nilesh felt a rush of victory. Though she'd kept the bangles and bindi, she'd ditched the mushroom barrettes for a lotus clip. Her chunky earrings were gone, and the necklaces hung out of sight. No one gave her a second glance, because she looked normal.

He watched Anil Uncle heft a sack of wheat flour over his shoulder while chatting with Kartik, and the rush soured. Ridhi had no clue how freaking lucky she was. *She* actually had a solid family, and all she wanted was to hop into some faerie story. What a waste.

"Beta," asked Meera Auntie, "can you go get me some cloves? A small package." She'd heaped her cart with baby eggplants, onions, fat red carrots, green beans, a knob of ginger, bunches of cilantro, one of the dudhi—and the mango he'd destroyed. So much for not being observed.

"Sure," he agreed. Any excuse to escape her scrutiny.

He took his time roving up and down the aisles. They were stocked with every possible variety of dried beans and lentils, Ayurvedic neem toothpaste and herb-infused hair oil, jars of ghee in different sizes, bottles of watermelon juice and aloe vera juice, oily pickles, dried dates, and soy nuggets. Clear pound bags of raw nuts: cashews, almonds, walnuts, pecans, and pistachios. Microwavable pouches of ready-made meals: aloo chole, saag paneer, jackfruit curry. Boxed mixes for idli and sambar. Savory snacks like chakli, chevdo, and far far; sweets like peda, jalebi, and kaju katli topped with silver leaf. Anything you wanted to cram down your gullet or plaster on your hair or skin, you could probably get hold of somewhere in the store.

Nilesh grabbed a three-pack of masala-flavored instant ramen noodles from a display stand, then tried the next aisle.

Bingo. Plastic bags of whole and powdered spices lined the shelves, along with colorful boxes of masala for all kinds of dishes. They made him nostalgic for Sunita and the feasts she whipped up every night.

Another thing Dad had taken from him.

Nilesh shoved that line of thought away and ticked off coriander seeds, cinnamon sticks, peppercorns, dried chili peppers, cumin seeds, and mustard seeds. There they were, cloves.

He was reaching for the nearest bag when a lilting Indian accent interrupted him. "Warming spices, the sweet fire in any true chef's arsenal. What delicacies will you be preparing with them?"

He almost snickered. *Sweet fire? Delicacies?* Who talked like that?

Then he saw the speaker. A girl his age stood there, pretty and willowy enough to model in an ad for haute couture. Her fire-colored sari and gold-and-flower jewelry were too glitzy for anything but a red-carpet event.

"Who, me?" he managed. "I'm no chef."

"A pity." The girl lifted a jar of cinnamon sticks off the shelf. "Surely you know these quills come from a tree? The inner bark is stripped down and left to dry in curls."

Nilesh's brain floundered. Curls like her black hair. It even had the same brownish tint, and its soft shine defied the store's harsh lighting. "'Quills'? Wow, you know a lot about spices."

She replaced the jar and helped herself to his bag of cloves. The curve of her dark-red lips was playful, a challenge. His heart beat faster in turn.

"And," she said, "these are the aromatic flower buds of a disparate tree. Tell me you knew that much, at least."

It hit Nilesh that he was enjoying himself. Random botany lessons from a hot girl? This was exactly his kind of diversion. "Can't say I did." He stuck out his hand for her to shake. "I'm Nilesh."

The girl's new-penny eyes sized him up. She didn't take his hand, so he let it drop. What was it about her coloring? Like—like autumn leaves, before and after they'd fallen. Yeah, that was it.

What a weird thought to have, as weird as this conversation. But he didn't want it to end.

Naturally, Ridhi had to text him. *Where are you? We're checking out now.*

It was surreal to see her name pop up on-screen after all these years. Surreal and unwelcome. He pocketed his phone without answering. "Sorry about that."

Smirking, the girl folded his fingers around the cloves. "It would be such a shame if you were to depart without these, Nilesh."

The words were throaty and amused, and Nilesh wanted more

of them. Without looking away, he scrabbled for the nearest spices. "What's so special about these?"

The girl raised an eyebrow. "Cardamom pods? A fair amount. For instance—"

"Ridhi!" Kartik shouted from somewhere close by. "He's over there!"

Oh, man. Nilesh really should have texted back so they didn't come searching for him.

The mysterious girl's grin widened. "Has she taken you to her forest yet?"

"Wait, you know each other?" And here he'd figured things were as bad as they could get.

"In a manner of speaking." The girl's lips twitched. "Is something the matter?"

That mouth. Nilesh couldn't stop staring at it. "Why?"

She leaned in to whisper, "Because you seem overwrought."

"Nah," he said, using her first question to dodge the second. "I'm not really into nature. Too quiet, and too many bugs. Boring."

Her eyes flashed copper, and displeasure flickered over her face. Crap, he'd offended her.

There weren't a lot of people whose opinions Nilesh still cared about, but this girl had somehow already made the list. Not only was she smoking hot, but she fascinated him, too. Who was she? What was she even doing in some dingy Indian grocery store?

"I must dissent," she said coolly. "Indeed, the wonders of the natural realm are second to none."

For a second, he smelled something earthy, like when he went for morning runs in October. His shoe crunched on bits of dead leaf. Somebody should really sweep the floors. "Oh, yeah? Like what?"

"*I* am one such wonder. Imagine never having encountered me." The girl tossed her head. "Would that not have been a tragedy of epic proportions?"

"I thought we were talking about nature."

"Did you say '*boring*'?" Ridhi interrupted. "You're kidding, right?"

Nilesh turned to see her advancing on him with an expression like he'd confessed to eating fried babies for breakfast.

Unreal. Shouldn't she be off communing with the tulsi plants or something? "So what if I did?" he asked. "It's an opinion. People have them."

Ridhi wrested the cloves from him. "Well, your opinion is wrong." Then she noticed the girl, who'd already gotten to the opposite end of the aisle, and went silent.

"Perhaps I should allow you two to resolve this in private," the girl called over her shoulder with a wink. She sashayed around the corner before Nilesh had gotten her name or number.

Ridhi gaped after her. "Who was *that*?"

"You should know," Nilesh said. "She mentioned your forest."

"I don't think so. But she's . . ."

"Hot? Yeah, I know."

Ridhi's glower told Nilesh he'd scored the point. He was still pissed—for five whole minutes, he'd forgotten about Mom and Dad—but getting under Ridhi's skin so easily almost made up for it. Almost.

Armed with the pack of instant ramen, he headed off to find

Meera Auntie's cart. And the hot girl, too, but she'd probably already left.

Ridhi walked beside him, apparently subdued.

Meera Auntie had parked the cart by the freezers and was arguing with Kartik. It seemed he'd cleaned out an entire section of frozen food and transferred it to the cart. Anil Uncle was removing package after package of kulfi, shrikhand, and khaman dhokla and restocking them.

"I'm *hungry*," Kartik whined. "You know I'll eat it!"

"I know you will," Meera Auntie said, grim. "You can keep one box of kulfi. We already have dhokla at home, and you don't need shrikhand right now." She frowned at the remaining loot. "Or three bags of chips."

"But I love shrikhand!"

"All right," Anil Uncle cut in. "That's enough. Nilesh, put that in the cart."

Nilesh obediently stacked the ramen on a jumbo tub of yogurt. Ridhi did the same with the cloves.

"How come he gets that if I can't have my chips?" Kartik asked.

"He's our guest," Meera Auntie said. "I already let you have the kulfi. Should I say no to that, too?"

Kartik shook his head hard enough to get whiplash, and Nilesh felt sorry for him. You didn't mess with desi mothers, not if you had half a brain.

Too bad, he thought numbly, that didn't stop *them* from messing with *you*.

"By the way, Nilesh," Anil Uncle said, "your papa has been

trying to call you since yesterday. Have you checked your phone?"

Nilesh's pulse went into hyperdrive. He'd been ignoring those calls. "It's dead. I don't know where my charger went."

"Beti?" Meera Auntie prodded. "Can you help him out?"

A beat too late, Ridhi said, "You can borrow mine."

She so clearly didn't mean it that Nilesh couldn't help himself. "Sure. That would be awesome."

His phone's battery basically *was* dead, so he'd recharge it and talk to Amar. As for Dad, he could wait the rest of his life, for all Nilesh cared.

Meera Auntie counted the items in the cart. "We still need serrano peppers. Can you go get them, Ridhi? Then we'll have everything."

"Nilesh," Anil Uncle added, "go with her. We'll meet you both at the register."

Nilesh's shoulders pulled tight. He didn't have to look to know Ridhi was just as pleased about her parents bulldozing them into being friends again.

But he could deal. He strode off, and she caught up.

"You're wrong, you know," she said. "It's never boring in nature. Not if you're paying attention. Just because some people need loud noises to distract them all the time—"

"You love nature. Good for you." Nilesh clapped twice. "Where're the peppers?"

"It's quicker if I show you." Ridhi led him past the row of refrigerators to a hidden cold-storage room with a heavy-duty plastic strip curtain. The curtain had yellowed with age. "I'll wait here."

"Whatever." Nilesh parted the dirty strips and went into the misty room.

Instead of the wooden bins of red and green peppers that should have been there, rows of stalls and tents in candy colors spread out before him. They extended back farther than they had any right to, until he couldn't tell where the room ended. It wasn't even cold. More like swimming in the ocean weather.

There wasn't a ceiling, either, just a night sky with lots of stars.

Nilesh didn't know what to think. This was a cold-storage room. Wasn't it?

"Hello? Is anybody there?" No one answered, so he took another step. And another, getting closer to the glittering marketplace. He could sort of make out the items for sale.

What *was* that fuzzy thing?

Ridhi poked her head in. "What's the holdup?"

Nilesh would have thought she'd flip out, but she just seemed impatient. When he looked again, the stalls and tents had disappeared, edged out by the frosty bite of a walk-in fridge and all the chili peppers Meera Auntie could possibly use. His arms broke out in little bumps, and his breath fogged up.

Great. Now he was hallucinating?

He tracked down the skinny serrano peppers and stuffed some into a plastic bag, which he pushed at Ridhi. Being around her was making him as loopy as she was. "Here."

"What's going on?" She sounded bent out of shape. "Or are you just being your usual charming self?"

Nilesh scowled. "I got your peppers. Quit being so weird all the time."

He trudged out of the little room. Not even his conversation with the girl in the spice aisle could redeem this wreck of a week, not when he hadn't gotten her number. "I'll be outside," he told Meera Auntie and Anil Uncle in the checkout line.

Busy with their groceries, they only waved for him to go. Good. All Nilesh wanted was to get to the exit.

When he hit the pavement, he was already zoning out—and walked right past the hot girl before doubling back. Now she wore a gold circlet with red, orange, and yellow leaves. It complemented her gulmohar flower nose pin.

"There you are!" she trilled. "Oh, I so hoped we would cross paths again. There are yet many more spices and their virtues to extol."

"More spices, huh?" Behind her, Nilesh saw a forest where the parking lot had been. She herself could have stepped right out of a tree. Every part of her belonged to these woods.

The branches swung near as she glided toward him. She smelled like the spices she'd praised—cinnamon and cloves and cardamom—and roses, too.

Nilesh couldn't think. She had clouded his senses with the sari-outlined curves of her body, the slyness of her wit, the promise of her mouth.

None of this was possible. Even through the haze, he knew that. This was a dream.

He also knew that he never wanted to wake up from it.

The girl's eyes blazed at him. "Come with me, and I will introduce you to far more than you could ever conceive of."

He'd gone off the deep end. He didn't care. Whatever this was, it had to be better than the crap he'd been dealing with. "What's your name?"

"Kamini." She held out her hand. "I will have you back before they know you left."

Nilesh took it and let Kamini pull him deeper into the trees.

5

I t was still dark when Ridhi arrived at her forest.

Oh, how she'd missed it, the rare sightings of rust-orange foxes prowling amid the bushes and cotton-tailed rabbits nibbling on clover. The wealth of treasures to be had, like molted snakeskins half buried beneath logs and abandoned nests with bits of blue-green eggshell.

And, of course, the multitude of trees.

While waiting for the rest of the house to fall asleep, she'd layered silk skirts over lace, pinned jeweled flowers and the amethyst deceiver clips in her hair, and pressed a crystal bindi to her forehead. By the pink glow of her lotus lamp, she'd dusted her eyelids with glittery purple-blue shadow and painted her mouth in bold red lipstick. Intricate necklaces, stacks of glass bangles, and a pair of jhumkas in her ears capped off the outfit. A touch of Sitayana, and she was ready.

Then, determined to win over her enchanted woods, Ridhi had stolen out of the house into the night.

She'd hardly parked her bike and shed her shoes before she was hastening toward the entrance, skirts swishing about her. It was dangerous to go barefoot—there could be rusty nails on the ground, to say nothing of rocks and roaches—but she wouldn't be separated from the land.

A great horned owl hooted somewhere above, mirroring her melancholy.

Ridhi gazed up at the treetops, where a gossamer web of moonbeams and murk had been woven over the boughs she knew so well. Beneath that netting, it was all so different, so mysterious and spectral, the colors and sounds muted. She'd planned for the occasional passing car or jogger making the most of the solitude, yet she was alone.

Curls trailing behind her like a cape, Ridhi sailed into her forest. The trees were glorious in their coat of silver, their branches shimmering, their leaves stirring. She could *feel* them singing to her, welcoming her home. Her golden anklets, like the ones Aranyani Devi wore as she danced through jungles, camouflaged but for their melody, tinkled in reply.

With the entrance behind her, Ridhi knelt, not caring that the loam would stain her skirts. She extracted Keeper of the Woodlands from her purse and tipped a single drop onto the mysterious leaf she'd received. Then she blew on the leaf, a spell that held at its heart a plea. *See me. Know me. Have me. I'm yours.*

Ridhi had been homesick as far back as she could remember. This was the realm where she belonged—this, and the land beyond it. Her latest offering had to gain her access. She'd seen the branch. The jungle crow had brought her a seed to round out her formula.

The night remained still, a snapshot of arboreal eternity.

She blinked, her eyes burning, and listened for the coming of the jungle crow, the murmurs of the trees. Maybe an opening in the air large enough for her to step through.

Had she gone to the wrong spot? Was the portal somewhere else, like her yard?

A tear trickled down, hot against her chilled cheek. "Please," she prayed, to Aranyani, to the yakshas and yakshinis, to the trees themselves. "Please."

Soft bleating caught her attention. Rather than the jungle crow, a golden deer, like the one Lakshman had hunted at Sita's request, had taken her leaf in its teeth. Then it galloped off, a specter in the moonlight.

Not about to lose it, Ridhi raced after the deer.

They darted through the woods, the doe sidestepping low branches and leaping over streams, but always at a pace that Ridhi could match. Then, as fleetly as it had materialized, it relinquished the leaf and fused with the darkness, marooning her much deeper in the woods than she'd ever been, with no clue how to get back.

She attempted the incantation again. Another misfire.

Could she have gotten both the location *and* the amount wrong? Ridhi tried a third time, pouring out the rest of the vial. If that didn't work, she didn't know what she would do.

Like a veil lifting, the blue-black sky altered, a threshold being crossed. From Earth to elsewhere. Ridhi's skin trembled in recognition, a shiver that had nothing to do with the frigid air.

In fact, the cold was gone, melted away by a temperature far too balmy for the middle of March. Her cheek dried, and she wriggled out of her coat and hung it over her arm.

After all her years of beseeching it, the forest had welcomed her in. She could scarcely breathe for triumph.

Even Lord Chandra shone more richly here, a silvery lantern by which she could navigate. His luminescence glazed the bushes and trees, thick enough that Ridhi fantasized about piping it over a fresh batch of blueberry velvet cupcakes.

Strains of music drifted toward her, a spring raga. Her ears picked out dilruba, sitar, and tabla, so skillfully played that the obscured musicians must have been gandharvas visiting from Lord Indra's court. A revel, she presumed, and where revels were, people would be.

A bend in the path terminated in a clearing where branches wreathed in Spanish moss formed a bower strung with fairy lights and strands of diamonds and pearls. Purple butterflies darted from bulb to bulb, their wings freckled with tiny stars.

When Ridhi looked closer, she realized the fairy lights weren't lights at all but noctilucent Indian jasmine blossoms. Their heady scent imbued the air, sweet yet sultry, laid over the familiar base notes of loam and decaying mulch.

A brooding yaksha detached himself from the tree he'd been leaning against and blocked her. "What is this influx of mortals tonight?" he groused, the contours of his face etched by a cluster of illuminated mangoes like lit diyas. "Your kind has no place here. Leave."

Ridhi couldn't believe it. After everything she'd done, all the years she'd waited, some guy she'd never met expected her to turn around and go home on his say-so? He might be beautiful, with those cheekbones and thick lashes, but really, who did he think he was?

"The forest let me in," she said, as sweet as honeysuckle nectar. "If you have a problem with that, you'll have to take it up with the trees."

With that, she bolted past him and into the bower.

Beneath the strands of jasmine and pearl stood a long table bedizened with emerald silk and set for fifty guests. Sprays of flowers, fruit, and leaves were interspersed with slender blue and green candles, whose flames had no effect on the icicle flute glasses. It was every fantasy she'd indulged, every film she'd watched over and over again, brought to life.

Now she was part of it all.

Yakshas, yakshinis, and shalabhanjikas paraded past, their hair woven through with gold and their diadems and turbans with berries. Ferns flowed across their leaf-silk saris and sherwanis; vines snaked about their bare arms like viridian bracers. And flowers, so many flowers, spilled from them like the jewels they wore, in madder, in mauve, in violet and teal and maize, in peach and powder blue and hot pink.

Wonderstruck, Ridhi drank in the procession. It was like having a front seat to the most glamorous fashion show ever.

The deep loneliness in her heart, as excruciating as if she'd ingested a wasp's nest, dissolved. The keepers of nature. Her people. She'd found them.

Food appeared on the plates, and liquid phosphoresced inside the icicle goblets, but only Ridhi paid the table the slightest regard. The other guests began to dance—great, flowing movements that ended in spirited twirls and swapping of partners. It wasn't anything like the stylized poses of bharatanatyam or even the wilder folk dances of garba and bhangra Ridhi had done at mandir events, but it swept her up, nonetheless.

She draped her coat over a chair. Then she was in the circle, her body swaying to the music.

Faces flashed past her, glimpses of wild, uninhibited loveliness. She spun and whirled, a wealth of grace coaxed out by the forest and transformed. Her arms rose, and her hips moved in supple figure eights, a shalabhanjika exiting her tree. The soft slap of her bare feet on the earth was the pulse of the trees made tangible. Her breath was their pine-needle fragrance.

Their susurrations enveloped her, and as she moved, she could almost work out what direction they had come from, which trees had spoken. Almost, but not quite.

"A mortal! How splendid," crooned a bewitching yakshini in a yellow-green sari. Her kajal-ringed eyes shone as she pulled Ridhi into the knot of her friends. Dwarf goldenrod and musk larkspur cropped up in her wake, carpeting the ground in festive colors.

The group cooed over Ridhi's clothes, her barrettes, her silver fingernails. She, meanwhile, coveted the mekhalas slung low about the women's hips. The golden girdles with their triple strands of jewels were said to have magical powers, but only yakshinis wore them, like a marker of an exclusive society. A sisterhood, through thick and thin.

Ridhi knew right then that she had to have one.

A yaksha in a sherwani of cherry blossoms introduced himself as Prakash. "Pray tell how you came to be with us this night," he said. Unlike the boy who'd tried to keep her out, Prakash waited keenly, clearly in the mood for an engrossing tale.

So Ridhi recounted the saga of the strange leaf, the jungle crow, and the golden deer. The Kalpavriksha sightings, though, she kept to herself, a secret too personal to disclose.

She was in the midst of describing her pursuit of the deer when the lantern-bedecked branches parted to reveal a lone yakshini in a plain lichen sari spooning arils from a pomegranate. She'd obviously been eavesdropping.

The gorgeous features of the peridot-garbed yakshini tightened with distaste. "Ishika. I had heard that the traitor crawled among us."

Her friends flocked nearer. "I shall never fathom how she was not ousted from the kingdom," declared a yakshini in a sari of violets. "A miscarriage of justice, to be certain."

Ishika's name rang a bell for Ridhi, yet the details evaded her. Something about a love affair?

"Surely you do not need to be told that you are unwelcome here,

Ishika," Prakash said sarcastically. "Or that my betrothed would be aggrieved to see you so brazenly trespassing. One would imagine that after four centuries, you would have mastered such basic notions of propriety."

Sneering, Ishika flung the pomegranate at the feet of the yakshini in yellow green. "You and your merry band of sycophants are as uncouth and opportunistic as ever. To think I once cared for you!"

"Do not blame her for your poor choices." Prakash put his hand on the peridot-wearing yakshini's back, and an intimate understanding passed between them. "Now, will you depart of your own accord, or do you require an escort?"

Ishika stalked off, leaving Ridhi uncertain as to what she'd just witnessed.

"You would be wise to give that one a wide berth, mortal maiden," cautioned Prakash's betrothed. "You speak of golden deer and jungle crows? She is naught but a viper." Composed once more, she produced a gilt pine cone the size of her hand and unscrewed the textured diamond cap. "Let us not squander another moment on conniving blackhearts. Allow me, guest of our forest, to offer you a beverage."

"You simply *must* try it," gushed a yakshini in wood sorrel. "Elixirs are Sulochana's specialty."

Sulochana. *That* was why Ishika's name was familiar. Mummy had told Ridhi tales of these yakshinis. Sulochana might look like a twenty-year-old, her cheeks full and unlined, her lips plump, and her streaming tresses as dark as ebony, but she was more like two thousand years old.

And four centuries ago, a princess named Ishika, of much higher standing than Sulochana's minor nobility, had been her lover. The pair had been so besotted that royal musicians had penned ballads venerating their courtship and how its depth lit up the very land.

That same ardor withered on the vine when Ishika nearly brought about the destruction of the yaksha kingdom.

Every ten years on Holi, or so the story went, Lord Indra had permitted the yakshas to wish on the Kalpavriksha to fortify their realm against the creep of mortal damage. Ishika had been selected to pluck the leaf that day, a coveted honor, and rumor had it that, as her reward, she would request a small parcel of land for the woman she loved.

Yet during the actual ceremony, Ishika had spat on Lord Indra's generosity, choosing instead to sunder an entire branch. Worse still, the wounded wish tree then succumbed to a rash of white spots.

Lord Indra had retaliated with hurricanes and blustery winds, pulverizing trees and incinerating homes with thrusts of his infamous thunderbolt.

Before the situation could escalate into all-out war, King Kubera and Queen Kauberi publicly denounced Ishika as an insurgent and sealed the portal connecting the worlds, forever cutting off the yakshas' access to the Kalpavriksha.

Ishika, once the darling of her people, became a pariah. Yet rather than return the branch and make amends, she'd hidden it, compounding her transgression.

Heartbroken at her lover's deception, Sulochana had withdrawn and spent a century out of the public eye. That time had amplified the hatred between the two until it overshadowed the passion they had once shared.

And Ishika dared show her face at this revel? Good thing Ridhi hadn't brought up the bejeweled branch. Poor Sulochana!

But with the others politely waiting, Ridhi set aside her questions in favor of the goblet Sulochana had decanted for her. The jade-colored liquid within had the clarity of spring water and the viscosity of maple syrup. She'd read enough folklore to know that tasting it was a terrible idea. "You made this?"

"I both produce and sell my elixirs." Sulochana gave a proud waggle of her head. "They are a challenge to keep in stock. I occasionally even gift them to the maharaja and maharani when they invite me to dine with them."

While it was impressive that Sulochana had restored her reputation with the monarchs, Ridhi couldn't picture buying these elixirs in Shivam Bazaar. It was as incongruous as spotting a rainbow among the aisles of cooking oils and canned chickpeas. "Where do you sell them?"

"Same place I got this," said the last voice she wanted to hear in any realm.

Wheeling around, Ridhi found herself face-to-face with Nilesh and his posse of eager yakshas and yakshinis. Her joy wilted like daisies in a drought.

"Kamini!" he called. "Look who I found!"

A familiar yakshini, wrapped in a filmy pumpkin-toned sari and wreathed in gold and dahlias, promenaded closer. It was the girl from the grocery store. "Namaste, Ridhi. I trust you have been keeping well?"

Ridhi frowned. "You know who I am?"

"A fellow lover of the arborescent?" Kamini asked airily. "How would you *not* be known to us?"

Behind her, the foliage warmed to spectacular autumn shades: prominent yellows, flamboyant oranges, reds as rich as garnets and rubies, even a smattering of mulberry. She slid a dahlia into Nilesh's collar.

Ridhi must be turning the single shade of green she couldn't stand—the green of someone about to be sick. That explained Nilesh's unusually peppy mood all afternoon. He'd known about this. And hadn't breathed a word, of course.

She pulled him to one side. "What are you doing here? You need to leave."

"More like *you* need to leave." Nilesh had the temerity to laugh. "You crashed my party."

"Your party? This should be *my* party. You don't even like nature."

He only shrugged. "Guess they like me better." Then he held up his goblet in a mock toast before clinking it against hers. "Cheers."

She gestured to his sherwani with its dupatta of red leaves and bark. "Where did you get that?"

"The Night Market. You can get pretty much anything there."

A Night Market? Like a Goblin Market? And Ridhi hadn't been invited?

Kamini and her friends descended on them, sparing Ridhi from having to comment.

"Where were you this morning?" one of them asked Kamini. "I hunted for you everywhere."

"Visiting my mother's grove." Kamini looped her arm through Nilesh's. "Come, silly boy! Your throne awaits."

Ridhi glanced over her shoulder in time to see a formidable wooden chair rise up from a stump near the table. Red clover blossoms spread to form a dense cushion on the seat, ivy sprouted over the armrests, and the backrest was enameled with mango leaves. It was a throne fit for forest royalty.

Her throat ached. Her eyes burned. Why hadn't Kamini picked *her*?

Sulochana drew closer, moving with assurance. The vines of hot-pink-and-purple fuchsia lanterns that showered her in gemlike radiance underscored her regal bearing. "Are you not thirsty?"

Ridhi started to say she wasn't. Who knew what this mystery drink might do?

But that hadn't stopped Nilesh. Nilesh, who'd discounted her for craving magic along with everyone else. He'd ripped the one thing she wanted out of her grasp—and he didn't even care.

The elixir might turn all food to ashes in her mouth or trap her between realms or strip her of her name. But always agonizing over what she'd passed up, always regretting that she'd held magic in her hand and spurned it while Nilesh had said yes, sounded like a much worse fate.

Ridhi tipped back the pine cone goblet. She tasted spring, the delicate flavor that was first shoots poking through thawing turf and virescent glades peppered with yellow crocuses and pale green buds protruding from dormant branches. Awakening inundated her, awakening and renewal. She could feel virtual fiddlehead ferns unfurling within her belly. *I'm drinking a season! With yakshas!*

Sulochana observed her, pleased. "Prakash and I decoct the flavors of the foliage."

"What's summer like?" Ridhi asked, intrigued by the option of a darker, more pronounced green, but an exclamation cut her off.

The yakshini in violets laid beringed fingers on Ridhi's shoulder. "I do not suppose you have any chocolate on hand? I have heard much of this mortal confection."

Ridhi hung her head. "No. I'm sorry."

"Oh, leave her be, Hamshi," said another yakshini, this one older. Her bearing held the sort of fierceness Ridhi associated with nature itself, ultimately untamable no matter how much modern society tried to subjugate it. "She has only just joined us!"

Sulochana reeled off more names: Hamshi, Shatapratika, Ghanta, Madana. Among them, these yakshinis were linked with riches, thaumaturgic powers, mysterious ointments, a pill that healed all ills and bestowed long life, and the secrets of sorcery.

Half drunk on the heart of spring, Ridhi gazed at them. She was talking to figures from folklore! She would never be able to go home and live a mundane life again. It had been hard enough before, but now, having experienced this . . .

She wandered to the little table Sulochana had set up, where carafes of various elixirs sat amid fairy-tale fruits. There were so many flavors, from something that might have been the yellow gold of ginkgo fans to the purple of the spearlike Persian shield plant. Purple was Ridhi's second-favorite color—after green, of course— and she was desperate to know what a purple plant might taste of. A gloaming wood?

As the yakshinis moved, tree buds burst into full flower. It was stunning. Unfortunately, it also triggered Ridhi's pollen allergy. She sneezed and sneezed.

"We have a lioness among us!" Shatapratika cried.

Everyone roared.

Though mortified, Ridhi roared, too. "I know, I know. How can I be allergic to flowers when I love them so much? Everyone always asks that."

That must have been the right thing to say, because the yakshinis formed a circle around her, and Hamshi offered her a pastille the orange pink of begonias. "This will help."

"I quite like voluble girls," Vikala asserted. "Being meek has its place, but only when it is chosen and not pressed upon another. As if men ever choose to be meek!"

Soon they were vying to tell her stories of times they had been loud or put a deserving yaksha in his place.

Sucking on the pastille, Ridhi launched into a memory of her own, turning the time Chetan Gopalkrishnan heckled her for talking to plants into a joke. Transmuting her pain and degradation in a sort of alchemy.

And the yakshinis *laughed*. They glided nearer still, weaving snowdrops and forget-me-nots into her hair. In that moment, she was one of them. Part of a sisterhood.

She held out her goblet, which Sulochana refilled with an elixir the burnt orange of maples in autumn streaked with yellow, as if the libation were liquid flame.

A voice at the back of Ridhi's head rebuked her for going too fast, trusting too soon. All faerie bargains had a true price, hidden in a loophole or masked by clever wording.

But this was what she'd spent her life waiting for. Hushing the voice, she clinked her goblet against Sulochana's, then sipped.

The taste of crisp autumn air, of distant woodsmoke and apples, and of a forest dressed up in its fiery finery for a last, defiant celebration before its wintry sleep spread over her tongue. A pleasant warmth shimmied along her solar plexus, the sensation of being rooted beside a pond as the leaves she shed danced down onto its surface. Fall was the sunset of seasons, and it smoldered in her veins.

Their foreheads touching, Prakash spoke in an undertone to Sulochana, and the adoration with which he beheld her was unmistakable. *Good for her*, Ridhi thought. She deserved a fresh start.

The other yakshas and yakshinis meandered toward the long table. Her heart overflowing, Ridhi lingered by the elixirs. She didn't think she'd ever been more elated.

A zephyr blew past her ears, and leaves rustled—the near

whispers of the woods. She sucked in a breath. "I hear them."

It had been a confession to the heavens, but Sulochana came closer. "Whom do you hear?" she asked, her gaze alert.

"The trees. They're speaking." Ridhi mimicked the whooshing noise, her arms rising in spontaneous arcs to emphasize it. "*Shh, shh, shh.* Like that."

Her candor must have convinced Sulochana. "Interesting. If they speak to you, there is promise. The forest, too, has its secrets. Few have the ears with which to hear them, and fewer still are given the chance."

"I have the ears," Ridhi said confidently. "I just need the chance. Teach me."

"Why is this so important to you, mortal maiden?"

Ridhi knew when she was being tested. Glibness wouldn't get her anywhere; this question required the truth.

"I've never loved anything like I love the forest," she began. "I even make perfumes from it. It's the only place I've ever felt at home, the only place I ever really wanted to be. Trees are my best friends, and I want to understand them." She paused. "So what do you think?"

Sulochana laughed, a high, tinkling sound. "Would that I could. Alas, between my stall at the Night Market and the Holi preparations, the hours in my day are spoken for."

"I could help with the preparations!" Ridhi proposed.

Sulochana appraised her. "Perhaps you could, at that. In any instance, I shall go have a word with my cousin. A talent such as yours should not be neglected."

A quarter of an hour had elapsed when the yaksha who'd sought to ban Ridhi from the revel joined her. He'd switched out his hostility for a more sociable gruffness. "You mortals have charmed my people this evening, it would seem."

Ridhi wasn't sure she liked the concept of working with a self-styled gatekeeper, no matter how nice he was to look at. But if that was the cost to eke out a position for herself, she would pay it.

She met his eyes, admiring the thick lashes that framed them. He might be a jerk, but he was really cute, too. Some small part of her wanted to crack that conceited exterior, to conquer him until he championed her as fervently as he had crusaded to drive her away. That would be fun.

"You claim to read the leaves. Demonstrate." He opened his palm, and the tree above him quivered. Ridhi recognized it as Indian fig.

"I said *almost*," she reminded him. "And Sulochana said you could help me get better."

"Indeed." The yaksha seemed to perform some internal calculation. "Holi is coming, and you might well prove useful to us. Very well; I will teach you, mortal girl. Consider this your trial period."

"If you're going to teach me, we should know each other's names. I'm Ridhi."

"I am Malav," he conceded. "Go now and enjoy the banquet, mortal girl. Our tutelage will commence soon."

"Ridhi," she corrected him. But he had already walked away.

She still wasn't certain why Kamini had brought Nilesh to the revel and not her, or why Kamini had sought him out in the store to begin with. There was the inevitable loophole in the faerie bargain, one Ridhi never would have thought to protect herself against.

Even in the yaksha kingdom, her old life could haunt her steps.

But she'd won a reprieve, and she would show Sulochana and the others that she could be of use.

She hurried to partake of the feast.

Nilesh had never felt so free. Not even the absurd stunts that got his blood racing came close. Kamini wasn't like anyone he'd ever met. The Night Market she'd taken him to, the same place he'd seen in the grocery store, had blown his mind. He'd eaten sky candy on a stick—it was blue and hard like rock candy, but it tasted like how flying felt—swung a sword that cleaved flames in two, and tried on a sherwani-and-churidar set made of leaves and bark. He'd figured it would be scratchy, but it was as sleek as satin.

It's like being inside a video game, he'd told her, *but cooler.*

Kamini had bought the outfit for him, laughing when he offered to pay. *Mortal currency has no worth in the Market. What is more, you will need it where we are going next.*

But where that was, she wouldn't say.

Later, on the way to the exit, she'd pointed out the vacant stall that belonged to her cousin Sulochana. Nilesh, still riding high from the candy, said it would be nice to meet her sometime.

Kamini had waggled her head. *That can be arranged.*

Then they'd gone through a portal and come out in a grassy clearing decorated with silk lanterns and glowing fruit. People good-looking enough to seem unreal mobbed him like he was a celebrity. More yakshas and yakshinis, he'd deduced, right before they started plying him with questions about the human world.

A revel in your honor, mortal boy, Kamini had whispered in his ear. *Are you not glad I dressed you for the occasion?*

I sure am. He'd slung his arm around her, and she'd introduced him to Sulochana, who'd been friendly, and to her brother, Malav, who'd barely nodded.

Before that night, Nilesh hadn't known magic existed. He gave a mental snort. Who would have guessed Ridhi had been right all along? It didn't make any sense. Hell, there he was in the yaksha kingdom, and it still sounded nuts. *Magic. Yeah, right.*

But he didn't want to think, and if magic could help him forget, he'd take it.

Nilesh refilled his goblet from a pitcher on the big table and swigged the purple contents. So far, the night had been exactly what he'd needed, lots of talking and laughing. It was like old times, if you didn't count the flowers sprouting randomly or the food and drinks out of some fantasy movie.

Even Ridhi and her weird barrettes had crashed the revel. They actually fit in there, which was the best argument for "never say never" Nilesh could think of. The one thing missing was Amar horsing around somewhere.

Best of all, Kamini hadn't left Nilesh's side. The others were cool, but she was the one he wanted to learn everything about. He liked not being able to predict what she'd say or do.

Malav, who'd kept to himself for most of the party, loped over. His snooty expression had been replaced by a nicer one. More affectionate. He didn't look at Nilesh, only Kamini. "May I speak with you?"

"You may," she said, "though you need not be so formal, dear brother." To Nilesh, she added, "Pardon me. I will be but a moment."

"Sure," he said, though he hated seeing her go.

Her friends immediately pulled him into their orbit. But he could still see Kamini standing with her brother. It was obvious they were related, what with the eyes and the noses and how they moved.

Something he had no desire to investigate pinged in Nilesh's chest. He faced his very attentive audience and spelled out the difference between motorcycles and cars.

"I still do not believe they could best our chariots," a yaksha said.

Maybe it was good Amar wasn't there. He'd be halfway to his car on his mission to prove the yaksha wrong.

After a few minutes, Kamini returned with a little silver bowl of fruit. "Open up," she said. The bronze berry she fed Nilesh was the ideal amount of sweet and juicy.

"Your brother didn't seem too thrilled I'm here," he said.

Kamini sighed. "He . . . is not fond of mortals. But do not

trouble yourself about him. The others are like me, and quite enam-ored of your kind."

"Glad to hear it." Nilesh opened his mouth for another berry.

When Kamini delivered it, she brushed his chin in the process.

Nilesh savored the caress and the splash of the juice on his tongue. He could've spent the rest of his life like this.

But way too soon, the sun peeked over the horizon, and the other yakshas and yakshinis were taking off.

"What now?" he asked. "Don't tell me you're ready to call it a night."

"Not in the least." Her smile coy, Kamini lay down under a young champak tree. "Surely you are in no hurry yourself?"

Nilesh, who believed there were only two valid reasons for being awake before ten—either the house was on fire, or he had to get ready for school—stretched out next to her on the dew-wet grass and watched the sky flip from night mode to day mode.

Lying there with a hot, magical girl made for a pretty persuasive third reason. He'd meant to keep his eyes on the dawn, but it was hard not to notice how good she looked in her orange belly-baring lehenga and choli. The mirror-worked vine embroidery matched the grass and clover patches she lounged on, and the orange and yellow flowers in her dark curls lit her up. There was no doubt about it; the modeling world had seriously missed out.

"Do you see how the sunlight uncovers the diamonds?" Kamini asked.

Nilesh shook his head. "All I see are the ones you're wearing."

"I am wearing rubies and topaz, silly boy. Shut your eyes and open them again."

He did. Dewdrops, the same stuff making his clothes damp, glittered on the blades of grass. Oh—dewdrops as diamonds. He went to nab one, but Kamini scooped it up first.

"Observe." On her fingertip, the droplet became a cut-and-polished diamond. "Is that not delightful?"

You're delightful, Nilesh almost said. Gods, she might have been the prettiest girl he'd ever seen. "You need money?"

Kamini laughed. "Hardly! I merely value the many charms of the forest." She plucked at his sleeve. "Charms such as a silly mortal wearing a proper sherwani."

Nilesh wanted to kiss her so badly. But a movement across the clearing caught his eye.

It was Ridhi, sitting alone and stealing glances while Malav talked to a family of blue jays. The longing written all over her made Nilesh uncomfortable. She really should've learned by then to hide how much she cared.

Not his problem, of course.

He turned to Kamini, who was twirling her diamond between her thumb and finger. "Let me guess," he said. "Only yakshas can do that."

It changed back to water, which she flicked at him. "Precisely. Yet better still are these."

The liquid felt cool on his cheek. He wished she would touch him again.

Kamini scoped out the grass until she pinpointed the droplet she wanted. It didn't look any different from the rest of the dew, at least not that Nilesh could tell.

"Occasionally, a ray of Lord Surya's light will become entrapped within the dew," she said. "It is in the vein of what your gemologists would term a precious opal. Like dewdrop diamonds, we also have dewdrop opals." She transformed the droplet into an opal. A rainbow flickered inside it. "See? Dewdrop opal."

Nilesh's knowledge of gemstones could be summed up in two words: *expensive rocks*. As far as he was concerned, anything that sat behind protective glass, waiting for people like his parents to buy it, was precious—as in worth thousands of dollars. Besides, precious or not, the dewdrop opal wasn't the jewel he was interested in.

He brought his face up to Kamini's on the pretense of getting a better look. "I'll take your word for it."

Kamini tipped her head to the side, clearly not fooled. But clearly not bothered, either. "It is a wise man who heeds the knowledge of a learned woman."

"Huh." Nilesh rubbed his chin in mock thought. "So what's it like to live for centuries, anyway? Creaky joints?"

"That you would have to ask Sulochana. Thus far, I boast a scant eighteen turns around the sun, and Malav is my elder with nineteen."

Nilesh would be eighteen in the summer, so no weird age gaps there. "That works."

He fingered a stray curl by her temple. She was close enough that he could count the row of white dots she'd painted over her eyebrows. That perfect skin—was it as soft as it looked?

Their eyes met. The gold and green sparks in Kamini's coppery irises riveted him. Her lips parted, and she licked them.

Nilesh thought his heart might rupture. Why wouldn't she tell him to kiss her already?

Kamini's gaze lingered on him. It felt possessive. She dropped the opal into the pocket of his sherwani. "Everyone and everything, particularly the most beautiful things, has its uses, Nilesh. Hold that close."

He tried not to grin. She'd said his name. "The opal? I can't. You already put it in my pocket. You know, if you want me to hold it."

She rolled onto her side, so near that he could smell the rose water on her breath, and ran her hand over his jaw. "Silly boy."

"Didn't we already establish that?" He reached for her, impatient to find out if she tasted like roses, too.

She sprang to her feet. "As loath as I am to part with you, I must send you home."

Home. The word hit him like an anvil. "But what if I'm comfortable right here?"

"That is a pity, as I have an errand to attend to. Call it a family affair."

Nilesh sat up and saw Malav grimly steering Ridhi toward them. She carried her coat and a twinkling blue bottle he must have given her, and a clump of the Spanish moss clung to her shoulder.

"Are you ready?" Malav asked Kamini, who nodded. "Sprinkle this at your doorstep before you enter the house," he told Ridhi, "and your absence this night will be known only to you."

Ridhi beamed so blatantly, Nilesh couldn't take it. What was she doing?

But it wasn't his place to interfere. "Thanks for the potion, man."

"You are welcome," Kamini said. "Now go."

Nilesh tried to sound casual. "First tell me how I can see you again."

She clucked in disapproval. "And here I thought you so clever, silly boy."

Oh, right. The dewdrop opal. He dipped his head and mouthed, *Use me.*

Clever boy, Kamini mouthed back.

Now that he knew how to contact her, Nilesh didn't mind leaving so much. He didn't even say anything about the moss to Ridhi.

"This tree is your gateway," Kamini said. She held out her hands to both of them. "Simply step forward. I will guide you."

Just one day before, that would have seemed bonkers. The champak's trunk was skinnier than Nilesh. But, he reasoned, how else would a yakshini get around?

Taking her hand, he went into the tree. Through it.

The passage was dark and woody, a lot roomier than it should have been. He barely had time to blink, and then he was at the entrance to the park.

Beside him, Ridhi practically had stars for eyes. "Wow. That was *amazing*! And so fast."

Until then, Nilesh had restrained himself. Seeing her all keyed up, though, he had to roast her. Just a little. "I like the wig. But it should probably be on your head."

"Wig?"

He pointed to her shoulder. "Aren't you going for the Muppet look?"

Ridhi shot him an incredulous glance. She ripped off the moss, then pitched it at him. It flew wide by a mile.

His work there done, Nilesh jammed his hands in his pockets and sauntered off.

The walk back had been quiet, with Ridhi ignoring Nilesh, and Nilesh only too happy to return the favor.

He knew he should be freaking out. He'd spent the night in the company of genuine yakshas and seen genuine magic, which no one except little kids and Ridhi believed in.

But for the first time in ages, he was excited about something.

While Ridhi uncorked the potion, Nilesh checked out her house, something he hadn't really done in years. Mom said Meera Auntie had considered painting the walls purple, but everyone had talked her into a more sensible pale yellow. It was still a nice house, with those shingles on the roof. He should sketch it.

What would Kamini think of his sketches? Maybe he'd show them to her.

Ridhi shook the potion over the doorstep like she was salting food. "It's not dinner," Nilesh teased. "You don't have to season it. Just pour it on."

"Can't you leave me alone?"

He held up his hands in surrender. "Whoa. What's your problem?"

"You!" She turned her key in the lock with a lot more force than necessary. "You are. This was *my* thing, but you took that away, too."

"Your thing?"

Ridhi scowled like she might dump the dregs of the potion over his head. "Magic," she said. "Obviously."

So it was his fault Kamini hadn't picked her? "It's not like I asked for any of this. Anyway, you seemed to be doing just fine, talking to Malav. I thought he didn't even like humans."

She had no comeback for that.

Nilesh should have been pleased, but watching Kamini with her brother had gotten to him. "Hey, remember you said I could borrow your charger?"

"In my room." Ridhi turned the knob and tiptoed inside. Nilesh slipped in after her. The door creaked shut behind them.

Dishes clattered in the kitchen. But the potion held, and no one showed up to yell at them. Nilesh plunked his shoes down. He stomped up the stairs, Ridhi behind him. Nothing.

Where had this invisibility spell been all his life?

"Pretty cool," he said.

Ridhi begrudgingly answered. "Yeah."

"Ridhi?" Anil Uncle called out. "Are you up?"

"Just a minute!" She hesitated, then turned back to Nilesh. "You don't know what you're getting into, but I do. All the stories say to be careful, so if you're going to do this, don't go looking for trouble, and try not to catch anyone's attention. Even Kamini's. I mean it."

Yeah, right. Kamini's attention was exactly what he was after. "The charger?"

"Forget it." Ridhi grabbed the charger from her room and shoved it at him.

Nilesh took it and went to his own room, where he plugged in his phone. Like it or not, he'd put off the reckoning with Hetal long enough.

If he was being honest, while his sister really had botched things, he missed her. Until recently, they'd texted at least once a day. Not talking to her felt wrong, like the rotten cherry on Dad's sordid mistress sundae.

He'd call her, and they'd move past all this. Things would go back to normal.

Nilesh changed into a T-shirt and flannel pants. After digging the dewdrop opal out of the sherwani, he hung the outfit in the closet, then flopped onto the bed and powered on his phone.

Notifications started popping up. Dad had called. He hadn't left a message, but he'd called.

Nilesh's throat hurt like he'd been strangled.

What had he been thinking? He couldn't call Hetal. She'd known what Dad had done, and she'd let Nilesh find out in the most horrible way possible. If she'd told him before, they could have helped each other through it. Her hiding it felt even worse than Dad's cheating.

Normal didn't exist anymore, and not because Nilesh had just teleported by tree.

Meera Auntie opened the door. "Ridhi said you were awake. Is everything all right, beta?"

Glad for the distraction, Nilesh dropped the phone on the bed. "Yeah."

Meera Auntie looked from the phone to him. "It would be good for you to talk to your family. This is hard, what you're going through, and you can't do it alone."

Nilesh stiffened. "Yeah, maybe," he said blandly.

Meera Auntie's smile was sad. "It's okay, beta. You can feel as mad as you need to." She checked her watch. "There's bhurji in the kitchen. We're heading out for the day after breakfast, so make yourself at home."

That was good news, at least. While Nilesh liked Ridhi's family, that meant four fewer people keeping tabs on whatever he did. He wasn't sure how much longer he could act like he wasn't on the verge of exploding out of his skin.

Maybe Meera Auntie could tell, since she fluffed up the blanket around him. "Everything will be all right, I promise."

It didn't get more delusional than that. But she was nice, so he nodded for appearance's sake.

Meera Auntie patted his shoulder, then left him alone again.

Whatever relief he'd found in the yaksha revel had been wrecked, torpedoed by Dad and Hetal. All that remained was the grief and fury.

They loomed over Nilesh, stronger than before. They threatened to eat him alive.

Sleep. He had to sleep.

Nilesh tucked Kamini's dewdrop opal under his pillow. With any luck, he'd see her in his dreams.

7

Ridhi breezed into the kitchen in her pajamas, the residue of the potion still sparkling beneath her fingernails. Malav might have been cold and surly, but he'd given her actual magic. She'd *drunk* actual magic. It was part of her now, making itself at home in her bones, her blood, and her brain. Everything from the cream cabinets to the bowl of bananas and apples on the counter gleamed brighter, more vital. She could sense the trees they'd once adorned like jewels, from the texture of the bark down to each and every stem.

The walk home from the forest had been like this, a profound link to each tree, each weed, each blade of grass. It was as if she'd had laser surgery to correct her vision, and the previously blurry world had come into focus, unveiling the enchantment she'd always known had to be there. It buoyed her, and despite the fatigue that begged her to close her eyes and snooze the day away, Ridhi twirled across the sunny tile floor to the table.

Her heart swelled at the sight of her family. There they were, radiant with light only she could see, connected like twigs on the same branch. Though she'd returned only five minutes before, they assumed she'd been home since their trip to the grocery store the previous afternoon. They had no reason to suspect her secret.

And what a secret it was. Just thinking of it made her giddy.

"Come eat," Mummy called from the table, where she stood shredding cilantro leaves over a plate of bhurji. In contrast to Papa's crisply pressed dress shirt and pants, she wore a unicorn T-shirt and jeans. "It's your favorite!"

Weird—Papa handled breakfast on weekdays. But the mouth-watering aroma of eggs scrambled with turmeric and garam masala overrode all Ridhi's questions. She'd been too sated from the elixirs to eat more than a few bites of the purple gajar halwa at the yakshas' revel, and her stomach threatened to consume itself if she didn't rectify that immediately.

"Yum! Thanks." She gave Mummy a kiss on the cheek and dropped into the chair next to Kartik's.

"Up so early on a vacation day?" Papa asked. Steam wafted from his mug of chai as he scrolled through the news on his phone. Across from him, Kartik wolfed down his bhurji and buttered toast. "I thought you'd be snoring away until noon."

"Ha, ha." Ridhi dug into her own breakfast. The combination of egg, tomato, onion, chili pepper, and savory spices hit her tongue in a shower of fireworks, and she couldn't help picturing the sumptuous banquet in the glade. And Malav.

She basked in the memory of their deal. Phyllomancy! She was going to learn how to divine leaves—after a long, long nap, that was.

Mummy scoffed. "This girl? When we're off to sell her perfumes? Please."

Eagerness dispelled Ridhi's fatigue. In just a few short hours, her perfumes would be on the shelves of local shops. Nothing but a revel in the yaksha kingdom could have made her forget that.

She did a little dance in her chair. This was how things should be, the way they'd been before Nilesh had blown up their lives.

"And you'll bowl them over and land accounts at every single store. I'm sure of it." Papa took his dishes to the sink and rinsed them. "Have a good day, kids, seeing as how you don't have to be anywhere in particular, unlike us old folks."

"'Old folks'?" Mummy bristled with faux umbrage. "Speak for yourself!"

Maybe her sleep-deprived brain was lagging behind, but Ridhi felt like she'd missed something. "Wait, doesn't Kartik have soccer camp?"

"Nuh-uh!" her brother said. "I'm coming with you."

Only then did Ridhi realize he wasn't wearing his uniform. Wow, was she slow on the uptake. She definitely needed some chai to wake her up.

Mummy smiled an apology. "The morning session got canceled."

Ridhi, however, could afford to be magnanimous. "You can be my assistant and carry the box. How does that sound?"

"Only if we get ice cream," Kartik said. "That's my fee—two scoops in a waffle cone. With hot fudge."

"Very funny." Mummy sipped her coffee. "But if you do a good job helping your sister, we'll see. In fact, why don't you start now and clean up in here? Ridhi, go get your stuff together once you finish. We have a big day ahead of us."

"Okay," Ridhi said.

For his part, Kartik must have really wanted that ice cream, since he didn't argue.

Papa walked around the table, meting out hugs. When he got to Ridhi, he shone with pride. "Remember, all you need is one yes to start your empire."

"Thank you, Papa." Ridhi swallowed her last bite and, once he'd left, went upstairs to fetch Keeper of the Woodlands.

A moment later, she returned to the breakfast table. "I thought you'd want to smell this first," she told Mummy, holding out the perfume. "It's new."

Though she spoke blithely, her belly sparked with nerves. When it came to Ridhi's creations, Mummy was a critic first and a cheerleader second. She never held back if she thought a blend could be improved, and she'd taught Ridhi to embrace experimenting. So much of the best art, she'd said, resulted from taking chances.

"Of course I do!" Mummy removed the lid and held the vial to her nose. Her smile turned contemplative, and she nodded to herself and inhaled again. "Oh, beti," she exclaimed. "I love it! It smells . . . green. Like the woods."

"Exactly what I was going for." Relief like tiny lights blinked through Ridhi, and a knot in her back relaxed. Mummy liked it! No, she loved it. "No pointers?"

"Not a one. You knocked it out of the park."

Ridhi had already known how good her perfumes were. They'd gotten her into the yaksha kingdom, hadn't they? Not to mention the effusive reviews of her online shop. Yet nothing compared to earning her mother's unmitigated approval. "My first forest blend, chock-full of leaves and branches."

Mummy laughed. "How is it you didn't already have one of those?"

"I don't know!"

"I'll mock up a new label for it as soon as I have a chance." Mummy sniffed the bottle again. "It takes me back to a class trip when I was your age. We went to a hill station, and I thought I saw something in the trees."

"What was it?" Ridhi asked. She'd never heard this story before.

"Just a piece of glass," Mummy said. "But this sent me right back to the Himalayas! If these stores don't jump on your perfumes, they have no taste."

That was all Ridhi needed to hear. She hugged Mummy, then ran off again to get ready.

Mummy parked in front of the first boutique, Treasures Ever After. "It's a numbers game," she reminded Ridhi. "We'll go in there and show them what we have, but owners are looking for a reason to say no."

Ridhi luxuriated in the beauty of the tree-lined street. Spring peeked around the corner, its harbingers permeating the city. "I know."

She adjusted her wisteria crown and tidied her lavender kameez. *Dress for the job you want.* She'd certainly done that.

And since she had three different obstacles in the form of three different shops to conquer, she'd sprinkled Damayanti and the Swan—a warm, honeyed blend of four fragrant varietals of rose; heady champak, with a floral note and a note of peach-apricot tea; uplifting green cognac; and sustainably harvested sandalwood—on her wrists. In the story, no matter how many people tried to keep Damayanti from reuniting with her husband, Nala, she never gave up.

Ridhi vowed to aspire just as high.

When she strode through the boutique's front door, Mummy and Kartik at her heels, a bell tinkled, heralding her arrival.

Ridhi waltzed toward the counter, where a salesman paged through a catalog. "I'd like to speak to the owner, please. I've brought samples of my original, handcrafted perfumes for their consideration. They're all made with essential oils, and I believe they'd be perfect for the store."

"I'll go get her," the salesman said.

Exchanging a jubilant glance with Mummy, Ridhi checked out the store's setup. Candles, cosmetics, racks of high-end clothing. Excellent. Her perfumes would fit right in.

But the owner, an older white woman with sleek blond hair, was already shaking her head as she approached. "I'm so sorry," she said, her smile practiced and flat. "We're not looking to take any products on consignment at this time. In the future, please call in advance to schedule an appointment."

How had that never occurred to Ridhi? What a silly mistake, when she was doing her utmost to seem competent.

Kartik raised the box. "They're really good, though!"

Aw, Kartik, Ridhi thought, wishing she could ruffle his hair. He typically complained that her perfumes smelled up their house.

The woman turned her insincere smile on him. "I believe they are, but as I said, we're not accepting products on consignment at this time."

"We could leave the samples and my daughter's card for you," Mummy proposed. She already held a stack of Ridhi's business cards. "Let you try them out when you have a moment."

"That won't be necessary." The woman began tapping at her phone. "If you'll excuse me . . ."

Ridhi shouldn't have been surprised. The store stank of chemical air fresheners. Still, she mustered every drop of geniality she could. "You have a lovely shop. Thank you for your time."

Then she pivoted and walked out.

Back in the sunshine, Mummy hurried to reassure Ridhi. "She doesn't know what she's missing. Her loss."

Ridhi lifted her chin. "Like you said, it's a numbers game."

At the Garden of Scentsual Delights, the owner at least agreed to try the samples.

Ridhi had gone in knowing she would have a harder time there, since the store itself was dedicated to perfume. Nevertheless, she arranged her top three bestsellers and the other two blends she'd brought next to the little ceramic dish of coffee beans on the counter.

The owner, a pretty Black woman in an ivory jumpsuit and a chunky statement necklace, had supplied the dish. Matching ones sat near all the displays. "Coffee is one thing we never run low on," she said with a laugh, and Ridhi made a mental note to pack some beans going forward. Not everyone would be as knowledgeable about the need to reset their sense of smell between fragrances.

The owner scanned each label. Minutes dragged by as she sniffed the samples and sniffed them again. Oddly, she skipped the bowl of beans in between, smelling the crook of her elbow instead.

Ridhi struggled to be patient. She was itching to ask which were the owner's favorites and did she want to carry all five? If so, how many vials of each? It would take some extra effort to fill a larger order, but Ridhi could manage.

For something to do, she studied the planters on the floor and the flower boxes on the walls. The plants within them, like the trees outside, epitomized the virescence of spring. Another day or two, and their flowers would be blooming.

The owner recapped the last of the vials. "You have skill," she said. "A good nose, too." Ridhi puffed up with pride. "But I'll be frank with you. Much as I'd like to, I can't buy in."

She wasn't sure she'd heard right. "Why not?"

The owner indicated a vial. "My issue is with the packaging."

Oh, *that* problem was simple enough to solve. "I've been sourcing some prettier bottles. They should arrive any day now."

"Not the vials. The labels. They lack polish." The owner pointed out the font and the flourish that Mummy had designed. "My clientele is used to a certain level of sophistication when it comes to aesthetics. I can't put that with the rest of my stock. I just can't."

Ridhi cringed. Mummy's work lacked polish? "But—"

Mummy, whose pleasant expression had waned, interrupted. "We understand. Thank you very much for your time."

"For the record," the owner said, "there's nothing special about coffee beans. Customers expect them, but your skin is the best baseline for getting over olfactory fatigue." She put out her hand, which Ridhi shook.

"Please enjoy the samples," Ridhi said, proud of how businesslike she sounded, when really, she was trying not to cry. Just how much of her inexperience had shown on her face?

The flowers in the window boxes had opened, but she didn't stop to appreciate them. While Mummy collected Kartik, who'd been playing with a perfume tester, Ridhi palmed the business card, then rushed toward the exit.

She burned with humiliation, both for herself and for Mummy.

They got into the car and buckled their seat belts. "That lady doesn't know what she's talking about," Kartik said from the back seat. "I think the labels are great!"

"It's all right, beta," Mummy said. "She has a point. Everything else in her store looks professional, and I'm not a graphic designer. We'll have to get Ridhi some real labels." Her face was soft with empathy. "It's the perfume that matters. If you don't have a good product, the rest is smoke and mirrors. You know that."

Ridhi didn't know anything. She hadn't called ahead. She'd

thought Mummy's designs were stylish. But she curved her mouth up in the pretense of courage.

"Still want to try that last shop?" Mummy asked before pulling away from the curb. "Or we could go straight to lunch. This is your day, beti. You tell me."

"I think you should," Kartik said seriously. "Because if you do, I'll get to be your assistant again, and then we *have* to get ice cream."

Ridhi twisted around in her seat and tweaked his nose. While she'd rather hide beneath the covers for the rest of the month, she had to rally for his sake. "Sounds like a plan to me."

In the third and final boutique, a specialty shop called Swati's Sweeties, Ridhi pasted on her friendliest smile and greeted the owner, an Indian woman about Mummy's age, with her best sales pitch.

"Perfumes?" The owner regarded Ridhi with puzzlement. "What kind of perfumes?"

"They're all based on Indian folklore and nature." Ridhi zeroed in on the dormant star jasmine plant near the register. That was, not counting a few random items on the white shelves, the only thing to look at. "I was inspired by the *Mahabharata* and the *Ramayana*, by dakinis, by the smell of trees on a summer day. My hope is to re-create that sense of magic for each person who wears my perfume."

"Interesting," the owner said. She made no move to pick up a vial.

"Would you like to try the samples?" Ridhi prompted.

"Oh, I don't know. We're such a new business, and I'm still

trying to find my footing. . . ."

Find her footing? What was left of Ridhi's goodwill crumbled. This woman didn't even have any real inventory.

Ridhi could have pressed her case, but the idea of foisting her perfumes on anyone galled her. This boutique—all three of the boutiques—would be lucky to carry them.

And yet they'd all said no.

Mummy, however, nudged Ridhi's card toward the owner. "How about we leave the samples with you for now? If nothing else, Holi is coming up, and what better way to celebrate than wearing a scent honoring the love story of Radhakrishna?"

The owner's reply was lost on Ridhi, because right then, Chetan Gopalkrishnan rounded a corner and addressed Kartik. "Hey, you're on my brother's soccer team! You better cream the other guys, you hear me?"

Ridhi quailed. Of course the guy who'd made it his mission in life to ruin hers would be there. He'd say something horrible meant to cut her off at the knees, like he always did, and worse, he'd do it in front of Mummy and Kartik, so she couldn't even pretend to save face.

Why had she ever thought this was a good idea?

Worse still, Shreya Prasad was walking over from the rear of the store, laughing with a pretty girl in an ebony lace dress. A teal streak peeped out from the girl's short black hair.

Chetan swaggered up to them. The girl's face dimmed, like she was caught between embarrassment and resentment. Whoever she was, at least she recognized a troll when she saw one.

Shreya's gaze drifted over. Her laughter died. It was three years ago all over again.

Ridhi noticed a new girl huddled in a corner of the mandir and offered to show her around. Shreya, timid and missing home, was grateful for the attention.

One afternoon, Ridhi brought Shreya to her forest, where they'd traded deeper confidences. Shreya had left a box of candy for the boy she'd lived next door to, but his father was the one who found the valentine. Even more distressing, he'd turned her down, saying she was too young for him.

Ridhi then confessed that her first and only kiss had been in a graveyard. She hadn't known what to do with her mouth, and neither had the guy, who'd coated her face in spit like he was trying to eat her. Shreya shrieked with disgust.

Later, Ridhi danced like she did for Mummy and her trees. You're really good, *Shreya said.* Like, TV good. You should show people!

Emboldened by her reaction, Ridhi took a gamble. There's something you should know about me.

Don't tell me you're, like, a secret ax murderer. That's where I draw the line. *Shreya giggled.* That, and people who don't like cake. How can anyone not like cake?

Oh, I like cake. *Ridhi toed the forest floor.* I know it sounds weird, but magic exists, and I'm going to find it one day.

Shreya didn't hesitate. For sure! I mean, all those stories about pixies and witches and demons came from somewhere, right? My dad always says the world is stranger than we could ever know.

Ridhi's heart sang with recognition. She'd found a kindred spirit.

They discussed bestiaries; what it would be like to have wings and fly away when things got to be too much; and whether a daayan's long, deadly braid ever had split ends. The words couldn't flow fast enough.

You know, you're really nice, *Shreya said shyly.* I was worried about moving here and not knowing anybody, but you made it so easy.

It was the best afternoon of Ridhi's life.

But at the next mandir gathering, it all fell apart. Shreya mentioned being thirsty, so Ridhi went to get them some water. She returned to find Shreya chatting with one of the popular kids. Though Ridhi's insides shriveled in alarm, she said hi to the other girl and offered Shreya a cup.

My friends are over there, *the other girl told Shreya.* Let's go.

Her gaze darting between Ridhi and the popular girl, Shreya awkwardly took the water. Her expression firmed up the moment she made her choice. It hadn't been Ridhi.

It was never Ridhi, not for anyone.

You're not going to stay here, are you? *asked the popular girl.* Not after what I told you about her?

Shreya stared straight at Ridhi. Then she whispered something in the popular girl's ear. Ridhi caught her name. She was glad she couldn't hear the rest.

The other girl nodded. Totally.

She snickered, and so did Shreya. When she flounced away, Shreya trotted after her, abandoning Ridhi to the growing hole in her heart.

She quit trying after that.

Ridhi came back to the present, where the single jasmine plant by the register had ballooned to twice the height of the pot. A wealth of star-shaped white blossoms covered it, the air ambrosial with their scent. As if that weren't bad enough, the plant was sending out feelers in her direction.

A signal. But why did it have to show up then?

Her heart pounded so hard, it left her woozy. The last thing she needed was Chetan or Shreya seeing *that*.

"We won't take up any more of your time," Ridhi said tartly to the owner. "Keep the samples."

Mummy examined her, visibly mystified. Ridhi lifted the box. Explanations could wait.

She blew past Shreya, Chetan, and their friend.

"A flower crown?" Chetan jeered. "Hippie-dippie Ridhi."

"I like it," the strange girl said.

But everything in Ridhi shrieked to get away, and she kept going until she was safely in the car with the windows up and the doors locked.

"I heard Chetan." Mummy shook her head. "Beti, you can't let him get to you. Or Shreya. They're not worth it."

Ridhi breathed in and out, in and out, so she wouldn't scream.

Mummy started the engine. "Anyway, I left your card. That woman was too discombobulated to decide anything today, but I think what I said about Holi got through."

Ridhi couldn't take it. Mummy always applied her programmer's logic to life. Her daughter wasn't yet where she wanted to be, but that was a problem with a simple solution: once people saw Ridhi dance, they would embrace her. Once the woman looked at the card, she'd realize her mistake.

Except it never worked for Ridhi. Not with dance, not with perfumery. Not with anything.

"Well, you shouldn't have!" she shouted. "You keep trying to make everything okay. To fix it. But I'm not you, and I never will be. Just stop. Just . . ."

"Is that what you think I do?" Mummy asked quietly. "Try to make you into me?"

"Yes! No. I don't know."

"I see." Mummy gripped the wheel hard enough that her brown knuckles paled. Without another word, she merged the car into traffic.

Ridhi dearly wanted to erase the last two minutes, if not the entire day. She opened her mouth, then let her worn-out head fall.

Kartik leaned forward from the back seat and squeezed her shoulder. "You can have my ice cream," he offered.

Her sore heart melted. "You don't have to do that. I'm fine. Really."

But she wasn't fine, and she wouldn't be.

Their booth in the diner overlooked the parking lot, so Nilesh and Amar had a great view of the motorcycle screeching into a space. The pure scorn in Amar's narrowed eyes was the funniest thing Nilesh had seen in days.

"Amateur," Amar grumbled into his chicken sandwich. He grabbed the ketchup bottle and squirted it over his already-drenched fries. Stray drops splattered his gray hoodie.

Nilesh made a face. "Want some fries to go with that ketchup?"

"They're only good if you drown them in the blood of tomatoes." Amar shoveled a handful of fries into his mouth. "Lots of it."

"You're getting weirder every day," Nilesh informed him.

Amar chewed. "Not my fault you have no taste."

"That's nasty. Close your mouth."

Amar opened it wider and swiped a few of Nilesh's onion rings.

Nilesh sucked his cherry soda through the straw. It was saccharine and fake-tasting. Everything in the diner felt like that, actually. Too bright, too loud. Too much. He'd thought going there would be like old times—the cheesy pictures on the walls, the porthole windows, the powder-blue vinyl booths like something out of the fifties.

Except it wasn't. Under the table, he rolled the dewdrop opal on his leg. He didn't want this food or this place. He wanted the fruit Kamini had fed him. He wanted to be back in the forest—with her.

Back in the forest. That was something he'd never thought he'd say.

When he'd woken, it had been to Ridhi's empty house. The silence had roared in his ears. So when Amar texted with the offer to break him out for lunch, Nilesh had jumped at it. But it wasn't working. He still couldn't unwind.

He must have been quiet too long, because Amar put aside his sandwich. "Hey, man, how are you really?"

Hearing Amar get serious was so bizarre that Nilesh almost cracked a joke to shut it down. "It's not great. I'll say that."

"I never told you this," Amar said. "I heard my mom and my uncle talking. They didn't know I was in the room."

"What happened?" Nilesh asked, not sure he wanted the answer.

"You know how my uncle's all famous around here?" Amar's uncle advocated for local human rights initiatives.

"Yeah?"

"Turns out some of the donations 'found' their way into his bank account. Only my mom knows. Okay, my mom and me. She made him promise to return them."

"Oh." Nilesh rolled the opal some more. *Well, that's depressing.*

"I was so proud of him, you know?" Amar dredged a fry through the red mess on his plate. "I mean, I still love him or whatever, but . . ."

Nilesh passed him another onion ring. "Dude, that's rough."

"Yeah. Family sucks sometimes, is my point."

"Look who it is!" A trio of girls from school, including Bhoomi Singh, Nilesh's ex-girlfriend, pranced toward the booth. "Nilesh!" She waved both arms.

"Hey." Nilesh nodded at her. Bhoomi was the most upbeat person he'd ever met. Not even getting grounded for three months after her super-strict parents figured out she had a boyfriend—thanks to one of Amar's pranks going wrong—could keep her down. She'd cried while telling Nilesh they had to break up, but ten minutes later, she'd been giggling again.

It was disconcerting to see her when Kamini still took up his thoughts. Nilesh wasn't sure he liked the two halves of his life overlapping.

"Go on without me," Bhoomi told her friends. "I'll be right there."

They left, and she hopped into the booth, next to Nilesh. "So? How are you? Tell me *everything*."

"I'm good, I'm good. Amar, too. Right, man?"

Bhoomi's nose crinkled. She still hadn't let Amar off the hook for the prank. To be fair, he'd never apologized for it. "Oh. You."

"Weren't you going to a cabin in the woods or something?" Amar stretched, making the vinyl seat squeak. "That's a horror movie reference. Meaning I didn't think I'd ever see you again."

She tossed her hair over her shoulder. "Simmer down. Just

because you don't like camping doesn't mean no one else should go."

"Nature's full of spiders. So many spiders." Amar shuddered. He looked to Nilesh for confirmation. "Spring break's for stuff like road tripping to see the world's biggest ball of twine or go hunting for chupacabras."

Amar's constant bickering with Bhoomi was legendary among their group, and like the good friend he was, Nilesh usually egged it on. That day, though, it had him wanting to flip what was left of that soggy plate of fries. "Camping, huh?"

His phone rang, and he silenced it without checking the screen.

Bhoomi flashed her orthodontist-perfected white smile, then rolled her eyes. "Yeah. My parents wanted to go to the beach, but it's still too cold, right? So we're going to get lots of board games and glamp it up. As if my sister won't be on her tablet all day. But, you know, *family time.*"

Family time. Nilesh studied her. She was cute, bubbly, and smart, and he knew she was still into him. But the world she was describing, his world, felt a million miles away.

He tried to imagine what she'd say if she knew about Dad. Besides spreading it to everyone else they knew, that was. Because that kind of news was too juicy not to share.

But he wouldn't give her the chance. "So, cabin in the woods? Nature's not so bad. A chance to get away, clear your head."

Amar, who knew how little Nilesh cared about nature until recently, couldn't have been more skeptical.

"Nature's okay," Bhoomi said, "but I'm going to be so bored. Oh! How's *your* family?"

"They're great." Nilesh smiled extra wide. "Everyone's great."

"Tell your sister I said hi." Bhoomi speared some of Amar's fries with the fork he hadn't touched. "So good! You really should eat them before they get cold."

Amar's scowl could have impaled her on the table.

"A bunch of us are doing this escape room thing when I get back," she went on. "You should come."

"Not my thing," Amar said snidely.

"Luckily for you, I was talking to Nilesh." Bhoomi shifted so she was facing him. "If you're not still in trouble, that is."

He could tell she was dying to ask about the suspension, but that wasn't happening. "Yeah, maybe," he lied. "I'll have to see what's going on. Who else is on the team?"

Bhoomi named a few people they had in common, and Nilesh gave her a thumbs-up. Amar didn't even pretend to be interested. But they all sat up when Nilesh's phone rang. It was Hetal. Again.

"Someone really wants to know where you are," Bhoomi said. She leveled a death stare at Amar. "Like my parents would."

"I guess," Nilesh said. His parents had never been the overbearing type like hers.

Maybe, he thought darkly, *they should have been.*

Holding the opal in his lap, he chatted about nothing with Bhoomi until she went to find her friends. Then he slapped down enough cash to cover the bill, along with a hefty tip. "Let's get out of here."

Amar draped his napkin over his plate like a burial shroud. "All right, but I gotta hit the restroom. Next stop, road trip to the beach."

"Why there?" Nilesh asked. "Why not just show up at that cabin?"

"Spiders," Amar whimpered.

"Yeah, yeah, yeah. Go do your thing."

Amar, though, stood there, hatching some plot. "We could, you know. Show up at the cabin."

"And listen to you scream like a baby every time you saw a cobweb? Nah, I'm good. I'll see you outside."

Nilesh made for the exit before Amar could suggest they pack it all in and head to Alaska.

Nilesh paced on the blacktop in front of the diner's chrome exterior. It had been ten minutes. Had Amar fallen in? Or gotten food poisoning? All that ketchup couldn't be healthy for anybody.

Three more minutes went by, so painfully slow that a snail could have crossed from one side of the parking lot to the other. Nilesh didn't love the idea of fishing Amar out of the toilet, but he might have to. *Dude*, he'd say, *for real, lay off the condiments.*

"Nilu!"

Even with the mild weather, Nilesh went cold. No wonder Amar had taken so long. He'd been arranging this little ambush.

Nilesh turned to find Hetal in her puffy red coat, leaning on her crutches for support, and Amar beside her. Since she wasn't in her wheelchair, it must be one of her better mobility days. Even though Nilesh had been conned into coming along, seeing that cheered him up. His sister didn't have a lot of those anymore.

Hetal slowly walked the few steps separating them. By her limp, he could tell she was hurting, but she pushed on until she reached his side. Then she squashed him like he was Amar's ketchup bottle.

He soaked in her warmth. That, at least, was right.

"Where have you been, you little troll?" she cried. She sounded happy and mad at the same time. Kind of like he felt. "I was worried sick! And you really need to call Dad."

Her last sentence slashed right through him. She could have said anything else, anything else at all, but she'd picked that.

Nilesh disentangled himself from her hug. "Shouldn't you be in California?"

"I texted her," Amar said, like it wasn't a breach of trust. "She told me you won't talk to her."

Hetal's smile had faltered. "Why would you disappear like that?"

Why did she think?

"What is this, an intervention?" Then Nilesh remembered people he knew might be watching from inside the diner, so he inched between the windows. "To get me back in line?"

Both Hetal and Amar eyed him like he'd said two plus four equaled lemon-lime. "Nilu," Hetal warned, "I am not in the mood for this."

"Yeah, well," he shot back, "*I'm* not in the mood for *this*. Since when do you fly cross-country to harass me?"

"Harass you? My baby brother disappeared. I couldn't sleep, not until we hashed this out."

The fire in Nilesh burned hotter. He hated that her little guilt trip was working. He especially hated that he'd just been glad to see her. "Quit being dramatic. Mom shunted me off to Ridhi's house, and I lost my charger."

"That's not what I mean, and you know it." Hetal's voice climbed higher. "Do you know how many times I've tried to call you? Text you? But you don't answer! What was I supposed to think?"

"I told you, I can't find my charger!"

She shook her head. "And you couldn't borrow one?"

Nilesh knew he was wounding her, but he couldn't stop. Not until she hurt like he did. "So what about how I feel? Are you even going to bother to ask? 'How are you, little brother?' 'I'm fine.'"

"That's not fair, and no, you're not." Hetal swiped at her eyes, smearing her mascara. "If you were, you wouldn't be doing this."

She was right. They had always been close, and she'd been one of the few people who really knew him, like Amar.

But that was before.

"I should have told you sooner," Hetal said. "I—I didn't want to hurt you."

That hitch in her words only fanned the flames. She'd come home so he'd have to forgive her? What the hell sort of attempt to mend fences was that?

"Well, guess what?" Nilesh retorted. "You did."

Hetal went still. She owed him an apology, and they both knew it. "Listen," she said, "I should have told you. I'm sorry; I really am. But do you know how *I* found out?"

"I'm sure you're going to tell me."

"I was thirteen." Her voice quavered. "I've actually known for years, Nilu. It's so cliché, but I saw a picture of them on his computer. Dad told me it wasn't anything, that I didn't know what I saw, but I did. I just . . ." She laughed bitterly. "It's funny what you can talk yourself into if you have to."

Nilesh didn't want to feel bad for her. "It doesn't matter. I don't care."

"I'm worried about you." Hetal bit her lip. It was chapped, like she'd been gnawing on it.

Nilesh's wrath came back in full force. *She* should feel bad. She'd known, and she'd acted like everything was fine. Because of her, he'd believed in a lie. "You said that already."

"The thing is, I love Dad, and I know Mom does, too, so I thought if I told myself it wasn't true . . ." She sniffled. "Nilu, how could I dump that on you? I wish *I* didn't know!"

"I don't want to talk about it anymore," he shouted. "I'm over it."

He wasn't, not anywhere near that, but she was so pitiful, with her red eyes and her bitten mouth. It made his chest ache.

It also made him really, really angry.

Hetal let out a sob. "What can I do to make things right? Whatever it is, I'll do it. Will you please just talk to me?"

"What's the point? You can't." The words were ugly, like venom-tipped darts. They felt good because of it.

Watching Hetal shrink back when they landed felt even better.

He fished out the opal. The rainbow trapped in its depths shimmered like a lodestar.

Amar's elbow jabbed him in the ribs. "Dude. You're being weird, and not in a good way."

Nilesh glanced from the opal to Hetal and felt numb. He was

sick of the entire conversation. "Go back to Berkeley."

"I know you're saying all this because you're hurt." She nodded unsteadily. "I don't like it, but I understand."

Nilesh fought not to laugh. "I thought you were majoring in business, not psychology?" He set off for the car. "Come on, Amar. You gotta get me home before they know I left."

Hetal called out from behind him. "I'm not leaving, Nilu. Not until we fix things."

He knew he should turn around. She was his sister, after all.

Instead, he kept walking.

9

The wall of rain doused the backyard in a cold gray light, the sort that made Ridhi yearn to curl up with a pile of books. Papa had left her a list of chores to tackle, but with no one except Nilesh home to check, she'd put them off to sit cross-legged on the sofa and watch the deluge through the bay windows.

Her beloved trees shook in the gusts, reminding her of Sulochana's tragic tale. Even now, Mummy had said, yakshas quaked at the sound of thunder.

Ridhi couldn't begin to fathom how demeaning, how heart-breaking, Ishika's duplicity must have been. What had she been hoping to gain aside from notoriety?

Yet Sulochana had risen above her past. She had rebuilt her life, founding a successful enterprise, taking a new partner, and surrounding herself with a loyal sisterhood. Were Ridhi in her chappals, she doubted she would have been half as resilient. But she had to try.

The previous day's rejections had clarified her purpose. She'd been looking in the wrong direction. Nilesh and Sulochana had both mentioned a Night Market, and Sulochana actually vended there.

Ridhi bounced restlessly on the sofa. Who cared about human stores populated by bullies and phony friends when she could sell her wares at a mystical marketplace?

She imagined presenting Sulochana with a sampler of her creations, crystal bottles aesthetically arranged in a velvet-lined box. One whiff would confirm Sulochana had made the right choice, and Ridhi was precisely what she'd been searching for.

But first, Ridhi needed to prove she could be useful. And to do *that*, she needed to impress Malav. Whom she didn't have the first clue how to get in touch with, any more than she knew how she'd convinced the plants in Swati's Sweeties to shoot up. A lingering effect of Sulochana's elixirs?

If so, maybe Ridhi could leverage it again. "Grow," she commanded the plants in the living room, envisioning them extending, spreading, so intensely green that they enhanced even the dull, cloud-clad day.

Though Ridhi detected a stirring, they didn't change. She sighed and slumped back against the cushion. If only she'd brought some elixir home with her. Sulochana's creations really were extraordinary, nature itself in tincture form.

The remembered taste of spring elixir sang on Ridhi's tongue. Its memory had rooted in her cells, marking them. Marking her.

Oh, to be a yakshini, she thought, closing her eyes, *and have flowers dripping from my fingers.*

Sunbeams as warm and bright as melted butter suddenly poured through the windows, erasing the storm. Like any good plant, Ridhi turned to face them.

What she saw should have been impossible: blooms covered the lilac hedges, far more than would normally fit. In fact, the yard had transformed into an oasis of edible flowers: roses, jasmine, cherry blossoms, cornflowers, marigolds, violets, hibiscus, moringa, and even lotuses floating in a lucent pool. An incessant flurry of petals billowed through the perfumed air like pastel snowflakes.

Had *she* done that? The possibility made her want to dance.

An irresistible urge to consume the flowers, to fill herself with their essence, came over her. The lilacs in particular demanded to be devoured, but how? Lemonade? Ice cream? Chocolates?

Lilac doughnuts. Ridhi had bookmarked the perfect recipe a few weeks before.

Still in her pajamas, she unearthed a wicker basket and ran outside. Her neighbors' yards were bare, and the usual noise of dogs barking and cars driving past had gone silent.

Whatever this was, it was just for her.

A bold mauve edged in white, the lilacs smelled luscious, richer and more complex than any she'd ever smelled before. And no matter how many she packed into her basket, more appeared in their place, a cornucopia of fragrance and flavor. The doughnuts she'd bake with them would be floral candy in pastry form.

A voice riddled with thorns like a devil's walking stick tore her from her reverie. "And here I thought you were defaulting on our bargain."

Ridhi whirled to her right, where a sylvan prince with kajal-accentuated eyes stood observing her. The hammered copper leaves on his hunter-green turban shone like amber in the noon sunshine. Beneath it, his skin glowed, the color of sheesham wood and flawless in a way no human boy's could ever hope to be.

No, not a prince. A yaksha. Malav.

"Defaulting?" she asked, hoping he couldn't tell how her pulse had accelerated. At least he hadn't commented on her clothes. "And what are you doing here? I thought you didn't like humans."

"A fair point." Malav treated her to a half smile. "But you are wrong to believe I ventured into your realm. If anything, you have stumbled into mine, where the blossoms you prize so highly grow in perpetuity."

It hadn't been Ridhi's magic, after all. She couldn't see her neighbors' yards anymore; ashoka trees had taken their place. "Where did my yard go?"

"An overlap. Yakshas are part and parcel of the natural world. We are tied to the water, the plants, the ground itself. For us, all terrestrial spaces are one." Malav's smile hardened. "Only mortals lay down artificial borders and stake claims to land they then proceed to ravage."

Shame poked holes in Ridhi's heart. She'd never understood how so many people behaved like they could separate themselves from nature and mine it without any consequences. "So, um, you *really* don't like us, then."

"Thus far, you have given me no reason to do otherwise."

Could she request another tutor? "What about our lessons?"

"Did you fail to see both instances of my signal?"

"What signal?" Ridhi grimaced. "Wait. The plants in the stores . . . ?"

"You were to journey to the woods at once. Henceforth, should you disregard my summons, I will assume our bargain nullified."

Ridhi bridled at that. He had no right to belittle her. But he blinked, once, twice, and his uncanny beauty pounced on her like a cat, those thick lashes trapping the light—and Ridhi—in their onyx length.

Malav flicked his wrist, startling her. "Attend to me!"

She'd been so caught up in the gold-burnished curve of his cheekbone that she'd missed the arrangement of leaves laid across the table he must have brought forth. "How did you want me to answer? Your 'summons,' that is?"

"By stepping outside." He let out a patronizing chuckle. "I would have brought you here, where we would have begun our study of the language of leaves. It is the same language yakshas and other nature spirits use to convey messages over great distances. A mother might use it to send for her son. A rani might use it to call home a warrior or a scout far afield."

Ridhi pushed away her awareness of both Malav's bone structure and his derision. "So how do I translate this language of leaves?"

He lifted a hand. "Patience. Choose a leaf. Intuit it. What about it feels unique to you?"

She touched the first leaf, a maple. Shutting out everything else, she focused on its vivid hue, its shape like a hand, the veins that ran along it like downturned arrows. Then she reported her list.

"That is merely the surface," he chided. "Consider not with your eyes but with your heart."

Though she felt foolish, Ridhi tried again. Imagining her heart as a lens, she peered at the leaf. In small details, it revealed itself.

The tree that had produced the leaf had been rooted far from there. In damp soil—it had recently rained, and the tree's thirsty roots had drunk up the moisture. New leaves had soon budded, each abundant with the resources to transmute the sun into nutrients. Over time, the tree strengthened, and through the passing wind, the leaf "spoke" to the grove around it.

Sure he'd approve of her progress, Ridhi briefed Malav on her discovery. "So? Isn't that better?"

"Nominally so." He sounded maddeningly dismissive. "Now forget the appearance and go deeper. See how each susurration is an idiom unto itself."

Nominally so? That stung. But how was she supposed to go deeper?

Malav waited, his expression stony. He'd obviously given her all the guidance she could expect.

After a bout of fevered brainstorming, Ridhi pictured herself imbibing the leaf's bright color like an elixir. It would taste and feel like a surge of spring. In her mind, in her heart, she drank and drank and drank, until she swam in the green.

Gradually, she heard soughing in the maple tree above, yet when she strove to tune in, it was to the equivalent of static. "I hear something! But it's just out of reach."

"A message may not always be intended for us, but for other

trees, for insects and birds." Malav paused. "Perhaps even for the sky. It is still accessible to us, if we humble ourselves."

"The sky? What would *it* talk about?"

"Precipitation? The speed of an eagle flying overhead? The nature of existence?"

Ridhi couldn't tell whether that was a joke and she should laugh. "The sky seems too flighty for that, sorry."

"Clouds, then. Certainly trees would have much to gossip about with cloud messengers."

"Like in Kalidasa's poem?" she blurted. The Sanskrit poet Kalidasa had composed an epic in verse, *Meghaduta*, about an unnamed yaksha who found himself exiled for a year from Alakapuri for shirking his duties to King Kubera. The poem opened with the distraught yaksha's plea to a passing cloud that it bear a message to his beloved wife, describing the myriad sights the cloud messenger would encounter along its voyage.

Ridhi had always felt for that exiled yaksha.

And if the poem was also beset with sensual imagery inspired by the yaksha's pining for his wife . . .

Malav's voice lowered in surprise. "You know of it?"

"Well, yeah," she said. "I read the English translation."

"Few mortals today would think to do so."

"I've never been like most people," she admitted, then winced. What was wrong with her?

"That," he drawled, eyeing her with new interest, "cannot be disputed. Shall we proceed with our training?"

"Yes, please." It couldn't be soon enough.

Without warning, Malav caught her hand, his grip sturdy and strong.

Her skin erupted into gooseflesh. He was holding her hand!

Yet all he did was guide her toward the maple tree before letting go. "You must set yourself aside," he lectured, as if touching her were no more stimulating than touching a twig. "It is a question of becoming a vessel."

Ridhi kept her gaze on the tree. So what if she'd liked the feeling of her fingers in his? So what if she'd liked it a lot?

Set myself aside. Okay. She drew in a lungful of air suffused with leaf mold, pine resin, and lavender shrubs. Another element lay beneath them, one her brain interpreted as sun-dappled shadow, then as the blast of flavor from a perfect, juicy boysenberry. Neither was right.

Was she smelling a future perfume?

"Do you want this?" Malav asked abruptly.

"Yes," Ridhi whispered. "I do."

"Then listen. Be one with the forest," he murmured.

His breath was warm against the shell of her ear, and she almost moved closer still.

But he stepped back, aloof once more. "Well?"

Her stomach plummeted. He wasn't thinking of her like that. He was there for his own reasons, and she should be, too.

So although his demeanor was anything but encouraging, Ridhi opened herself up to the trees. They stood vigilant like sentinels, their slow exhalations keeping time with the beating of her heart. She sensed their sap like emerald blood. She sensed it flowing within her own veins.

If she squinted, she might have been one of them in motion, having uprooted itself for the chance to arch its elegant trunk and bend its slender branches, encompassing the sky. She raised her arms and angled her head, a shalabhanjika striking a pose.

The rustling returned, yet rather than entering her ears, it slipped beneath her skin as she danced.

Malav crossed his arms. "I suppose that will do."

Maybe it was the giddiness, but Ridhi grinned at him.

"Phyllomancy is no dry, static art," he said sternly. "You cannot puzzle it out through analysis. You must *experience* it." A breeze set the woods undulating once more, and he made an impatient gesture. "Go on."

Chastened, Ridhi nodded. She settled on the ashoka tree as her focal point and invited it to speak.

Her attention never strayed from the leaves, and bit by bit, their sibilance came together like speech. A vision of her perfumes crystallized in her mind. She saw herself in the role of customer, opening a beautiful bottle and dabbing its contents on the inside of her wrist.

Ridhi inhaled the fragrance. She saw the sun-dappled shadow again, tasted the succulent boysenberry. She heard a strain of melody, as silver and distant as the stars.

And then it was gone, a half-captured whisper.

Immersion.

If her perfumes could truly induce immersion, the trees seemed to be suggesting, that should be enough to qualify her for the Night Market.

"It is not about the dancing," Malav said, as if she hadn't already put that together. "It is about—"

"Connection," Ridhi interrupted, fighting to retain the feel of the leaves' missive. Was there something she needed to do to create an immersive effect? Something she should add to her blends?

"Excuse me! Miss! *Miss!*"

Ridhi glanced up to find the mailman at her fence, wearing a plastic poncho over his uniform. "I need you to sign for a package," he said. "I rang the doorbell, but nobody answered."

She stared at him, baffled. Didn't he see all the flowers?

But Malav's glade had faded, replaced by the usual features of her backyard—the swing, the still-dormant bushes, the branches only beginning to produce new foliage. The gray rain fell once more, and tires splashed through puddles as cars zoomed past.

"Miss!" the mailman repeated.

"Oh," said Ridhi. Her pajamas were sodden, and her arms prickled with the chill. "Sorry. I'll be right there."

Malav had sought shelter in the peach tree, and once the mailman had gone, he reappeared. "It is wise to heed the advice of a tree when one is favored enough to receive it. That is your first lesson."

Her first lesson. Ridhi had done it. She'd performed actual phyllomancy and received the tree's message.

In hindsight, it had been easy, almost shockingly so. "But I still don't know how I did that."

"My presence was the catalyst," he explained. "To do so alone, you must cultivate the patience you lack. That is your second lesson."

He turned to depart, and she grabbed her basket of harvested lilacs, grateful those hadn't absconded with the rest of the yaksha kingdom. "I'm going to bake doughnuts with these. Do you . . . do you want to come in and have one?"

"I do not, no." Malav strode into the afternoon. No umbrella for him; the rain skirted his form.

"How do I reach you again?" Ridhi shouted through the curtain of water dripping down her face.

Over his shoulder, he called, "Divine the leaves."

10

Nilesh parked himself on a mostly dry fallen log and looked around. Green, lots of green. All the bushes and trees you could ask for. Flowers, mushrooms, and some berries. It was nice in the post-rain sunshine.

That wasn't the reason he'd gone to Ridhi's enchanted forest, though. Kamini was, and she still hadn't responded to the dewdrop opal.

His phone rang. It was an unknown number. Maybe Hetal thought he'd pick up if he didn't know it was her.

A pair of birds in a nearby tree chirped like they were scolding him.

The ringtone *was* pretty loud. "Sorry," he muttered and turned down the volume.

They didn't react, of course. He was losing his mind.

The phone kept ringing. To make it stop, he answered. "Hello?"

"Beta!" Dad boomed in his ear.

Nilesh felt like he'd been slugged in the stomach. He hung up.

The unknown number. *Oh, gods.* Was that the mistress's phone?

He didn't even have the chance to freak out before it rang again. Palms sweating, Nilesh sent the call straight to voice mail and let his phone fall to the ground. Too bad it didn't break.

Ding—Dad had left a message.

Nilesh rubbed the opal between his finger and thumb. *Kamini, where are you?*

But she didn't come.

"Fine," he got out through gritted teeth. Bending forward, he grabbed the phone. "You want me to listen, Dad? I can't wait to hear your crappy excuses."

The trees kept swishing in the wind. Dragonflies with blue wings still flittered past. A rabbit plunged through the undergrowth. But the forest was listening, waiting for him to live up to his bravado.

He set the phone to speaker and pressed Play.

"Nilesh, pick up," Dad wheedled. "I know you're there, beta." His tone roughened. "You want to judge me? You don't know what I've given up for you and your sister. Your mother and I haven't been happy in years."

What *he'd* given up? Nilesh thought he would choke. How dare Dad put that on him?

"I thought we'd come to love each other. That's what happens in arranged marriages. But for us, it didn't."

So what? No one had forced Dad to get married. Once you made a commitment, you kept it. Simple.

"I stayed for you," Dad went on. "To give you children the life you deserved. But I needed an outlet. I needed to feel something."

The rest was a jumble under the pressure building in Nilesh's ears. *Dad* needed to feel something? How selfish could he get?

"Dilip?" a female voice called in the background. "Ready to go?"

Nilesh tasted acid. The mistress. It had to be her. *To hell with Dad. To hell with all of this.*

But that voice mail had gotten its hooks into him. He couldn't move. He couldn't do anything.

The phone vibrated. A group thread, started by Dad. *I rented an apartment. There's plenty of space for you both, and Janaki can't wait to meet you.*

An apartment—with the mistress. Who'd been promoted to girlfriend.

Then it really was over.

A message from Hetal appeared. *I call dibs on the bigger room! Older sister privilege.* 😉

Nilesh couldn't have read that right. He looked again.

I call dibs, the message still said. *I call dibs.*

Black ice dammed up his insides. His sister had said she was sorry. She'd said she hadn't known what to do. But in reality, she'd sided with Dad and the now girlfriend.

Nilesh's eyes stung. He had nothing left.

He raked his hands through his hair. Somehow the phone's camera had switched on, and it hurled his reflection back at him like an accusation. *Chump. Pathetic.*

Everyone always said he took after Dad, and Nilesh had always been flattered. *So pathetic.*

He threw the phone at the log. It bounced off some lichen and landed on the ground. When that didn't help, he launched himself to his feet and swung out.

His fist slammed into the nearest tree.

Pain blasted through him. Swearing, he jerked backward. His knuckles were raw and bloody where the bark had abraded them, and the skin had split from the impact.

"What do you imagine you are doing?" Kamini shouted. Out of nowhere, she loomed over him like an avenging nymph. "*You attacked a tree.* In *my* forest."

The joke broke free of Nilesh's mouth before he could hit the brakes. "Would it have been okay in somebody else's forest?"

Kamini rushed at him, her eyes two slits. The jeweled belt around her waist glittered like knife blades. "Have you forgotten who I am?"

"It's not a big deal." Still, he dropped his head.

"What did you say?" Her question was hushed. Deadly.

Nilesh glanced back at the tree. "It's just a tree. I mean, isn't it?"

Sunlight flashed in Kamini's copper irises. "There is nothing in this world that lives and yet knows no pain, *mortal boy.*"

"Look," he said, trying to seem contrite, "I'm sorry if I upset you. I guess I don't understand."

Kamini pressed her lips together. "It would appear, then, that you do not understand *me.*"

She sounded so bleak. If she left now, he'd never see her again. His chest writhed with panic. He couldn't accept that.

Nilesh had never invested real effort with the girls he'd dated. He'd never had to. Light and easy was how he liked it.

This girl, though, this yakshini. They'd only met the other day, but being around her helped take his mind off the catastrophe his life had become.

Was he really about to lose her over something so small?

"Kamini—" His voice cracked. "Don't go. I'm sorry."

She was already gone, vanished into the trees.

The forest was so much bigger without her. So much emptier. Even the judgmental birds were silent.

There was no reason for Nilesh to hang around. Except he had nowhere to go. No one to go to. It wasn't like he could trust Amar.

His shoulders slumped. He couldn't stand the thought of ending up at Ridhi's house and watching her perfect little family being all cozy and sweet to each other. Nothing would ever tear *them* apart. And Ridhi didn't even see it.

It made Nilesh want to throw up.

So he sat on the log and watched bugs crawl over his phone. Then he shook them off and replayed Dad's voice mail on loop, like the message might change if he listened long enough.

He tried again. And again. And again and again and again.

Every single time, Dad failed him.

At some point, the phone's battery gave out. The angle of the sunlight had shifted by then, and Nilesh's legs were numb. He must have been sitting there for hours.

What was he going to do?

"You struck a tree."

Sure he was dreaming, he jumped up. He winced as the pins and needles kicked in.

"You struck a tree," Kamini repeated, but less enraged. More probing. "The blood of the forest runs in my veins, mortal boy."

She'd come back! Nilesh felt hope skewer the black ice inside him.

He tapped his throbbing hand. "If it helps, the tree didn't take it lying down."

"I suppose," Kamini said, with a sly tip of her head, "you have learned your lesson. Refrain from venting your foul temper on my woods in the future, and perhaps I will absolve you this once. Perhaps."

Nilesh grinned. "So you're saying you're *not* going to banish me to the dark, scary part of the forest where no one but ghosts will ever find me again?"

"Do not entice me." She gestured for him to join her. "Come."

Nilesh walked arm in arm with Kamini down a shady lane on the outskirts of Alakapuri, where he'd been telling her about Bhoomi and Amar. She'd swabbed his knuckles with ointment, and the wound had already healed.

"So that's camping," he finished. "I still don't get why anyone would do it. No offense."

Yakshas and yakshinis passed them, some carrying bundles, others just enjoying the day.

"Yes, yes," Kamini mocked. "After all, nature is so very boring, is it not?"

But she didn't remove her arm from his.

Nilesh laughed. "You're never going to let that go, are you?"

"Certainly not. Not for another century, at the very least."

"Okay, so that was stupid of me," he agreed. "But have *you* ever tried sleeping on the hard ground with rocks digging into your back every time you move? You'd hate it, too."

"Mortals are beyond my comprehension. Why would they choose to torment themselves so when they might opt for mattresses of moss and silk? Is this camping some form of penance?"

Nilesh snorted. "Believe it or not, people do it for fun."

"Alas, poor Nilesh. It is clear that your fellow mortals have been led astray." Kamini smiled wickedly, and the gulmohar flower in her nostril glinted red orange. "How fortunate for you that I am on hand to elucidate the multiple pleasures to be gleaned from slumbering beneath the sky."

"I'm slow sometimes. I think I need another lesson." Nilesh slid his hand around hers. He'd expected her to tell him off, but she laced their fingers together. "Didn't you say something about your mom's grove the other night?"

"Perhaps," Kamini said shortly. She didn't elaborate. "It is rare that I play tour guide. I would not fritter away this opportunity if I were you."

He took the hint. Who understood better than he did what a bummer family could be? "Show me your city, oh, great tour guide."

Her cheek dimpled. "I shall."

Alakapuri was incredible, Nilesh conceded as they got nearer to the river. Sure, Earth, or Prithvi, as Kamini had referred to it, had its fair share of beautiful places. But in all his travels, he had never seen trees like these. Gold, silver, and copper fruit hung from their branches, along with more conventional things like bananas, lychees, and pistachios. Flowers sprayed petals over the green-and-gold pathways in more colors than he'd known existed.

And the buildings, with their gold and jewels. They could have been the backdrop to a movie, with Kamini and him in the starring roles.

An obvious question stared him in the face: Why had she brought him there?

But Nilesh didn't care about her motives. She'd taken him back. That was all he needed to know.

He would, however, love to get Hetal's reaction to this place. She'd been all about set design in high school and was always sending him snapshots of quirky things she found in Berkeley. A picture of the yaksha kingdom would blow her mind.

His free hand was in his pocket when he remembered almost breaking his phone—and why.

The hurt gutted him all over again. No. Even if his battery hadn't run out, Hetal didn't deserve to see this. Neither did Amar, no matter how hilarious watching his jaw fall would be.

They walked onto a golden bridge that spanned the river. "Are you hungry?" Kamini asked.

"I could eat." Nilesh looked down at the water. It was clear and ran over shining rocks, carrying away the dirt. He wished he could dunk his head in.

They ambled to the other side and into an orchard of fruit trees. Nilesh plucked something that looked like a big green blackberry. "What's this?"

"Sitaphal!" Kamini snatched it from him and peeled off the skin with a gold knife from her mekhala. She excavated the white pulp with a similar spoon and tossed the black seeds to the ground, where they sprouted into seedlings.

"*That's* a custard apple? Huh." He took the spoon from her. The sitaphal was creamy, like the custard it was named for, and smelled a little like vanilla. "Nice."

Kamini waved her hand, and a tree with long, spearlike leaves bloomed, pushing out tiny white flowers that ripened into yellow-orange fruit.

The glowing mangoes from the revel. Their scent had Nilesh drooling.

Kamini picked one and cut a slice. "Try this."

She looked on with amused approval as his teeth tore the flesh from the skin. Juice dribbled down his chin, but he was too busy chewing to mind. It was sweet. Tangy. Perfect. A million times better than the tasteless grocery store garbage.

"That's the best mango I ever had," he said, "and I've had a lot."

She fed him the rest of the fruit. When nothing was left but the pit, she leaned forward. "You do intrigue me."

Nilesh was no stranger to kissing. But with Kamini so close, her mouth right there, he felt as nervous as he had the first time. "Can I—"

She extended a finger. The fire opals on her ring smoldered.

That same red-hot current pulsed through his body, wild and electric. He couldn't breathe. Forget the fruit—he wanted *her*.

If they didn't quit now, he knew, he would drown.

A slow smile curled over his lips. That was fine with him.

Kamini twirled a lock of his hair around her finger and tugged hard enough that his scalp tingled. Her gaze scraped his mouth. "Shall I forgive you, then, mortal boy?"

"Kamini." Nilesh caught her around the waist, making her bangles clink together. "I really am sorry. About the tree. It won't happen again."

"Of that I am certain, or you would not be here." Kamini freed herself and relinked their arms. "Now come. The palace awaits."

Her withdrawing hurt, but he could wait.

Nilesh had visited palaces before, in Europe and Asia and South America. He'd met the royalty who still lived in some of them. But when he saw the maharaja and maharani's residence, he had to wonder how it didn't dominate the city. It was that big and that impossible to ignore, with ornamented gold walls and plants growing all over. Definitely a master feat of architecture with magic involved. He'd need days just to wrap his head around one small section.

If he'd had his sketch pad and the crowds weren't moving in, he would have tried. "It's really busy here."

Kamini maneuvered him into a grand courtyard. "Holi fast

approaches. The city is preparing for the royal celebrations."

"Oh, yeah." Nilesh never remembered the lunar calendar. "I bet it's a huge production around here, huh?"

"You might say that." She reclined against an ivory pillar swimming in flowers. "How are you finding the tour of my city? There is so much yet to show you."

"I've seen better." At her disgruntled expression, he cracked up. "It's pretty great. Better than the Taj Mahal, even."

Kamini huffed. "I should hope so!"

Nilesh drew a check mark in the air. "No joking about the palace. Got it."

"It is so very important to me that you like it here," she said, so urgently that it felt like she was testing him.

"Really, it's awesome," he said. "I haven't seen anything like it." When she didn't seem convinced, he added, "This is what every garden on Prithvi wishes it could be."

Another wave of Kamini's hand, and a tangle of branches to their right separated, displaying an alcove set with goblets and a pitcher. "I thought we might indulge in a beverage before continuing on."

But Nilesh wanted to see what was happening in the pavilion ahead. A square outlined in gold and constructed from other squares covered the marble floor. Two pairs of men and women stood at the square's corners.

"Mortal boy!" Kamini whispered. "We intrude. Let us go."

The women swapped cagey looks. Then the one with brambles in her hair spoke. "It is hardly an intrusion. We were about to embark upon a new game. Would you care to participate?"

The floor was a chessboard, but Nilesh hadn't recognized it at first, since the squares inside the boundary were all the same golden-brown color. His uncle in India had teakwood furniture that same shade. "Are you playing chess?"

"The pieces move at our command, yes," said a yaksha with a gold torque. "Yet you are mistaken about the game."

The bramble-wearing yakshini popped a berry from her circlet into her mouth. "It is chaturanga. Do you not know it?"

Nilesh shook his head.

"Chaturanga," said the other yakshini, "is the game a pair of mortal brothers once invented to decide ownership of their kingdom. Its offshoot is what you refer to as chess." Her smile broadened in challenge. "Shall we teach you the rules?"

He didn't know how to play modern chess, never mind some antiquated version he'd never heard of before, but he was curious. "Yeah, why not—"

"We must be on our way," Kamini interjected. "Play your games with someone else."

"Such as your mother?" The yaksha with the torque leered. "Do tell, Kamini. How is she?"

Kamini hissed like he'd stabbed her. "Enough. Come, Nilesh."

The yaksha stretched lazily. "If you should change your mind, mortal Nilesh, you need merely recite this phrase: *Rakesh, my lord, I beg of you, let me in—*"

"Do not listen to him. He speaks nonsense." Kamini had stiffened. Whatever that nonsense was, she did *not* want Nilesh to hear it. He couldn't blame her.

"That I might play your game," Rakesh concluded. He made a sardonic bow.

Kamini practically shoved Nilesh out of the pavilion, then let him have it. "I would have taken you for many things, but not a fool. If you were to play and lose—which you most assuredly would—the price would be far more than the most desperate among us would pay."

"Like what?" Nilesh asked, trying to keep up. "And I never said I wanted to play. That guy's a jackass."

"Like being transformed into one of their playing pieces for eternity." Kamini quivered with fury. "Or being trapped here, unable ever to leave. In other words, you would belong to them. They are abhorrent people, preying on mortals and worse, and they have been sequestered in this area, where the guards can monitor them. Wise folk maintain their distance, as should you."

"Worse? How do you get worse than that?"

"They turned my mother into a tree," she said bluntly. "Because I was the antithesis of wise and mingled with them."

Whoa. Nilesh's annoyance dried up. That was nuts. No wonder she'd avoided getting into it earlier.

Before he could figure out how to reply, Kamini switched subjects. "In any case, *I* found you, mortal boy. Therefore, if anyone should keep you, it is me, not some stuffy old mischief makers." She pointed to the alcove. "If you are done dawdling?"

Nilesh knew he should leave. It was late. But Kamini liked him.

144

She'd just kept him safe. He didn't need to go back to Ridhi's house, not yet.

"Sure," he teased, "as long as you tell me more about this 'intriguing you' thing."

She sputtered. "I said nothing of the sort!"

Inside the alcove, he pulled her to him. "We'll see about that."

11

Ridhi drew her curtains to find that an unseen artist had painted spring into existence, shading in foliage here, stippling flower pistils there. The last sleepy breaths of winter had subsided overnight, yielding to a palette of chlorophyll and pastels, and the drowsy land, having yawned and stretched, then shook off its hibernation, rejuvenated for another year. When she opened the window, a warm breeze enfolded her in a hug.

She felt so alive, so renewed, that her skin hummed with it. This was her season, full of freshness and possibility, a season to be relished. The plants in her room glimmered their agreement.

Yet, out of habit, her phone made its way into her hand. Chetan Gopalkrishnan, she learned, had thrown a party at his house. Pictures of girls in sequin tank tops and makeup and boys with T-shirts and messy hair flooded her screen, like everyone in the world but Ridhi had been invited.

She scrolled through the deluge of photos, steeling herself for the usual ill feeling of being unwanted. Running into Chetan—and

Shreya—at the boutique had been awful enough.

It didn't come. Because while the kids from the mandir were off at their boring party, Ridhi had been learning magic from yakshas and baking enchanted lilac doughnuts. She might not be showing off online, but she didn't need to.

Ridhi closed the app. In the silence, trees rustled. *Sulochana*, she deciphered. *You. Morning.*

The remainder of the message escaped her. She'd been too impatient, too antsy, to listen as though she, too, were a tree, her pulse slow, her sap thick. How frustrating that she couldn't yet manage phyllomancy without Malav's assistance.

But she thought she'd gotten the gist of it: Sulochana wished to meet with her that morning. Ridhi could barely tame the energy zipping through her. She would go to Alakapuri with alacrity.

First, however, she needed to see her family off for the day. She brushed her teeth and ran downstairs.

In the kitchen, Mummy and Papa had pulled out the platter of doughnuts and were examining her handiwork. The pastries, which she'd frosted in light-purple glaze and topped with candied lilacs, might have been a magazine spread.

Their delectable aroma wafted through the air, whisking Ridhi back to her lesson the day before. She still couldn't quite believe that Malav had brought the yaksha kingdom to her yard.

"Where did you get these lilacs?" Mummy asked, her forehead vaguely troubled. "It's too early for them."

Ridhi plated doughnuts for her parents, then chose one for herself. "A good magician never divulges her secrets," she teased.

"Here, tell me what you think."

Papa bit into his, and the weariness around his mouth eased into smile lines. "Wherever you got this extract, buy them out. It's delicious!"

Enchanted lilacs were pretty spectacular, it was true. Ridhi had sampled a few prior to stirring the rest into the batter. "Hooray!"

Kartik thundered into the kitchen. "Ooh, doughnuts!" Like a hawk in search of prey, he pounced, ripping a chunk out of his fluffy quarry.

"Beta!" Mummy chastised him. "Stop and chew before you choke."

"Hey, so you're going to bake cookies for my game on Friday, right?" Kartik asked Ridhi through his mouthful. "But not those cashew cardamom coconut things you like. You can make oatmeal chocolate chip. We'll eat those."

"Wow, that's *so* generous of you." Ridhi pretended to faint. "I don't know how I'll *ever* be worthy of such an honor."

Kartik smirked. "I know, right?" He looked at Mummy. "Aren't you going to try yours?"

Mummy finally pecked at her doughnut. "Your baking is getting better and better," she said dreamily to Ridhi, who couldn't have been prouder.

She tucked into hers. It tasted like a confection a yaksha might snack on, and she lingered over each bite.

Once everyone else had left to start their mornings, she sat and listened to the trees, absorbing the play of the wind through their branches like a song. Trees, it occurred to her, were part of a greater family, too.

At last, anticipation tugging at her, Ridhi showered and paired moss-green leggings with a stretchy lavender slip dress in a medley of ruffles, crochet lace, vintage roses, and butterfly appliqués. Then she donned bangles, an emerald kundan necklace, a lotus choker, faux-flower earrings, and her paayal, and made herself up with royal purple lipstick, gold eye shadow, and a purple gem bindi.

For luck, she dotted her wrists with Keeper of the Woodlands.

Finally, Ridhi rifled through her closet until she located her box of flower crowns and jasmine gajras. She selected a circlet of aubergine poppies and light-pink primroses, then scrutinized her reflection in her dresser mirror. The crown perched atop her loose curls, transforming her into a storybook queen.

A queen didn't passively sit around, nor did she prostrate herself for scraps. She went after what she wanted—and for Ridhi, that was a place in the yaksha kingdom.

But something was missing.

Her gaze stopped on the bag Mummy had commissioned last year. The fiber artist had crafted a wearable garden from blossoms she'd felted in an assortment of shapes, sizes, and shades. Each bloom's rich details had been highlighted in gold accents like powdered magic.

The morning of her seventeenth birthday, when Ridhi had unwrapped the purse from its nest of tissue paper, she'd cried. Her mother knew her like no one else.

Slinging the green velvet strap over her shoulder, she slipped out the back door into a fairyland. *Sulochana, find me.*

A few more steps, and her neighbors had vanished, so she must have entered the yaksha kingdom. Everything was so green, so bright, touched by the patina of Lord Surya's effulgence. The trees had bedecked themselves in saris of white dogwood, pink apple, and peach champak blossoms, while the bushes flaunted azure juniper and orange mountain-ash berries. Their beauty salved her heart, and their fragrance intoxicated her spirit as she knelt to gather offerings for her altar.

This was why Ridhi adored botanical perfumes. Nothing could match nature's inherent virtuosity and complexity.

Birds sang a merry tune, and butterflies and bees pranced from plant to plant. The back of Ridhi's hand skimmed a stalk of light-purple downy skullcap blossoms as she went. A few red alpine strawberries peeped out from amid the lacy ferns, living rubies promising minute bursts of flavor. She helped herself to one, savoring its sweet tang.

How many times had she anticipated a portal opening up within a ring of toadstools, or a yakshini dancing forth from an ivy-wreathed tree trunk, slender finger crooked in summons, to welcome her home to the land where she belonged?

And now there she was.

Her breath flowed in and out, as calm and stable as the trees, the bushes, the berries and blooms. Ridhi's pulse slowed, the sense of her skin roughening, as if she were one more sapling rooted among many. A spectrum of green sluiced across her vision, and her eyes drifted shut. Her ears caught the sibilating of leaves someone else might mistake for a whisper, a collective sigh.

Why, it wondered, did she care about kids at school or the mandir when she was bound to the forest itself? When its sap ran through her veins?

I don't, she told the trees, *not anymore.*

A shrill cry roused her from the trance. "Meh-aao! Meh-aao!" She glanced down to see a peacock watching her curiously. Its white talons scratched at the grass.

She hadn't been up close to a peacock since she lived in India. The sight was arresting, from the crown-like crest on its head to the cobalt plumage over its chest to the five-foot-long train of blue-eyed green feathers trailing behind it.

Then she remembered the golden deer and the yakshinis' counsel. "You're not Ishika by any chance, are you, pretty peacock?"

The peacock blurred, and the switch had barely dawned on her before Malav stood there, miffed. "That traitor? Hardly."

Ridhi would have given anything to turn back time right then. Of course haughty Malav would go for a pavonine aspect. She should have known. Now he'd berate her for comparing him to Ishika and maybe keep her from Sulochana, just as he'd tried to keep her from the revel.

One side of Malav's mouth lifted in amusement. "You think me pretty?"

He was so finely drawn, an illustrator's portrayal of all that was both inspiring and inaccessible about nature. You could admire the beauty of a tree in bloom. You could even cut down a forest to clear its land for development. Yet no matter what you did, you could never truly possess it.

Ridhi's palms were sweatier than they had any right to be. "Most people think peacocks are pretty, yeah. I mean, maybe some don't? But they have bad taste."

Her prattle garnered her one of his rarer-than-rainbows smiles. "And so they do."

She fussed with the strap of her purse. "Um, I was looking for Sulochana? She called me."

"Come, then." Malav held out his arm. "I will bring you to her."

Remembering how comfortable Kamini had been with Nilesh, how comfortable Malav had been when he'd taken her hand, Ridhi maneuvered herself into the bow of his arm.

He started at the contact, and the crimson berries on the ground bulged with juice. Had she misunderstood?

But he only closed his arm around her and started walking.

"And," Sulochana said, reading off her scroll, "Devisha is the mother to Lakhit, a princeling from the far reaches of the Western Ghats."

She sat back in her ivy-wrapped golden chair and studied Ridhi across their leaf-mosaic table. Despite her ethereal sari of azalea petals and her hair like an ocean of black waves flecked by jewellike flowers, she resembled a businesswoman with a clipboard, checking items off her jam-packed agenda. "You will likely meet them during the opening ceremonies."

Ridhi felt dizzy just listening to the winding roster of names. She would never survive as a courtier. Too many faces to keep straight, too many incomprehensible rules and practices. The fabrics and colors they wore, how they styled their hair—all that sent clues she couldn't begin to gauge. Something as basic as a hello could be interpreted as a grave insult, if spoken with the wrong inflection. On Prithvi, people trained for years to become diplomats, yet egos still got pricked, setting off international disputes and, in the worst cases, wars.

Too honest, she'd overheard Papa say when she was a child, with a face like an open book, her thoughts and feelings available to anyone who cared to read them.

Ridhi didn't think she was quite that bad nowadays. But as for political intrigue? Hardly. She'd be found out on day one. "That's a lot to keep track of. But unless I'm mistaken, I don't think you brought me here to talk about the court."

Sulochana rewarded her with a smile. "Not in so many words, no, although it is always prudent to acquaint oneself with the current state of affairs." She placed a piece of rose-mango barfi on Ridhi's golden plate. "Malav apprised me of your recent attempt to divine the vernacular of the trees. He says it has borne fruit. Immature fruit, to be certain, yet fruit nonetheless."

"It's how I knew to come here today," Ridhi said. She tried her honeyed jamun lassi. It was fantastic.

"I am pleased to learn that my first impression of you was correct." Sulochana's teeth shone like pearls under moonlight. "You said you wished to aid me with my preparations for Holi. Is that still the case?"

"Yes." Ridhi kept her voice dispassionate. She couldn't let herself be swept away without hearing more first.

"That gladdens me. You see, I have been giving the upcoming celebrations a great deal of thought. Holi is a time when supplicants might petition our rulers for a boon in return for a bit of entertainment. I plan to make use of that."

Sulochana's expression turned bitter. "Four hundred years ago, the one I loved cost me everything I held dear. We were to reap the highest honor that blighted day—she would pluck a leaf from the Kalpavriksha, and in return for her service, she would request a parcel of land for the two of us. Our own solitary retreat."

"That sounds nice," Ridhi ventured. *Romantic.*

A nostalgic smile touched Sulochana's ranunculus-red lips, then crumpled. "It would have been. To my dismay, she elected instead to risk us all, and for what? A chance to grandstand? I still cannot comprehend it."

What a terrible situation. Ridhi couldn't think of a single response that didn't sound trite.

A few minutes passed before Sulochana spoke again. "By dint of hard work, I was able to preserve my reputation and rebuild our lieges' trust in me. Yet it must go deeper. I have been deliberating how I might repair the rift Ishika caused and shield Alakapuri once more. And I believe I have found a solution, albeit one that will require help."

"What is it?"

Before continuing, Sulochana checked that no one else was within earshot. "I have located the missing branch of the Kalpavriksha."

Ridhi almost slipped from her chair. "You *what*? Where was it?"

"Right here in our city." Sulochana reached across the table for Ridhi's hands. "You say you care for nature. And that you wish more mortals felt for the natural realm as you do."

Ridhi's head was spinning. The missing branch—that had to have been the branch she'd seen. "Of course I do."

"Then aid me." Sulochana squeezed firmly.

"How?"

"Help me reopen the portal to Svargalok by presenting the maharaja and maharani with a gift of your botanical perfume, perhaps a dance." Her voice fell to a whisper. "The Kalpavriksha will manifest for a minute or two, held in place by an anchor. In that time, I will heal the branch, you will pluck the leaf, and together we will complete the protective ritual."

The Kalpavriksha, with its gold and silver branches and gemstone leaves. Even there in Alakapuri, with its wealth of mythic grandeur and forests as lush as daydreams, even having spotted the branch, Ridhi could scarcely imagine interacting with the fabled wish tree. Never mind addressing King Kubera and Queen Kauberi.

"But why go through all this?" she pressed. Tantalizing as the proposal was, there had to be a simpler solution. "You're close with the maharani, right? Why not just give her the branch and let her take care of it?"

"The obvious solution, yes?"

Ridhi nodded. Wasn't it?

"Alas, it is not so simple as that. If you but knew how many times I have broached the subject of recommencing negotiations with Lord Indra. The maharaja supports it, yet the maharani—well, I have had some time to come to know her, and while she is generally wise and expansive of perspective . . ." Sulochana sighed and released Ridhi's hands. "That he beat her to the Kalpavriksha remains a thorn to her pride. And then being made to rely on him for its wishes, well!"

"Queen Kauberi doesn't like to lose," Ridhi joked weakly. "Got it."

Sulochana's own half smile was wry. "Indeed. Were I to hand over the branch now, I fear she would rather incinerate it than return it and see the tree healed."

"She hates him that much? What about the forest?"

"Going without the Kalpavriksha's protection has convinced her that such protection was superfluous all along. Were it not for your mortal technology encroaching on our lands, I might be inclined to agree. Yet the reality is that someone must intercede before it is too late."

Sulochana sagged in her chair, and Ridhi could see how much it cost her to keep up a genial front. "I am tired, Ridhi. Four centuries ago, I nearly lost everything. My people may tolerate me now, yet until the wish tree is restored to itself, I can never move forward. They will forever associate me with the loss Ishika incurred."

In *they*, Ridhi heard *I*. Sulochana felt responsible for what Ishika had done. Four hundred years of carrying that burden would exhaust anyone.

Sulochana wasn't the culpable party, and Ridhi thought to tell her as much. But countless other people must have said the same thing over the years. Actions would help her, not more words. "You said something about an anchor?"

Sulochana sipped her jasmine-berry cooler. Her guise in place once more, she trained her fierce stare on Ridhi. "Another tree, but one in this territory. That I will manage. The question is, are you up to your task?"

Ridhi squirmed under its vehemence. "I mean, I hope so?"

"You must *know* so," Sulochana said brusquely. "If you are not, tell me now. Too much rides on this to allow doubts."

"Okay." Ridhi straightened her spine. She hadn't done more than pick at the first round of sweets, as scrumptious as they appeared, but she munched on the soft barfi for something to do. It melted into a floral pool in her mouth. "I am. But why do you need me to do this?"

"That is quite simple." Sulochana took a delicate bite of her chum chum. "I cannot risk another yaksha or yakshini reporting my plan to the monarchs before I am able to carry it out. A mortal does not have the same prejudices against reopening the portal that one of my kind would."

"No, I got that. But why *me*?"

"In truth? You remind me of someone I once knew, who also cared deeply for the world around her." Sulochana cast Ridhi a devious glance from beneath her eyelashes. "Furthermore, Malav seems quite taken with you."

Malav, huh? Though Ridhi recognized the flattery for what it was, hearing it was still nice.

"But." She hesitated. "You didn't say how it'll work."

Sulochana tossed her nightfall of hair behind her shoulder. "As I mentioned, we will have an anchor, and the transfer should last a moment or two at most, before anyone in Svargalok notes the wish tree's absence. Essentially, it will instruct you as to which leaf to pluck, and, utilizing the phyllomantic skills you have been honing, you will listen and act accordingly."

Ridhi weighed the proposition. It was a risk, uprooting the wish tree for any length of time, but if that meant they could prevent humanity's careless plunder of Prithvi from tarnishing the yaksha kingdom, how could she refuse?

Besides, if Sulochana pulled this off—if Ridhi pulled it off in her name—she would become an instant darling. A heroine. Securing a wish from the unattainable Kalpavriksha for the maharaja and maharani of the yaksha kingdom *and* potentially restoring relations with the monarch of Svargalok? No one else's tribute could ever top that.

And since Sulochana couldn't do it without her aid, Ridhi could get what she'd always desired, too.

"I'll help you," she declared, "but I'm not going to do it for free."

"I would expect no less. Name your price."

"I want to sell my perfumes in the Night Market." Ridhi knew how to haggle—start high, appear to settle in the middle, and let the other person walk away believing they got the better of you.

Yet Sulochana merely waved her hand. "Done."

"Just like that?"

"You craft perfumes of plants. I decoct elixirs of the same," Sulochana enthused. "Indeed, I will make space for you in my stall. It would be a fine match for us both."

While Ridhi thrilled at the compliment, the win felt too easy. She inhaled the perfumed air, exulted in the flowers underfoot, tasted the rose and jasmine on her tongue. "I wasn't done."

"Oh?"

She forged ahead. "You told me to name my price. Then I also want a mekhala and my own tree. I want to be a yakshini. That's my price."

Had Ridhi really said that? Surely Sulochana would tell her to take a hike. She should backpedal, come off as more amenable.

But she didn't. She belonged there in Alakapuri, and not for the span of an afternoon.

When Sulochana replied, esteem tinted her tone. "The yearning in you burns hot, and you would make a fine yakshini, with your devotion to the natural realm. Yet are you certain you wish this? It is no small thing, you realize."

"Yes," Ridhi said as evenly as she could, considering her pulse stuttered. "Utterly certain."

"Then deliver what I have asked of you, and not only shall you enjoy ongoing vendor access to my stall in the Market, but I will see to it that you become a yakshini with a mekhala and a tree of your choosing."

"*You* can do that? You, personally, can make me a yakshini?" Ridhi didn't mean to antagonize Sulochana, but this was too serious, too significant, to let slide through some loophole.

"It is within my power, yes, and I swear to do so in return for your service. The deal is struck."

Not trusting herself to speak, Ridhi held her goblet aloft.

Sulochana's smile might have rivaled Ridhi's lassi for sweetness. "The forest itself chose you when it sent the jungle crow. How could I do any less?"

The server arrived bearing a fresh tray of food, which she acknowledged with a gracious tilt of her head.

Once they were alone again, she resumed the conversation. "I trust you not to speak of this to anyone. If you do, our bargain is off, and the forest will close itself to you."

"I won't. I promise." Ridhi had never meant anything more. "How about we go over that list of courtiers again?"

Sulochana started the recitation from the top, but from behind her, Malav watched Ridhi. How long had he been standing there?

Their gazes locked. Then he smiled. A smile just for her.

Her heart turned a handspring. Maybe Sulochana's claim hadn't been mere flattery. Maybe Ridhi truly could have more.

As if she'd already wished on the Kalpavriksha, all her dreams were coming true.

12

It was twelve thirty by the time Nilesh made it down to the kitchen for breakfast and one o'clock by the time Ridhi came back from wherever she'd disappeared to that morning, all dreamy smiles. Weird.

She took a foil-covered baking sheet from the fridge. "I baked these," she said, helping herself to a doughnut with purple frosting. "Enchanted lilacs. Yum."

"Huh." He waited for her to offer him one. She didn't.

"You'll have to amuse yourself today. I've got a few blends to work on."

Nilesh finished his last spoonful of cereal. "I'm heartbroken, flower girl."

The second she was out of sight, he filched a doughnut. It smelled amazing. No surprise, really; Ridhi always had been a great baker. He remembered having a thing for her rosewater brownies.

Something scratched at the kitchen door. When Nilesh

opened it, a fox peered up at him.

Weird. It—she—was a beauty, with her silky fur, black paws, and keen eyes. If foxes could be said to have human expressions, this one would be indignant. *What took you so long?*

Nilesh crouched and presented his hand. The vixen could bite him. She might have rabies. But he doubted it.

She sniffed him. He must have met her cryptic requirements, since she nudged him with her wet black nose and licked her chops.

"Oh, you're hungry?" He split the doughnut in two and held out half.

She lunged under a bush.

Nilesh knew it was stupid to feel let down. It was a miracle the vixen had approached him in the first place. Most people would never get near enough to feel a fox's nose or see the brown striations in its yellow eyes and the individual orange and yellow strands of its fur.

He'd barely stood up again when the vixen reappeared. She danced toward him, then back.

His mood skyrocketed. Maybe she was asking him to come outside.

"Going for a walk!" he yelled, on the off chance Ridhi was listening. "Thanks for the doughnut."

When he reached the sidewalk, the vixen blurred and shifted shape. "Namaste," Kamini trilled.

Nilesh should have guessed. Even he knew yakshas were shape-shifters.

Her big eyes provoked him, making his blood run faster. "I am questing after a mortal boy named Nilesh," she said. "Might he be available for a ramble?"

"I hear his schedule's open. Fox, huh? I'm into it."

"Are you? Then where is the treat I was promised?"

"All you had to do was ask." Nilesh gave her the other piece of the doughnut.

They strolled down the street, chewing, and he took advantage of the slow pace to check her out. She wore a blue lehenga and choli—made out of lobelia and butterfly pea flowers, she informed him—and sapphires and juniper berries glinted in her black braid. She was as pretty as a garden.

Kamini finished her doughnut. She looked forlorn, like when she'd mentioned her mother at the revel. "There is something I wish to experience. A task that has naught to do with my preparations for Holi."

"Anything. You name it."

Her perfect teeth shone in a sudden cheery smile. "I wish to play these video games you spoke of."

Nilesh couldn't believe his luck. "I know we just had dessert, but how do you feel about pizza?"

The automatic doors parted, and Nilesh and Kamini entered the blue-lit indoor amusement park.

Nilesh bought two afternoon passes with the credit card Mom had left him for emergencies. He was pretty sure teaching Kamini about video games counted.

She surveyed the flashing lights, the arcade machines blaring sound effects, and the tables of people munching on pizza and nachos. "Fascinating, but it is sorely in need of some greenery."

"Yeah," he said, "places like this don't really have plants. It's not a thing, you know?"

But Kamini was already yanking him toward the nearest unoccupied machine, which happened to be vampire-themed pinball. She rapped her knuckles on the glass case. "What is this?"

Nilesh explained the rules and showed her how to use the plunger. "See how there are two scores? We can take turns."

Except once Kamini got the hang of it, she refused to share the machine. She was too busy groaning when the bumpers smacked the ball down and whooping when the flippers knocked it into the higher target zones.

Nilesh faked a sulk, but this was the best date he'd ever been on.

"I like the doorbell noise best," she announced. "It sounds like clinking coins."

"Man, casinos would love you," he said.

From there, they attempted a zombie shooting game, a martial arts tournament, and a platform game with plenty of leveling up. Kamini loved that last one. Even though she kept running into enemies and flatlining, she couldn't resist all the treasure chests and hint-dispensing cats.

"Would that we could stay here all day," she mumbled after her character fell down a hole for the fifth time. Her head was bowed with that gloom from earlier.

"I mean," Nilesh said, concerned, "we can if you want to."

Then he remembered they hadn't had lunch. Even yakshas needed to eat.

While she battled another overpowered boss, Nilesh ordered them slices of greasy cheese pizza with red pepper flakes. The server behind the counter barely looked at him. "Is that all?"

"Actually, no," Nilesh said. "Can I get two sodas, too?"

The guy put two souvenir cups on the tray. "Over there."

Kamini came up beside Nilesh and beamed at the server. "If I torment my character any further, she will surely leap free of the game and curse me. Perhaps more later."

The server's jaw slackened. "Uh, hi there."

Nilesh knew how he felt. Seeing Kamini—or any yaksha or yakshini—was like being kicked in the gut, but in the best way. He nodded at the dazed guy. "Thanks."

After he'd filled the cups at the soda fountain, Nilesh carried the tray to an open table. He grinned and toasted Kamini. "To the authentic arcade experience."

She grinned back and imitated him. "To the authentic arcade experience."

The food was okay. Way better was watching Kamini try it. The straw confounded her, and she scrubbed so hard at the grease by her mouth that she ripped the paper napkin. But she got through the meal, calling it "another game."

Whatever had been bothering her seemed to have drowned under the layers of cheese and canned tomato sauce.

They headed to the Skee-Ball alley, where Kamini went on to

rack up a bunch of tokens. With Nilesh's input, she cashed them in for a cotton candy–pink teddy bear the size of her forearm.

"Want to try the claw machine?" he asked. "No one ever gets anything out of there."

"In a moment." Kamini waved her hand. Wildflowers pushed up through the epoxy floor, and vines crept between the arcade machines. She waggled her head. "Now I feel at home."

Nilesh snickered. "You can't do that."

"And yet I did." She cradled her teddy bear to her chest. "I will tame this claw machine in much the same manner."

"How? You'll sic vines on it?"

"Perhaps."

"What the hell?" someone bellowed. "Who did this? Jason?"

Nilesh and Kamini choked down laughter. "No claw machine, then," he said. "Run?"

"Run," she agreed. Hand in hand, they did, out the doors and into the tree that had brought them to the arcade.

They tumbled out of a skinny tree that smelled of cinnamon and onto a pile of silk and moss cushions. Kamini's tree, Nilesh was sure of it.

"That was wild," he gasped when he finally stopped laughing.

Kamini glanced up at him through her lashes. Her braid had come undone, and tendrils dangled around her face. She had to know that suggestive pout drove every other thought out of his head.

"As wild as roses!" She snuggled her teddy bear. "Yet I would have you know that, had we stayed, I would have mastered that claw machine."

"Next time for sure," he lied. But it would be fun to watch her try. And try. And try.

"I know you do not believe me!" She poked him in the stomach.

Nilesh didn't remember rolling over, but then they were kissing, their mouths hungry and hunting. She was all flowers and fresh air, a plant incarnated as a person. He pulled her closer, tighter, his fingers knotting in her hair.

Kamini murmured his name. Her breath was sweet on his lips. "Oh, silly mortal boy. What a day you have given me."

His last thought before his mouth found hers again was that maybe he wasn't the only one of them looking to disappear into somebody else.

Later, once Kamini had straightened her clothes and recovered the teddy bear from the grass, once Nilesh had sneaked another kiss and then another after that, once he'd finger-combed twigs from his hair while flowers bloomed in hers, he unlocked his phone and snapped a few shots. "You look like a painting, lying there like that."

Kamini examined the screen with relish. "You even incorporated my tree!"

Capitalizing on the view, Nilesh propped himself up on one elbow. He'd been right about the tree. "I'd send them to you," he teased, "except for the thing about you not having a phone."

It hit him then. He hadn't thought about Dad's voice mail or the apartment in hours. He was . . . happy.

Kamini and he could have the best of both worlds—his world and hers. Concerts and movies alternating with forest parties and court functions. Why not?

"That *is* a problem." Kamini put down the phone and flicked a polished fingernail over his mouth. She wasn't smiling anymore.

"Nah. I'll just get you a phone. Or get them printed." But Nilesh didn't think she was talking about the pictures.

Kamini pored over his face like she was memorizing the details. Then she kissed him. It felt different from before, though he couldn't put his finger on why.

"Thank you for this day," she said, her voice low with regret, "for the doughnut, the games, the teddy bear. I swear I will not forget it. Or you."

That was what had been off. The kiss felt like an ending.

"What do you mean?" Nilesh's happiness curdled. "We can do this every day. There's nowhere I want to be but here with you."

She jumped to her feet and began pacing.

He got up, too. Had he come on too strong? Hurt her feelings? "Hey—"

Kamini kept her back to him. "You must leave now. Goodbye, Nilesh."

Feeling sick, he took her by the shoulders. "Look, if I scared you, I'm sorry."

She twisted away. "Foolish boy. You are not listening. Hear me well. Purge your memory of me. Of us."

Why was she doing this? Hadn't they had a great day together?

Her tree wasn't so nice, now that she didn't want him near it. He laughed. "Don't you think you're overreacting?"

"This is no jest," she said icily. "Go home to your family and stay there."

"No!" Nilesh tried to meet her eyes, but she wouldn't let him. "Talk to me. Kamini, what's wrong? Is it your mom? Something I did?"

"I said *go home*, mortal boy." Catching hold of his arm, Kamini touched her tree.

And then he was careening through its cinnamon-scented trunk, alone.

Nilesh emerged in Ridhi's front yard to see Amar opening the passenger-side door of his car so Hetal could get out. *What a gentleman*, he thought bitterly.

The abrupt transition from the yaksha kingdom to the stupid mundane world didn't do much to improve his mood. He shouldn't be there.

Excitement spread over Hetal's face. She must not have seen him arriving via tree. "Nilu, Mom said you can come back home! Which, if you'd checked your phone, you'd know already."

A few days ago, this would have been the best news. But that was before the yakshini he liked more than any girl he'd ever met had dumped him.

Amar jingled his keys. "Your mom's waiting at the restaurant. Get in the car."

"You two sure have gotten cozy, huh?" Nilesh accused. "Every time I turn around, there you are, together."

"Look, I get that you're mad at me." Hetal's smile was watery. "But can we please stop fighting? I miss you."

"Fine, whatever. Let's go." Nilesh plopped down behind her in the back seat, resigned to his fate.

The atmosphere on the drive was heavy. Amar cranked up his music so loud that no one could talk, not that Nilesh wanted to. He kept reliving the moment Kamini had given him the boot.

Why would she do that?

Finally, Amar pulled up in front of the restaurant and handed Hetal her crutches.

She hugged him. "Thanks for the ride."

Nilesh grunted and stalked toward the spicy aromas wafting out at them. Why did this dinner have to be right then?

Hetal caught up with him at the hostess station. "Mom really misses you, too, you know."

Not sure what to say, Nilesh nodded.

The hostess guided them to a table in the center of the dining room. Mom stood to greet them.

"Hi, beta! How are you?" She flashed him a thousand-watt smile. Her hair was pulled back at her neck, and she looked as put together as usual.

Nilesh helped Hetal into her chair, then slouched into his. "Why are we here?"

Mom laughed, false and tinkling, like Nilesh was a client. "To have a nice dinner out, of course. I missed my baby boy!"

"Isn't it nice?" Hetal cooed. She'd set her crutches against the empty fourth chair. The one where Dad should be. "All of us together again!"

"Not *all* of us," Nilesh muttered.

A waitress brought their menus. "My name is Pragna," she

said, "and it will be my pleasure to wait on you this evening." If she noticed the tension in the air, she didn't let on. "I'll give you a few minutes to decide, shall I?"

She left, and Nilesh took in the restaurant with its orange-and-pink palace-themed décor, the crystal chandeliers raining sparkles, the gilt arms on the velvet-upholstered chairs. He tried not to make eye contact with anyone, but he picked out faces from his parents' social circle.

Suspicion built in him. There was no shortage of good Indian restaurants in the city where you could be anonymous over your tandoori chicken and naan. If you dined here, you wanted to be seen.

Or you wanted to make a statement that you knew would get around.

Mom sat ramrod straight in her chair, and she kept her mouth in that smile no one could miss. She didn't relax it once while paging through the menu.

A family could go to a fancy dinner without it meaning anything. Their family used to. But that wasn't what was happening. Aruna Batra was bragging to the world that she was doing great and her children stood by her.

The waitress reappeared at Nilesh's elbow. "Have you decided?" she sang out. "We do have a tasting menu, and I'd love to tell you about tonight's specials."

"Go ahead," Mom urged Hetal.

She nudged Nilesh. "You start."

"I'm not hungry." He barely registered Mom ordering him a thali and a coconut rose mocktail.

"Nilesh," Mom began, once the waitress had gone, "you know things have been difficult."

"You mean, Dad has a mistress, and you never told me." Nilesh grinned, big and insolent. "Yeah, that was pretty difficult, all right."

Mom sighed. "You don't understand. When you're a parent, you do what's best for your child."

"So you lied to me."

"I shouldn't have sent you away. I wasn't thinking."

If she had said that any other day, Nilesh might have felt better. But not then, when it was meaningless.

"You don't have to stay at Ridhi's house anymore," she continued. "We'll find a way to get through this as a family. A new kind of family, a little smaller, but still a family."

"Mom," Hetal cut in, "just tell him."

Nilesh's anger corroded into fear. "Tell me what?"

"I've spoken with Bindul Das," Mom said in her formal lawyer voice. "He's initiating divorce proceedings on my behalf."

Nilesh needed to break something. But he'd promised Kamini he wouldn't do that again. So he crumpled up his napkin instead. "I don't believe you."

He did, though. Why would Mom stay with someone who was shacking up with his mistress? Really, the question was, why hadn't she filed for divorce sooner?

And why, after everything else, did this feel like such a betrayal?

Mom took a breath. "Nilesh. Please."

"That's why you brought us here, right?" he asked, just as bright as her glued-on smile. "Because it's all about making sure you look good. That's what matters."

"Of course not!" Hetal insisted. "It's . . ."

Mom, however, had no issue completing the sentence. "It's exactly why. The rumors are all over town. You can't ask me to sit back and let that happen."

The pressure to punch something felt like steam rising from a geyser. It scalded Nilesh's insides.

All those eyes around them. Those people had known. They'd been waiting for his reaction, as if his family falling apart was popcorn worthy.

The waitress brought a basket of papad and dishes of tamarind-date and green-pepper chutneys and began laying them out. "And how are we all this evening?"

Nilesh staggered to his feet. "I'm going to wash my hands."

He made it across the dining room and into a restroom stall before he started shaking. His stomach roiled. Tears burned salty tracks down his cheeks.

He wasn't sure who he was maddest at—Dad for starting this, Mom for ending it, or himself for caring.

Himself, he decided, staring at his reflection in the mirror over the sink. It was stupid to get this upset when no one else was. Mom wanted the picture-perfect show? He'd give it to her.

Nilesh splashed water on his face, dried it, and balled up the paper towel as small as he could before chucking it in the garbage.

When he came out, Hetal was waiting for him. "The food's here," she said. "It looks really good."

"Uh-huh," he muttered.

She cuffed him on the shoulder. "It'll be okay, little brother. We can get your stuff later."

"Uh-huh."

"Sunita planned a welcome-home dinner for tomorrow. All your favorites." Hetal dropped into a conspiratorial whisper. "Mom and I made the rasmalai."

"Mom and you, huh?" he echoed. "So what, you're playing both sides now? Is that it?"

Hetal recoiled. "They're our *parents*, Nilu."

"So what Dad did is fine? And now you're on board with a *divorce*?" He laughed. "Happy-go-lucky Hetal. Nothing bothers her. You should work for the UN."

Hurt had dimmed her over-the-top cheer. "What do you want from me?"

Nilesh studied this person he'd grown up with, who'd told him jokes when he was sad, who'd treated the first sketch he'd done like architecture gold, and felt his heart close off. "What do you think I want? For you to tell Dad to get lost."

She looked like she was confused, or like he was. "Dad messed up. Big-time. But he's still our dad. And Mom made her choices."

Clearly no one but Nilesh gave a damn that their family—their lives—had turned out to be one gigantic lie. "Don't worry about taking me to get my stuff. You don't need to do anything for me. Go suck up to Dad some more and then come make Mom feel better when you're done. Diplomat of the year."

Hetal didn't say a word.

Nilesh knew he was hurting her. Good. "What difference does it make what's really going on, when we can all pretend it's fine?" He shot her finger guns and a wacky grin. "Am I right?"

"Stop it!" she whisper-shouted. "You're being horrible."

It should have been a victory. But the fire inside him had burned both of them. "Let's just get through dinner."

Side by side and worlds apart, they plodded back to the table.

It felt so weird, being home again. Like Nilesh was another person now, a stranger.

He went up to his room. His phone was still under Kamini's tree, so he turned on his computer. He had to see for himself.

His feeds loaded. Then notifications filled the screen, one after another after another.

Word had spread fast. The rumors Mom had expected. Comments full of performative sympathy that made Nilesh ill. Their community loved the drama, that was for sure. What was more entertaining than watching one of its golden families brought to their knees?

Some people had sent him private messages. He closed the browser without reading them.

Everything had disintegrated in one fell swoop. His whole life, Nilesh had been standing on shallow ice and hadn't known until it fractured and plunged him into the freezing water below.

He'd give anything to be with Kamini. He didn't care about the magic, only her. Why had she thrown him away?

The evening dragged on. When Mom knocked, he didn't answer.

Later, Hetal, who couldn't really navigate the stairs anymore, shouted up to him. "Come watch a movie with me, Nilu. I made popcorn!"

"Don't yell!" Mom called. "Use the stair lift! That's why we had it installed."

"Yelling's faster!"

How many nights had they had that same debate? Nilesh could fall right back into the pattern with them. All he had to do was ask what movie.

The words stuck in his throat. Hetal might be able to act like nothing had changed, but not him.

Nilesh flipped through old sketchbooks, jammed on his guitar, and loaded some car-chase video games. None of it held his interest.

He'd seen the reluctance on Kamini's face. She hadn't wanted him to go. That had been obvious. She'd thought he had to.

The problem was, Nilesh was tired of other people making his decisions for him. Dad, Mom, Hetal, and even Kamini—they'd all done it. They'd all believed they were keeping him safe.

Well, no more.

If Kamini had wanted him to stay away, Nilesh reasoned, she shouldn't have introduced herself in the grocery store. She definitely shouldn't have brought him to the yaksha kingdom.

He grabbed a backpack from the attic and stuffed a new sketchbook, a set of fineliner pens, and his game console into it.

If humans wanted to play out their sick dramas and keep disappointing one another, he wouldn't stop them. But that didn't mean he had to be part of it.

Around nine thirty, once Mom had retired to her—not Dad's anymore—study, and Hetal was in the den, midway through her movie, Nilesh sneaked down to his car. He hadn't driven it since getting suspended.

Even that left him cold.

He parked near Ridhi's house, then jogged the five minutes to her woods. Holding the dewdrop opal tight, he addressed the dirt. "Kamini, I know you told me to go home, but I don't like it there. I want to be with you. Let me in. Please. I miss you so much."

It felt like a thousand sets of ears were listening to Nilesh debase himself. If Kamini's were among them, she didn't answer.

"Please, Kamini," he begged. "I'm sorry for whatever I did. Don't leave me here. Please."

She still didn't answer. No one did.

But . . .

Oh, right. He'd been asking the wrong person.

Repugnance crawled up Nilesh's throat. He hadn't forgotten how Kamini had dissuaded him from talking to Rakesh, or that he'd splintered her family.

But it was the only way to get back to her for good.

"Rakesh, my lord," Nilesh forced himself to say, "I beg of you, let me in, that I might play your game."

The words were gross in his mouth, but the air around him

wavered, and the night's chill turned to warmth. The plants around him began to shine. A circle of mushrooms sprouted before him.

Nilesh jumped through the circle and trailed the glowing flowers to the pavilion with the game board.

A new round of chaturanga was in progress. The players had only advanced a few squares. He was sure they could fit him in.

"I'm ready to play," he called.

The yakshas and yakshinis sneered. The bramble-wearing yakshini asked, "Your bodyguard is not here to protect you?"

Nilesh crossed his arms. "This is boring. Are we playing or not?"

The same greedy look passed over all their faces. "The price for losing is to become trapped here. A bird with clipped wings, bound to the land."

Exactly what Nilesh had in mind. "Let's get started."

PART TWO

*D*id you know a papaya tree once became a witch? Oh, yes.

It was late summer when this transpired, and our tree was festooned in fruit as radiant and green as tourmalines. Each and every summer before, her kin had joined her in celebration, their communal canopy offering shelter and sustenance to all who passed beneath.

Alas, that year, a blight had befallen her orchard. None but our papaya was spared. No longer might she trade tidbits about the heedless squirrels that misplaced their large stores of nuts. No longer might she dissect the avian family dramas being enacted in her boughs.

Cut off from community, no longer might she thrive.

All trees, from new-sprouted plantlets to towering elders, are schooled in the art of patience, and our papaya was no exception. Anchored in the earth as she was, she shed seed-rich fruit and waited. Through drought she waited. Through monsoon she waited. Through bloom and dormancy she waited.

No seed took root. The tree surveyed the soil and the sky. The land had become sandy and insubstantial. The air had become harsh and dry. Worse, the changes were spreading, and soon she would lose even herself. Already white blemished her leaves.

Unlike in the past, deduced the tree, it was not enough simply to wait; she needed to act.

So she stretched her branches up, up, up and drew down the flame of the setting sun. Her veins distended as she drank. The few abiding squirrels and birds and insects paused their chirping and cawing and flitting to watch.

In the silence, the tree cast her very first spell. It was an orange-and-red spell, made of fire and flora and the sheer joy of freedom.

Sun sap poured out her branches and sparked in the air. When its embers accumulated at the base of her trunk, a pool the color of the sun came into being. Our tree peered within its waters, and what did she see but a ring of other trees?

A coven! She needed a coven.

She directed more of her gathered flamelight at her meager audience: the chirping squirrels, the cawing birds, the flitting insects. "Go," she commanded, the word as rough and miraculous as bark. "Bring others to me."

The animals and the winged things scurried and soared away, leaving the tree to wait once more.

At daybreak, her woodsy coven arrived: neem, jamun, hawthorn, magnolia, pong-pong, and champak.

The jamun was the first to speak. "The land itself is under siege. It is the work of the mortals and their endless avarice!"

"I would unleash my wrath upon them," hissed the pernicious pong-pong, "that they might at last conceive of what they wreak on those around them."

The magnolia's creamy blossoms blushed a sweet pink. "I would shower them with flowers that strike their hearts with beauty and their nostrils with pollen until they are too stupefied to chop down a single tree."

"I knew a mortal and her clan," the neem said woefully. "She sought succor beneath my branches and sang songs in my shade. In return, she embraced me often and with true affection. I would not see her injured, not ever."

"I, too, know gentle mortals," the champak offered. "They make incense of my blossoms and burn it in their rituals, so that I fly high enough to touch the stars."

"That is a bit romantic for my taste," mocked the jamun, "but I agree that we need mortals, and whether or not they know it, they need us, too." She angled her purple fruits toward the pong-pong. "Therefore, we cannot permit you to poison them all."

"What would you have us do, Papaya?" asked the neem.

When our tree became a witch, she had felt a truth inscribed in the air, in the soil, in the water; in the storming of the clouds, in the shining of the sun: what ailed one would soon ail another, for all things were inextricably connected, many trees entangling their roots.

She relayed her plan to her coven.

"Yes," said the hawthorn, and the other trees agreed.

"Then, sisters, let us commence," intoned the papaya.

Together, our tree and her coven sent a web of sorcery into the world.

It penetrated dream and imagination alike, a constant reminder of the mortals' childhoods when they had loved crunching through dry leaves or climbing trees. When they were young and openhearted enough to hear those same trees speak rather than cut them down.

Of course, there were those who refused to capitulate, to acknowledge their selfishness and cease their harm, and for those intractable individuals, the coven made liberal use both of its pollen and of its thorns.

Sometimes, the papaya knew, dry underbrush had to be burned away to allow for new growth.

"Forgive me," one such man pleaded, unable to withstand the coven's barrage. "I failed to remember. We all did."

The coven gilded him inside and out with the gift of its sun sap. "Infect them all with the itch of your vision," charged the pong-pong, "or else I will infect you with mine."

The new-forged artist had no need to be told twice. Off he went to acquire clay and glaze.

Back in the papaya's orchard, rain cleansed the sky and moistened the soil. It darkened and gained nutrients. Our tree's discoloration vanished, and her seeds found purchase in the earth.

Then the coven dispersed, with plans to meet again at Ashvin Purnima.

Content, the tree meditated. She had become an accomplished witch. Where, she mused, should she apply her skill set next?

She was a witch, so she would call up the fireflies and the walnut-gathering squirrels and the fine-plumed birds and begin to plot.

But she was also a tree, and for now, she would rest and reflect.

—FROM *THE TALES THAT TREES TELL*,
A COLLECTION FROM ALAKAPURI AND BEYOND

13

It had taken Nilesh two moves, not one, to lose the chaturanga game.

The irony burned in that gallows-humor kind of way. His first move had been a lucky guess, delivering him to a safe square on the board rather than the sudden death he'd intended.

Well, well, well, Rakesh had said, like Nilesh might be a decent opponent, after all. *A possible contender.*

Then, of course, he'd blown it.

When his feet had touched the second square, a cavity had opened under him. The next thing Nilesh knew, he was hurtling through blackness, wind slapping at him. He'd skidded on impact, arms thrashing, and landed face-first in noxious mud. It clogged his nose and made his throat raw.

The pit's steep walls were too smooth to climb. He couldn't find any rocks to stack or anything to stand on, except for a single poison-green briar with red roses that radiated their own gory light.

Imprisoning him down there hadn't been enough for Rakesh

and his buddies. A lazy wave of the bramble-wearing yakshini's hand from above, and the briar had clamped into place over Nilesh's wrists and ankles. Whenever he shifted, dull red thorns impaled him. Blood trickled from the wounds into the mud, where they made a toxic soup.

That was when Nilesh knew for sure he'd screwed up.

But he hadn't joined the game so his new jailers could have some fun at his expense. He'd done it to be with Kamini again. So, figuring they'd snub him, he'd spat out the grit in his mouth and pleaded for them to call her.

They'd bared their teeth with glee. Another chance to torture him.

But Kamini had shown up to save him. Each time she paced into his line of sight, acorns and pine needles hailed down.

All Nilesh could do to dodge the onslaught was swivel his head. Even deep in the hole where he'd been trussed up, he knew exactly how mad she was. He could measure it by the tree parts accumulating at his feet.

Overhead, the bargaining continued.

His jailers ringed the pit. His heart raced on seeing them. They were definitely the sort of predators that liked to play with their food before killing it. If Kamini couldn't talk them into freeing him, he was toast.

Nilesh had been so desperate to shake off his family and get back to her that he hadn't thought past losing the game. But the way the yakshas pondered him, like he was a doll they couldn't wait to break, sent acid churning in his stomach.

He recalled Kamini saying something about the two types of yakshas—the ones like her, and the nasty ones. She had been warning him, but Nilesh hadn't listened. He hadn't wanted to.

A pine cone ricocheted off his head. Then a crab apple with its stem.

Kamini looked down at him for the first time since she'd arrived. He saw storm clouds in her glare.

Nilesh made his own eyes huge. *Please*, he tried to say through them. *Yell at me all you like. Just get me out of here first.*

Kamini projected her voice so that it carried to his ears. "The mortal boy is here at my behest. Therefore, my claim on him supersedes yours."

Sulochana and Malav stood watching alongside her. Nilesh hadn't even known they were there.

Rakesh growled low in his throat. "He is ours. He entered our game of his own free will."

"And now," the bramble-wearing yakshini said, "we have a new toy with which to amuse ourselves." Her lip curled viciously. Like her comrades, she was the scary version of beautiful. "Such an auspicious turn of events, yes?"

Nilesh shuddered, even though that just made the thorns bite harder. He did *not* want to be left alone with these people.

"What of the ramifications?" Sulochana's question was pure ice. "Was he cognizant of them?"

The yakshini tittered. "You may ask him."

"We admit no one without their consent," Rakesh said, so

pretentious that Nilesh wanted to deck him. "But a mortal who volunteered himself? Only a fool would turn away such a treat."

Sulochana waggled her head in submission. "Then I am afraid there is nothing to be done. Come, Kamini."

Nilesh's breathing sped up. She was kidding, right?

Kamini didn't argue.

The circle of faces disappeared, taking the conversation with them. Nilesh strained to listen. Unfortunately, the yakshas had strayed too far from the pit for him to catch anything.

They'd left him there. They'd really left him there.

She'd left him there.

The reality that he might be trapped forever in this hellhole was unbearable. He wouldn't accept it.

No, he'd get out somehow.

But the moon moved overhead, and no one came.

The mud dried and flaked on his skin. Nilesh's hope deflated like it was a balloon, literally punctured by the thorns.

He waited for hours, and still no one came, not even the yakshas and yakshinis who'd stashed him there.

This was it. Nilesh was going to live out the rest of his life in the slimy, rancid pit, however short that was. He wished he'd thanked Amar for the ride to the restaurant. He wished he'd hugged Hetal and Mom. He was never going to see them again.

Would they think he'd died or just run away? He would never know.

Since he couldn't do anything else, Nilesh slept.

Cold water splashed Nilesh's face, rudely waking him.

"Bestir yourself, mortal," Rakesh ordered. "You have slept long enough."

Then a vine ladder was being lowered. The briar binding Nilesh's wrists and ankles loosened. Bloody holes marked where they'd been.

He hesitated. Was he still dreaming? What if the yakshas were tricking him before they terrorized him some more?

Rakesh appeared over the lip of the pit. The roses' red light turned his handsome face demonic. "Come, mortal creature. It seems someone believes your pathetic life worth paying for."

"Kamini?" Nilesh had known she wouldn't leave him stranded.

Rakesh's laugh was harsh. "It is good you have a fertile imagination. You will need it to keep you afloat."

What a scumbag.

Nilesh grabbed his muddy backpack and pushed himself upright. Almost immediately, he toppled backward. "Oof."

More mud leaked into his wounds. He hissed at the pain. He'd need some disinfectant, stat. The skin behind his ear was itching, too.

It wasn't until he'd hooked one arm through the bottom rung of the vine ladder that he found any purchase and could climb out. Part of him was sure Rakesh would jerk the ladder away and let him crash again, but he made it to the top.

Rakesh was nowhere to be seen. Neither were the other yaksha and yakshinis from the chaturanga game.

When Nilesh glanced down, the pit had been covered over again. It must be lying in wait for the next victim.

He ran as fast as he could to the courtyard exit. The sooner he put this nightmare behind him, the better.

Outside, the fruit trees greeted him. His breathing slowly calmed. *You're free*, he told himself. *You're free.*

He was out, and he'd survived. Soon he would be with Kamini, and it would all be worth it.

Something scratched his ankle. He jerked away. It wasn't the green briar. It wasn't.

Patches of stinging nettle, foxgloves, and little bell-shaped white flowers that seemed harmless but were probably anything but bloomed on the ground. And there was Kamini.

She'd come back, after all.

"You absolute *idiot*!" she roared. Her eyes glinted like she was about to throttle him. "You dunderhead! You . . . you foolish mortal boy! I told you not to do this! I forbade you!"

If Nilesh had thought she was mad before, this was on another level. But he could cope with that.

"Aw," he said, as the adrenaline spike started to fade. "I missed you, too."

"Do you possess even the slightest sense of self-preservation?"

"What?" he asked innocently. Playing the game had been stupid, yeah, but didn't she get that he'd done it for her?

Kamini shoved some moss at him. "Apply this to your wounds."

Nilesh tore the moss in four pieces and wrapped them around his wrists and ankles. The pain reared up, hot and angry, then went out in a cool *whoosh*. When he checked, the bloody spots had scabbed over.

"I'm sorry," he said. He was—for upsetting her.

All at once, her rage fizzled out. "Why did you not heed me?"

"Because." Nilesh shrugged. "I want to be with you."

She laughed, but it was glum. "You had a full life in the mortal world. You could have reaped its benefits into your dotage. I would much rather you had chosen that."

"But you saved me from those ghouls."

"Me?" Kamini shook her head. "I did no such thing."

Nilesh's throat ached. He felt like someone had spun him around and around until he couldn't tell which direction was up anymore. "Then who did? Your cousin?"

"Hardly." Kamini pointed to his ear. "It seems the forest itself has claimed you."

He scratched the skin there, which felt rough and scaly. It would be just his luck if he was allergic to that mud.

She sighed. "Oh, mortal boy. Why could you not remain among your kind? I never should have given you the dewdrop opal."

Why not? Because he'd come back?

Nilesh didn't see what the issue was. If he'd listened to her, then what? Graduate high school, go to college, get married—all while pretending he bought into the mass delusion that he was happy?

He thought he might get why Ridhi was so obsessed with

nature. It was a reminder that most of the things people built their lives around ultimately didn't matter. Everyone was so frantic to make an impression, leave a legacy: *I was here*. But for what?

Seriously, who would ever remember what you wore to prom or how many cars you had in your garage when you died? Nilesh had never understood that. You'd be lucky if your grandkids remembered your name.

Birds molted their feathers. Snakes shed their skins. What was stopping him from doing the same thing? Just tear off this Nilesh Batra persona and see what lurked underneath?

He was finished being the son of Dilip and Aruna. Time to try on an alternate life.

Kamini stayed at arm's length. "I am sorry, truly."

A strange comfort washed over Nilesh. He'd been fighting his destiny. Now he would embrace it.

He closed the distance between them. "You did me a favor. If someone's going to use me, *I* decide how."

Kamini's eyes drilled into his. "I do not desire for you to be the forest's tool. Or even mine."

"But it's what I choose." Nilesh reached for her.

She backed away, trembling. "You do not comprehend what that means, mortal boy."

"That's what I'm trying to tell you." He stepped forward again. "I don't care."

Kamini stroked his arm like she was consoling him. Apologizing. But he didn't need her to apologize. He needed her to hear him.

"I chose this," he reiterated.

She had to recognize that. No one had made him join the cha-turanga game. That had been his decision.

He wouldn't let anyone take it from him in a misguided attempt to help.

That was what people like Ridhi would never learn. You couldn't wait for people to let you in. You inserted yourself in the center of the crowd and charmed everyone, like Nilesh did, and before you knew it, they'd be orbiting around you. To put it in her terms, you'd be the sun to their plants.

What plant didn't need the sun?

Nilesh flashed Kamini his most easygoing smile. Unlike with Bhoomi, he didn't have to fake it.

Kamini palpated his ear. "Perhaps I can find a liniment for this. Perhaps also a loophole through which to send you home."

"No. I *want* to be here," he reminded her. "You don't need to feel bad."

She inclined her head, but he could see how grudging it was.

Nilesh, however, had never felt more validated. He was putting down roots. Dad could learn something from that. "I mean it. It's okay. Now that you're here, I'm fine."

"Fine? How can you say such a thing?"

He cupped her cheek in his palm. "Because I am."

She did an about-face. "Do as you will, then. I cannot be part of this."

Her shape blurred, and a vixen dashed away from him into the trees.

Nilesh's hand dropped to his side. It felt like she'd hacked

194

through his skin and pulled apart his rib cage to expose his stupid, defenseless heart. The pit had been bad enough. Now she didn't want him anymore?

His legs started to shake. He couldn't have lost her. She was all he had.

No. He refused to believe it. He'd gone through too much for that to be true.

Nilesh stared out at the horizon, willing her to wait. To look back.

Then he saw it. Outlined by the dawn was a fire-furred silhouette. It seemed to be observing him.

His whole body relaxed. She hadn't left. She still cared.

He cobbled together a plan. As soon as the sun rose, he'd find the other yakshas and yakshinis he'd met and chill with them until Kamini got over her guilt. She'd come around. It was just a matter of time.

And then, despite what she thought, everything would be all right.

14

The house was calmer, less chaotic without Nilesh, and Ridhi couldn't say she really minded. She rubbed a sprig of the rosemary in its windowsill pot. Well, except for the part where she'd never gotten to confront him about the doughnut he'd stolen—or the sample vial of Damayanti and the Swan she'd found while stripping the guest bed earlier. And the part where he was the one other person who knew her secret.

The rosemary's fresh, pungent aroma left her mind clear and alert. No point in getting sentimental. Just because Nilesh and she shared a secret and he'd had her perfume for some reason didn't mean they were friends.

Kartik, on the other hand, wasn't handling the news well. "I never got my rematch!" he complained. He was supposedly helping Mummy with the towels from the dryer while Ridhi pruned the kitchen herb garden and Papa cleared the dinner dishes, but so far, he'd accomplished more whining than folding.

"So play me," Ridhi offered, snipping off a strip of basil flower buds. Like the other herbs, the basil had shot up seemingly overnight. "We were on for a rematch, too."

Kartik thwacked a towel into a messy hump. "It's not the *saaaame*."

She brandished the bright green buds at him. "Oh, yeah?"

"Speaking of games," Mummy interjected, refolding the towel, "what should we play?"

Ridhi loved family game night, but with Holi only a couple of days off, she'd never be able to concentrate on playing. Who knew when the next signal from Malav might come? "Do we have to?"

Papa whipped out a deck of cards. "How about crazy eights?"

Mummy voiced what they were all thinking. "Have you been carrying that around with you, just waiting for me to ask?"

"Fortune favors the prepared," Papa droned in a spooky, exaggerated oracle's cadence. His wiggling eyebrows and light-blue polo shirt only heightened the absurdity. Even Kartik laughed.

Ridhi obviously didn't have a choice, so she separated herself from the neatly trimmed oregano, which had curled around her finger, and put away the kitchen shears. "Fine, give me the deck. I'll deal."

They'd scarcely arranged themselves around the coffee table, Papa pretending to tell Mummy's future—how she'd soon be bowled over by a tall, dark man in a polo shirt—when her phone rang.

"Hi, Aruna," she said. "Everything all right? You must be glad to have Nilu back with you."

The mirth slid off her face as she listened. Ridhi froze mid shuffle.

"Achha, achha, I see. I'll ask her. I'm so sorry." Mummy hung up and addressed Papa. "Nilesh is missing. They think he ran away last night."

They held one of their silent conversations, and Papa nodded.

"Ridhi, Kartik," he said, "there's something we need to tell you. Aruna Auntie and Dilip Uncle are getting divorced."

Divorced? Ridhi felt like she'd been knocked over. And it wasn't even her parents.

"That's why Nilesh went home," Mummy explained, "to be with his family. But this morning, he wasn't there. Amar doesn't know where he is. No one does."

"Why couldn't he stay here?" Kartik asked. "Then he wouldn't have run away."

"He's not our child, beta."

As much of a pain as Nilesh had been, Ridhi ached for him. What would it be like to have your parents hate each other so much they ended their marriage? She remembered how she'd once thought Nilesh guilty of a charmed life. Not anymore.

She picked her own phone off the floor and texted him. *I heard. Are you okay?*

No reply. But he wouldn't have cell reception in the yaksha kingdom. If she were him, that was where she would've gone.

"Ridhi," Mummy asked, watching her carefully, "you don't happen to know where Nilesh is, do you?"

Ridhi hesitated. She didn't know how to lie to her parents, because she'd never really had to. "No. Why?"

"Do you know where he might be?" Papa pressed. "If you do, you need to tell us."

"I—"

"Kartik," Mummy said, "go find us some snacks." She waited for him to run to the pantry before continuing. "Did he go out while he was here? Tell me the truth."

A blend of anger and guilt surged through Ridhi. Nilesh wasn't her responsibility. "I don't know. To the forest, maybe?"

Mummy and Papa exchanged dubious expressions. "Why didn't you go with him?" Papa challenged. "Did we not instruct you to keep an eye on him?"

"A walk would have been fine," Mummy added, "as long as we knew where he was."

"I'm not his babysitter!" Ridhi had never heard anything more unjust. "I already have one little brother."

Papa crossed his arms. "I don't know what's gotten into you, but enough is enough."

"But I didn't *do* anything!" she objected.

The worst thing was, Nilesh was probably fine and hanging out with Kamini in Alakapuri. If only Ridhi could say that.

Papa's dour visage softened. "I know this seems harsh. But you're too young to know what the world is like, and my job as a parent is to keep you safe. That went for Nilesh while he was here, too."

Behind him, a spider plant dangling from the ceiling let down a runner, then a second. At once, Ridhi smelled all the herbs in their pots, succulent and vital. In her palm, she felt the ghost of the mysterious leaf from Alakapuri.

Well, that was a signal if she had ever seen one. At least the plants were on her side. "I'm going to my room. Like you said, enough is enough. Good night!"

Before anyone could argue, she fled.

All her life, Ridhi had been waiting for a door.

It would be a portal, a door that shimmered, perhaps within the confines of a castle, perhaps apart from any building, under a star-speckled midsummer sky. A door shaped by icicles that shone a soft frost blue. A door fashioned from sunbeams and scattered with efflorescent vines, deep in the heart of the woods.

As soon as she entered her room, light flashed behind the slats of her closet's double doors. A portal in her own bedroom? For all her daydreaming, she'd never considered that.

Seizing the door pulls, Ridhi yanked them apart.

A glitter-dusted, otherworldly marketplace twinkled out at her, lined with stalls and tents in whimsical hues and designs. An enigmatic fragrance greeted her nose, a blend too multifaceted, too fluid, for her ever to re-create. Yet Ridhi recognized it at once—the tang of magic itself.

The Night Market. Sulochana had kept her word.

Ridhi breathed deeply, her rancor at her parents for blaming her and her pique at Nilesh for putting her in that situation extinguished like stale air canceled out by a scent diffuser. She packed six of her most popular perfumes, plus Keeper of the Woodlands, into a naga scale–patterned pouch, retouched her makeup, and braided jasmine through her hair.

Then, pouch tied about her waist and felt-flower bag slung over her shoulder, she set foot in another realm.

The Night Market spun past in a stream of spangles, figures from fairy tales, and treasures both gruesome and gorgeous. Its spell, its surreptitious allure, its starry song all swept over Ridhi in ethereal strains, a charm she had no desire to fend off. She could already visualize her vials being exhibited, one batch of fanciful and impossible wares among many.

Ridhi passed merchants selling bottles of fog and bottles of inspiration. She tried on a pair of beaded chappals that would bear their wearer to other dimensions. She perused the undelivered love letters of apsaras to their mortal consorts and thumbed through a tattered volume of the mouse kingdom's most arcane paradoxes. She waved a net meant to catch the shades of the dead before they embarked on their next incarnation.

Her heart, her spirit, nearly combusted from the sheer magic, the sheer *wonder*, of it all.

But she'd come to vend at Sulochana's stall, not to browse, so she hurried on.

Across the aisle, a narrow gold chain dangled in the air, attached to nothing but darkness. "When tugged," claimed its vendor, a sly-eyed daayan whose ankle-length black braid lassoed the ground in search of new victims, "one may switch the cosmos on and off like a lamp."

Ridhi was staring up at the chain before she realized she'd stepped toward it, her arm held high. The prospect of turning off the universe chilled her, and yet she itched to pull the chain. She had to.

No, she reprimanded herself. *No getting sidetracked, remember? Besides, what happens to* you *if the cosmos goes out?*

Before the daayan could persuade her otherwise, Ridhi hastened past. A cabinet of feathers from birds that had never been cajoled her closer. The colors and patterns thwarted her brain's ability to classify or even properly perceive them. Daunted, she turned her head . . .

And caught the wink of a mirror edged in starlight, promising to reveal the state of her soul. Another offered the ability to see through a cat's perspective—for the right price, of course.

"A good night's sleep eluding you?" called a shadowy, red-eyed figure. "Then recline upon this divan and slumber soundly for a thousand years! Upon waking, all your problems will be as dust."

Shuddering, Ridhi sped to the next stall.

The charcoal flames burning on the pearl candles there both diverted and disturbed her, as did the helmet that counseled its wearer during battle.

"You need only don it," hissed the purveyor, "and its surplus of wisdom will be yours."

"No battles for me, thanks," she said.

For that same reason, she declined the bow and quiver of arrows sharp enough to rob the target of their dearest delusions.

In a brightly striped tent, musicians touted a pair of tabla that linked the player's heartbeat with the thrum of the instrument until death, compelling them to drum without cease, and a flute that either created or destroyed worlds, depending on the song played.

"A concert beyond your wildest imaginings!" crooned the gandharva merchant. Ridhi had to agree.

Farther on, a parrot squawked. Its owner, a girl who might have been Ridhi's doppelgänger but for her sharklike dentition, interpreted the message. "For the measly cost of your oldest dream, my familiar will pronounce your fate. Yet only half of what he speaks is true."

"How do I know which half?" Ridhi asked.

The girl bared her rows of many-cusped teeth, still bloodstained from her last meal. "That, sweetmeat, is up to you."

Somehow Ridhi kept her composure. "Another time, maybe."

So many curiosities, some horrifying, some hypnotic, yet not even the pleasant ones could tempt her as much as the thought of locating Sulochana and her elixirs.

At last, a stall of flowering branches studded with bronze and teal berries came into view, and with it Malav. He wore a sherwani of indigo blossoms and a silver turban that set off his copper irises. "I had not anticipated encountering you again so soon," he remarked with an approving nod.

Ridhi struggled not to stare at his full lips as he spoke. Naturally he'd be there. It *was* his cousin's stall. "Um, hi?"

"Ridhi!" Sulochana's lilting tones were regal, in keeping with her golden-leaf sari. She'd been hidden behind Malav. "Bear neither right nor left, lest you become ensnared."

But Ridhi had already peeked at the neighboring tent.

Blue-white bolts of lightning danced out and molded themselves into a belt around her waist. She didn't dare move, terrified she'd be electrocuted yet transfixed by the bolts' sauciness. Nowhere but in an enchanted Night Market would lightning come to life with the aspiration of being worn.

She could scarcely breathe for awe. *I'm wearing lightning like jewelry!*

"For a bit of spark in your life!" exclaimed the vendor, a makara with the head and torso of a crocodile and the fins and tail of a fish. "In return, I ask only a bit of that life."

"I would not make that bargain," advised a familiar voice. "There are cheaper means of procuring such spark."

Kamini! She had emerged from the makara's tent, the jalebi pop in her hand a perfect accessory to her sari of red-and-yellow blanket flowers.

"Call off the bolts," Sulochana commanded the makara. "While on the premises, she is under my protection."

He resentfully complied, and the bolts milled around him.

Ridhi forced a smile at Kamini. "Where's Nilesh? Shouldn't he be with you?"

Kamini laughed, though she appeared discomfited. "Surely you did not come all this way to ask me that?"

"He's missing." The fight with Ridhi's parents had no place in the Night Market, and she was already regretting having brought it up. "I just want to be sure he's okay."

Kamini looked at her askance. "I was under the impression you did not like him?"

Ridhi really had to learn how to dissemble. "Never mind."

"He is resting as we speak." Amusement played over Kamini's face. "Shall I produce him for you? Would that ease your fretting?"

"No, I—"

"Young woman, do you prefer your meals on the spicy side?" inquired a merchant across the aisle. "Well, *I* can do you one better. I will give you fiery! Heat to rival Lord Surya's heart!"

Though Ridhi instinctively recoiled at the preta's mummified skin and grotesque bloated belly, she welcomed the respite from Kamini's baiting and approached the stall. "Oh?"

The stall needed no lanterns or candles to drive away the dark; crystallized flames sat piled in neat pyramids, their hues ranging from orange to blue, with refulgent flickers of purple and green. They radiated warmth and light, insinuating themselves into Ridhi's bones.

Oh, how she yearned to sample those treats.

The preta cast a sunken but cunning eye over her. "It costs me much to isolate these flames. More still to then roll them in my cumulus sugar."

She nodded. "How much are they?"

The merchant's expression was the purest distillation of greed as it bent its long, skinny neck. "I may ask no less than one rice ball rite per sweet."

Ridhi opened her mouth to haggle, then snapped it shut. This was a preta, asking her to liberate it from its ongoing state as a hungry ghost. The request was nothing to be taken lightly.

"If you do not perform the rites within one month of purchase, my string will claim your hand as payment," exhorted the preta. A bracelet of plain black cord materialized on its skeletal palm. Ridhi didn't doubt that the cord, innocuous though it appeared, could slice her wrist in half. "Extend your arm, and the bargain will be sealed."

She knew she should be aghast. She was, distantly, but she'd gleaned a valuable lesson, too. Rather than foisting goods on unwary bystanders, like the makara, the trick was building on the customer's inherent fascination with them and with the Night Market itself, like the preta. Patrons journeyed here to be wooed. To be enthralled and forget the travails of their lives.

Above all, to buy.

"No deal." Dismissing the preta's blandishments, Ridhi faced Sulochana. "You said I could vend here. I'm ready."

Sulochana waggled her head. "Then let us get you situated."

Within the stall, a pink-and-gold platform bore a curated selection of her elixirs.

"I would estimate there is space enough for the three of us," Malav said, and only then did Ridhi notice the knot of miniature forests beside the elixirs. "What do you think, Cousin?"

"I feel the same." Sulochana waved her into the stall, where Ridhi saw the other thing she had missed: a vacant area on the platform reserved for the seven vials she'd brought to sell.

Her stomach felt as carbonated as a hot spring. It was really happening!

Before she could lose her nerve, Ridhi arranged her vials next to Malav's forests. If only the replacement labels Mummy commissioned had already arrived. But Ridhi had her perfumes, and that was what counted.

As she worked, a pretty woman poked at an elixir, its liquid so pale a blue that it gleamed the silver of moonlight. "Dare I say winter?"

"You are correct!" Sulochana portioned out thumb-sized emerald goblets and distributed them among Ridhi, Malav, and the woman.

Ridhi sipped hers and tasted the coolness of mint, the sharp bite of sunshine on a snow-drenched day. The elixir swaddled her in the sensation of being bundled up and snug among bare branches crusted with rime. How cerulean the sky, how crisp the cold.

In that moment, Sulochana's beauty resembled that of a snow leopard, all coiled power and careful evaluation. "You wish to vend," she murmured to Ridhi. "Then begin with this one."

Ridhi's palms were slick with sweat, but she gifted the woman her most winning smile. "Welcome to our stall. Would you like to try one of my custom fragrances while you sip? They're stories, but with scents instead of speech."

Humming, the woman selected Savitri and Satyavan. "A story, eh?" She extended her wrists. "I would see it for myself."

Ridhi felt the woman's stare on her like a spotlight. Worse, that spotlight was drawing other patrons. How was she meant to perform a magic she didn't have?

Malav, too, watched with as much interest as he had that day behind her house. His gaze, in contrast to the woman's, warmed her. *Prince of the lilacs*, she thought.

She recalled Sulochana's comment about their perfumes and elixirs complementing one another, and how it would benefit them both. This was the test.

Ridhi uncapped the vial and dabbed it on the woman's wrists.

In the fairy tale, Princess Savitri and her husband, Prince Satyavan, strolled through a ripe and verdant forest. She alone knew he was about to die, yet she never breathed a word to him. Weaker and weaker he became, until he halted and laid his head in her lap. She did not sorrow. The life departed his body, and still Savitri did not grieve. For Lord Yama, steward of the dead, was coming to collect her husband's shade, and she had a plan to outwit him.

Ridhi sensed as much as smelled the finer details blooming around her customer: the woman heard the wind in the forest like a scale of musical notes. She felt the series of caresses between Savitri and her beloved, soft and tender. The wildflower honey they had eaten that morning manifested on her tongue, as rich as sunlight.

It was the immersion the trees had mentioned, and it left Ridhi inspired.

She'd been overcomplicating things. *She* was the magic, the secret ingredient. It was in her cherished daydreams—in her connection to the enchanted woods, and without Malav's direction among the lilacs, she never would have figured it out.

When the scene had dissolved, the woman sighed with contentment. "How much for this wonder?"

Ridhi ran through her options. No one paid in cash there. How should she price her fragrances if the local currency took the form of things like broken promises and the color of strangers' hair? Which was more valuable?

The woman glanced at the adjacent stall, which advertised a garland of bells that rang in the future if played from top to bottom and the past if played from bottom to top.

No. Ridhi wasn't going to dither and lose this opportunity. "A wish you regret making."

The woman raised her chin. "A wish I never made."

Ridhi countered with a lower offer, and the woman met her in the middle. And just like that, the transaction was complete—a vial of Savitri and Satyavan for a wish that only partially came true.

The next customer stepped closer. Had Ridhi made a good bargain? She didn't know, but she also didn't have time to worry about it. "Do I ever have the fragrance for you!"

In due course, the line thinned out, and only one of Ridhi's seven perfumes was left. Her cheeks strained with glee. The moment she got home, she'd have a ton of blending to do.

Kamini had wandered off, possibly to find the resting Nilesh, and Sulochana was still occupied with her customers, leaving Malav to observe Ridhi's success.

"You continue to surprise me at every juncture," he said.

"Thanks." She pointed to his miniature forests. "Are you going to tell me what those are?"

Like a set for dolls, each was rendered in perfect detail, down to the most minute petals and pine needles. But they weren't for dolls, nor were they ornaments. Ridhi didn't need to touch them to tell they were true forests, organic and alive. She could feel it.

Malav lifted one, its russet and gold leaves a perfect encapsulation of autumn. "My recent innovation. The forests of Alakapuri are known for their profound fecundity. There are few who would not surrender something of great value in order to obtain access. When placed in the ground, this has the same power to repopulate mortal territories."

Reforestation. Healing. Ridhi could have swooned. This boy spoke her language.

"They're wonderful," she said with utter sincerity. "And I'm all for rewilding. But what about the people who own the land where these trees would go? What happens to their houses? Or their neighborhood?"

"Is it fair that they paved over that land with no concern for the flora and fauna residing there?"

That was a fair question. "No, of course not."

Malav nudged her wrist. "I am pleased we agree on that point."

Ridhi's belly was turning somersaults. Pretending to reorganize the fastidious array of Sulochana's elixirs, she asked, "If you could buy one thing here, what would it be?"

Malav simply fiddled with his miniature forests.

It hurt, but Ridhi should have known better than to think the moment would last. She turned back to the Market with its glowing stalls, luminescent butterflies, and stars so near that she could pluck them like silver apples. Some things were too impossible even for a place like this.

"I would not purchase anything," said Malav, startling her. "Rather, I would present something of my own, a bouquet that will never fade." He touched the purse Mummy had given Ridhi. When he withdrew his hand, the felt flowers had become a living, aromatic garden. "As I said, mortal girl, you continue to surprise me."

A purse of genuine blossoms that would neither bruise nor wilt. Ridhi stumbled over the right words to thank him.

She glanced up to find him studying her. The depth of Malav's regard made her want to hide at the same time she doted on it. He was so good-looking, and he'd been so sure all mortals were terrible. Yet he didn't believe that anymore—because of her.

"I suspect," he said softly, "it might be time for your next lesson."

Sulochana bustled toward them. "You seem to be doing a lively trade. Tell me, what other sorts of barter have you made so far?"

A buoyant Ridhi checked her basket. "So far, a lock of hair, a gold coin that will always return after being spent, a vow never uttered, a skeleton key that opens all toolsheds, a phoenix feather, and a love of popcorn. Caramel popcorn, to be specific."

Sulochana's smile was as bright as the crescent moon in the sky above. "For your first time out, you might have done far worse." She patted Ridhi's head as though she were a young child. "That said, you also might have done far better. Next time, I shall instruct you in the art of striking a proper bargain."

Next time. There was going to be a next time. Ridhi's insides detonated in a burst of confetti.

Her perfumes had been a hit. Malav was softening toward her like the best butter. And Sulochana was inviting her back to sell again. After all that, Ridhi didn't even need to walk on clouds to float.

But for now, she had to go before Mummy and Papa discovered her escape route.

15

Before the pit, Nilesh would have said he never thought every yaksha was great. Most humans weren't, so why would yakshas be?

But the experience with Rakesh had taught him that he'd been way too trusting. He still didn't know who had freed him from the pit, only that it wasn't Kamini, and he couldn't count on getting lucky again.

The pit—or whatever the forest had done to him—must have worn him out, because he'd lain down for a quick nap and it was Friday when he woke up. The day before Holi.

Now, using the palace as his compass, he explored, on the hunt for anyone he knew.

Merchants sold nimbu pani and flowery sweets; shoppers cruised through an outdoor market; friends chatted in the streets; attendants hung garlands and images of Radha and Krishna for Holi.

It was nice at first, but the longer he walked, the more one avenue blended into another—stores, restaurants, open spaces filled with trees. More stores, more restaurants, more open spaces and more trees. And then even more trees. He didn't recognize a single person.

Alakapuri was the capital of the yaksha kingdom, and Nilesh had traveled enough to know that capital cities were oversized, sprawling metropolises. Had he seriously thought he'd just bump into Kamini's nearest and dearest?

At the edge of the palace grounds, right in the middle of the servants starting their day and the guards changing shifts and all the visitors, Nilesh admitted defeat. His head ached, he was ravenous, and his throat was bone-dry.

He needed a new plan.

A group of yakshinis wrinkled their noses at him. They could have been royalty sneering at a peasant who had dared cross their path.

One girl in a sari of pansies made a shooing motion. "You are in our way. Kindly move along."

Her rudeness was a turnoff on its own, but the fact that she was wearing Hetal's favorite flower just made Nilesh dislike her more. "Go around," he said. "It's a big street."

She sniffed in disbelief. "The swamp monster dares to address us?"

Nilesh almost laughed. *Swamp monster?* What was her problem?

A putrid odor assaulted his nose, and he gagged. *He* was. He reeked. It hadn't sunk in while he'd been walking, but it sure did now.

All the flowers in Alakapuri weren't enough to mask the stench. Kamini had healed his injuries, but she couldn't fix his torn, dirty clothes or his hair, stiff with the same mud.

He would have been embarrassed if he hadn't been so tired. His top priority was getting hold of a shower and a big drink.

"So befouled with muck he is!" the pansy yakshini's friend said. "I can scarcely bear it."

Yeah, yeah, yeah. Nilesh didn't have time for this. He raked his eyes over the droves of people—and locked stares with Kamini's cousin's fiancé. What was his name?

Prakash. That was it.

Nilesh had found his new plan.

"Prakash!" he hollered. "Hey, Prakash, over here!"

The snobby yakshinis glowered. But hearing that he knew someone important, they took off.

Prakash himself looked taken aback. No surprise there—they hadn't said more than hello at the revel.

Still, he came right over. "Goodness, boy. What is it?"

Nilesh tried to flash his usual crowd-pleasing smile, but the corners of his mouth were still caked with dried earth. "Know where a guy could get a shower around here?"

Prakash's eyes bugged out, and he slapped a silk handkerchief over his nose and mouth. "You are in dire need of a bath!"

"Yup. And some food and clothes. Think you can help me out?"

If Prakash said no, Nilesh would just chase after him. He was the best lead for finding Kamini.

Prakash must have sensed that. "Fortunately for you, my

215

dwelling is nearby. While you bathe, I will see about securing proper attire."

They trailed some rich-looking people into a ritzy residential neighborhood for a while. Trying hard not to breathe in his own miasma, Nilesh studied the curving lines of the houses, the way they merged into the sky.

When they reached Prakash's front door, it was the same as all the others. The arc of the flowering lychee tree branches. The scalloped arches, done in gold without being ostentatious. Organic plant life and artisan metal.

The two shouldn't have gone together in any world, but they did, united by the canopy of ceiling, whose glassless skylights created the illusion of something greater. The house, while its own thing, belonged to everything around it, kind of like—

The thought finished in Ridhi's voice. *Like a tree in a forest.*

Yeah, like that. Nilesh wanted to draw it.

"Give me a minute," he said. "I'll be right in."

Prakash sighed like he wanted to remind Nilesh how gross he was. "A minute, then." He opened the door and went inside.

Nilesh pulled his sketch pad from his backpack. Luckily, the mud hadn't penetrated the nylon.

He uncapped a pen and got drawing. There had to be a secret to this. He'd crack it, and then maybe he'd understand the yaksha kingdom better. Figure out how to win Kamini over again.

Alakapuri wasn't just her home anymore. It was his, too.

But no matter how many lines he put down, no matter how much cross-hatching and shading, the house bucked his attempts to depict it. Something about the sketch was always off: the curve, the arches, how the house sat between the ones around it.

Nilesh didn't let himself think about what would happen if he *couldn't* figure it out. Because Kamini had to take him back. There wasn't any other option.

The rough patch behind his ear itched. What he wouldn't do for some calamine lotion. . . .

"You appear quite taken with that building, mortal."

Nilesh jumped, and his pen left a scraggly streak across the page. A yakshini about Sulochana's age, but in a threadbare sari and no jewelry, had crept up on him.

"I can tell you who lives there," she said. "What is such knowledge worth to you?"

Something about her was familiar, but what? "I already know who lives there, so nothing."

"You certainly observe the house as if it matters to you."

"I'm drawing," he pointed out. "What's your excuse?"

"The trees speak. Did you know that?"

Nilesh ignored her. Hopefully she'd give up and go away.

"They speak the truths no one wishes to hear. One such truth is that Kamini failed even to attempt to rescue you. She simply forsook you, as did her cousin."

Whoever this woman was, now she'd pissed him off. "Mind your own business."

The front door swung open, and Prakash stormed back out. In contrast to his spotless turban and sherwani, the woman looked even shabbier.

"You," he said, "are banned from this quarter of the city. Or have you forgotten, to be skulking about again? I have told you multiple times already to keep your distance, Ishika!"

"I will 'skulk about,'" Ishika hissed, "as long as you align yourself with Sulochana and her lies. You and the maharani and maharaja, that is."

Prakash's eye twitched. "Queen Kauberi and King Kubera were merciful not to have exiled you!"

"Merciful." She laughed hard enough to make Nilesh nervous. "Prakash, you will never mean a tenth to her of what I did. Even now, she loathes me more than she will ever love you."

Prakash's neighbors, as posh as he was, were piling out of their luxurious homes to witness the commotion. *Just like on Prithvi*, Nilesh thought. Everyone loved a good train wreck.

Prakash, though, kept going. "Take your leave," he demanded, "lest I summon the guards."

Ishika didn't budge. "You are as false as she, so the opportunist with your betrothal. Tell me, is it the whiff of scandal you find so attractive, Prakash? You were once my friend."

"Guards!" he called. "Guards!"

"I acted as an agent of the kingdom and its people," Ishika said. "If you wish to imprison me for that, perhaps some self-reflection is in order."

The neighbors started shouting insults at her. But she only looked at Nilesh. "You have come in on the wrong side of this battle, mortal. You think you know Kamini and her heart. Yet you do not."

Like he cared what some random person had to say. "*You* don't know what you're talking about."

Armored guards marched toward Ishika, swords raised. Even then, she kept her eyes on him.

"Ask her," she said, almost obstinately. "Ask her why she did not save you."

Shape-shifting into a golden deer, she galloped down the street.

Prakash persuaded the guards that he was fine, and they sheathed their swords and went back to their posts. The neighbors, though, took their time disbanding, gossiping like there was no tomorrow.

They were probably all thinking the same thing Nilesh was. Talk about out there. Sulochana had been engaged to that yakshini once?

He couldn't imagine them in love. It was laughable, popular Sulochana together with that bitter woman only looking to stir up trouble.

Being an outcast for four centuries had really messed her up. She'd done it to herself, but still.

"Pay her no mind," Prakash said, escorting Nilesh into the house. "She would see everyone wounded as she is wounded and speaks whatever fabrications necessary to accomplish that goal. Let us focus on readying you for society once more."

The place was a mansion, built from plants and gold. Even the furniture looked like someone had fused it out of sunlight. Nilesh could analyze it for hours.

But Prakash didn't stop until they reached a spiral staircase.

"Tread softly," he whispered, "for my parents and brother have not yet arisen from their nap."

On the third floor, they turned through an archway, where a servant holding a bundle of clothes and a dish of scented oil waited by a golden door. He bowed, then opened the door onto an enclosed meadow. A small stream with no source Nilesh could make out ran through a grassy riverbank, and thick pockets of trees formed the walls.

"*This* is the bathroom?" he exclaimed.

"It is. Dharmendra?" Prakash signaled to the servant.

Dharmendra left the bundle and scented oil by the water and exited again.

Prakash smiled his thanks. "We will leave you to it, then," he said to Nilesh.

After they left, Nilesh stripped off his ruined jeans and hoodie and chucked them into a corner. Maybe Dharmendra would burn them.

Then, sure it would be liquid ice, Nilesh gingerly poked a toe into the water. But it was actually warm, like a hot spring. The grass was a pretty green, and the ceiling was blue sky that never ended.

Using the scented oil like soap, Nilesh scrubbed away the layers of mud, sweat, and dried blood. The pit, the fights with his family, and Kamini bounding into the night peeled off with the filth, followed by the encounter with the rude yakshinis and the even stranger one with Ishika.

The clear water hauled them all away, transforming him from swamp monster back to human.

Well, that beat any sauna he'd ever been in.

It was awesome to float like this, free of anyone's expectations, with the water splashing over him again and again. It soothed the scratchy patch behind his ear. Even his headache went away. He caught himself dozing, he was that mellow.

A nagging thought cropped up. He let it.

The truth was, Nilesh kind of owed all this to Ridhi. If he hadn't been at the Indian grocery store that day, he never would have met Kamini. And without Ridhi's dogged belief in magic prepping him, who knew if he would have accepted it without freaking out?

Honestly, he'd been giving Ridhi a hard time for way too long. He'd have to make it up to her.

Rolling his head back, he snoozed some more.

When Nilesh eventually got out, dripping, his hair plastered to his head, he made a beeline for the bundle Dharmendra had given him. It contained a comb, a gold-rimmed hand mirror, a sherwani-churidar set, and a pair of juttis with little mirrors on the curling toes. But, weirdly enough, no towel.

Seconds later, he knew why. The yellow sunlight slanting in from above had completely dried him, even his waterlogged fingers. His skin was as toasty as if he'd been sitting in front of a fire. *Very cool.*

He got dressed and slipped his feet into the juttis. Running the comb through his mud-free hair, he winked at himself in the hand mirror.

If those snobby girls from before could see him now, they'd be singing a different tune.

Nilesh emptied out his backpack and gave it a good dunk in the stream. The nylon came out clean, and every drop of moisture vaporized on contact with the sunny air. More thorough than any washing machine, and faster than any dryer.

He reloaded his good-as-new backpack. Magic could be pretty useful, with those kinds of tricks.

The hollow in his chest howled for food. He opened the door to signal that he was done.

Poking his head in, Prakash surveyed Nilesh. "That will do. Now come. I have an appointment, yet I would converse with you beforehand."

Nilesh nodded. "Sure, but food first."

"That has been attended to."

Prakash brought him to a sitting room, then sat down on a green leaf-velvet couch. "Eat," he said, "and tell me how it is that you came to be standing like a lost lamb in the heart of my city."

The table before the couch had been set with onion and potato pakora and two gold goblets of illuminated mango juice. It all looked and smelled so good that Nilesh demolished three of the fried dumplings in one go. The spicy chickpea batter was still warm, and he washed the rest down with huge gulps of the juice.

With his blood sugar back to normal, he could think. If Prakash didn't already know about the chaturanga game, that meant Sulochana hadn't told him.

Good. Nilesh needed his compassion, not his contempt.

222

"Kamini and I had a fight, and I didn't know what else to do."

"A fine stroke of luck that I was in close proximity, then," Prakash said dryly. "That girl is as changeable as the tides. She will relent, I am certain."

Gods, Nilesh hoped so. His chest went hollow again, and not because he was still hungry. "Yeah."

"Did Ishika harm you?" Prakash sounded concerned. Maybe he thought being nice to Sulochana's cousin's friend would earn him brownie points. Maybe he just wanted to spite Ishika.

Whatever the reason, Nilesh would take it. "No, but man, does she ever have it in for *you*."

Prakash tapped his goblet. "I do not think she has forgiven me for winning Sulochana's heart," he said after a minute. "Yet she has had four centuries in which to accept her own complicity in her loss."

"You two are engaged, right?" Nilesh didn't really care, but he did want to learn more about Kamini's family and Alakapuri in general. After all, he lived there now.

"Betrothed, yes. Originally my parents had thought to make a match with a courtier of our standing, yet once I laid eyes upon Sulochana, I knew there was no other for me. Did you know . . ."

Prakash launched into a list of Sulochana's qualities in painstaking detail. It was like a love poem on steroids—not exactly the research Nilesh had in mind. He almost fell asleep again.

In fact, he was half dozing off when Prakash cut the lecture short. "We must be going. We are already late."

Thank the gods. Nilesh raised his head. "So what's this appointment of yours, anyway?"

"An elixir tasting," Prakash said. "And now you may repay me in kind for my aid. We have a cart full of beverages to dispense to our guests."

"I never signed up for that—"

"And who can say which errant maidens might be in attendance?"

Nilesh wiped his hands on his napkin. "Well, what are you waiting for? The people are thirsty!"

16

Sunshine streamed down Ridhi's closed eyelids, richer and more buttery in Alakapuri. It cascaded over her arms, her bare midriff, and her ankles, nourishing them. The springy turf tugged at her toes, drawing them into the fecund earth below. She basked in the warmth of the air, in the touch of the soil, at peace like the plant she'd always believed herself to be.

Leaves sighed and susurrated about her, and she could almost discern them. . . .

A honeyed voice, one not made of branch and breeze, infiltrated her reverie. "Ridhi?"

Ridhi opened her eyes to find Sulochana regarding her with amusement. Set against the panoramic landscape, the forest in all its glory rising up behind her, she looked as lovely and inhuman as the nature spirit she was.

Oh, right. Ridhi dragged herself back to the present, and with it, the fact that she still couldn't divine the leaves without help.

She'd been waiting at a respectful distance for Sulochana to emerge from her get-together with the maharani and her retinue. They met weekly at the palace for chai pani, as Ridhi had learned, Queen Kauberi speaking of the trials and tribulations of running a kingdom, and Sulochana supplying the maharani with advice and samples of her most recent elixirs. When she had described the feast the royal chefs laid out for what was ostensibly a modest snack, Ridhi's mouth had watered in envy. The affair sounded unbelievably decadent, something within a story.

Awe and fear bubbled in her belly as the maharani's attendants took her measure, their saris of multicolored wildflowers fluttering in the sunlight, their long tresses waving in the fragrant wind. They must be Sulochana's political friends, some of the courtiers she'd mentioned. Ridhi could only hope they liked what they saw.

Sulochana laughed. "I have been calling your name for some time. Am I so dreary to listen to, then?" She made no effort to moderate the volume of her words, as if unconcerned who might overhear.

But that was the reason for this public meeting. Judging by Sulochana's satisfied tone, the probing glances from passersby were exactly what she'd anticipated. It reminded Ridhi of a saying from Prithvi: *no publicity is bad publicity.*

"Never!" she exclaimed. "It's so lovely here, I lost myself for a minute. That's all."

"That is certainly understandable, mortal daughter of the forest," noted one of the maharani's attendants. "Sulochana told us you are a nemophilist."

Ridhi would have to research the definition later. In the moment, she tried for a noncommittal smile.

"Indeed! My companions have been keen to meet you," Sulochana said, loud enough to carry, "knowing as they do that you will be joining me on Holi. They are beside themselves with anticipation for our grand offering." Mischief danced over her mouth. "I have promised them quite the spectacle."

Ridhi hadn't yet fully accepted that she would be invoking the Kalpavriksha, or that she had little more than a day to get a handle on phyllomancy if she wanted to pull that off. The notion of the maharani trying her perfumes felt remote enough to be a joke, an entitled daydream. "A spectacle it will be," she agreed.

"She is charming, this one," said the first attendant. "The maharani will be very pleased."

"I could not be more curious as to what the pair of you have concocted!" said another. "A hint, perhaps?"

"Oh, um, we couldn't. We don't want to ruin the surprise!" Ridhi's neck heated with both shyness and gratification. If the courtiers liked her, surely Queen Kauberi would, too.

But a divot appeared on Sulochana's brow. Had Ridhi said the wrong thing?

No, Sulochana was gazing past her, at Prakash and Nilesh jogging up to them.

"Please excuse us," Sulochana told the ladies-in-waiting. "It was a pleasant occasion as always, and I send my compliments to Queen Kauberi."

They made their farewells and paraded off, petals and silk swishing along the grassy path.

"Nilesh!" Sulochana looked him over. "Is all in order with you?"

The sight of Nilesh in his dapper outfit brought up the argument with Mummy and Papa, which Ridhi had been working so hard not to think about.

Guilt panged in her chest. She'd missed breakfast that morning, feigning sleep when Mummy checked on her. Fighting with her parents hurt. It left a hole she had yet to repair.

But with Holi around the corner, Ridhi didn't have time to be scolded for something she hadn't done, much less risking being ordered to stay home altogether.

Standing there, among such refined company, only underscored what was at stake.

"I'm fine," Nilesh said. In his leafy sherwani and juttis, he might have been a noble yaksha, but his cocky half smile was a shade dimmer than usual.

Odd that he wasn't with Kamini. Ridhi couldn't help but suspect they'd had a fight.

Prakash took Sulochana's hand. "That is actually what we have come to speak with you about, meri jaan."

"What is it?" she asked. "What harries you so?"

"I was stepping out the door to meet you," he said, "when whom did I come across but Ishika, haranguing this boy? It was not until I summoned the guards that she disengaged."

A range of emotions from frustration to dejection to ire played out in Sulochana's expression. The ashoka branches above stirred as if to comfort her. "She is bent on ruining this for us. Because she is miserable, so must I be."

The two of them moved a few feet away, to a bench of engraved gold beneath a tree weighed down with aquamarine lychees, and began to talk in animated murmurs.

Now that she was alone with Nilesh, Ridhi's anger at him came flooding back. Not even the serenity of the forest could mollify her. "I almost got grounded because of you taking off without telling anybody! Thanks a lot."

His laugh sounded strangled. "Oh. Parents, huh?"

"Yeah, parents." Ridhi poked him in the shoulder, a little rougher than strictly necessary. "Your mom's ready to call the cops. Luckily, my mom convinced her to hold off and see if you would come home on your own."

She waited for him to retaliate, to make her responsible somehow.

Instead, he shook his head. "Listen, I'm sorry. They have no right to blame you for what I did."

He'd apologized, and sincerely, no less? Ridhi was so non-plussed that she forgot the rest of her tirade. "Thanks?" She found herself picking at her wearable-garden bag.

Nilesh noticed. "Night Market special?"

"Not exactly." Her lips stretched into a giddy grin. "Malav did that. But I sold my perfumes there last night!"

He looked downright smug. "I told you that place was cool."

So proud of himself. It usually would have ticked Ridhi off. Yet she'd already begun to confide in him, and he *was* being nicer. "*So* cool. I'm going to take even more perfumes with me next time."

She waxed rhapsodic about her customers and her bargains, then braced for Nilesh's usual biting reaction. He only nodded. "Not bad."

For some reason, Ridhi believed he meant it. Maybe everything with his family had made him reevaluate his life. Stranger things happened every day. "Where is Kamini, anyway?"

"According to Prakash, off crushing tons of dried flowers into powder." Nilesh shrugged. "But she's going to be at this 'gathering,' so I guess I'll see her there."

Ridhi was delighted by the idea of Kamini creating the colors that would be flung in the air and at other players on Holi. But the fact that Nilesh had gotten that information secondhand? Definitely a fight.

Well, it couldn't be that bad. She was sure they'd make up before long.

Sulochana glided over, apparently done with her own private chat. "Come along, both of you. As Nilesh is already aware, I am hosting a small gathering to debut my elixirs before the impending festivities. It would be terribly gauche of me not to be home to welcome my guests."

Ridhi detested having to decline. She was so rarely invited to parties. "I would, but I have to meet Malav."

"Yes, another lesson, if I recall correctly?" Sulochana smiled impishly. "How fortuitous! Malav is on the guest list."

Ridhi let her curls fall forward in a curtain, blocking her from view, and pretended not to hear Nilesh cracking up.

By unspoken agreement, Ridhi and Nilesh made their way to the creek near Sulochana's bungalow. Nilesh should have been inside already, helping Prakash unload a cart of elixirs, and Ridhi should have been seeking out Malav for their next lesson, but after the past hour, she needed a moment to breathe.

A plethora of mushrooms peeped out from beneath ferns, between leaves, at the base of tree trunks—one of the very best things about being in a forest.

Ridhi lifted the hem of her skirt to form a bowl and began foraging. Wrinkled peach, with its pinkish grooved cap, was the first to go in. Then indigo milk cap, with its dark-blue gills. The showy, lacy white skirt of the veiled lady. Golden chanterelles, shaped like meaty funnels. The cone-headed blue pinkgill. Parrot waxcap, as glossy and green as its namesake. Velvet-topped violet webcap. Even devil's tooth, its fruiting body leaking drops of red like blood.

At last she arranged the mushrooms in a circle on the ground, an offering.

Pleased with her design, she joined Nilesh where he sat, his legs dangling in the warm, clear water. On its surface, the sun broke into countless shards like a relucent mosaic. A flight of dragonflies zipped about, the metallic purples, carmines, and teals of their wings as rich as airborne gemstones. Fir, cedar, and almond trees grazed the sky, their pulse of life a parallel for the leisurely beat of Ridhi's heart, of her breath.

She flapped her hand through the diamond-clear creek. The resulting ripples, which looked like blown glass, dwindled almost as soon as they'd come into being, as evanescent as the notes of a perfume. "So you're working with Prakash?"

"Yeah." Nilesh kicked out, splashing her knee. "I get to be his serving boy, if by *get* you mean I don't really have a choice."

Ridhi splashed him back extra hard. "Fun times."

"I bet you'd like the other end of it. The elixirs, I mean. You like making perfumes and stuff."

He'd been paying attention? Remembering the sample vial she'd discovered on the guest dresser, she blurted, "Like the one you took from my room?"

The air between them thickened with anticipation.

Ridhi hadn't intended to say that, but there it was, out in the open. She held her breath, her body on high alert.

Nilesh didn't answer immediately. "Your mom told me what went down at those stores. They were stupid. You're really talented."

Oh.

Ridhi kept her eyes on the water so he wouldn't see how pleased she was. Nilesh wasn't exactly known for his compliments—not when it came to her, anyway. "I did just finish a new blend. If you want to try it, I could, I don't know, make that happen."

That elicited a surprised laugh. "I might take you up on that. You think there're any fish in there?" He was playing with what might have been an opal, rotating it on his thigh. "Like that story about the fisherman who saved the golden fish and it made him rich?"

As kids, they'd read that story in a book of fairy tales, and Nilesh had argued that, had the fisherman's wife not gotten greedy, the couple could have had everything. Was he thinking about that day, too?

"Could be," she said. "But I wouldn't try to catch one. Chances are good they're just yakshas who went for a swim."

Nilesh snorted. "Yeah, the last thing I need is another curse."

A pale green-and-violet lily coasted past, and Ridhi snared it. He probably assumed she knew about the divorce, but she would let him bring it up.

"Hey," he protested, "how do you know some mermaid didn't need that?"

The lily's satiny petals dripped sunlit beads of water on the grass. Ridhi shook them loose and tucked the flower behind her ear. "I doubt you'll see any mermaids around here. Nagas, on the other hand . . ."

"Ridhi!" Sulochana called. "Malav is here. And Nilesh, Prakash requests you bring the cart around to the rear door for unloading."

"Be right there." Nilesh turned a diabolical smirk on Ridhi. "So, Malav and you, huh? Making you purses, giving you lessons?"

It cost all her willpower not to react. "You should go. They're waiting."

Nilesh didn't move. "For a while there . . ."

"Yeah?"

He hesitated. "I wasn't sure what the point of any of this was, you know?"

Was *he* confiding in *her* now? "What do you mean?" she asked cautiously.

He angled his chin toward the palace far in the distance, which Ridhi still couldn't bring herself to take in directly, and the trees in the vicinity. "When I got dumped off at your house—"

"Dumped off? You're *lucky* you ended up there!"

"When I got dumped off at your house," Nilesh repeated, as if she hadn't spoken, "it felt like—" He gnawed on his thumbnail. "Like someone had taken a giant hammer to my life. Everything too broken to ever be fixed, and then, like some sadistic bonus punishment, I had to come stay with *you*?"

Ridhi fumed. "It's not like that made my day, either!"

"I thought there was nothing left. But you showed me what else was out there, and it got me thinking." Nilesh rummaged around in his backpack and retrieved a sketchbook. He tore out a page and thrust it at her. "To make up for taking the other one."

He'd drawn Sulochana's stall at the Night Market, with Ridhi's perfumes prominently—and beautifully—displayed.

Will wonders never cease? Something old and irate thawed inside her. "This is really good. You could design houses for real."

Nilesh scratched behind his ear. "Not exactly a big call for architects around here, unfortunately."

Ridhi wasn't sure why that mattered, so she concentrated on the art. He might not do portraits, but he really had a knack for buildings. "What about when you go home?"

"No one told you?" He shrugged. "I'm stuck here. Forever."

She would have assumed he was joking, if not for the strain in his voice. "What do you mean?"

"Turns out it's not that smart to play old-school chess with people who think thorn tiaras are trendy. I lost, they threw me in a pit, and even though they let me out, I can't go home." One side of Nilesh's mouth curved in a lopsided grin. "Guess we both belong here now."

"What?" Ridhi felt blindsided. *Poor, poor Nilesh. And Auntie and Uncle! And Hetal!*

The urge to hug him overwhelmed her, and she barely managed to resist. "*That's* your curse," she whispered.

"It's all good." Nilesh rose and slung his backpack over one shoulder. "Anyway, I better go help Prakash. See you inside."

He headed toward the bungalow.

Ridhi stared after him, then back at the sketch, her mind and heart reeling.

17

Even though Sulochana had told him to go on into her bungalow, Nilesh loitered under an amla tree out back, in the company of Prakash's gold-and-emerald cart. He should've been bringing in the elixirs, but Kamini was probably inside.

It was one thing to think about seeing her again. It was another to actually face her. What if she didn't want to talk to him?

He studied the little house's mix of gold and branches, then let out a low whistle. Lots of curlicues and flourishes on the door and the roof. Leaf-shaped emerald borders on the windows. Runners with fat tangerines corkscrewing around the walls, making the air smell like citrus. Kamini had said Prakash was some kind of medium-rank lord, so his mansion made sense, but apparently even the minor nobility lived it up in the yaksha kingdom.

Alakapuri was so perfect and clean, Nilesh kept comparing it to a theme park. None of the amla tree's round yellow-green fruits lay decomposing on the ground. The whole city was like that, orderly.

Conserved. He'd seen fallen leaves and petals, but no fruit. Not a rotting lime or apple anywhere.

Nothing aged there. Flowers didn't wilt, and plants didn't die. Fruit was never over- or underripe. Yakshas lived long enough to qualify as immortal, and their seasons matched them, never changing. Even the snow and ice on the peaks of the Himalayas didn't melt. They'd always be commercial beautiful, all pure and glittery.

In the human world, a few decades meant the difference between a baby and an old man. One season ran into the next. Hurricanes and wildfires and plagues decimated entire countries. Past the boundary, the yaksha kingdom didn't have natural disasters. No aging, no destruction, no illness.

Nilesh needed to nail down that timelessness. Wrap his head around it. So he got out his pen and sketch pad and drew. He sketched Prakash's mansion, then Sulochana's bungalow, and finally the palace. He even sketched Kamini in the arcade.

The drawings of the buildings were better than his attempts outside Prakash's house. Still not accurate, but closer. The rendering of Kamini, not so much. Her proportions were almost comically wrong, more like a caricature.

He was proud of it, anyway. Maybe he'd gift it to her, once they'd fixed things between them.

But what if that didn't happen?

Only one way to find out. Nilesh packed up his drawing supplies and wheeled the cart behind the bungalow.

All frayed nerves, he strode inside.

The interior was less fancy than Prakash's mansion, but it was a lot nicer than comparable human houses. Opulent furniture, gold and plants everywhere, moss for carpet, torans over the windows, and flowering vines hanging from the ceiling.

An assembly line of different-colored thick syrups, bottles, and corks lined the far wall. That must be where Sulochana bottled her elixirs.

In the middle of the room, a long buffet had been stocked with sabzis, rice, flatbreads, fruits, creamy dishes, and sweets. A ton of people milled around it, laughing and gossiping and serving themselves from the banana leaves and coconut shells.

Some "small gathering."

A handful of faces jumped out at Nilesh, Kamini's friends from the party. But where was she?

Prakash's voice accosted him. "Where have you been? We must bring in the elixirs!"

Nilesh had half-heartedly started toward Prakash when two words halted him where he stood. "Mortal boy."

Kamini had barely breathed them, but his ears had been primed for her. Prakash and the elixirs shrank into the background.

Nilesh turned, and there she was. Pretty in peach, like a flower on a tree.

"I am glad you came," Kamini said. She almost sounded shy. "I was hoping you would."

He reined in the compulsion to fling himself at her. "I thought you wanted me to leave?"

She sighed. "I have pondered what you said, and you are correct in that it is not my place to deny your autonomy. If you choose to be here—"

"To be with you," Nilesh clarified. "As long as *you* want that."

"Then"—she removed a pink rose from her hair and twirled it—"who am I to forbid you?"

The tension leached out of him. He'd been ready for another argument, another futile round of trying to get through to her, and instead, he'd won the lottery.

"What are you ogling, mortal boy?" she teased. "Do you not know parties are meant for rejoicing?"

Nilesh opened his arms, and Kamini glided into them. Her cheek pressed against his chest. It felt like holding autumn.

He'd never been happier. She'd taken him back.

"Come," she said finally. "My friends await us!"

Nilesh let her lead him around the room. They paused every few feet to talk to her friends. He felt so light with relief that her touch might have been the only thing keeping him tethered to the floor.

They passed Ridhi and Malav, who were chatting with Sulochana and another yakshini from the revel. Nilesh was glad Ridhi seemed like she'd gotten over his big revelation.

Just as he nodded at them, a bird soared in through the open window. It was purply black, with shiny feathers, and it alighted on Sulochana's shoulder.

Ridhi's eyes went wide, like she'd been smacked in the face. "A jungle crow!"

"Oh, yes," said Sulochana. "The local wildlife has quite the talent for surfacing when there are morsels to be had." She massaged the crow's feathers, and it butted its head against her hand. "Is that not so, Cousin?"

"Which one of us could you mean?" Kamini asked sweetly. "My brother or me?"

Malav grimaced at her, and Nilesh squeezed her hand. Family would be family. He didn't let himself think past that.

At the revel, people had been talking about a jungle crow that helped get Ridhi into the yaksha kingdom. What were the chances this was the same bird?

Zero. That would be one hell of a coincidence.

Ridhi must have come to the same conclusion. She pointed to Malav's pista barfi. "Are you going to eat that?"

"I had not yet decided," he said.

She plucked the barfi out of his grip. "Not deciding is a decision."

Wow. Nilesh had never seen her so confident before. "Hungry much?"

She dangled the barfi in front of Malav, totally flirting, before popping it into her mouth. "It's mind-blowing. That's what you get for being so slow."

"Indeed. I suppose I will have to obtain more." Malav traipsed toward the buffet, and Sulochana excused herself to check on her other guests.

Kamini laughed. "Do keep my brother in line," she told Ridhi.

240

"That would behoove him highly."

Nilesh put his arm around Kamini's waist, and she leaned into his side. "Seems like you're having a good time."

"Yes!" Ridhi said. "Oh! Have you met Hamshi? She's one of Sulochana's best friends."

Hamshi bowed her head. "I believe I glimpsed you at the revel. I do not, however, recall you dancing. Shall we remedy that?"

"There's music?" Nilesh hadn't seen any instruments.

"Oh, we do not need music." Hamshi lifted her arms and shimmied her hips, simulating a tree.

Ridhi copied her without missing a beat. She could have been a shalabhanjika, the way she danced. It was so self-assured, a word Nilesh never would have associated with her. Even at mandir events, she'd held back.

Kamini joined in, spinning toward Nilesh, then away from him. That was how things were supposed to be. The two of them happy and having fun.

For his part, Malav abstained with a drink, but even he smiled.

When the improvised dance ended, Ridhi put her hands together in front of her face. Hamshi hugged her before joining their friends at the buffet, and Malav took his place at Ridhi's side.

Kamini touched Ridhi's shoulder. "That was a lovely showing. You truly have a gift."

"Yeah," said Nilesh. "That was awesome!"

"Thanks!" Ridhi got giggly. "You never knew I could do that, did you?"

"Nope."

"Well, I can." She gestured to her yakshini friends. "Want to come sit with us?"

"I don't think there's room," Nilesh said. He smiled. "But thanks."

"Sure thing. See you later." Ridhi grabbed Malav's hand and practically skipped over to the buffet.

"How like one of us she is," Kamini remarked. "You mortals perplex me."

Nilesh made his voice exaggeratedly low. "And charm you, too, I hope?"

Before she could answer, Sulochana rang a small golden bell. "Shall we begin the tasting?"

Cawing, the crow flew off her shoulder. It landed at the edge of the buffet table, but no one acknowledged it. They were all too busy deciding which elixir flavor they wanted to try.

It must not have liked that, cawing again and shooting out the window as fast as it had come in.

With a start, Nilesh realized he'd never helped Prakash with the elixirs. "I should go bring in the cart."

"On the contrary," Kamini said slyly. "The jungle crow has the right of it. I could do with some fresh air. As could you—through the front door."

A chance to be alone with her? It wasn't even a question.

"Sorry, Prakash," Nilesh said, already swerving toward the front door.

Nilesh and Kamini hiked past the bungalows, just talking and talking. Though Kamini asked about his family, she didn't push him to make peace with them or to find a way to go home. She didn't give him *any* advice.

Nilesh couldn't get over how refreshing that was.

"But," he said, "you never told me about *your* family."

"Hmm." Kamini tensed. "You know my mother became a tree when Malav and I were but children. We make occasional pilgrimages to her grove. It is quite picturesque." She adjusted her nose pin and gazed at the bungalows in the distance. "Not long after, our father took a new wife, a shalabhanjika. She is kind enough, if inconstant in her affections, and her ambition rivals Sulochana's."

Nilesh's stomach clenched. He shouldn't have asked.

"Hey, look!" Taking her hand, he pointed to a theater that ranged over three treetops. Onstage, a troupe reenacted the love story of Radha and Krishna. Of all the gopis who adored the cowherd Krishna, Radha was his favorite.

Kamini sighed. "A morose tale for such a jolly occasion, do you not agree?"

"Huh? How so?"

"They fall in the truest and most profound of loves, yet he abandons it to become king and wed Princess Rukmini. Poor Radha is left behind, bereft, forever pining for the one she will never see again."

"I never thought of it like that." Nilesh hoped Kamini wasn't pulling away from him. "Is something wrong?"

"Ah, but I am being silly," she said. "Pay me no mind."

She dropped his hand and ran to a river birch tree covered in mushrooms. Nilesh remembered learning about them in school. Turkey tails, with their orange and white stripes.

A line of little kids used the turkey tails like a ladder, chasing after squirrels and birds and then diving into a bed of flowers. A chaperone oversaw the line, and when two boys started fighting over who got to go next, she quickly separated them.

"We have a similar thing on Prithvi," Nilesh said, "except you go down a slide." He'd done that with Hetal, sliding to the bottom and landing in the grass. Dad had been content to catch them as many times as they shrieked for while Mom took pictures.

A painful knot unwound in Nilesh's chest. When would he quit thinking about Dad?

"Come on," he said, his voice rough.

Kamini must have sensed the shift in his own mood, but she was smart enough not to comment.

They drifted away from the kids and down a path tunneling through the trees. Ground cover grew up on either side, and in the yellow-green light that filtered through, everything felt calmer. More remote.

Neither of them spoke until Kamini bent to pick some splashy red-violet flowers. Her voice was stilted. "Go on. I will find you."

Nilesh wasn't wild about that—she was definitely upset about something—but he didn't argue. "Pick one for me," he said.

He walked ahead slowly so she could catch up. But she didn't.

Why did she need those flowers so badly, anyway? There were flowers all over.

The grassy path curved in front of him, and he stopped short of the bend. For a second, he thought about turning back for Kamini, but that would probably make things worse. So he kept going.

Ishika stood on the far side of the curve, smiling like he was the person she'd been waiting for. "Have you asked her why she did not free you?"

That again? Nilesh sneered. "Do you always stalk people?"

"Only those with good hearts," Ishika said. "That you have one is apparent. You did not immediately write me off as so many have."

"We're talking about you, not me."

"Permit me to tell you a story." Ishika closed her eyes. "Once there were two lovers, both young, one a noble of high standing in the court of Alakapuri, the other a ladyling of minor import. The two women had pledged their hearts to each other, their love a flame so ferocious, a force so potent, that those around them revered and envied it by turns."

Where was Kamini?

"Don't tell me," Nilesh said, deadpan. "The story's about you."

Ishika opened her eyes, and he saw annoyance there. "If you do not wish to hear this, I will not tell you."

"I don't, actually."

"Ah, but it is imperative that you do." Ishika resumed her story.

"Those lovers' bond, once so passionate, burned out as swiftly, as irrevocably, as a fireball in the night. Dazzling, and then darkness. I was so lovesick that I desired not to share her with a soul."

She paused. "Have you heard of the Kalpavriksha?"

Against his better judgment, Nilesh nodded.

"Then you know it resides in Svargalok. Every ten years, on Holi, Lord Indra condescended to open a portal to his realm for two minutes. In that time, a yaksha or yakshini honored by the maharaja and maharani would select a leaf and wish for the continued fortitude of the yaksha kingdom."

Ishika's smile warped into a snarl. "I saw a means to eliminate that dependence once and for all, and I acted. How could I know it would fail? Yet, fearful of the aftermath, Sulochana proved herself a coward and shunned me. Because of that, they call me a menace. I am the one they hold in disdain.

"But I am also the fool; I loved her and believed she loved me. What she loved was what I represented—an opportunity to ascend in the court. She is a grifter who has ingratiated herself with the maharaja and maharani. Prakash will learn the truth forthwith."

Nilesh ran a hand through his hair. "That's quite a speech. Why did you tell me all that?"

"You long for roots," she stated. "You recognize the strife that others, with their selfish desires, bring."

"Huh? You're harassing me because you think I want roots?"

"I know it to be so. You have been seeking a place where you cannot be shaken. Where the wind might bend but never break you. Where the rain, even at its most malevolent, can sever a branch yet leave the trunk intact."

Clutching a bouquet of flowers, Kamini charged around the bend in the path. "Leave him be!"

Ishika looked amused. "As you will, Kamini—for now. As for you, Nilesh, do not discount what I said." She sashayed off into a thicket of pine trees.

Nilesh raised his eyebrows. What was *that* all about?

Kamini pinched his arm. "Do not even entertain it!"

He flinched. "Ow! What was that for?"

"To make you think thrice before you do something so foolish as to heed a word from her poisoned lips."

Nilesh rubbed the sore spot. "Thanks, but I hadn't planned to. No more pinching, okay?"

Waiting for her to answer, he had the feeling he was being watched. For all that Ishika claimed to be okay with being ostracized, maybe she wasn't.

"Stay away from that one," Kamini advised. "She brings misfortune with her."

"Don't worry," he said. "Whatever she's selling, I'm not interested."

"I am glad to hear that." Though Kamini waggled her head, she looked rattled. "After the chaturanga game . . ."

Nilesh felt like an ass. He'd really scared her in the pit, more than she'd let on. He couldn't stand to see her upset, so he brought out the drawing he'd done of her. "For you."

She accepted the gift with a kiss on his cheek. But instead of taking in the sketch, she rolled it up. "Whatever shall I cash it in for?"

Her playful tone was too flimsy to be convincing. Nilesh glanced at the thicket. No sign of Ishika. "I'm not going to listen to her," he said. "I promise. But if you don't like the sketch, I can hang on to it—"

"Alas, it is mine now." Kamini preened, seeming genuinely pleased this time. She held the drawing out of his reach. "All mine!"

Her free hand found his, and together, they walked on.

18

A waterfall arced down the rocky cliff, its lacy white ribbons scattering rainbows along its descent into the creek. On either side, autumn foliage blazed in all its splendor, vivid red oranges, the yellows of ground mustard and cooling butterscotch, scarlet and burgundy, sprinkled against a clump of evergreens.

More than ever, Ridhi understood why Sulochana was so determined to reinforce the yaksha kingdom's defenses. No trash dirtied the streets of Alakapuri. No concrete roads choked the earth; no barbed-wire fences defiled the terrain. Animals moved around at will, with no fear of being pursued or pushed out of their natural habitats. Like her once-felted purse, the realm was a garden, a haven.

But where was Malav? He'd told her to wait for him there at the edge of the mossy peninsula while he went over some last-minute arrangements with Sulochana at her bungalow. They'd promised it wouldn't take long.

It had better not, she thought. Kartik's game was that evening, and she had yet to bake for it.

Shh, shh, shh, said the leaves above, perhaps whispering to Ridhi, perhaps to one another, but without Malav's presence, their message remained nebulous. No, she wasn't a plant, as much as she wished otherwise, let alone a yakshini. Not yet, anyway.

She thumbed her pendant. How, by Aranyani Devi, was she going to manage the Kalpavriksha if she couldn't even hear the more common trees?

"And what do we have here?"

The baritone question startled Ridhi from her musing, and she yelped. A yaksha maybe five years older than Malav had appeared next to her.

"Hi," she said. "I didn't see you there."

"My apologies." His mouth quirked. Nearby, a cherry tree fruited, its crop lush and tempting. "It is so rare that I have the opportunity to speak with a mortal. Particularly the mortal who, it is said, captured the lordling Malav's interest."

Something about him struck Ridhi as off. "Have we met?"

"Your reputation precedes you." The yaksha's long fingers toyed with a cluster of the plump mahogany cherries. "What in all the worlds, I find myself pondering, could be so titillating about *you* to have turned his head?"

What a hateful thing to say. Ridhi struggled to maintain a neutral expression. "Why don't you ask him?"

"And if I prefer to ask you?" The yaksha snapped off the cluster and sank his pointed teeth into a fleshy cherry. "Such an opportunity might never present itself again."

She waved him off. "I'm not that interesting, I promise."

He closed the gap between them. "I highly doubt that. Malav is not known for his—how shall I put it?—love of your kind. You must be quite a specimen."

"You flatter me." Ridhi's ire was rapidly mutating into unease. "But we actually have a lesson, so I shouldn't keep you any longer."

"Ah, yes. I am certain he will turn up eventually." The yaksha scanned her from head to toe like he might a sculpture for purchase. "It would be coarse of me not to keep you company until then."

"Really, you don't need to. I'm fine." She would have backed up, but the water was behind her.

The yaksha ate another cherry, then drew his juice-smeared thumb down her cheek in a mockery of tenderness.

Her muscles tautened. What was he doing?

Too fast to register, his fingers burrowed into the soft hollow under her chin. "Is something amiss?" he asked, all innocence.

Ridhi strained in vain against his unyielding frame. The yaksha swiped the side of his face over hers, and she felt him leer. "Tell me, paltry mortal girl, when you pine at night for Malav, is this how you envision his clinch? Do you wish to reprise *Meghaduta*, feebly fancying that someone such as he would ever desire someone such as you?"

The reference to the poem couldn't be an accident. Had he been spying on them?

Revulsion pooled in her throat. "What do you want?"

"Not everyone is so servile as to entertain the whims of mortals," growled the yaksha. "You would do well to learn that sooner rather than later."

Around them, the woodland had changed. The difference was

subtle, almost imperceptible; the colors still shimmered in a gardener's palette of ground emerald and peridot. But a pernicious gloom had fallen over the trees like a mantle on a hook.

Bullies, even here in Alakapuri. Even among the yakshas and yakshinis.

The yaksha's handsome features contorted. "Surely you recognize that the forest is more than sunshine and sweet flowers, would-be princess? That it also harbors poison ivy and predators?"

They were mere inches from the creek. He was going to knock her in, Ridhi was certain of it. She attempted once more to wrench loose, but his hold was impossibly strong, locking her in place.

Her heart juddered against her ribs until she was sure she'd vomit.

"You contaminate our lands and sicken our people, and yet you have the temerity to fraternize with us?" The tips of his fangs sparkled. "It nauseates me to see you here."

Ridhi had known that yakshas came in two main classes: the mischievous but generally benign nature spirits, and the malicious, bloodthirsty type similar to rakshasas. But for that second kind to be there, so near Alakapuri?

"Let me go," she begged.

The yaksha seized her shoulders. His jagged nails cut grooves in her skin, and she smothered a cry.

"I was curious what Malav might see in a mortal. I regret to say the appeal remains opaque." He snorted. "You are common, mortal girl. As drab as a starling among peacocks. An affront to our realm and our kind."

Ridhi's throat closed, but she didn't have the chance to do more than blink before the yaksha had pinned her arms behind her back. "You do not belong here. Heed me well and quit this place."

"Get away from her, Rakesh. Now." The command was cool. Authoritative.

The strange yaksha shoved Ridhi to the ground, and she crab-crawled to safety. "Did you believe this ludicrous dalliance would pass unremarked, Malav?"

He'd planned for Malav to witness that, Ridhi realized. It was a message.

Malav glared at him. "This mortal is not for you to concern yourself with."

They argued for another minute before Rakesh stormed off.

Ridhi's breath came in harsh bursts, and she distantly noted that she was shaking.

Strong arms encircled her. "Are you injured?" Malav asked, his body firm and solid against hers.

"My knee's a little scraped," she said, expecting him to let go.

But Malav stroked her hair, disturbing the flower crown and sending tingles over her skin like golden grains of pollen.

"Rakesh will never trouble you again," he pledged. "On that, you have my word. But I would know what he said to you."

"He threatened me. And then you showed up."

Malav brought his forehead to hers. A kaleidoscope of images swirled behind her eyelids, of her feeding him floral sweets, of him tipping spring elixir into her mouth. Of him grazing her bottom lip with his thumb, of her licking off the shoot-green droplets, and the two of them kissing, first hesitant, then wild and hungry and torrid.

All of which she wanted to steer out of the fantasy and into the realm of the real.

Ridhi pulled back to find an odd intensity had supplanted Malav's solicitude. Her belly thrilled, and her palms prickled.

"Do you feel threatened now?" he asked, his eyes heavy-lidded and searing.

Again, Ridhi felt like she couldn't flee. This time, she welcomed it. "No."

"I am glad," Malav said. "For it is not intimidation I wish to inspire in you."

Good. It was one word, but it stalled somewhere between her thoughts and her throat. Ridhi brought her fingertips to his cheek in answer. His skin was hot, as flushed as hers. His burnished irises glinted like fresh-minted coins, holding her captive.

Branches intertwined overhead, their canopy cloaking Ridhi and Malav from potential onlookers. Petals drizzled down, pale pink and peach and plum, as if invisible hands had shaken the branches. It was idyllic, a scene from an anime.

Yet folktales had taught her far too well how everything had a dark and ugly side, the rot beneath the varnished surface.

Rakesh filled her vision. His fangs. His sneer. That primal brutality. Her calves bunched, prepared to run. How far might it have gone?

No. Ridhi banished the memory. *You're fine. Malav saved you.*

"I'm human," she made herself say. "I thought you despised that."

Malav traced his lips over her knuckles, and Ridhi shivered. "Perhaps I was too hasty in my judgment," he admitted, so soft it might have been the whisper of a spider crawling across its web. "Did I not say that you have surprised me at every turn?"

Her heart glowed as bright as daffodils. He *had* said that.

More than that, he'd rescued her.

The breeze switched direction, carrying his scent of sandalwood and pine resin to her nose, and her knees almost buckled. He was a yaksha noble, the essence of the woods, and he wanted her. Who cared what Rakesh or anyone like him thought?

Ridhi tilted her head until the briefest of spaces separated her from Malav. Need thudded in her chest, her temples, her trembling fingers. She skimmed his lips with hers, an invitation.

The world beyond them stilled, as if awaiting his response.

For a moment, Malav didn't move. Then, like a tiger pouncing on its prey, he was kissing Ridhi, consuming her.

His mouth was so warm and wet. She kissed him back, guardedly, then eagerly. If this was being devoured, he could have every bit of her.

Flowers shot up around her ankles, infusing the air. Malav gently, so gently lowered her onto the bed of blossoms. Through a haze, Ridhi cataloged roses, sunflowers, poppies, jasmine, orchids, morning glories, daisies—each propping her up in a profusion of color and scent. And Malav, drinking her in as if she were the fairest bloom of all.

My fairy-tale prince.

Ridhi inhaled as deeply as she could, inflating her lungs with the intoxicating bouquet, with *him*. She had just recalled that each of those flowers was classified as an aphrodisiac before Malav's mouth was on hers again. Her hands tousled his hair, cupped his jaw.

The universe had shrunk to three things: how good it felt to kiss him, how his breath quickened at her touch, and how that and the hoarse sounds coming from him made her long to kiss him even more.

So she did.

When Malav finally released her and stood, Ridhi had no clue how much time had passed. Her lips felt bruised, and she could already tell her hair was a hopeless mess, sticking up and tangled with leaves and petals. But she didn't care.

Kissing was its own kind of spell.

Her flower crown had tumbled to the grass, and she retrieved it, replenishing it with unwilted blossoms. "Thank you," she whispered to the plants, then braced for the creased foreheads, the ridicule. But the one person listening—the yaksha she'd just kissed—didn't laugh.

She got up and turned to him.

Unlike her, Malav was immaculately put together, clothes unwrinkled, hair kempt and bare of stray twigs. Only a slight frown marred his refined profile.

Ridhi's stomach tightened. Did he regret what they'd done?

This part never happened in wonder tales. *Tell me you're not sorry we just did that.*

The ponderous silence stretched between them. Ridhi shifted

from foot to foot, admiring how the grass, the bhumi amla ferns, the plantain, the vetiver, and the wild strawberries all sprang back no matter how much she trod on them. She plucked a blade of the vetiver. "I use this in some of my perfumes."

"I must confess, I do not know much about perfumery." Utter business once more, Malav beckoned to her. "We should, however, begin our lesson."

Ridhi's spirit grew as dense as wet earth. He was right, but it would have been nice if he'd needed another kiss or two to recover.

She drew herself up. "I'm ready."

"Then look around." Malav gestured to the waterfall, to the rocks, to the trees and the blue-peaked mountains. "What do they evoke in you?"

Ridhi breathed in the scenery. "Everything good and alive."

His austere expression brightened. "Kamini and I have frequented this place since we were small."

Ridhi pictured him at Kartik's age and bit down to keep from smiling.

Kartik. The cookies. But it wasn't a complicated recipe, and a hurried calculation told her she still had time.

Malav opened his fist to reveal a miniature forest. It possessed the same delicate detail as the others, but one aspect set it apart. The leaves were teal and violet and rose, and the fruit gold and silver and copper. Enchantment hung over it like an aura. A forest from a daydream.

"I cultivated this specifically for you," he said, placing it in her hand. "For what we have to accomplish this day."

The quiet thrum of life in its roots resounded through Ridhi's palm. She'd been worrying for nothing. He liked her. He must, to have made her a present. "It's perfect."

Malav smiled. "Visualize what we might achieve if we were able to repopulate the forests in your world and undo the damage your kind has caused. What we might yet do together."

She petted the forest, then gave it back. "I want things to be better, too. You know that."

"Good." He stashed it in his satchel. "Then let us convert that desire into deed. In this lesson, I shall teach you how."

"But what about phyllomancy? I still can't do it. I—"

Ridhi broke off, ashamed to say that she might not be good enough. That Sulochana had chosen badly.

"You are perfectly capable of performing phyllomancy. It is your fear hindering you, nothing more. I would not introduce you to my friends if I did not believe that."

His friends? She glanced sideways at Malav. "What do you mean?"

He gazed into her eyes, so near that she thought she might be engulfed in molten pennies. "Hear me well, Ridhi. I have been seeking a partner for some time now. You know of Sulochana's scheme to recall the Kalpavriksha to our world."

Ridhi nodded, her pulse as aflutter as a hummingbird's wings.

"It is a fine plan, one I endorse. For too long, Alakapuri has been vulnerable to the blowback of mortal expansion."

Adrenaline still coursed through her veins, and she felt like she could run for a thousand miles or swim across Lake Lanier or dance until the moon rose. She dared to lean against him, and his arm curled around her waist. The heat he radiated set her aflame.

"Yet it fails to take full advantage of the options available to us." Malav kneaded the space where her shoulder met her neck, and she shuddered. "A single leaf, taken from the Kalpavriksha. A single wish, and we could reclaim not only my world but yours as well, on a far greater scale."

Ridhi had been so worried she would disappoint Sulochana that she'd never dared dream that she, too, could have a wish. That, as Malav hinted, she could wish better.

The prospect left her breathless. No more litter. No more woods cut down for strip malls. No more concrete jungles. Just the forest, alive and unbound.

"Think on it," Malav said, his lips at her ear.

He bent to kiss her again, sending more of that golden pollen up her spine, then escorted her to a tulip poplar bespeckled with yellow-and-orange flowers. Its leaves rustled a salutation.

Malav pressed his palm against the trunk. Ridhi did the same.

"Today," he said, "you will meet others like me, and after our lesson, you will see the possibilities I speak of. Together, we will restore the natural realm. I believe you termed that *rewilding*?"

"Yes!" Beaming, Ridhi accompanied him into the tree. It was all happening so fast, a whirlwind of a day. But she didn't mind. Whatever he had in store for her, she knew it would be an adventure.

And if that adventure involved more kissing, well, she wouldn't complain.

When Ridhi and Malav disembarked outside an abandoned warehouse in Atlanta, two yakshinis and a yaksha received them with toothy grins.

"Compatriots, this is Ridhi, the mortal girl I spoke of," said Malav. "Ridhi, may it please you to make the acquaintance of Phoolan, Saanvi, and Harsith."

"How *lovely* to meet you," Saanvi said, low and challenging. "A mortal girl!"

"Such a treat," Phoolan agreed, while Harsith joined his palms in greeting.

Maybe it was Saanvi's prickly attitude or Phoolan's choker of bloodred currants and black belladonna berries, but the welcome left Ridhi inwardly squirming. For now, at least, Rakesh had spoiled her for meeting new people.

"But what of our strategy? She cannot shift her shape," Saanvi noted.

"No," Malav said smoothly, with an admonishing glance, "she cannot. Yet the forest has chosen her, and so shall we."

"Are you certain?" Saanvi placed her long-nailed hands on her hips.

Ridhi knew what these yakshas saw when they looked at her, a human who cared far less for the world than she did for her material comforts, whatever those comforts cost.

If, like Saanvi and Phoolan, she already had a mekhala, they would view her very differently.

260

"I am. She is a champion of the natural realm, someone familiar with mortals and their customs. Precisely what we have been lacking." Malav reached into his bulging satchel and divvied up the miniature forests, reserving one for himself. "As I said, we will break off into two groups and cover the deserted buildings in this area."

"I would be on *her* team," Harsith said, oozing innuendo.

That comment galvanized Ridhi into action. She *did* know what she was doing. She *had* been chosen by the forest. Hadn't Sulochana entrusted her with a monumental task?

This was her lesson, and no obnoxious yaksha, not Rakesh and not this jerk, would stand in her way.

"There's nothing I love more than trees," she said, "and if I can help them, then I will." She smiled. "But I'm staying with Malav."

That did the trick; Harsith and Phoolan, sheltered by the shadows, transformed into a squirrel and a raccoon, respectively, then skittered into the warehouse.

Good riddance, Ridhi thought. She looked at Malav. "What about security cameras?"

"What about them?" he asked. "We cannot be captured by your technology unless we choose it. As for you, our presence grants you camouflage."

Saanvi, still in yakshini form, darted down the street. "Well, come along, mortal," she called. "We are here to frolic!"

The three of them were in a run-down section of the city Ridhi had never been to, rife with trash and boarded-up windows, but the yakshas, the trees lining the street, and the scattered bluish-purple chicory flowers lent the gritty area an otherworldly ambience. She was going tree planting with a fairy-tale prince who wanted her for his partner as he endeavored to protect the natural realm. It didn't get more magical than that.

They hadn't gone far when a dilapidated storefront came into sight. Brown beer-bottle shards littered the entrance like remnants of a broken tiara.

"This," Saanvi said, baring her sharp teeth, "is how it is done." She squatted at the base of the store, uncaring of the slivered glass, and drove her hand into the ground. Then she set her miniature forest into the hole she'd created and leaped back.

The forest instantly began growing up and out, first enveloping and then burying the building. It continued spreading until it had overrun the lot and then some.

Where seconds prior there had been wreckage and eyesores, rampant life now thrived, a thicket where animals would nest, where trees would provide shelter and shade and the solace of green. Flowers and fruit, creepers and twiglets poked out everywhere.

It was the most rewarding thing Ridhi had ever seen.

Thanks to Malav, five spots around her city would be returned to the wilderness. So his friends were a bit odd. So what? Getting to heal the devastation her people had wreaked more than offset any peculiarities.

She should get home. But judging by the sun, it was only late afternoon, and she still had to rehabilitate her own scrap of urban wasteland.

"My turn," Ridhi said. "And *I'll* show *you* how it's done."

Malav waggled his head in approval. "I am pleased to hear that, for your building awaits you down the street. Shall we?"

Her miniature forest clasped to her chest, Ridhi was already running as fast as she could.

As Malav had promised, the derelict building—ironically a gardening center—was only a block from where they'd been. Ridhi tallied up the numerous broken windows, the graffiti tags, and the strips of peeling yellow paint. This business had been prosperous once.

She might not be able to resurrect the past, but she could do something better.

Recalling Saanvi's posture, Ridhi crouched and began to dig. Though hard, the soil parted beneath her diligent fingers. She inserted her miniature forest in the ground, then stood back, her nerves sparking.

Vines and branches and runners swathed the decrepit garden center like a yakshini's sari. Blossoms burst forth, even more abundant and colorful than Saanvi's attempt, trailed by a flood of animals and insects. Ridhi spotted a cottontail rabbit among the vibrant green.

No, she thought. She'd been wrong. *That* was the most rewarding thing she'd ever seen.

Engrossed in wonder as she was, it took Ridhi a few moments to register that Malav and Saanvi had come up on either side of her. "You performed superbly," Malav said, his handsome face aglow with admiration. "And now you see the valor of what we shall achieve together."

Even Saanvi gave a reluctant nod. "It seems Malav was correct, and you may be of more use than I had initially believed."

Ridhi couldn't stop grinning. She felt amazing, so full of power and pride and purpose. So like the yakshini she was meant to be. She could ride this high for the rest of her life. And with Malav and his miniature forest, she would.

"I am next," Malav said, with a soft stroke of her cheek. "Surely you will accompany me?"

"Yes," she replied, breathless. "Of course I will." A few more minutes couldn't hurt. Just long enough to watch him. Then she'd go.

The house was as dark as Malav's hair when the wise old oak tree deposited Ridhi in her front yard.

How was that possible?

But she knew how. She knew exactly how.

Ridhi let herself into the shadowy house and flipped on the lights, hoping against all evidence that she wasn't too late. "Hello? Mummy? Papa? Kartik?"

The only answer was silence. The plants, however, hummed in a chorus.

No, she pleaded. *No, no, no.*

In the kitchen, the stove clock blared *8:14* in an accusatory blue. Worse, adhered to the refrigerator with strawberry washi tape was a note addressed to her.

Ridhi tremulously unfolded it.

I tried to call and *text you. I'm assuming you must be lying in a ditch somewhere, because I know you'd never miss your brother's big game otherwise. Text me when you get this.*

Love, Mummy.

The paper crinkled in Ridhi's sweaty palm. The regionals. She was missing it, and it was her own fault.

Guilt smacked the wind out of her, and she dropped down onto the purple couch in the family room. How many times had she cuddled with Kartik there, at least back when he'd still put up with her cuddling?

She imagined his excitement souring to hurt when he worked out that his big sister wasn't coming, and it made her sick.

If she'd left after activating her miniature forest, she'd have arrived home with time to spare. Yet she'd stayed, unable to bear the thought of missing the other restorations. Unable to bear the thought that Malav might decide he didn't need her, after all.

Ridhi had to be the worst sister in the cosmos, past, present, and future.

It wasn't that she'd blown off the cookies she'd promised to bake, though that was bad enough. She'd blown off her brother. She should have been cheering Kartik on from the stands, not running around the city with cute boys and their friends.

It was far too late to feed the team, of course, but after Ridhi had texted Mummy to apologize and wish Kartik luck, she assembled the ingredients for a smaller batch of the oatmeal chocolate-chip cookies he'd requested. She could do that much for him.

His inconsolable little face—she couldn't stop seeing it as she stirred in the chocolate chips. For their part, Mummy and Papa must be so upset.

Yet as she spooned out dough over the baking sheet, questions broke through her guilt like a lotus through muddy water, recalcitrant and irrepressible. Why did she always have to be responsible, the good daughter? The reliable, self-sacrificing daughter?

Why wasn't she allowed to mess up once in a while, too?

I want to be free, Ridhi thought. *Just let me be free.*

She didn't really know what she meant by that. Mummy and Papa never pushed her to tone herself down. If anything, they empowered her to be who she was. They loved her.

Yet that wasn't sufficient. Ridhi yearned for the forest. To be with the yakshas and the yakshinis.

To be one of them.

And come Holi, she would be.

19

Grunting, Nilesh unloaded another pallet of Sulochana's elixirs from the cart into the little kiosk. It was Holi, Prakash's big day.

Prakash's neatly trimmed mustache bristled. "Mind you do not spill so much as a drop. If that is too arduous a parameter for you, I can manage it alone."

Nilesh mouthed the words along with him. Prakash had repeated them at least four times already. "Like I said, it's not. We're almost done, anyway."

Kamini, who'd met up with them after visiting her mother's tree earlier that morning, smirked. She was, in Nilesh's opinion, enjoying this way more than she should be. He made a face at her.

The official celebrations weren't scheduled to start for another hour, but that hadn't deterred the crowds wearing white and raring to play colors. They congregated around the jeweled lampposts, under green banners with the devices of noble families and, of course, lots of leaves, chatting and exchanging bouquets.

Kids chased a golden ball past the kiosk. The girls' saris, tied around their legs, didn't slow them down, which Nilesh thought was pretty cool. Families crouched on the ground, telling fortunes in twig patterns and playing shell games with acorn caps and berries.

Down the lane, archers tested the tautness of bowstrings before aiming their arrows at copper apples set in tree branches or clay targets shaped like dogs with open mouths.

"Wasn't there some story about that?" Nilesh struggled to remember. "In the *Mahabharata*? Yeah. Prince Eklavya got so good at archery that he could shoot five arrows into a dog's mouth to make it stop barking without hurting it."

"Seven," Prakash corrected.

"What?"

"Seven arrows, not five. And that is nothing to one of *our* markspeople. Watch."

Sure enough, an archer nocked an arrow and shot it straight into the statue's mouth. Then she followed it up with nine more. Another archer speared three apples with a single arrow. No one seemed especially impressed by either feat, not even the archers themselves.

"We are of the land," Prakash said. "Naturally, we train, yet it is the land that guides our hand, instructing us how and when to loose the arrow."

"What about hunting?" On Prithvi, Nilesh knew, there were rules for where to stand and whistled commands to keep everyone safe, and even then, people got hurt. He didn't see any markings or signs anywhere.

"We do not hunt for sport," Kamini said. "There are the monstrous among us, with a taste for mortal flesh, but they are not at liberty to hunt in Alakapuri, so they find other ways to satisfy their craving."

Nilesh was about to ask another question when she added meaningfully, "You have already encountered them."

Not wanting to think about his time in the pit, Nilesh took a closer look at the bows. They were masterworks, carved from sheesham wood and inset with golden leaves. He liked the archers' uniforms, too, leaf-scale kurtas and salwar kameez. "I did an archery unit at school. It wasn't anywhere near as cool as this."

Maybe Kamini and he could give that a go. Or the old woman painting flowery designs on her customers' cheeks with a paste of juice and clay.

Shh–shh–shh.

The trees' rustling got him thinking of Ridhi. He hoped she was up to something fun.

"Sulochana has been through far more than anyone should ever have to endure." Prakash arranged cups made from scooped-out roses and sighed. "I can only pray that her attempt to atone for the past will allow her some peace. Four centuries is far too long to bear such regret."

Damn, was the guy ever smitten. Now that he had a willing audience, all he could talk about was Sulochana. To hear him tell it, she was the smartest, prettiest, most interesting woman to have ever lived, and no one was as fortunate as he was.

It was a lot. Nilesh couldn't really complain, though, not after Prakash had put him up the night before even after getting ditched at the tasting.

Besides, he understood. The business was Prakash's baby, not to mention Sulochana's, and Holi was their big debut. "I hope she gets the piece of the forest," Nilesh said, meaning it.

Prakash and Sulochana were the perfect example of a couple ready to settle down for the long haul. But thinking about that reminded Nilesh of something Ishika had said. That he needed to put down roots?

Hadn't he already done that, getting stuck there? What was left, apart from avoiding Rakesh and his crew?

Nilesh doubted the yakshas wanted his thoughts on their houses, so that was out. Gardening wasn't his thing, and he definitely didn't have any magic.

Running his own little business, maybe? Prakash seemed pretty content.

That didn't fit, either. Nilesh still felt like he was watching from the outside. He'd compared Alakapuri to a theme park, but it was more like visiting a Renaissance Faire and pretending to be a knight. He could play a game or two, talk in fake medieval lingo, but he wasn't part of the show. Not yet.

Though the kiosk wasn't technically open for business until the parade got going, Kamini nicked a sunset elixir. Organic, and it smelled great. Like her.

Who cared what Ishika said? As long as he had Kamini, Nilesh would make it work.

Prakash emptied the last pallet of bottles. "Four hands do make a swifter end to labor than two. I am much obliged for your assistance."

"No problem," Nilesh said. He leaned against the kiosk counter, watching the shell game in progress.

One player, a young girl, kept guessing the correct acorn cap and winning the berry underneath. That riled the man operating the game so much, he hopped up—just in time for the golden ball to come flying at him.

Nilesh dashed out of the kiosk and snared the ball before it could hit the man. "Watch where you kick that thing," he told the boy and the girl running after it.

They hung their heads, and the boy blinked like he might cry.

"Hey, hey, it's all right." Nilesh swiped a bottle of autumn elixir from the display. Whatever Prakash said about holding off, a treat couldn't hurt. "Want some? If you don't let anyone see, I'll give it to you."

Both kids nodded vigorously.

Nilesh poured them each a cup. He grinned at Kamini, but her smile was sad. He would bet she was missing her mom, so he gave her a quick hug.

The girl gulped down her elixir. "You are tolerable for a mortal."

"Thanks. I think." Nilesh tossed her the ball, and she kicked it into the street.

The boy finished his elixir and tore after her. "Wait for me!"

Prakash's mouth crimped. "You know that we were not to serve anyone until the parade begins."

"But how can you deny those little faces?" Nilesh snarked.

"With a modicum of effort," Prakash replied, so earnest that it hurt. "It poses no difficulty. Should I be concerned for your well-being, if you are asking such questions?"

Nilesh shook his head. "Forget it." Prakash might be a nice guy, but no one could accuse him of possessing a sense of humor. "Let's get some food, Kamini. I'm starved."

Kamini linked arms with him. Her nearness felt like drinking one of the elixirs. He couldn't imagine ever getting tired of it.

"A growing boy must nourish himself," she said, "and I have just the thing."

"Go ahead," Prakash said archly. "I would never dare stand against Lady Kamini and her desires."

Huh. Maybe he understood being irreverent, after all.

The golden ball zoomed toward them again, but it was too far for Nilesh to catch. He tracked it through the plaza and fished it out of a fountain.

Shh-shh-shh.

Bizarre. This time, it almost sounded like . . . someone whispering?

"Did you hear that?" he asked Kamini, who'd kept pace with him. She carried a gold-trimmed parasol in a bunch of colorful patterns.

"Hear what?"

Shaking his head, Nilesh kicked the ball across the plaza. "Nothing. What do you want to eat?"

Kamini grabbed his hand. "You shall see."

"Oh, yeah? Sounds ominous."

"What if I told you that I procured you a gift, and you may have it after we dine?"

"A gift?" Nilesh squeezed her hand, loving how it felt in his. "Now that's my kind of thing."

Leaving the plaza behind, they roamed the forest. Kamini showed him into a dip in a hill whose overhang would hide them from anyone who came by. Sunlight spilled into the grotto, green and pinky red and orange where it filtered through the trees. It reminded Nilesh of a stained glass window he'd seen in Italy.

"Up there," Kamini said, setting down her parasol. A vine with turquoise grapes dangled above them like mistletoe.

She broke off a bunch and hid it behind her back. "Mortals fear that consuming fruit of other realms would imprison one forever, both physically and spiritually. Are you certain you would risk it?"

Nilesh feigned snatching at the grapes. "I think we missed the boat on that a few days ago. But I'm pretty sure I can't get any more stuck here than I already am."

He'd been poking fun at himself, not Kamini, but her mouth turned down. She let her hand fall without another word.

No. They were not doing this. Nilesh took the cluster from her and tore the fat globes from their stems. He'd had plenty of amazing fruit since the revel, with smells and tastes like nothing he'd ever had before, so he wasn't expecting much.

These grapes, however, had his senses wobbling. Each one popped in his mouth, coming to a juicy crescendo that was both sweet and like eating shadows, the gray kind that came after dawn. Even the seeds cracking between his teeth were a delicacy.

Kamini watched him knowingly. "Delectable, are they not? They are my secret stock, shared only with you."

"Every time I think the food here can't get better, it does." Nilesh fed her a grape, and her eyes closed in ecstasy.

Together, they polished off the bunch.

Kamini threw the stems to an interested oriole outside the cave. "Tell me, my Nilesh," she said softly, "are you fulfilled here, in my city, in my forest?"

He brought his face to hers, and their noses bumped. "I am. I really am. This is all I want—to be with you."

Her lips curved in a vulpine smile. She couldn't have been more like a fox, so sure of itself. "How very darling you are, my silly mortal boy. Yet what if I were to tell you that things are not so simple as you conceive of them to be?"

He shrugged. "I'd say it doesn't matter."

Kamini gave the scaly patch behind his ear a skeptical glance. "I would claim otherwise."

Nilesh's good mood tanked. She was doing it again, withdrawing with no explanation. "I don't get it. Do you not like me?"

It would kill him if she said yes, but better that than her running hot and cold.

Kamini pressed herself against him. "It is not you."

"Then what is it?" Tightening his arms around her, he waited.

"Nilesh . . ."

Normally he liked when she used his name. This time, there was too much pain in it. "Whatever it is, it can't be that bad. Just tell me."

She pressed little kisses down his jawline, obviously trying to distract him.

He shivered but stood firm. "Kamini. Tell me. Please."

"It is difficult . . ." Kamini raised her head. Her coppery eyes were wet. "It is difficult for me to see my mother so. More difficult still to know that I am responsible." She blinked away the tears, but more came. "One would think I would have grown accustomed to it by now."

Even crying, she was magic.

"Sometimes things suck," Nilesh said, "and that's just how it is. It's not like you meant it."

"Would that intention could excuse the result." The turmoil in her words cut deep. "We could rescript history."

He thought of Hetal and her apologies. "Maybe not excuse, but it has to count for something. We all mess up, don't we?"

She smiled through her tears. "That is generous of you."

"I try, I try."

Kamini kissed him, and Nilesh tasted the enchanted grapes she'd eaten. She was so warm in his arms, and he couldn't get enough of her scent. They kissed again and again, until she seemed to have forgotten her sadness.

"You do intrigue me," she confessed. A group of trees outside the grotto turned the orange and red of autumn.

"Even though you told me I was stupid for not listening to you?" he teased.

"Even then." Kamini nibbled on his bottom lip, making him groan. She really *was* like her cousin's elixirs. Wild. Capricious.

Every dare he'd ever taken rolled into one.

She pulled back. "As delicious as this is, it would be discourteous to keep my surprise from you any longer."

"I don't mind."

Kamini tugged on his arm. "Ah, but it cannot wait."

Nilesh didn't want to let her go. He definitely didn't want to stop kissing her. But they had the rest of their lives for that.

So, hand in hand, they left the grotto in the hillside. The branches sloped close to Kamini, like they were greeting her.

Nilesh loved that. He loved pretty much everything that had to do with her. She was why he'd returned.

Shoulders touching, they entered a tunnel of trees.

A large group of yakshas and yakshinis had gathered in the meadow. Everyone wore white. Even though he knew they'd be splotched with color soon, Nilesh felt like he was at a funeral, rather than celebrating the holiday Holi was.

Then he saw why.

The yakshas and yakshinis were marveling at a wheelchair. His sister's wheelchair. Vines and flowers and berries had grown over it, and someone had given her a flower crown. Others posed for Amar, who was taking pictures with his phone.

What was Hetal doing there? And Amar?

Nilesh turned to Kamini, who smiled. Her smile was off, though. Brittle, like she was the opposite of cheery.

"Meet your surprise—my new friends," she murmured. "I believe they are old friends of yours."

Hetal rolled her wheelchair closer, Amar at her side.

"Dude," he said, "I can see why you ran off." Then he punched Nilesh in the arm, hard. "Not that it's okay. Your mom's going nuts!"

"That is patently untrue," Kamini reproached him. "I sent a draught to assuage her fears." She turned to Nilesh. "Both your father and she presume you will return any moment now."

"Okay, well," Amar amended, "she *was* going nuts."

"Not us, though." Hetal held out her arms. "Nothing could ever make me forget you."

In spite of his conflicting feelings, Nilesh bent down for the hug. How could he have made her cry? His own words from a few minutes before came back to him. *We all mess up, don't we?*

When Hetal finally sat back, he saw they had an audience. The yakshas and yakshinis all watched them with avid interest.

"This place is wild!" Amar said. "And you really thought you could keep it from us?"

"Hold that thought." Nilesh took Kamini by the arm and led her away from the prying eyes. "What's going on? Why did you bring them here?"

"If you cannot go home, perhaps you will at least cleave to them." Her voice was reserved, almost off-putting. "And since they are here, surely the three of you should make merry as the family you are?"

Something else was going on, Nilesh realized, a different kind of chaturanga game, and he was the only one who didn't know the rules. "But they couldn't have gotten here if you didn't let them in."

He'd assumed Kamini would defend herself or deflect outright.

She didn't do either. "They are your home," she said. "Not me. Not Alakapuri. You need to fathom what you are giving up."

"I already gave everything up!"

Her laugh was harsh, a vixen's bark to go with her earlier smile in the grotto. "Hardly that." She gestured to her friends and his. "Did you think this would last? Oh, Nilesh, what you have yet to renounce is more than you can dream of."

"Quit speaking in riddles." Nilesh scratched the rough patch behind his ear. He wasn't going anywhere even if he wanted to. "Leave them alone. Send them back."

She looked almost angry. "So sharp of wit, yet you see only that which you wish to. You did so that day in the grocery store, you did so that day in the palace courtyard, and you do so still." She pointed to Hetal and Amar. "Hold fast to them, and stay out of sight."

"This isn't you," he insisted. "Someone's forcing you to do this."

Kamini tapped her temple. "Ponder, Nilesh. Who would do that?"

He couldn't shake the hunch that this had been a game. "Ishika said I couldn't trust you. Was she right? Don't tell me she was right."

"I told you to keep away, mortal boy." Kamini sighed. "Why did you return?"

The blow knocked the breath out of him. Ishika *had* been right. "You keep saying you told me to stay away, but you're the one who invited me here in the first place."

"Perhaps you should ask the one who bought your debt." Kamini flounced off.

"Why? Why won't *you* tell me?"

But she was already carousing with the other yakshas and yak-shinis. With his sister and his best friend, who she'd brought to Alakapuri.

Nilesh turned and slipped through the gap between the trees.

20

Ridhi had always known she was a daughter of the forest, a devotee of Aranyani, a yakshini in training—if not in practice. Blending plant-based oils into perfumes, making flower-flavored desserts, learning the art of receiving messages through leaves, and dancing barefoot amid the grass and moss—what more could she need?

Yet now, when Mummy wouldn't meet her eyes, Ridhi felt like she'd lost everything.

It hurt enough to have Kartik rebuff her, to have Papa look at her like he didn't recognize his own daughter. Both those things ached down to the marrow of Ridhi's bones. But for Mummy to be cold to her on Holi, their holiday, well, nothing was worse.

Just in case, she'd already showered, and her plain white salwar kameez had been ironed and lay on the bed. She'd left her bedroom door open, also just in case.

Sitting cross-legged before her altar, Ridhi ran her hand over the African violet and rang the small golden bell in honor of the goddess of all forests. The potted plant put forth another blossom, a palatial purple, which she plucked and set on the altar in offering.

"Get dressed," Mummy said from the doorway.

Chilly as those two syllables were, hope glistered in Ridhi's chest. For Mummy to come deliver them meant she still wanted to perform their private ritual.

Ridhi leaped to her feet. "I'll be right down."

Ridhi found Mummy in the backyard, which had outdone itself for the occasion. Everywhere she turned, she met with a plenitude of blossoms from palest lily of the valley to deepest black iris, each sharply delineated against the blue sky.

At the mandir, the focus would be on Radha and Krishna and their immortal, larger-than-life love, but there at home, Ridhi and Mummy chanted quiet mantras to Aranyani Devi. Both wore paayal on their ankles and jasmine in their hair. They danced to the melody in their hearts, and when they finished, Mummy left a paper saucer with scraps from a lilac doughnut by the base of the peach tree. Some wild creature would soon be very happy.

Yet the friction between them persisted.

Please, Ridhi prayed, to the goddess, to the trees, to anything at all. *Help me.*

Petals soared up from the bushes and eddied through the air, obscuring her sight like a pastel maelstrom. When they came to rest, the trees had transformed. A great pinkish-purple sweep of jacaranda bloomed in their place, robbing Ridhi of her breath.

Mummy gasped. "What is this?"

Ridhi saw no reason to shy from the truth. "The yaksha kingdom."

"The leaf you showed me. I thought . . ." Mummy trailed off when the sisterhood of yakshinis melted out of the thicket and knelt within the circle of jacaranda trees. In unison, they laid their palms flat on the ground.

Shoots burst forth from the dirt, first a few, then bushels, and finally far too many to count. Like a time-lapse video, they swirled and straightened and grew. Leaves unfurled and lengthened, flowers budded and blossomed, and at last nectarous fruits covered the plants in gold, silver, and copper; in aquamarine, royal purple, and cinnabar.

The noise Mummy made was one of joy, an adult relearning a truth she'd known as a child. "It's so beautiful," she whispered.

Ridhi nuzzled her. She hadn't felt this close to her mother since before the audition. "Yakshinis, Mummy."

"Yakshinis, beti," Mummy affirmed.

Hamshi clapped in satisfaction, and the group set about going over the yield and harvesting the ripest, most appetizing gourds, berries, oranges, limes, cherries, peaches, pineapples, and pears, as well as fruits Ridhi didn't recognize. All she knew was that she intended to eat them.

Their labor executed, the sisterhood reclined on cushions of gold-worked silk beneath the robust jacarandas. Vikala gestured at the treasure trove of produce. "I hope you know you need no invitation. We do not stand on such formalities among friends."

"Yes, do partake!" urged Shatapratika. "The pears in particular are a variety our maharani called into being long ago, and we have been entrusted with its cultivation ever since."

"Twist my arm, will you?" Ridhi plucked a pear the silver of moonlight, exulting in the *snap* of the stem parting from the branch. After mangoes, pears were her favorite fruit. She ran her finger and thumb over the velvety skin before plunging her teeth into it.

The amethyst flesh bled a juice so dark, she first misread it as black. Like eating a night devoid of stars. Then the cloudlike texture lit up her tongue, making her groan with pleasure. And the flavor! It was pear yet utterly *other*, something phenomenal that defied description. All other pears might as well have been boulders, insipid and tough.

She'd meant to draw out the experience, but the pear was gone before she knew it, leaving her fingers sticky and purple black.

"I think you've ruined me for fruit," she said, earning a round of laughter before the yakshinis pushed more on her, a copper banana and a gold-shelled coconut with glittering juice. Each piece astonished her afresh, the banana soft and sweet, the coconut creamy and immeasurably invigorating.

The fruits were, Ridhi thought, as lush, as alluring as the women who had brought them into being. How lovely each yakshini was, how full of life. It wouldn't be hard to nurse a crush on any of them, no more difficult than longing for nature itself. But becoming one of them was just as good.

Ridhi, sang the trees, and it was the most exhilarating sound she could have envisaged, *things are not as they seem. Everything is a tale. You must take care.*

They murmured bits of stories, of rose sisters and autumn jewels and covens of tree witches. Without trying, she comprehended every word. She almost whooped with glee.

But what did they mean, take care?

"You are radiant," said Hamshi. The others chimed in. "I would say our harvest is a success."

Ridhi lowered her gaze to see that her own skin had grown lustrous. Even the plain cotton of her salwar kameez had been substituted with gardenias, their white petals as creamy as custard and their fragrance divine, and a dupatta of porcelain berry hung across her neck, its fruits as blue and purple as gemstones. She looked like magic, and she felt like it, too.

Mummy, however, stood in silence.

Ghanta held out a peach to her. "Eat this, Meera. Eat and relive your adventure."

Sighing, Mummy took a single bite. As she chewed, her dumbfounded expression dissolved. "Sulochana! I remember."

"Yes," said Shatapratika. "Now share it with your daughter."

Before Ridhi could ask what Mummy remembered, Hamshi blew on a palmful of jacaranda petals, so they rained down in a diaphanous shower that once more blanketed the air.

For thirty seconds, the world was the pinkish purple of twisting, twirling fragments of flowers. But for the lack of water, Ridhi might have been inside a snow globe.

When she could see again, the yakshinis had decamped, and she sat facing Mummy on the backyard swing. Not even the beauty of what she'd experienced could drive the foreboding from her heart. "Share what with me? What did you remember?"

Mummy tugged a hand through her hair. Right when Ridhi was certain she wouldn't answer, she relinquished the peach. "Here. I don't know why, but I think you're supposed to eat this, too."

Curious, Ridhi bit into it.

"I told you," Mummy began, "about my school trip to a hill station in the Himalayas."

As Mummy narrated, the scene played out in Ridhi's mind.

Mummy was seventeen, and her class had gone deep into the woods, taking notes on the plants they observed. Out of the corner of Mummy's eye, she caught a gleam of gold. While the class moved on, she slipped away to find it.

But no matter how long she looked, it hid from her. Maybe the sun had hit a drop of water at the perfect angle to look like gold.

Then she heard mysterious singing in Sanskrit. It lured her into a glen with a pond of lambent pink lotuses. Mummy recalled her grandmother saying Kashmir had been like that once, a paradise on Prithvi even the gods would visit. Everything was so green, as if the plants had been sculpted from emeralds.

The singer appeared, a goblet in hand. She looked like a princess who'd come from a rana's estate, too stunning to be real. How thirsty you must be after your excursion.

Mummy took the goblet from her, a swirl of gold and copper and silver worked with a jade-and-peridot vine, and swigged the contents to lubricate her suddenly parched mouth. They tasted like imbibing summer. All its heat, all its plants, all its flowers, with a hint of the monsoon. Dizzy, Mummy became certain that she, too, had roots.

I really love trees, *she said*. Sometimes I think I was one in a previous life.

Indeed. *The singer's smile was as pretty as the moon.* Tell me, do you know of the Kalpavriksha?

Of course. It's Lord Indra's wish tree.

What if I told you that, in return for a slight service, something insignificant in scope, you could leave this mortal world behind?

What a question! It left Mummy flabbergasted. Why would I want to do that?

The singer tossed her head. Oh, I do not know—to experience a realm beyond your most outlandish imaginings.

She touched her sari of roses. The lure of apparel as soft on your skin as swansdown.

She nibbled on a kumquat. Fruit so sweet and ripe that one bite would turn your heart to gold.

She pointed behind her to a fish in the pond. Companions the like of which would entertain you for the rest of your days.

Mummy gave it some thought. For a vacation, those things might be nice. But Mummy liked her life, and she would be sad to leave her friends and family for good. No, thanks. The rest of my days is a long time.

Meera! *The call came from far off. Mummy ignored it.*

No? *The singer edged closer and assessed Mummy with a clinical eye.* No, *she decided*. Not you. Your daughter. She will inherit your affinity for the woods. Tell her about Sulochana the yakshini.

That threw Mummy for a loop. I'm going to have a daughter?

The call came a second time. Meera!

But the drink, whatever it had been, wore off. Mummy found herself at the spot where she'd veered off the path, her teacher shouting her name.

"I forgot about that until now, when the peach brought it back." Mummy laughed drolly. "Though it seems her orders have stayed with me."

Mummy had met Sulochana. Sulochana had originally selected her. That was more than Ridhi knew what to do with.

You remind me of someone, Sulochana had said. Now it made sense.

"Are you still mad at me?" Ridhi asked.

Mummy didn't speak for a minute. "I knew something was going on with you, but I thought it was the audition and Nilesh staying with us."

Ridhi flailed. "I wanted to tell you. I did. But I thought you might stop me."

A thousand questions alternated across her mother's face, and she let out another sigh. "I wonder if I made a mistake teaching you all of this. You wouldn't love it like you do if I hadn't raised you to."

"Don't be sorry. I'm not. Not about that, anyway."

"You're brave, my sweet girl. You always have been." Mummy shook her head. "I can't imagine what Aruna and Dilip are going through. If I ever thought you'd run away . . ."

"Papa would never cheat, though," Ridhi pointed out.

"No, but we all have our weaknesses, and we all make mistakes." Mummy hugged her tight. "Just make sure you talk to me instead of disappearing, okay?"

The lump in Ridhi's gut tripled in size. She might be about to do exactly that.

"I will," she said, hoping it was true.

She thought of Malav's request. Of how Sulochana had chosen her over Mummy, and her own role in Sulochana's scheme. Of everything she still didn't know.

Things are not as they seem. She gnawed on her fingernail.

"You asked if I'm still mad." Mummy gently pushed Ridhi's hand down. "A little. But we'll be okay." She bent to kiss Ridhi's forehead. "Come on. Papa and Kartik are waiting."

The long white mandir with its carvings of deities seemed as prepared to celebrate as the masses of people flowing in and out its entrance. Tents brimmed with food and items for sale, including packets of powder for playing colors. One stage had speakers blasting bhajans, and from another, a man broadcast announcements that echoed across the grounds, but which very few people were actually listening to.

It should have felt like home.

That day, though, the mandir was the last place Ridhi wanted to be. The vial of Keeper of the Woodlands she'd packed to gift the maharani practically burned a hole in her blossom-bedecked bag. *Soon.*

She spotted Kartik and caught up to him.

A scowl distorted his face. "Leave me alone!" He plunged into the crowd.

It's fine, Ridhi assured herself. *It's fine.*

So what if her own brother had rejected her? She'd make her rounds with each of the deities and then continue on to Alakapuri.

She left her shoes on top of the already teeming cubbies and went into the mandir proper. Wisps of incense-heavy smoke gyrated through the space. Along the walls, individual niches showcased the murtis of Radha and Krishna, freshly bathed, arrayed in silk clothing, and garlanded with marigolds and roses.

Ridhi halted before her favorite statue, the one featuring Krishna playing his bamboo flute while Radha leaned against his side in rapture. Nothing existed for them but each other. What was it like to be that blissfully in love?

Her imagination flew to Malav, trying to view the two of them in that light, but it didn't quite gel. Maybe she was too nervous to think straight.

She'd circulated halfway around the room, pausing before each murti to pray and leave dollar bills in silver dishes, when a familiar voice called her name.

"Ridhi! So nice to see you," Varsha Auntie said. "I'm disappointed you couldn't join us, but at least you can enjoy the show. The girls are outside, getting ready. Would you like to come say hello?"

Ridhi had forgotten the dance team was going to be performing. "Sure," she blurted, even as her brain was screaming at her mouth to stop. "I mean, I can't—"

But Varsha Auntie was already directing her to where the troupe, decked out in full bharatanatyam dress, was warming up before the main stage.

Ridhi took in the girls' blue-and-red silk saris embroidered with gold zari and fashioned with pleats that would fall into tasteful fans as they danced, their dark-red lipstick and the pronounced kajal around their eyes, their lengthy braids and white gajras, and wished she could kick herself.

Worse, upon seeing her, Shreya broke away from the team. "Hey, can I talk to you?" she asked.

Ridhi gripped her pendant. The other girls were watching with far more interest than they had at her audition. It was silly to feel cornered, but she did. "Um, okay?"

"I like your outfit." Shreya chewed on her lip. "It looks so real. Where'd you get it?"

Real? Ridhi boggled. She didn't tend to wear fake clothes. *Oh, right, the gardenias.* "It was a gift."

Shreya hopped from side to side, making the ghungroo around her ankles tinkle. "Your audition was really good."

"Thanks?"

"What I'm trying to say is, thanks for not taking the spot." Shreya chewed harder. At this rate, she'd eat off all her lipstick before the show. "I mean, I don't think you would have felt at home there, anyway."

All the wounded feelings Ridhi had been nursing since the day Shreya had traded her in for a better model ignited. "I heard you at the audition, you know."

Shreya's eyes widened. "What?"

Now that she'd begun, Ridhi didn't care who heard her. She'd been holding this in for far too long. "That was really mean of you and your friends. *That's* why I turned it down. You know Varsha Auntie kept begging me to say yes, don't you?"

Shreya laughed. It was a flustered laugh. "Um—"

290

"Didn't you wonder why it took so long for you to join the team? Well, now you know."

"I'm sorry." She wore the same lost look she'd had when Ridhi had first met her.

The look that, irrespective of her flawless hair and makeup, let slip how unsure of herself, how frail she was in the first place. It didn't excuse any of Shreya's poor choices. But it did tell Ridhi that she hadn't missed out. Shreya wouldn't have been what she needed.

Shreya's teammates were already closing ranks around her, commiserating, yet she gawked at Ridhi.

No, Ridhi didn't think she'd stay to watch the show. "Break a leg," she told the girls, then walked off.

It took every ounce of calm she could summon not to run past the tents and away from the crowds. Once she reached the thicket bordering the grounds, she'd be free. Both Malav and Sulochana had promised that, for all of Holi, any tree would act as a portal to Alakapuri.

"Beti!" Mummy cried. "Where are you going? I just saw Swati Auntie from the store in one of the tents."

Her heart crumpling, Ridhi glanced back. Her expression must have given her away, because Mummy's exuberance faded.

"Forget all that," she pleaded. "Stay here, with us. With me. Don't go there."

Even now, Mummy didn't understand. The letdown was more than Ridhi could bear. "I have to," she said.

Because that was where she belonged, not Prithvi.

The line of trees swished in the wind, and she sprinted toward it.

21

When Nilesh stopped running, he was in a small grove he'd
never seen before.

How was he supposed to tell Hetal and Amar that he couldn't
go home—not then, not ever?

Kamini's voice kept looping in his head. *Make merry as the family you are. Cleave to them.*

Well, since she was so hung up on family togetherness, *she* could
fill them in.

Nilesh laughed sourly. Gods, he'd been stupid. He'd thrown
away his life for a girl who just wanted to jerk him around. First she
said he intrigued her and let him get close. Then she said he should
have stayed away.

What hurt most was that he still wanted to be with her.

He needed something to do. Something to keep him busy.

Nilesh took stock of the grove. Trees, trees, and more trees.
Some plants, too. He couldn't name most of them, but he might
as well work on learning to tell them apart. He was going to be in

Alakapuri for a long, long time.

He poked at a pine cone and fingered a low-hanging branch. Needles. Those, at least, he could identify. Prior to meeting Kamini, he would have said pine tree, no question. But she'd told him that other kinds of trees dropped cones and grew needles, too.

So was this one pine, fir, or spruce?

Nilesh buried his face in his hands. No way around it—he was in over his head. With everything.

When he glanced up, something bright grabbed his attention. The flash of color stood out in the mostly green grove.

It was probably just a dupatta someone had lost, but Nilesh went to investigate.

A tree with wide branches and red-orange flowers towered above him. A gulmohar tree. Like the jewel one Kamini wore in her nose.

Feeling like he was in a dream, he walked over to the tree.

"It seems you happened upon my mother's grove, mortal boy."

She'd found him. He hadn't really expected to hide from a yakshini in her forest, but still.

Nilesh whipped around to see Hetal and Amar watching him, all wide eyes and concern, while Kamini stared in anguish at the tree. Her mother.

So that was why Kamini was such a fan of fall colors.

"Nilu!" Hetal said. "Kamini told us what happened. I don't care what anyone says; it's not too late. We'll get you out of here one way or another."

He was so sick of everyone telling him what to do. "Did it ever occur to any of you that *I* picked this?"

"No." Hetal eyed him in confusion. "Why would it?"

"Well, I did." Nilesh made himself take a breath. "Can you all just please stop talking? You don't even know what you're talking about."

"*You're* the one who doesn't know what you're talking about," Amar retorted. "They're using you. They want you to be an anchor for the Kalpavriksha."

Nilesh wasn't following. "Huh? What anchor?"

Amar nodded. "Exactly. So maybe you should shut up and listen, seeing as how we came to save you and all."

Nilesh aimed his answer at Kamini. "Did I ask you to?"

No one said anything.

Kamini's gaze finally swung to him. Her nose pin twinkled in the sun. When she spoke, her voice was miserable. "It is no accident that we encountered each other that day among the spices."

"What do you mean?" Nilesh asked. He hadn't meant to reach for it, but the dewdrop opal was in his hand. He rolled it back and forth, back and forth.

Like he'd summoned her with it, she edged forward until only inches separated them.

"I was measuring your suitability for Sulochana's plan," she said. "Someone must hold the Kalpavriksha in place while she restores it to us. An anchor. But when the time came, I could not permit it. Not at the cost of you."

Nilesh's impatience ratcheted up. "If that's true, why are you telling me now?"

"You deserve the truth." Kamini clutched his shoulders. "You must know I tried to prevent it. I told her no."

He shrugged her off. "So let me get this straight," he said slowly. "You didn't care about me at all? You just needed an anchor for some plan?"

She made a frustrated noise. "Of course I did! I would not be here now if I did not."

"But you still went through with the scheme? Doesn't sound like you cared to me."

"It was a ruse, yes," she cried desperately. "The trappings—"

Her confession was starting to sink in, and a sick knot was forming in the pit of his stomach. "The trap, you mean."

"No, Sulochana's plan. I evicted you that day because I could no longer adhere to my role in it, not once I began to know you. I could not rob you of your freedom, even if that meant losing you. Yet despite my efforts, you returned!"

Kamini's forehead furrowed, and a strong wind blew through the trees. It knocked fruit from branches and stripped petals from flowers. She must really be upset.

Nilesh didn't get what she wanted him to say. *"You apologized, so it's all good"? "So what if I lost my family and my best friend and my life on Prithvi"? "It's okay; I don't mind"?*

But he knew what he wanted to tell her. "Because of you, I'm stuck here for the rest of my life. *My life.* I'll never talk to my parents again. I miss my dad, you know that?"

Kamini twisted her fingers together. "I—"

"I don't *want* to be here." It felt like someone had lit a bonfire

295

inside him. "Sure, no one made me play that chaturanga game. But if you hadn't shown it to me—if you'd left me alone in the first place, I never would have had the option to play it. That's on you."

"Nilu—" Hetal said at the same time Amar chided, "Dude—"

Nilesh held up a hand. "I don't want to hear it, okay?"

The knot inside him was getting bigger and bigger. Everybody let him down if he waited long enough.

"You know what?" he asked dully. "You shouldn't have told me. If I didn't know, I might have been all right. I would have thought we had something real and you were just in a weird mood or something."

"We *do*!" Kamini angled his jaw so he couldn't avoid her misted-over copper eyes. "That is why I told you. Because this is no scheme, not anymore."

Nilesh thought she might even have meant it. "But it was."

"Nilesh—"

"You didn't do it for Sulochana." Funny how he could suddenly see so clearly. He pointed to the gulmohar tree. "*She* was your reward, wasn't she? If you got me to be the anchor, Sulochana would turn your mother back into a yakshini."

Kamini looked stricken. Amar and Hetal didn't meet Nilesh's eyes.

"She would plead my case to the maharani, yes," Kamini whispered.

"Why me? What did I do to you?"

She let go of him, more despondent than she'd even been about her mom. "You would truly know? We saw how shattered you were.

296

How fragile. You were the consummate anchor."

Shattered. Fragile.

She hadn't picked him because he was cute or interesting or anything like that. She'd picked him because he was broken. Easy to manipulate. He'd even told her, at her prompting, to use him.

Pathetic. No better than a character in the video games he'd taught her how to play. The video games she'd asked him to teach her while laughing behind his back.

A farce. That was all this had ever been. One big farce, with him as the punch line.

Nilesh felt like he was meeting the real Kamini for the first time. Still pretty but alien, too.

He made his voice as hard as Mom's had been the night when everything had gone to hell. "You should go. All of you."

"Buddy—" Amar started.

"I said go!"

When he looked up, he was alone.

A thick, pea-soup type of fog was swamping the grove, like a blanket thrown over someone so they couldn't see. From inside it, Nilesh felt someone's eyes on him again.

"Ishika?" he called out.

Her voice made it through the mist before she did. "So at last you are ready to listen?"

"Just tell me what's going on."

The fog lifted enough to show her standing just a foot from him. Ishika swirled her hand through the air, and a baby persimmon tree burst up in front of her. Nilesh watched impatiently as it developed from sapling to mature and pushed out tomato-shaped orange fruit.

Ishika plucked one. "Fancy a nibble while we converse?"

"No. But I do want to know who bought my debt. You know, don't you?" He'd meant to dig into that, but tracking down his mysterious benefactor had fallen off his priority list.

And he'd let it. Even then, he'd thought he'd been deciding for himself. What a joke.

Ishika smiled at the sky. "I will speak plainly, then. I did. Kamini could not help you, yet I could—and still can."

"But *why*?" Nilesh didn't bother to hide his skepticism. "You don't even— You didn't know who I was. Why would you help me?"

"I saw another soul in pain. Another soul Sulochana condemned to suffer while she thought only of herself and her goals."

Did Ishika really think he would buy her whole high-minded act? "You don't care about me. What do you really want?"

"You may believe as you will," she said. "In you, I saw someone who understood what it was like to be discarded."

"Sure you did." But after Kamini's little bombshell, Nilesh was feeling more charitable toward Ishika. "They wanted me to be an anchor for the Kalpavriksha."

Ishika waggled her head. "Without obtaining your consent, naturally. I am not surprised. I *did* attempt to warn you that something was afoot."

"Yeah." He should have listened.

"Did you ascribe finding Prakash when you were in need of him to mere chance?" she asked pityingly. "Hardly. It was that opal you keep so close."

I never should have given you the dewdrop opal.

Every time Nilesh thought he'd hit rock bottom, another thing stabbed him in the chest. Feeling like a chump, he threw down the opal.

Ishika and he stood there without talking. It was so nice. No drama. No arguing.

She must have thought so, too. "Do you see the peace inherent in this environment?" she asked. "Do you feel it? It is why your friend Ridhi prefers trees to people."

Trees didn't judge. Nilesh got that. But he'd never thought they might actually be giving her something.

Ishika was right though. Back on Prithvi, or even out in the heart of Alakapuri, the world was always rushing, rushing, rushing. It didn't slow down. He *couldn't* slow down. But in the grove, it was so quiet.

"Spiritual seekers retreat to the forest for this very reason," she went on in a sedate tone that made him think of a rainy afternoon. "But eventually, they must leave and return to their problems. A tree, however, never does."

He nodded.

"Do you wish to achieve that permanent peace? I can show you how."

Kamini would have killed Nilesh for considering it. But the gulmohar tree, blazing through the mist, taunted him. "I guess."

"Doff your shoes and plant your bare feet in the ground," Ishika instructed. Nilesh did what she said. "Trees are grounded. They are moored by their roots, and those same roots connect them to their neighbors. Can you feel it?"

Something pleasant swooshed through him. "Yeah. Yeah, I can!"

She smiled. "Close your eyes and think on that."

Nilesh's eyes fell shut. The inside of his head came to a standstill. It was as peaceful as she'd said it would be.

When he finally looked again, Ishika wasn't there anymore.

The trees around him, however, had joined their branches in an arch. Sunlight had burned off the fog, and their shadows moved over him. These shadows had substance. Purpose.

They were telling him to choose.

He should be flipping out, but eerie floating orbs bobbed in front of him, blue and red and yellow, disarming him.

Chir batti, the marsh lights Nilesh had once observed in the Rann of Kutch. They'd been fun then, decaying matter going wild. Now they held him immobile, so all he could do was wait to see what happened next.

Something scuttled past. What felt like claws scratched his leg, and he yelped.

He thought of his parents' deception. Hetal and Amar, banding together.

And Kamini. How she'd never actually liked him, only how broken he was. How pathetic and suggestible.

But it didn't help. She had been his safe place, and now he didn't even have that.

A ring of spotted mushrooms sprouted at his feet. Ishika's words about being with the trees came back to him.

Nilesh squared his shoulders. "You want me? Fine. Then take me."

Another branch swiped at his arm. The woods, the place Ridhi had always thought was a wonderland, were claiming him, and it was a little scary.

Was this what she was talking about when she said she could feel the forest?

Because Nilesh could feel it, too. Just for a second, but in that second, his thoughts and feelings slowed again.

Then the trees released him. The rough, barklike patch behind his ear had spread all over.

Nilesh was a tree now, washed in green. Lots and lots of green. Around him, animals squawked and snorted. Insects hummed and buzzed. The wind rustled. He could decode it all.

A picture appeared of a girl. Ridhi. She was the one who'd said she could talk to trees.

More pictures sailed by. Nilesh knew every person in that montage. He'd been there for it. It was his life, flashing past him. But it felt like something that had happened to someone else.

He tried to remember what it felt like to have arms and legs. It wasn't going well. Then he realized why.

They'd vanished.

Should he be panicking? He didn't know.

He felt pretty sturdy. His roots had gone into the soil, so he was getting nutrients and water. The sun beat down, and the chlorophyll in his leaves grabbed the rays to store as energy.

Yeah, he felt good. Still, he thought later, maybe minutes, maybe hours—it was hard to say—something was bothering him. Almost like a voice shouting from miles away.

Nilesh tried to tune in to that voice. The snatches he caught sounded familiar, but he couldn't make sense of them.

Another picture, this time of Amar carving both their initials into the bark of a young tree. Nilesh felt the pain in his own trunk. How had they not known better?

Good thing the knife had been in Amar's hand, not his. Nilesh didn't want anyone to carve him up now in some morbid form of karma.

It was so calm there. Trees didn't sleep, but Nilesh could go into a reverie. There was nothing he had to do. Nobody he had to answer to. He could see why that girl liked trees so much.

What was her name again? Right, Ridhi.

At some point, Nilesh realized a squirrel was leaping from tree to tree. It touched down on one of his branches and started gnawing on the acorn in its paws.

Hey, Nilesh protested. *I didn't say you could sit here.*

The squirrel flicked its tail but kept eating. Nearby, a songbird tweeted.

The forest he was part of inhaled and exhaled. It was soothing, like the sea. Nilesh wasn't sure how he knew what that was like. Something about the crash of waves on sand?

Don't go deeper, a voice cautioned him. *Don't push. Don't look.*

Too late.

Four people played at the edge of the pond, up to their ankles in the water. It reflected the blue sky, but Nilesh could still see all the way to the bottom.

Look! *Dad called.* A turtle!

Mom bent down and waved to the little turtle. Imagine being able to go anywhere you want and bring your house with you. Plus you never have to worry about uninvited guests. No one else can fit in there with you.

They all laughed. Everyone knew that Mom loved hosting parties and visitors. She would never be happy alone in a shell.

Yeah. *Hetal scrunched up her face.* I'd never let Nilu into my shell. *She nudged him, and he splashed water at her.* Hey!

Don't make me feed you to the fish, *Dad teased.* They look pretty hungry.

Hetal squealed and jumped back onto the sandy shore. Her legs, healthy and strong, let her dash off.

Mom jogged after her. Stay where I can see you!

Dad got out of the water, too. He pulled a candy bar from his pocket. For you, Bablu, *he said, his nickname for Nilesh that he saved for when it was just the two of them.*

Suspicious, Nilesh grabbed the bar. It's not my birthday until tomorrow. *He tore open the wrapper anyway and took a big bite.*

Dad chuckled. I know. *He tapped a rhythm up and down Nilesh's arm while Nilesh drummed on his knee. It was their two-man band, and Dad liked to joke about how they'd go on tour one day.* But we can get a head start, can't we?

303

Yeah, *Nilesh said*. We can.

Good. Because I want you to have everything. You're my favorite son, you know.

I'm your *only* son.

Dad smiled and pulled Nilesh in for a hug. Still my favorite.

The memory plagued Nilesh, as much a part of him as his bark or his leaves. It had been years since Dad had called him Bablu. About as long as it had been since the last time Hetal could still walk unassisted, never mind run.

Some distant part of him mourned. He would never see Hetal again. Never talk to Amar or Ridhi.

A golden deer cantered up to investigate him. Nilesh checked it out, too, just as curious.

The deer seemed to approve, because it cantered away again.

He couldn't guess how much time had passed when he heard his name. "Nilesh!" Warm fingers trailed over his trunk. "Are you able to hear me?"

The sap in Nilesh's veins flowed faster. Kamini! She'd come. He recalled being mad at her once, long ago.

At least now she'd get her mother back.

A few of his leaves fluttered down to greet her. She put her arms around his trunk and rested her forehead against his bark. "What have you done? This is far beyond my ability to set right."

How could he let her know that, this way, he was rooted? Nothing could shake him. He would be there through the ages, no matter what.

A tear ran down her cheek. "I am sorry, mortal boy. Why did

you not heed me and keep to your world?"

She sobbed, her shoulders shaking. Nilesh, who was still figuring out his new shape, struggled to tell her not to cry.

If she heard him, it didn't help.

Pain spread through him. All he wanted to do was comfort her, but how?

Nilesh *pushed* within, and then his branches were in motion. He moved them too quickly at first. Something cracked. Slowing himself, he brought them down across Kamini's back and into a hug.

She clung to him, warming his branches. "Remember," she murmured. "Remember who you were. Who you still are."

Nilesh resisted the call. He didn't want to remember.

"Please," she begged. "Wake up, mortal boy. Return to me."

But Nilesh was already fading again.

22

Ridhi, bundled between Sulochana and Prakash among the masses assembled for the parade, did her best to focus on what they were saying. If she had thought the city of Alakapuri fabulous before, she had no word to describe it now. *Resplendent, magnificent, sublime*—all fell short of the vision before her. *Transcendent*, perhaps, came closest.

Delicate mushrooms and dew-strewn grass garmented the ground, the latter a balm to the soles of her feet. Above them the trees, dignified beings on the most ordinary of days, radiated a verdancy that could only come from magic, an ancient alchemy wrought from sun and stream and soil. Even the foliage that was hot pink and violet and teal, even the fruits and nuts in gold, silver, and copper, exuded that luster, paving the streets of the already breathtaking capital.

And, scattered as thickly as coins in a wishing well, flowers bloomed in every imaginable tint and shade, as if the forest itself were offering up a benediction on this most auspicious of occasions. Their diverse and often discordant fragrances combined into something ineffable, the quintessence of which girded Ridhi like wings.

She needed no words, no gestures, merely this.

The *shh–shh–shh* of the wind through the leaves, the swirling dance of air on matter whooshed through her with the piquant delight of a summer day. The trees murmured so many stories, Ridhi was awash in them. They soaked through her skin and into her blood, and while she might not recall the specifics, she would never forget their core.

Yet as much as she longed to lose herself in their whispers, now that she finally comprehended their arcane language, she couldn't. *Things are not as they seem.*

Which things?

Sulochana, bent upon keeping her promise of introducing Ridhi to the upper echelons of the court, sustained a vivacious conversation with the nobles who came by. "The forest itself brought her to us!" she chanted again and again, like a spell designed to lure in the haughty courtiers. "Such a dream Ridhi has been, this mortal friend to our kind."

That mortal friend circumspectly combed the droves of people for Malav and Nilesh. She'd searched for them earlier, but in a throng this size, they could be anywhere.

"How perfectly sweet!" cooed an elderly lady, her white hair in a bun worked through with jasmine and marigolds. Her husband agreed, making Ridhi feel like she was a five-year-old being fed a bonbon. It had been this way all morning. Either the nobles were overly indulgent, or they refused to be talked out of their glacial demeanor.

She put her palms together and articulated what she hoped was a passably polite reply.

Ridhi recognized that Sulochana was granting her an incredible opportunity, and these connections would prove advantageous when she became a full-fledged yakshini. But she found herself missing the sisterhood. Sulochana had explained that they weren't much for court affairs, although she was certain they were observing from a safe distance.

A traitorous part of Ridhi wished she were with them. Deep inside, where she could barely hear it, she thought, *Maybe I'm not cut out for court affairs, either.*

She wanted to belong, she did. But . . .

The procession, which had commenced at the city gates, wound past. A band of musicians played bansuris, the bamboo flutes high and wistful, and beat dhols to a rhythm that had Ridhi swaying where she stood. It felt as though they were channeling the heartbeats of the trees into melody, but sped up, and all around her, the other spectators moved gracefully to the music.

Ridhi was thankful for the excuse to stop talking and just appreciate the parade. The organizers had spared no effort, featuring a menagerie of animals, shalabhanjikas dancing with sprays of leaves, archers with silver-tipped arrows, swashbucklers with buffed golden swords, and giggling children pitching fruit to the onlookers.

Her breath hitched at the quartet of caparisoned elephants, their gray skin set off by the green and gold of their headdresses.

Sculpted gold umbrellas balanced on their backs, which were insulated by green-and-gold blankets. The silk had been worked with mirrors and richly embroidered, and gold ribbon gleamed along the edges, matching the ribbon tied around the elephants' tails and the cloth caps on their heads. Even their ivory tusks had been touched with gold.

The elephants trumpeted joyously, then linked their trunks together two by two to form an archway through which a calf, also robed in green and gold, trotted along. It gladly accepted copious pats from the nearest yakshas and yakshinis.

No trainer pushed them. No groom commanded them. Like the other animals in the parade, the elephants had elected to take part of their own free will. They, too, wanted to celebrate.

Ridhi's eyes pricked. It was all she could do not to run forward and embrace the little calf. How blessed was she, to be a witness to this?

The musicians passed out of hearing, and the nobles fell back into their dialogue. Though she smiled and nodded, Ridhi could scarcely feign interest in what they were saying. The past hour had drained her, and the knowledge that she would have to engage in small talk every day from there on out had her sinking inside.

It also terrified her. What if, in the course of courtly repartee, she accidentally agreed to something that would hurt her or someone else? The responsibility was too big, too dangerous.

Slowly the susurration of the trees stilled her inner tumult. It was as if they yearned to compensate for lost time, imparting every tale they had, and the collective tapestry of their narratives bore her away. As long as she made the right noises, none of her conversation partners noticed.

A single message coalesced in her mind's ear. *The foundation has been laid.*

The message jarred Ridhi from head to toe. It was no mere sylvan missive but a personal telegram steeped in triumph. Not only that, it had the same energy as the leaf she'd first received from the forest.

Malav had mentioned other agents besides trees being able to communicate via leaf, but he hadn't expounded on that, and it hadn't occurred to Ridhi to ask him to. If she could, she would go back and give her past self an in-depth talking-to.

Because this message disturbed her. Unable to put her finger on why, she reached for her pendant, then the vial of Keeper of the Woodlands in her purse.

A jungle crow soared overhead, circling Sulochana and Prakash before continuing on its journey.

"That bird really likes you," Ridhi noted, a little envious. Sulochana wasn't doing anything to catch the bird's notice. She hadn't even fed it at her tasting party.

Maybe that would change for Ridhi once she was a yakshini, too.

Sulochana brightened, her expression softer than her normal reserve. It made her less of a tactician and more of a person. What had she been like before the Ishika fiasco? "Such a charming creature, yes?"

Prakash smiled his adoring smile. "Who among us would not be devoted to you?"

Sulochana waved him off, then went back to chatting with her neighbor. It occurred to Ridhi that she seemed more tolerant of his overtures than actually reciprocating them.

Well, if he didn't mind, it was none of Ridhi's concern.

Their little band grazed on the fruit they'd caught from the children in the parade while another unit spun flower-petal and butterfly-wing pinwheels and blew amber bubbles of conifer resin. A handful of acts remained, after which the maharaja and maharani would officially kick off the game of playing colors.

And then the line of querents would start taking the stage.

What was left of Ridhi's appetite evaporated. She gave her kiwi to a girl her age and concentrated on breathing. She would get through the afternoon, and Sulochana would gift her everything she'd ever yearned for.

At last, the final act of the procession came through. A golden palanquin transported the murtis of Radha and Krishna snuggled on a swing while Krishna, the peacock feather on his turban fluttering, played his bansuri. The familiar sight filled Ridhi with guilt at how she'd run off, leaving her family to worry.

She batted it away. She couldn't think about that now.

The crowd dispersed, seeking out refreshments and preparing for the colors to come.

"There go our customers," Prakash said. "It would be cruel to deny them your divine elixirs a single moment more."

"Indeed." Sulochana laughed and kissed his cheek. "Go appease their thirst, then."

He took his leave, and she clasped Ridhi's hands in hers. "I wish to thank you for all you have done. Without you, I would endure in my holding pattern. Four centuries, even by our standards, is too long to remain stagnant."

"But I haven't done anything yet!" Ridhi demurred. "Not really, anyway."

Sulochana's smile was kind. "*Yet* is but a marker of time, nothing more. You will make a fine yakshini, of that I have no doubt."

"What about my mom? Didn't you offer that to her, too?"

A series of emotions played across Sulochana's beauteous face: surprise, vexation, and even something approaching respect. "Ah, so she told you. At the outset, I had believed she would do, but she lacked your depth of devotion. That is why the Kalpavriksha did not appear to her." She released Ridhi's hands. "Only you can do this, and I know you will prevail."

Servants in green and gold livery brought out enormous, gem-encrusted thrones and arranged them on the vacant stage, a golden dais large enough to support the maharaja, maharani, and a selection of their most loyal advisors and trusted guards. At the front of the dais, cunningly positioned between stylized carvings of trees and famous characters from yaksha lore, was a large staircase of marble.

It was that staircase that would allow petitioners to access the dais and request the royal blessing—and Ridhi to perform her task.

Behind it, the palace, which she had succeeded in avoiding over the past few days, rose into the heavens, as stately as the forest. Vakeshvara itself.

Ridhi forgot everything, the enchanted forest around her, the yakshini accompanying her, and stared. The yaksha kingdom had shown her so many marvels since she'd arrived, but the abode of King Kubera and Queen Kauveri eclipsed them all.

Vakeshvara extended for a good quarter mile across the land, its gilt walls artfully overgrown with plants and gold and jewels. Large diamond windows flashed in the sunshine, interspersed with carved pillars ringed with ivy. Filigree balconies lined the upper levels, coyly hinting at the luxuriant rooms within. Lush garlands of multicolored flowers swathed ornamental brackets and scalloped entrances and spiraled delicately around slender turrets. On the roof, onion domes of emerald, ruby, sapphire, and amethyst blazed like beacons.

The structure with its celestial halo was, unmistakably, the domain of demigods.

Viewing it, Ridhi felt like a saturated sponge. She was too small for this. Maybe she should turn tail and run.

Sulochana lay a steadying hand on her arm, then decanted a dram of spring elixir. "I saw you did not eat your fruit. Drink this and be rejuvenated."

Ridhi did. Her jitters calmed, replaced by a placid alertness. "Much better. Thank you."

Sulochana waggled her head. "If you will pardon me, I should check on my betrothed and the elixirs. Why do you not also take some nourishment? It will be some time yet, and there is nothing to be achieved by burning up from nerves beforehand." She slipped some coins onto Ridhi's palm and prodded her in the direction of the food stalls. "Go on."

Ridhi disguised her disappointment as best she could. It would have been nice to have some company, and so far, none of her friends had surfaced.

She headed toward the nearest stand, where she ordered a cup of thandai and a plate of gujiya. Though Prakash had referred to the visitors to his kiosk as customers, this vendor dismissed her attempts to pay. "You are Sulochana's mortal friend, yes? For you, everything is free."

Feeling a little lighter, Ridhi thanked him and hunted for a place to sit.

But before she'd gone far, Malav waylaid her. "Holi greetings!" He embraced her as though he hadn't been absent all afternoon.

"Where were you?" Ridhi asked, trying to sound like it didn't matter. "I've been here for a while."

"I was attending to some family matters." He stood back to look her over. "How fetching you are. You lack only a crown to match."

Though she was right there, she missed the moment when he fashioned a gardenia circlet out of thin air. Malav set it on her head alongside the jasmine and daisy clips. "There," he said, like a stylist pleased with his client's appearance. "Now you are complete."

"Thanks." Ridhi couldn't help noticing it felt more desultory than when he had brought her purse to life, an afterthought. Had he already forgotten their kisses? The miraculous rewilding that had made her late for Kartik's game?

"Remember what I said," Malav whispered against her hair. He tugged on the gajra at the end of her braid. "Today will alter everything."

Listening to him, Ridhi recalled the trees' warning. She kept her eyes lowered so he wouldn't see her doubts.

He was already striding off, like the bone of affection he'd tossed her should be more than enough, and he could move on to the things that mattered.

Shouldn't their first Holi together be one of those things?

Ridhi thought about how Malav hadn't shown any interest in her until he'd been sent to teach her phyllomancy. About how he'd neither shared anything personal nor asked her to. About how uncomfortable she'd felt around his friends, and how their plans lacked provisions for people like her mother, who loved the natural realm every bit as much as he did.

It was starting to add up to something she wasn't prepared to examine, so she finished her snack and fixed her mind on the imminent throwing of colors instead.

A multitude of tables wreathed in leaves and tuberoses held silver dishes heaped with candy-bright powders, each grouped by hue. Attendants in white garb encouraged everyone to help themselves.

The maharaja clapped twice, the sound booming in Ridhi's ears. "Let the colors begin!"

Beside him, the maharani dipped her hand into a miniature version of the silver bowls and lobbed powder the green of oak leaves into the air.

Rainbows spread across the sky, culminating in sparkles that sprinkled down on the guests. It jogged a memory of a cartoon Ridhi had seen once, but this was the real thing. Far lovelier, and far more beguiling.

A gandharva quartet broke into a wild song. The thrumming of their tabla set the ground vibrating.

At the signal, the guests cheered, some ululating, and began throwing colors at one another. The saturated powders clouded the air like pigmented smoke, billowing scarlet here, violet there. Yellow struck Ridhi's torso, staining her gardenias with sunlight. She shrieked with laughter.

A few feet away, a boy flung tangerine powder in a girl's face. Blinking it out of her eyes, she launched some cobalt at him. It landed in his hair, and though he shook his head like a dog, he failed to dislodge it.

"You will pay for that," he warned, but his cackle undercut the threat.

His jovial attitude reminded Ridhi that this should have been the moment when Malav and she were giddily chasing each other, fistfuls of powder at the ready.

Pushing the sadness from her, she grabbed a spectrum's worth of colors and hurled them at her nearest neighbors, tinting their pristine saris and sherwanis with jewel tones. They returned the favor, besieging her so that she could only see a kaleidoscopic haze. It was as though a tremendous prism had cracked open over Alaka-puri, smudging everyone with its contents.

Ridhi dashed around, greedily cramming her hands with as

much powder as she could hold and slinging it with abandon. Of course, she soon found herself in another chaotic cloud of color. Rather than fight it, she twirled and skipped, welcoming the chromatic rain.

Once that subsided, she spotted Hamshi and Shatapratika. Armed with plenty of magenta and teal, she forged a path toward them.

"Yo, Ridhi! Over here!"

Amar? What was he doing there? And Hetal?

Hetal waved wildly. Except for her tearstained cheeks and the streaks of color, she could have been a fairy-tale princess in her wheelchair covered with ivy and flowers. She even wore a thin circlet of jasmine and tuberoses. "We were looking for you everywhere!"

Ridhi gathered herself. "Where's Nilesh?"

"We don't know! We can't find him." Hetal groaned like she might be sick.

Amar shook his head. "He's been acting nuts ever since his parents split up. But yakshas? I mean, come on." At an elbow in the side from Hetal, he added, "No offense, Ridhi."

"Just tell me what happened," she urged him.

Ridhi listened in growing horror as they recounted the showdown between Kamini and Nilesh. Sulochana hadn't said anything about an anchor, had she?

Things are not as they seem.

No, wait. She had. She'd just omitted the details, and Ridhi hadn't pushed. "But Kamini didn't tell him how to do it, right?"

"No." Amar ran his hands through his hair. "The thing is, they're both gone."

"And you've been here ever since?"

Hetal rubbed her eyes. "Yeah. How could we go home without him?"

"We've been in the woods," Amar said. *The woods.*

He looked so woebegone that Ridhi laughed and threw her powder at him. "You remember who you're talking to, right?"

"So what do we do?" Hetal asked.

Ridhi had no idea, but she couldn't say that. "He has to be around here somewhere. You said he's upset at Kamini?"

Amar and Hetal exchanged glances. "And at us," Hetal said.

"Then give him some time to cool off." Ridhi paused. "Listen, I know this isn't how you planned to spend your Holi, but at least you can celebrate spring in the prettiest place ever. That's not so bad, right?"

"It is pretty and all that," Hetal allowed, "but full disclosure—I don't think you should be here, either. I don't think any of us should."

Ridhi turned a charged stare on Hetal. She knew one thing: no one was taking away her chance to become a yakshini and win her tree and her mekhala.

"I'm sure he's safe. He'll find us," she promised.

He had to, right?

23

Nilesh had gotten so used to his branchy body that he could hardly remember what it had been like before. He could distinguish the plants around him and identify the animals flying, scampering, and hopping past. And he'd figured out what type of tree he was, with his broad trunk and upside-down heart-shaped leaves with tapered tips.

A peepal tree. The same type that Siddhartha Gautama had sat under when he'd achieved enlightenment and become Buddha, except in that story, it was called a bodhi tree.

Nilesh sincerely doubted anyone would ever figure out the nature of the universe by sitting in *his* shade.

A third name for it was ashvattha, the sacred fig. The Kalpavriksha was a sacred fig, too, except the Kalpavriksha could actually grant wishes.

Another realization came to him, lethargic and from a million miles away. He might be isolated, but he wasn't alone. Or rather, he wouldn't be.

He finally understood what being an anchor meant.

Until then, Nilesh had assumed he'd be holding a door. Propping it open. Something simple.

But the reality was a lot worse.

In the wild, peepal trees relied on a host tree or building to grow. Birds ate their fruit and deposited their seeds on the hosts, and the seeds that successfully wedged themselves in cracks and clefts germinated and sent down roots. Those roots got so big and thick, they essentially qualified as second trunks, and sometimes they garroted the host.

Nilesh didn't have a host, but he would soon be one. He was going to be a literal anchor.

Ridhi, that human girl who loved his kind, probably would have been able to recite all that data on command. Nilesh hadn't known any of it, but thanks to Ishika's magic—or was it Kamini's? He couldn't tell—information was seeping through him, thorough and relentless. He felt it like he was aware of the bark on his trunk or the breeze rustling his leaves or the ants marching over his roots, and he couldn't stem the flow.

With each thing he learned, his sense of being Nilesh faded. Before long, it would be gone.

He heard voices before anyone showed up, carried on the wind. The air blurred. Then he realized he'd been transported to the palace gardens. He might be a tall tree, but the walls of the palace went up a lot higher than he did.

Nilesh felt the trees around him reaching out, trying to

320

communicate, but it didn't work. Even though his roots pushed into the earth, he couldn't make contact with his neighbors.

Because he didn't have any.

He'd been isolated. The nearest trees were hundreds of feet away. He was part of the forest, but he stood by himself.

Sometime later, a yaksha or yakshini sneaked up to him, holding a branch with glowing jewel leaves. The branch's aura kept the strange person hidden. But when the stranger broke out a knife and nicked one of his limbs, Nilesh could feel their presence just fine.

Then the stranger grafted the branch onto him.

Pain screamed through Nilesh, and he rejected the branch.

The perpetrator tried again twice. Nilesh rejected it twice. On the third try, the graft while still horrible, finally took.

When the perpetrator withdrew the knife, the pain stopped. Nilesh knew he should be worried, but he wasn't, not really. His perspective was becoming too sluggish, too big.

"Excellent," the unknown yaksha or yakshini said. "You shall perform your duty well enough."

They slipped away, leaving Nilesh with the branch.

It didn't hurt, but it felt weird. A piece of another tree was attached to him.

The sap inside him moved with drawn-out surprise. Not just another tree—the Kalpavriksha! All foliage recognized the king of trees.

But what did it mean? Nilesh couldn't begin to guess.

More time passed, and then the yaksha called Prakash jogged toward him in a palace gardener's uniform and probed the grafted branch.

"Well done," Prakash said, then waved an arm and began chanting. The air around Nilesh blurred again, and the distance separating him from the rest of the gardens closed.

Nilesh didn't feel any different, but he knew he didn't look like an ashvattha anymore. He'd been smushed in among shala trees, the kind shalabhanjikas dwelled in, and going by his leaves and flowers, he'd been camouflaged to look like them.

He wanted to wonder about that, but all his thoughts, all his feelings, came at a snail's pace. It was like someone had put them in slow motion and dialed back the intensity.

So Nilesh wasn't bothered when yakshas and yakshinis dressed for Holi started streaming into the gardens. Somewhere between his gradual, rhythmic inhalations, tables of food and drink had appeared. So had the guests. Prakash wasn't among them.

But those yakshas and yakshinis, all done up in white clothes made of flowers—Nilesh felt tied to each of them. The cruel, the caring, the young, the old. Even Ishika, Sulochana, and Prakash, wherever they were.

Little by little, the crowd's enthusiasm infected him. He felt it with them. He *was* them.

But underneath it, he picked up on small currents of dread. Ridhi's. Kamini's. Malav's.

And somewhere, too, worry from Hetal and Amar. Nilesh

322

could feel Hetal trying to tame hers before it escalated into full-blown panic.

It was like being battered by a hurricane. He got why Kamini had almost ripped his head off when he'd socked that tree. A beech, he knew now. The beech hadn't deserved it, any more than the human Nilesh had deserved Dad's recklessness.

But taking in all the joy in front of him, the celebration of spring, love, and the eternal union between Radha and Krishna, Nilesh admitted he could've reacted better.

The hurt from his family's betrayal was still there, sure, like someone had chopped off one of his branches. But it wasn't the end.

In what felt like just a few breaths in and out, carbon dioxide metamorphosing into oxygen, the feast had been eaten, and King Kubera and Queen Kauberi sat on their thrones on the royal dais.

Nilesh spotted Ridhi. She was coated in rainbow colors, like an extra in a Bollywood movie, with her wild curls that leaked flower petals whenever she moved. Malav was there with her, holding himself like he was waiting for something.

Ridhi, Nilesh thought.

Ridhi frowned in his direction, obviously puzzled. But she turned away and whispered something to Malav. Nilesh got a nervous energy off her.

Another bruise he couldn't do anything to heal.

Malav and Sulochana swapped glances across the way. Nilesh tried to analyze the feeling between them, but the other guests' anticipation diluted it.

He located Ishika. She was farther back in the crowd, watching while pretending to take part. Prakash and Kamini were actually playing, but Kamini didn't look like she was having fun. More like she wanted to kill Prakash. If she'd been throwing stones and not powders, he'd be bleeding on the ground.

And there was Hetal, looking dazed and laugh-crying. The blackish brown of her hair had almost disappeared under patches of blue and orange and green, like jelly beans had melted on it.

Nilesh knew she had no idea where he was. But again, he was powerless to do anything except watch.

Amar cleared a route so Hetal could navigate her wheelchair through a bunch of kids pelting one another with colors. A girl flung some pink at her.

"Hey!" Hetal lobbed powder right back from the golden tray on her lap. The girl squealed and ducked. Both of them giggled.

On the outside, it was a terrific celebration. A bash for the ages, Amar would've said. He'd moved on to flirting with a couple of yakshinis. All three of them were caked in powder.

But why hadn't he gone home like Nilesh had asked? Why hadn't Hetal?

Nilesh knew the answer. They'd stayed for his sake. That made him sad, but he didn't feel it so hard anymore. Being a tree was calming. More calming than he'd ever dreamed.

Time changed everything if you waited long enough. Time would change this, too.

The guests eventually ran out of colors. Some collapsed in

delirious piles on the grass. Attendants gave out fresh coconut water in addition to barfi, pink chum chum, and saffron penda. Someone had also restocked the spicy snack tables. Nilesh felt the ghost of hunger.

Ridhi, however, wasn't looking at the food. She stuck by Sulochana, who was chatting with Prakash and some nobles Nilesh didn't recognize.

The round, deep sound of a conch shell being blown cut through the drone of talking. At the royal dais, a herald announced, "Their Majesties will begin receiving their guests. Please present yourself at this queue if you wish to offer tribute."

A lot of people must have wished to. A line instantly began to form at the base of the dais.

Ridhi hurried toward it, but Sulochana hung back. She was too busy scouring the crowds. Her gaze stopped on Ishika, who was watching her just as intently.

They glanced away from each other, but when Sulochana strolled past Ishika to join the line, Nilesh could have sworn their hands brushed. It was so fast, it didn't seem real, but he was pretty sure something had passed between them.

A message? Why would Sulochana have anything to say to her?

Nilesh thought again of how Ishika had bought his debt.

As far as he could tell, no one else had seen a thing. Not Ridhi, who'd been at Sulochana's side. Not even Prakash.

Still, Nilesh was willing to bet he hadn't imagined it. Trees had clearer sight than humans, since they didn't allow themselves to be influenced by what they wanted to be true.

He strained to get through to Ridhi. She needed to know he was there.

Ridhi! he called, shaking his leaves. *Ridhi!*

24

Ridhi had lost count of the hours she'd stood in the massive line with Sulochana, even with attendants waving everyone along. Every living yaksha and yakshini in the kingdom must have come to curry favor with the maharaja and maharani and receive their blessing in return.

No one else appeared to mind the wait. The aspirants were chatting and laughing, greeting old friends and reuniting with family members, and gorging themselves on goodies from the various refreshment stands. A royal enchantment had transformed their clothes into priceless botanical silks and cleansed the lingering traces of powder from their arms and faces. Their ornate gem-and-blossom gold jewelry seemed a net designed to capture Lord Surya's light.

Ridhi was certain they had never looked more distinguished. She herself sported a delicate sari of lantana inflorescences, each cluster composed of concentric circles in orange, pink, yellow, and purple. It was spring made substance and shone against the brown of her skin.

Yet she felt like throwing up. If Sulochana weren't dosing her with elixir as necessary, she would have.

Ridhi rocked back and forth on her heels. Despite what she'd told Hetal and Amar, she *was* concerned about Nilesh. He'd already gotten himself in trouble once in Alakapuri.

Where was he?

"Patience," counseled Sulochana. "I have waited four centuries for this. I can afford to wait a few minutes more."

The supplicants before them presented all manner of goods from carved furniture to new breeds of plants to wares that might have come from the Night Market, like a necklace of stars that bestrewed constellations over the wearer. One even had a troupe of humans perform a dance that involved juggling fire and swords. Sulochana, though, didn't appear perturbed in the least.

Ridhi supposed that was fair. Her dance was merely the prelude to their tribute.

She could see why Sulochana was content to wait. The contrast between the other supplicants' largesse and her own would lend hers even more brilliance. Her name would once again be on the lips of singers and storytellers, but for a far different reason.

Up to then, all the petitions for small favors, like a new house or a blessing on an orchard, had been granted. Of those seeking parcels of land, however, only five met with a yes. The recipients were directed to schedule a meeting with the minister of holdings.

To the best of Ridhi's knowledge, Sulochana remained unconcerned. Her own palms were slick with nervous perspiration. She reached into her bag and tapped the vial of perfume she would soon offer up before initiating her dance.

A breeze blew, causing the bells on her anklets to tinkle. Aranyani Devi might be laughing on her way past.

Ridhi had to smile. *Just a dance and a wish*, she told herself. *Then all of this will be yours, too.*

As Sulochana and she neared the dais, lampposts wreathed in pink and red roses kindled with metallic flames and emanated a magnetic fragrance. Rose was such a complex smell, caught somewhere between seductive and sweet to overpowering and even repugnant—it varied from cultivar to cultivar and from day to day—but Ridhi had never smelled anything like these.

The extract of desire and mystery—oh, the blends she would make!

But the image was swept out of her head as she took in the wealth piled before the dais. Sulochana had told her any material gifts would be redistributed among the guests, chiefly the commoners, yet seeing it collected there made Ridhi realize just how many people would be watching her dance and deliver her perfume. That left her more ill at ease than ever.

Eight supplicants separated Ridhi and Sulochana from the dais. Ridhi glimpsed the dual thrones and the majestic monarchs who sat upon them, and her palms dampened.

Malav and Kamini approached them together, winsome in fresh outfits of leaf and flower, twig and ivy. Malav's turban glimmered with the same gold that looped through his earlobes and adorned

Kamini's neck, wrists, fingers, and ears.

Yet for all their glamour, they still lacked something—Nilesh.

"Where have you been?" Sulochana demanded.

Malav inclined his head in apology. "I was conversing with some friends and lost track of the time." He brought a hand to Ridhi's cheek. He was so warm, so suave.

But would he still be if she chose not to make his wish?

She waited until he was deep in discussion with Sulochana to lean close to Kamini and whisper, "Where's Nilesh? No one can find him!"

The tiniest of tremors crept across Kamini's lovely features. Her gold-dusted eyes rolled to the side, alluding to Sulochana. "I regret to report that he is otherwise occupied."

"Occupied how?"

"We have our anchor," Sulochana said, without looking over. "That is what matters."

Ridhi's stomach felt like she'd been hurled into Nilesh's pit. "But you said our anchor was a tree."

"Oh, he is," Kamini replied grimly. Her voice dropped. "Ridhi, it is too late. Do your best and accept Sulochana's recompense. Perhaps one day, we will be able to free him."

Free him? Nilesh was a tree? What?

But the opportunity for asking questions had ended. Attendants were beckoning their party forward.

Part of Ridhi wanted to make it stop. It was too soon. She wasn't ready. This was going to blow up in her face.

Malav must have intuited the waves of frantic energy rolling

330

off her. "Remember what I told you," he murmured. It wasn't as supportive as Ridhi assumed he meant it to be.

Kamini only twisted her fingers together.

"Come," Sulochana said. "This is our moment."

Somehow, Ridhi strode up the staircase without tripping over herself.

And then they were onstage before King Kubera and Queen Kauberi. The maharaja and maharani, imposing in silks of palm frond and frangipani petal, sat straighter on their thrones.

Sulochana bent to touch their chappaled feet. "Your Majesties, I come before you today in supplication."

As she straightened, King Kubera dabbed her forehead with a resin like a hunter-green version of the vermilion kumkum Ridhi was accustomed to. "Rise, Lady Sulochana. What would you ask of us?"

"My king, my queen," she declaimed, "I have thought long and hard about how I might prove my devotion to you. Four hundred years ago, a grave wrong was committed on these very premises. With your leave, I would create for us a much more pleasant memory in its stead."

Queen Kauberi rested her chin on her hand. "Do continue."

"As you will." Sulochana addressed the audience. "Fellow citizens of Alakapuri, Holi is a time of renewal. A time when we may repair sundered relationships. A time when we may rid ourselves of the many impurities acquired through the very act of living. In that vein, may I—"

"Your Majesties, Lady Sulochana is not to be trusted!" Malav

331

vaulted onto the dais with the grace of a gazelle.

The crowd had hardly broken into gasps and exclamations when Rakesh and Saanvi joined him. Saanvi wore a circlet of dewberry brambles, like a darker version of Ridhi's flower crowns.

"He speaks true," Saanvi affirmed. Rakesh raised his golden mace high.

Ridhi had to have fallen into an angst-induced hallucination. Malav, allied with sinister Rakesh? It made zero sense. "Malav?"

Malav didn't spare her a single glance, only gave the monarchs a perfunctory bow. "You see, Majesties, this mortal girl deceived my cousin and her tender heart, just as you have chosen to be deceived. While you allow mortals to run amok in our kingdom, they commit vile trespasses behind your backs!"

"What buffoonery is this?" snapped Queen Kauberi.

Undeterred, Malav held up a miniature forest identical to the one he'd cultivated for Ridhi. "This is the very same tool with which she instigated crimes in Alakapuri's name, ripped from my hands."

Ridhi felt like he'd slapped her. *You liar.*

Sulochana's lips pursed. "Your Majesty, I assure you that I know nothing of what my cousin rants. Have you taken leave of your wits, Malav?"

"Hardly." Malav insinuated himself between his friends. "My companions and I witnessed her desecration of mortal buildings. She refers to it as 'rewilding,' with no care for who, mortal or yaksha, might be harmed in the process."

Rakesh and Saanvi both grinned, a horrid collage of teeth like spearheads. "We attest to the validity of this allegation, Your Majesties," Saanvi hissed.

Brambles. The thought was almost buried under Ridhi's growing shock and shame. Hadn't Nilesh mentioned someone like that? *Thorn tiaras.*

They must be the yakshas who had trapped him in the pit!

Cringing, Ridhi flashed back to kissing Malav by the waterfall and how romantic she'd found it. How he had "rescued" her from Rakesh. Some fairy-tale prince.

It must have been a setup, all of it. How could Malav have done that to her?

Suddenly she was hyperventilating. Rakesh winked at her, and, still wheezing, she shied away.

Things are not as they seem, indeed.

Gods, was she the most gullible person in all the worlds?

Scores of fanged yakshas and yakshinis charged the stage, armed with maces and swords. The onlookers' exclamations turned to screams, but packed in as they were, they couldn't flee.

"Be calm, citizens of Alakapuri!" commanded the herald.

Ridhi didn't move, her pulse as rapid as a bunny's.

"My companions and I have come to call for changes, Your Majesties," Malav asserted.

The trees within range all shivered, trying to address Ridhi, but she couldn't listen. What good was that comfort when she'd been played for a fool? When she was being humiliated before the yaksha kingdom and its rulers?

She wanted to pummel him. *And to think I liked you!*

Sulochana and the maharani shared a weary look as if to say, *Upstart.*

Queen Kauberi murmured to her counselors and her husband, then settled back against her throne.

"Child," she said, conferring an imperious smile on Malav, "you are but a sprout, with an undeveloped sense of discernment. These allies with whom you have cast your lot? They have exploited you."

Rakesh laughed. "You have sequestered us in Alakapuri, yet you claim that we are the ones in the wrong? The whelp merely showed compassion for our predicament. Free us, *Queen.*"

Then, in a blur of motion, he leaped into the audience, captured Kamini, and hauled her onto the stage. "You wish to heal relationships?" he asked, his blade at her throat. "Then redress this injustice you have done to us."

Ridhi's petrified body went cold. Poor Kamini!

"What are you doing?" Malav shouted. Ridhi almost—but not quite—pitied him. Had he really believed he controlled the situation? "This was not part of our agreement!"

The guards moved to converge on him, but some of Rakesh's cronies had mounted the dais and stymied them.

"Ah," said Rakesh, "perhaps I wish to revisit the terms." He jiggled the dagger. Kamini stood so still in his clutches, she might have been one of the sculptures carved on the front of the dais.

Saanvi bared her teeth. "The kingdom is long overdue for new rulership. And we are the ideal candidates."

"Is that so?" The maharani gesticulated, a negligent swivel of her bangle-covered arm. In response, a vine of Indian jasmine burst from the stage in full bloom and coiled around Rakesh's dagger.

Another gyration, and the blade clattered on the platform near the feet of the guards, who scrambled to confiscate it.

A third, and vines twined around the wrists and ankles of Rakesh, Saanvi, and the rest of their horde.

Kamini tore free a beat later, seeking shelter with Ridhi. The desolation on her face as she beheld her brother struck Ridhi harder even than Rakesh's leering by the waterfall.

"I do not suppose," said King Kubera, "that Rakesh detailed why, precisely, his ilk and he have been sequestered?" When Rakesh deigned not to speak, the maharaja addressed Malav. "Naturally not. They have repeatedly violated the injunction against feeding on mortals. We had no choice but to seclude them."

Feeding on mortals? Ridhi let out an involuntary squeak. Rakesh could have chewed on *her* if he'd been in the mood. And Malav had, deliberately or not, put her in that situation.

"It might have been worse," said an advisor to the maharaja. "We should have relegated them to solitary confinement."

Queen Kauberi frowned him into submission before turning to Malav. "Without you to open the channel," she noted, "they would have been unable to travel to Prithvi. What if they had dined on the mortals there?"

Malav's slitted eyes were mutinous. "If they are so dangerous, then why permit them a game?"

"Everyone needs an occupation," said King Kubera. "As you, child, have newly proven."

"Stand down, Malav," warned Sulochana. "Do not worsen your plight."

He stuck out his chin, unrepentant. "I will not. Not until you remove the mortals."

"Guards, you may collect the miscreants," decreed the maharani, her tone fatigued. "As they have shown they cannot be trusted to value a more lenient penalty, remove them to the dungeons."

More royal guards surged across the stage, making swift work of Rakesh's associates. Ridhi and Kamini stared at Malav, who looked past them both.

Sulochana grasped Ridhi's chin, forcing their gazes to meet. "Breathe."

Ridhi did, counting in sets of four, until her nervous system calmed. Kamini, meanwhile, had disappeared back into the audience.

"Now," said the maharani warmly, "I believe you were saying, Lady Sulochana?"

The sea of spectators hushed, and Sulochana resumed her speech. "Your Majesties, I have thought long and hard about how I might prove my devotion to you. I once sought a parcel of land. Today I would bestow upon you a gift."

The trees rustled again. Ridhi sank inward, beyond her impression of being apart, into her affinity with the forest.

A bough bumped against her mind.

Nilesh! She'd found him. Or, more accurately, he'd found her.

Be careful, he warned.

But the threat was already eradicated. Wasn't it?

The Kalpavriksha. The branch. I have it.

Ridhi wasn't sure what he meant, but something that had been niggling at the back of her head clicked into place. She'd been careful not to tell anyone she'd seen the Kalpavriksha's branch. And yet Sulochana had known. She'd mentioned it not appearing to Mummy.

Sulochana had befriended the jungle crow, potentially the same crow that had brought Ridhi the seed for the perfume that had gained her access to the enchanted forest. Had Sulochana also been the golden deer that had guided her to the portal?

Did Sulochana do this to you? she asked Nilesh.

He didn't answer.

His reticence worried her, but this was her chance. She couldn't think about how she'd left her family behind without so much as a farewell. She couldn't think about how Nilesh had been turned into a tree, or that Sulochana had kept her in the dark and that she had been fine with it.

Only Ridhi was going to divine a leaf from the Kalpavriksha. Her knees grew wobbly at the notion.

Sulochana indicated Ridhi with a sweep of her arm. "In tribute, this mortal girl would dance and gift you a fragrance bearing the very heart of our woodland. Yet it is no mere perfume; it wields the ability to wake remembrance even in other mortals. A sylvan sousing, if you will."

The monarchs regarded each other thoughtfully, then waggled their heads. "Show us," said King Kubera.

Showtime, Ridhi thought.

She touched the monarchs' feet just as Sulochana had. "Your

Majesties, it is my privilege and immeasurable honor to present this humble perfume to you today. It was inspired by that pearl above all pearls, the Kalpavriksha, and with it, I can invoke for you an image of that blessed tree. May I bring it to you?"

The monarchs' mien instantly sharpened. Until that moment, Ridhi had been a mere oddity to them, a momentary diversion. They were as old as the hills they inhabited, and little existed in the way of novelty to captivate them.

But a chance to view their beloved Kalpavriksha again? *That* warranted their interest.

Careful to contain his emotion, King Kubera waved her on.

With a nod at Sulochana, Ridhi passed the vial of Keeper of the Woodlands to the maharani. If hearts could inhale, hers was holding its breath.

Queen Kauberi took the perfume and uncapped it with beringed fingers. She tipped a drop onto the leaf that had appeared in her hand, sniffed deeply, and sent the leaf oscillating through the sky. As the scent reached their noses, the faces of King Kubera, the advisors, and the guards all shifted subtly.

Wonder burgeoned in Ridhi's chest. Had Sulochana known this would happen?

"Now," Sulochana whispered, "dance."

Ridhi proceeded to sway, her movements augmenting the fragrant immersion.

She danced the forest itself. Its sheer majesty flooded her with reverence. She could feel how she belonged there. How it would be less without her tiny presence within it. Gold coins of sunlight dappled the grassy floor. Butterflies flitted like sprites from bush to berry-laden bush. The mossy sari that wove over her was as soft as any velvet, and streamers of wisteria hung from her hair like ribbons. And, of course, she wore her jewel-strung mekhala, identifying herself as a creature of the trees.

The audience of yakshas and yakshinis below observed, quiescent, transported by the aromatic story Ridhi spun. Although she still had a decision ahead of her, she wouldn't have traded this moment for anything.

She danced a rainbow in the role of a door. That door—that portal—opened on the dais, and golden beams cascaded through.

At first, all anyone, even Ridhi, could see was the glint of metal. Then branches of gold and silver. A trunk of gold and gemstone leaves, which reflected the light of Lord Surya like highly polished mirrors until it seemed to gild the city.

Alakapuri and its guests watched, agog, as the Kalpavriksha materialized within the portal. Unlike the intangible impressions of Ridhi's perfume, the wish tree's physicality couldn't be denied.

Nobody said a word. Even the maharaja and maharani could only gape.

Sulochana put her palms together before her face. "A gift of the mortal girl. Ridhi, pluck the leaf."

The Kalpavriksha towered over the dais, anchored by Nilesh's unseen presence. The crowd's stunned silence erupted into an uproar.

"Lady Sulochana," demanded the maharaja, "cease this insubordination!"

Sulochana ignored him. "Now," she insisted.

The seconds were ticking away. Ridhi's body moved into autopilot, responding to her training. She left off dancing and gazed up at the gold-and-silver tree with its leafage of precious stones. It was at once ancient and ageless. She could easily imagine it rising from the mythical waters of the cosmic Ocean of Milk during Samudra Manthan, one of fourteen treasures to come forth.

The Kalpavriksha. All Ridhi had to do was comply, and she would be part of the sisterhood. She would never be alone again.

The potency that radiated from the wish tree submerged the city, the possibilities of wishes she could never apprehend fanning out alongside wishes that her heart sympathized with all too well.

Everyone was connected, a root system in the great forest. How was this so hard for people to grasp? She could feel it in every capillary in her body, each one a branch.

More cries rent the air. Yet having no desire to break the tenuous bond, she kept her awareness on the wish tree.

Tears filled her eyes. This was the Kalpavriksha of legend. She was about to pluck a leaf from the most mystical of trees, whose might was said to rival that of the gods themselves.

The amethyst, said the tree.

Ridhi was vaguely aware of guards approaching, of the maharaja and maharani commanding her to halt. But she chose an amethyst leaf, which fulgurated with an inner radiance. Of her own volition, she fell into that radiance.

It was the magic, the wish tree's warm, living enchantment.

The tree, however, was in pain. A piece of it had been stolen.

Without the missing branch, it had become diseased. The branch, too, longed for reunion, but it had been grafted onto another tree. Another sacred fig—the anchor holding the portal open.

Ridhi ached at the loss. Her eyes had adjusted to the tree's dazzle, and she spied the sickly white riddling the healthy aureate and argent, the bulbous scar where a single branch had been severed.

"You see," Sulochana proclaimed, "this is my tribute to you. The truth. Four hundred years ago, a falsehood was spread, a falsehood that caught fire and burned innocent lives to ashes."

A falsehood? Ridhi glanced over to see the jungle crow on Sulochana's shoulder. Suddenly she understood. No, the golden deer hadn't been Sulochana.

Ridhi knew even before the bird transformed, becoming the comely yet reviled Ishika. All along, the trees had been telling her.

Sulochana had lied. She had no intention of healing the Kalpavriksha.

The audience bellowed with outrage. "Ishika the Immoral!" someone jeered. "Degenerate wretch!"

"Deceitful reprobate!" yelled someone else.

Queen Kauberi sprang to her feet. The noise of the crowd, even of the nearby advisors and guards, cut off like a door had been closed, yet her voice still rang out. "Lady Sulochana! What is the meaning of this?"

Ridhi assumed the maharani had insulated the principal players on the dais, blocking them from being heard by the populace. With that much power at her disposal, Rakesh's attempt at a coup must have seemed like a child's tantrum.

"Enough!" Ishika barked. "Do you truly believe we care for what you, of all people, have to say?" She didn't appear the least bit harrowed by the guards that had hemmed them in, weapons trained on their heads. "*We* possess the branch, and for once, you shall do what we say."

She took Sulochana's hand with a smile as tender as new shoots.

Sulochana's righteous fury softened into unabashed ardor. "At last, my jaan." She curled Ishika's fingers around her own. "It has been torture without you."

"After today, never again," Ishika said fiercely, kissing her.

Lovers. They were still lovers. This was the true spectacle Sulochana had promised.

Ridhi saw the same realization dawn on the monarchs. Sulochana and Ishika had played them for fools in a long game. But what could possibly have been so terrible that they gave up being together for the sake of revenge?

"You sacrificed us without a second thought, and you thought it would simply be forgotten?" Sulochana's face was a wrathful mask. "Disclose the truth, or we will summon Lord Indra ourselves."

"And this time," Ishika added, "war will be inevitable."

25

Before he'd made contact with Ridhi, Nilesh had virtually forgotten being human. He'd been losing more of himself with each second that went by.

But the same way he served as anchor for the Kalpavriksha, she served as anchor for him.

It felt like two trees interlacing their branches. Nilesh held on tight. He sensed that Ridhi was, too. In the past, his human self would have busted a gut laughing at the suggestion of a bond between them.

But now that it was a thing, it helped him remember who he really was.

The jeweled branch grafted onto him was calling for its real tree, the Kalpavriksha from the portal. The Kalpavriksha, covered in ugly white marks, was calling back. Nilesh could feel how the two parts of the wish tree begged to be one again.

If they were going to be reunited, it would take both Ridhi and him. It was his turn to be the anchor for her.

He shook his leaves. It was a message no one else could intercept, and she heard him.

Don't let that stump you. It's not like you'll get in trouble for being knotty.

He might be a tree, but he could still mess with her.

Ridhi was gobsmacked. *Did you just make a tree joke?*

Maybe. I'll never tell.

She surveyed Sulochana and Ishika. Malav and Rakesh. King Kubera and Queen Kauberi. Through her eyes, Nilesh could see details on the human scale.

Unfortunately, that meant that he could feel with the heart he didn't have anymore, too. All the memories of Dad and Mom. Of Hetal. Of Amar and their shenanigans. All the anger, all the pain.

All the misery of learning that no matter how well you thought you knew someone, they could always shock you.

But Nilesh felt something else. Regret.

He'd run away, but in the end, it hadn't changed anything. Like his fellow trees with their roots in the earth, he was linked to his family in a network he couldn't pretend didn't exist.

Sometimes, Nilesh knew, you had to burn deadwood and never look back. And other times you had to get through the drought or the blight or the people trying to chop you down and grow another ring.

It had taken her a while, but even Kamini had figured that out.

Ridhi's forehead puckered. *I don't know if I like being attached to you like this. Get out of my head.*

Yeah, well, you don't have much of a choice. What happened to being such a fun girl?

Trees couldn't make faces, but Nilesh tried his hardest to get the sentiment across. Ridhi twitched, so it must have worked.

Below the dais where she stood, yakshas and yakshinis fidgeted. The guards had detained Malav and Rakesh and were carting off the members of their gang, and only the people still on the dais could hear what was going on up there.

His larger perspective notwithstanding, Nilesh was glad for his front-row seat. Sure, Malav had a point about the yaksha kingdom and its politics and human interference. That said, his solution was just as bad.

But gloating would have to wait. The Kalpavriksha had talked to Ridhi, and she'd plucked the leaf. Now she had to make her wish.

Nilesh could feel how unsure she was. Sulochana had claimed she would use the leaf to heal the wish tree. But that had been a trick. A front for her own scheme.

So what should Ridhi do?

What about the future she'd been promised? Should she wish for that?

Not so fast, he warned her.

You don't get it. I . . . I can't lose magic, she whimpered. *I can't.*

Nilesh knew what she would be giving up if she didn't make that wish, because she showed it to him. Her chance to live in her enchanted forest and be part of a sisterhood that got her at the deepest level.

He felt how scared she was to be deprived of that. He saw how lonely she'd been, how everyone had told her how weird she was. How he'd been just as crappy as the rest of them.

345

Another blunder he'd take back if he could.

No, he didn't owe her his friendship. But he wanted her to have it, which was better.

Easy for you to say, she said. *Everyone's always liked you.*

More people would like her, too, if she colored inside the lines. Like he'd gotten her to do at the grocery store. Except that would be a mistake. More than a mistake—a waste.

Friends don't let friends wish on magical trees alone, he quipped. *Especially if that friend is a tree.*

Ridhi traced the veins on her jewel leaf. *You can't stay like this, you know.*

Why not?

Because you can't. People need you. You have to go home.

I'm trapped here—

You know what I mean, she said. *We'll fix it.* With a smirk, she added, *You're not so bad as a tree, though.*

Nilesh thought about that. Everything—everyone—he'd deserted would still be waiting for him, and he'd have to deal with all of it. All of them.

He gave the branchy equivalent of a shrug. *You try having squirrels climb all over you and never shut up and see how great it is.*

It was far from his best line, but Ridhi choked out a laugh. *So I really have to do this, huh? I have to make this wish.*

Whatever you pick, he said, *I've got your back. You know that, right?*

She sighed. *Malav—*

Malav's a two-faced twerp. You can do better.

Ridhi bit her cheek. Her fear of going back to how her life had

346

been was so strong, it would have knocked Nilesh out if he weren't rooted in the ground.

Luckily, he was.

Harnessing Alakapuri's soil with those roots, he sent a flicker of spring into her. She glanced from him to the Kalpavriksha.

The guards were almost on her.

You get to choose, he said. *But you have to decide, one way or the other. Now.*

She raised her head high. *So* I'm *saving* you, she said with a mental cackle. *You make a cute damsel in distress.*

Nilesh rattled his branches in mock offense. *Hey, watch it!*

Ridhi took a long breath. *I think I'm ready—*

Then Prakash appeared on the dais beside her.

26

Ridhi's insides went into free fall as Prakash, with a self-congratulatory strut, ascended the stage to stand at her side.

Wait, he'd known about Sulochana and Ishika's ploy? And gone along with it?

"Four hundred years later," Ishika accused the maharani, "you remain too great a coward to expose your complicity. And to think I was once flattered to sit at your feet! To call you my liege and serve in your court."

"What's happening?" Ridhi asked. She was so confused.

Both Sulochana and Ishika turned to her. "Her Majesty has always desired to propagate a wish tree of her own," said Sulochana. "Yet why sully her royal hands when she could request that her devoted subjects dirty theirs in her stead?"

So Queen Kauberi was behind the idea of stealing the Kalpavriksha's branch? That certainly seemed to be what Sulochana was implying.

But that would mean Ishika . . .

It was almost too much for Ridhi to process. Was anyone there *not* embroiled in labyrinthine schemes?

Whoa, said Nilesh.

Whoa is right, she agreed.

Ishika waggled her head. "I also thought it unwise to bind ourselves so to another kingdom and its charity. What if that should be rescinded one day? And with mortal gadgetry and greed progressing as they were . . ."

Ridhi dared a glance at the monarchs. They sat motionless but infuriated.

"Fool that I am, I did as I was bade. And believed it an honor to boot! None of us could have presaged the Kalpavriksha's deterioration as a result of the theft." Ishika glowered at the maharani. "Yet when Lord Indra attacked, you chose to conceal the truth and cast me in the role of villain."

Again Ridhi felt the Kalpavriksha's agony, now coupled with Ishika's. She could picture the scenario in lucid detail: Ishika had believed herself the maharani's darling tasked with saving the kingdom, for which the monarchs and she would be showered in glory. But if it failed, as it had, the blame would land squarely on her shoulders.

How cruel and cold, yet how politically savvy. No wonder she was livid.

"All to save face." Sulochana's animosity might have been its own entity. "We trusted you, liege. And this is how you repaid our dedication?"

King Kubera looked away, but to her credit, Queen Kauberi didn't.

"You devastated us, our very existence, all without a single qualm. I vowed that I would not permit Your Majesty to bury this, that I would bring it to light no matter how many centuries it took." Sulochana's smile was rueful. "I had not foreseen that Malav would seek to usurp my moment, but the young are full of surprises."

"As we speak," Ishika said, "Lord Indra doubtless leads his army forth. Confess, Maharani! Cancel this curtain of silence so the many worlds might learn how willing you are to sacrifice your adoring subjects for the sake of your pride."

"A true queen would defend those subjects even at the cost of her reputation." Sulochana stared witheringly at the maharani. "How many times over our luncheons did I hint that you might reconsider? How many times did you make light of it? I think you wished to forget this machination was your idea."

Queen Kauberi heaved a beleaguered sigh. "What do you know of ruling? The people must have faith in their leaders. Without it, our realm would fragment and fall. The maharaja and I must ensure the sovereignty of Alakapuri at all costs."

Poison oak shrubs pushed up around Sulochana's ankles. "You find the life and dignity of my love an acceptable price to pay?"

"If that is the case," put in Prakash, "who is to say you do not view your other subjects as equally expendable?"

The maharani took no account of their questions. "There is yet time to reinstate the wish tree. Do it now, and Lord Indra need not darken our door."

"That will not occur until you confess to our kingdom who is truly at fault," Ishika said stoutly. She caressed Sulochana's cheek with a touch so ardent, Ridhi felt like a voyeur just being on the same dais with them.

Queen Kauberi appeared scandalized. "I cannot do such a thing. Surely you see that!"

"Then we are at a stalemate," said Sulochana, "and the war you had hoped so fervently to avoid will ensue."

Ridhi thought she could make an argument for both sides. She wouldn't deny that the monarchs had gravely misused Ishika, but she could also see why they had kept the reality of the situation under wraps.

This was why she had no interest in court politics. Where did you begin untangling such an old, thorny dilemma?

Oh, to have her tree and go there now, where the only drama was between the squirrels and the birds fighting over nuts.

What does the Kalpavriksha think? Nilesh asked. *It was talking to you, right?*

It had only told her which leaf to choose, but if she were to ask, maybe it would have more to say. Bejeweled leaf in hand, Ridhi reached for the wish tree.

Another voice entered the fray. "Cease this," said Hamshi.

The sisterhood had arrived.

"Sulochana, Ishika, Your Majesties," she continued, "you know this is wrong. Innocents should never be made to pay for the misdeeds of a few."

"And what of Ishika?" Sulochana countered. "Was *she* not an innocent?"

The calls of the Kalpavriksha and the amputated branch drew

Ridhi in, overriding the argument onstage.

Heal me, rustled the wish tree. Its voice was pure and bright, with the resonance of a thousand trees. *Only you can.*

Its shimmer bathed her heart, its wisdom her mind. Ridhi could feel her bond to it, to the forest at large. To the land itself and beyond.

She could feel Kamini and Hetal and Amar. She could feel the sisterhood and Mummy. Nilesh, who was grounding her. Kartik and Papa. Aruna Auntie and Dilip Uncle. Even Shreya and Chetan Gopalkrishnan. All of Alakapuri, all of Prithvi was connected like the network of tree roots nestled in its soil.

It was when people forgot that, when they thought solely of themselves or swindled others so they might prosper, that problems arose.

Life was about balance. When that balance was disturbed, the repercussions rippled outward. Neither humans nor plants were always good to one another. Some were parasitic. Some were invasive. When the balance was upheld, however, the world flourished.

The mistake was always in the taking without permission, the hoarding. Lord Indra had been too proud to share more of his prize than the periodic leaf, and Queen Kauberi and King Kubera had been too proud to reprise their petition that he do so.

They had failed to recognize that the Kalpavriksha, while one of the fourteen great ratnas, was, fundamentally, a tree. And trees could be propagated, through cuttings and seed and grafting. Through doubling.

Things are not as they seem. Things are not as they seem. Things are not as they seem! susurrated the forest.

What Ridhi had misconstrued as comfort was exactly the inverse.

She still craved magic. She would always crave magic. But not like this.

The Kalpavriksha was right to say only she could heal it. That wasn't technically accurate; nothing was hindering Ishika or the maharani from doing so. But because they were locked in their pattern, they were oblivious to a third option.

Ridhi wasn't. It had all sounded so simple before, when she'd fancied herself the heroine of her daydreams. But no one had to look over in daydreams and see their old friend transformed through trickery.

Neither was Nilesh. *Are you ready?* he asked.

Yes.

Before the others could piece together her plan, amethyst leaf in her fingers, perfume on her wrists, Ridhi began to dance for a second time.

All around her, through her, proliferated a realm of sun-dappled greenery. Of blossoms and branches, foxes and fireflies, sparrows and serpents. Moss, pine needles, twigs, rocks. Berries everywhere she stepped, the lethal ones rendered edible within the boundaries of the yaksha kingdom.

She visualized a door opening in that forest, a glimmering rectangle taking shape in the air, its edges spreading until she could see into another domain altogether.

A glorious, supernal place, home to Indra, lord of the demigods, and his queen Indrani. Ridhi glimpsed scintillating beings, their skin a radiant brown and their hair as luminous and rich as starlight, gathered within a splendid silver palace while concurrently burning bright against the vast expanse of the universe.

But it was not the stars she sought.

Ridhi danced another story, one of a tree birthed from a cosmic ocean in the sky, that darkness some called a void, and others termed the origin of all things. This tree, formed of wish magic, had come forth from that ocean, yet now it resided in the pleasure garden of the maharaja and maharani of Svargalok.

Ridhi's fingers splayed to form petals. Her hip jutted out in summons. Her body told a tale of invitation, of conjuring. Of a golden tree that could, for the space of a moment, propagate itself in two places at once. How, in that same moment, its dual nature might go unobserved by any in the paradise garden.

How, once the deed was done, peace would predominate in both its abodes.

"Stop her!" someone ordered, suspending the spell.

Keep going! Nilesh urged.

The blood roared like a waterfall in Ridhi's ears, making it nearly impossible for her to hear his encouragement. All the stage fright she'd believed conquered struck her like Lord Indra's thunderbolt, paralyzing her.

So many pairs of eyes on her. It was like the dance audition again, but a thousandfold more pivotal.

Ridhi's throat constricted. What had she been thinking? She was just an overly trusting human girl, a mortal horribly out of her depth among otherworldly beings.

Oh, why had she listened to Nilesh, let alone to Sulochana?

"Guards!" cried Queen Kauberi.

Hurry! Nilesh mentally poked her in the ribs. *We're running out of time!*

Ridhi couldn't do it. She shook her head.

You have to, he insisted. *Don't worry about the dance. Just heal the tree!*

The sound of the guards grew louder, more threatening. In another second, they would have her in shackles.

Lord Indra's thunderbolt rumbled. The wheels of his chariot could be heard on the other side of the portal.

Leaves and branches spiraled through the air in a cyclone of foliage, scattered as if by a celestial hand. The desperation it transmitted was so stark that Ridhi barely needed to listen before the message rang in her ears.

You must persevere, said the trees. *There is no one else. And you must do it now.*

She looked at the amethyst leaf, then at Nilesh.

A hundred possible variations sprouted in her mind, half measures and defenses. She eschewed them all. *I wish for the Kalpavriksha to be healed.*

The purple leaf sparkled. A venerable power coursed up Ridhi's spine and out the crown of her head, leaving her dizzy.

She felt the grafted branch vanish from Nilesh, and she saw it then reappear on the Kalpavriksha, whose white blotches converted to gold and silver once more.

Shooting light in all directions, the Kalpavriksha receded. Without the anchor of Nilesh tying it to Alakapuri, Lord Indra's claim on it was recalling the wish tree to his paradise garden.

A few guards flung themselves at the contracting portal, arms outstretched, but it was too late. It closed as if it had never been.

Ridhi's heart was on the brink of imploding. She'd forfeited everything she'd ever hungered after.

But a rainbow gemstone dropped into her hand. A seed.

"Queen Kauberi!" she shouted. "Your Majesty! You have to listen!"

The maharani glared at her. "What did you do, mortal child?"

Sulochana and Ishika clutched each other. "Yes," echoed Sulochana, "what *did* you do?"

Dodging the guards' drawn swords, Ridhi raced toward the monarchs. "The Kalpavriksha gave me this."

"A seed," breathed King Kubera.

Ridhi thought of what the tree had shown her. "A seed for a Kalpavriksha all your own. But I want something in return."

Queen Kauberi snapped her fingers. "We could simply unburden you of the seed with ease."

"You're right," Ridhi said. "You could. But the thing is"—she grinned cheekily—"it will only work if freely given."

Her words were met with dead silence. Both Sulochana and Ishika looked as though they might fall over.

"You see," Ridhi went on, "that's where you went wrong. You didn't ask before you took. If you had, the Kalpavriksha would have helped you, regardless of what Lord Indra said."

"Aha," snarled Queen Kauberi. "Everything has a price. What is yours?"

Unlike at the Night Market, Ridhi wasn't going to haggle. "Two things. First, let's talk somewhere more private—"

What about me? Nilesh grumped.

He was rooted in the forest, a piece of it. The Kalpavriksha had emphasized that his time there would have lasting side effects. Even so, Ridhi was determined to take him home with her.

Be patient, will you? she scolded.

If I have to.

"Second," she concluded, "you restore my friend to his mortal body." She bowed her head. "Your Majesties."

The sisterhood of yakshinis, led by Hamshi, rallied around her. "I would pay her heed, Your Majesty," said Hamshi, her smile deceptively soft.

"Oh, I intend to," said the maharani. "This mortal girl has me quite intrigued, indeed."

PART THREE

*T*he broad bush, home of the rose sisters, is a sight to behold, with its pink-red thorns, dark-green leaves, and, of course, the garnet blossoms themselves, their sensuous fragrance a perfume even the maharani cannot resist. Listen, past the buzz-buzz-buzz of bees and the shh-shh-shh of butterfly wings, to the gossip of those little sisters still budding. Hear the supercilious observations of their elder sisters in full bloom. See how they hold themselves apart, petals ruffled by the commentary of their loquacious kin.

Oh, how the rose sisters quarrel! How they sulk and shout one moment, frightening the most inquisitive of squirrels. How they make amends the next, tempers calming, laughter flowing. Rejoicing in their own beauty, they preside over their realm, a court of preening, crimson-clad queens tangled together.

All but one.

She was rather shy, this one, and her thoughts, though nimble, came quiet, like the shadows her sisters cast in the noontime sun. While they sat in judgment on the peculiar daisies and the prideful hyacinths, she speculated about these others, envisioning herself a sun-bright dandelion; a melodious bluebell; a sweet yet wild honeysuckle flower.

One morning, a golden silk spider who frequented the rosebush returned to check the web of his ever-industrious mate in search of sustenance. He himself lifted not a leg to hunt, content to live off the spoils of her labor.

"Good morning!" he greeted our rose, anxious to recite the tales of his travels. She was the perfect audience, patient and wistful, unlike her sisters, who talked right past him.

The spider chittered his story over his purloined breakfast, but it was evident the rose was not listening. "What is it?" he queried.

"I no longer wish to hear about your grand adventures," replied the rose. "I am ready to experience them for myself!" Her petals shivered in anticipation. "Will you take me?"

Appalled, the spider could not speak. "You would leave your bush? Your family?" he asked, when at last he had recovered his wits. For such a meek blossom to trumpet her intentions like that—surely the skies themselves would trade places with the ground next!

"I would. Let us be off." The rose, who had already disconnected from her stem, descended onto his back. Uncertain how he had permitted this to occur, the lazy spider abandoned his repast and bore her away from the bush. Her sisters, too busy bickering over whose bloom was the loveliest that day, failed to mark her departure.

The rose and her mount soon passed a clump of dandelions, and she asked him to halt. So incandescent were the sunny flowers that the spider threw up his forelegs to blot them out. "Tell me," implored the rose, "what makes you special? I would learn your ways."

"We are tenacious," a dandelion said. "And you may stay as long as you wish." Her sisters and she recommenced their conversation, and the rose made herself comfortable beside them. Over time, her sepals grew greener with their optimism.

Yet all things end, and the rose knew she must resume her journey. She thanked the dandelions for their hospitality, and her new friend gifted the rose a dollop of their stamina. In return, the rose offered one of her thorns.

"Now I am tenacious, too," she said, and climbed aboard the spider's back.

They then traversed a field of bluebells. With their six upturned petals in blue violet, the bluebells appeared as distinct from the rose as the dandelions had. "Tell me," implored the rose, "what makes you special? I would learn your ways."

"We are uplifting," a bluebell said. "And you may stay as long as you wish." Her sisters and she tinkled with music that floated away on the breeze. Over time, the song chimed within the rose, enlivening her.

Yet all things end, and the rose knew she must resume her journey. She thanked the bluebells for their hospitality, and her new friend gifted the rose a sequence of notes from the song. In return, the rose offered one of her petals.

"Now I am uplifting, too," she said, and climbed aboard the spider's back.

They roamed until they came to a vine of honeysuckle. With their tubular blooms in pale pink and orange and their yellow pistils, the honeysuckle flowers appeared as distinct from the rose as the bluebells had. "Tell me," implored the rose, "what makes you special? I would learn your ways."

"We are wild," a honeysuckle blossom said. "And you may stay as long as you wish." Her sisters and she revealed the droplets of nectar that glistened at their centers like a secret.

Here the rose resided the longest, the honeysuckle guiding her to compose poems laced with daring, to dance freely with the breeze, and to dream.

Yet all things end, and the rose knew she must resume her journey. She thanked the honeysuckle flowers for their hospitality, and her new friend gifted the rose a droplet of nectar. In return, the rose offered a trace of her sultry scent.

"Now I am wild, too," she said, and climbed aboard the spider's back.

But when the weary spider asked where she desired to go next, she found she missed her sisters, their chatter, their bush. *"Home."*

The spider, fearing being saddled with yet another burden, delivered the rose to her stem and then fled the bush, to the acute relief of his long-suffering mate.

Oh, how the rose's sisters wept to see her again. *"We thought you had left us!"* accused one.

"We were so worried!" confessed a second.

"When did you become so bold?" pondered a third.

All together they cried, *"Tell us everything!"*

Our rose did precisely that, passing around the gifts she had gathered and relating what she had learned, to the amazement of her awestruck sisters, and never again did she feel unseen.

—FROM *THE TALES THAT TREES TELL*,

A COLLECTION FROM ALAKAPURI AND BEYOND

27

A solution so tidy, so perfect, it might have been a gift, took root in the loam of Ridhi's imagination. The Kalpavriksha's seed snug in her fist, she listened breathlessly as the notion sprouted.

We chose you, rustled the trees. *Go forth with our blessing.*

Ridhi located the link she shared with the Kalpavriksha. Although the wish tree had returned to Svargalok, she was bound to it, as was Nilesh. They always would be. The thought bolstered her spirit.

So, while chaos reigned—people shouting accusations she couldn't hear, guards storming the dais—Ridhi felt deep inside for the network of roots connecting her to the yaksha kingdom and beyond. The mayhem of the external world ebbed, displaced by the knowledge that she could salvage this situation.

Your perfume, whispered the Kalpavriksha. *Be prepared.*

The vitality encased in the seed throbbed in her hand. *I am.*

The Kalpavriksha, the yaksha kingdom itself, was counting on her. Not to mention poor Nilesh.

That part of her plan had succeeded; he stood there with her, human again and blinking rapidly in the sunlight. "You saved me," he mumbled.

Ridhi ducked her head. "Yeah."

When he smiled, it was warm, real. "Thanks, fun girl."

The guards swarmed them like rankled bees, trussing their hands behind their backs. At least the sisterhood had been able to slip away.

"Your Majesties!" Ridhi called. "The perfume. Use it!"

She'd been worried that the maharani might not hear, but Queen Kauberi unscrewed the lid and let fly the vial's contents. Borne aloft on a magical wind, the scent spread across the city once more, adroitly wielding its immersive spell. The clamoring for answers below abated, as did the shoving.

In their wake, peace glossed the city, peace and joy, accentuated by the lustrous wealth of petals still drizzling from above.

Ridhi tasted awe. *Her* perfume had done that.

What if that power functioned on Prithvi, too? She could take people like Shreya and Chetan Gopalkrishnan down ten pegs and influence them to treat her as she deserved to be treated. She could inveigle people like Nilesh's father to put his children first.

Ridhi could center herself in the chronicle of her life, the vision she'd nurtured with such care. She could be more than a pawn in other people's plots. She could be a yakshini *and* have her family.

The guards interrupted her contemplation, pushing with their gleaming swords and marshaling the monarchs, their advisors, and the members of Ridhi's wayward band into the palace.

It was the palace of her daydreams, with its extravagant furnishings, the intricate art wrought of plant interwoven with gilt, the abundance of flowers forming a garden that was both organic and conformed to an underlying motif. The chairs alone were an ivy lover's delight, and she should have been tempted to curl up on one. Yet with her task a neon sign flashing at the forefront of her thoughts, the details caromed off her, ephemeral.

The guards led Ridhi and her companions into a prodigious throne room, its ceiling cerulean sky. On the walls, portraits framed in leaves told of the yakshas' illustrious history. At pleasing intervals, golden fountains flowed with crystalline waters. And everywhere, trees rose high into the heavens, as old, as wise as the forest to which they belonged.

Engrossed in their susurrations, Ridhi failed to notice when the maharaja and the maharani assumed their royal seats, two immense chairs carved of gold and embellished with blossoms.

Nilesh bumped her shoulder with his, jerking her into the present, where the monarchs beheld the unlikely coterie before them with discontent.

Although she had just seen them outside, there in the throne room King Kubera and Queen Kauberi appeared less like people and more like mythical archetypes come alive, sweeping her along in the unfolding of their lengthy tale. Her anxiety mounted.

"It seems," King Kubera remarked wryly, "we have a problem."

Queen Kauberi's brow knit. "And how, precisely, shall we address said problem, my love?"

Ishika and Sulochana, whose wrists had been secured as firmly as Ridhi's, leaned defiantly against each other. With four centuries of separation to make up for, Ridhi doubted they'd get tired of being able to touch in public for years.

Sulochana scoffed. "The problem *you* created?"

"Your Majesty!" exclaimed Queen Kauberi's advisor. "Such disparaging of your character is not to be tolerated!"

"How does speaking the truth equate to disparaging one's character?" asked Prakash from where he flanked Sulochana and Ishika. "Did our liege not originate the scheme to pilfer the branch?"

The advisor tutted. "Facile accusations benefit no one."

Sulochana had scarcely begun to retort when the doors to the chamber swung wide and another pair of guards ushered in Kamini and the sisterhood.

"Your Majesties," said a guard, "this party insisted on being admitted to your presence. They invoke their right to witness this audience."

His voice leaden with irony, the maharaja intoned, "Is that so?"

"Yes," said Hamshi. "We have come as representatives of the kingdom—and of the mortals on examination here."

"As I am feeling generous," said the maharani, "they may stay. For now."

The guards bowed and withdrew.

Queen Kauberi's frosty glare found Sulochana. "You would censure Malav's impetuous rebellion. Yet far more lamentable are the actions of his cousin, who thought to revenge herself upon me in this manner."

Sulochana seethed. "It was no less than you deserve, *Your Majesty*."

"And you!" Ishika lambasted the sisterhood. "What do you have to seek here? The mortals are of no import to you."

"On the contrary," said Ghanta. "Though we stand by Sulochana and you as always we have, the girl has earned our allegiance."

The advisors started speaking at once. Though Ridhi couldn't discern a word, she wasn't troubled. None of them knew the truth of the maharani's schemes, and Ridhi, as much as Queen Kauberi, aimed to keep it that way.

Ghanta smiled and murmured, "Your mother sends her greetings."

Mummy. Ridhi felt warmed down to her toes. Mummy had sent a message of faith, and, as the trees above pointed out, it hadn't even required any enchanted perfume.

That warmth reminded Ridhi that she had a job to do, and it didn't entail twisting her perfume for her own ends. Immersion was one thing, but she would never rob anyone of their agency.

Nor was it about gaining prestige she'd never yearned for in the first place. She wasn't a queen or a diplomat, and she had no designs on becoming either.

All Ridhi wanted was to set things to rights.

Yes, urged the trees. *Do so.*

Ridhi glanced at Nilesh. The yakshas couldn't fix this. Only she could. The Kalpavriksha itself had said as much. So why did she feel shy?

"Ready when you are," he said.

The simple statement shocked her out of her misgivings. Wasn't she expected to do this by herself?

But Nilesh was nudging her toward the thrones.

Ridhi swallowed, then projected her voice above the advisors' bickering. "Pardon me, Your Majesties, but may I speak now?"

Nilesh gave her an encouraging nod.

Maybe it was the mark of the forest on him, that rough patch of skin behind his ear, but Ridhi didn't think she'd ever be able to view Nilesh as cool again. He'd always be the goofball who'd gotten himself trapped in the yaksha kingdom and become a tree. A tree!

If the kids at the mandir only knew.

Of course, they never would; friends didn't rat out friends. Ridhi smiled in gratitude.

"Hush, children," said the advisor who'd been so concerned about the maharani's character. "We are preoccupied with matters whose significance far exceeds your comprehension."

What a pompous jerk. But Ridhi was done being bullied.

"Well," she said, so sweetly that the advisor's lofty arrogance deepened to venom, "since I *did* just help forestall a huge war between your kingdom and Svargalok, perhaps you can allot me a minute of your valuable time?"

Queen Kauberi quelled him with a look. "We shall hear her out, Vairaj. It is meet." She treated Ridhi to a favorable smile. "Ridhi, is it?"

"Yes, Your Majesty." Ridhi met the monarchs' gazes, one after the other. She was no simple toy Sulochana had brought forth for an afternoon's entertainment. She was the mortal who had liaised with the Kalpavriksha. The one appointed as its representative. "My thanks to you for hearing me out."

"It is true that you have aided us," said the maharani, "and we do not hold you accountable for Sulochana's treachery. Whatever she offered you, we will grant in her stead. You need merely set forth the terms—and, naturally, surrender the seed."

Caught off guard, Ridhi drew in a breath. Her mouth automatically formed the shape of *yakshini*. She'd already planned to hand over the seed, and it wasn't like Sulochana would be in any position to fulfill their bargain after this.

"No," she managed to say. "It's not that. I need to talk to you about Sulochana and Ishika. Oh, and the future."

"I see. Proceed."

"Y-yes." Ridhi cleared her throat. "So these subjects of yours have gainsaid you and brought the threat of war to your doorstep. I may have averted it, but unless you can resolve this situation, that's just a stopgap."

"This is old information," carped Vairaj. "Desist with your lolly-gagging."

Not so long ago, his rudeness might have caused her to shut down. Now it spurred her on. "Okay, but you don't know the solution."

"And *you* do?"

Ridhi answered slowly, deliberately. "I'm pretty sure I do, yes."

The advisors broke into a second round of vehement chatter. Sulochana and Ishika watched Ridhi with hopeful curiosity.

Queen Kauberi appraised her. "Do enlighten us."

"Your Majesty," Ridhi said, "please trust me when I say you will want to clear the room for this."

The monarchs held the sort of tacit conversation her parents were so partial to, an exhaustive dialogue carried out through slight muscular movements and head waggles. "A highly irregular request," King Kubera said, "yet we shall allow it."

"Your Majesty, I must contest this!" Vairaj protested.

"Overruled." The maharaja motioned curtly. "Clear the room. All but our prisoners."

The guards frowned. "Your Majesty—" one began.

"They are fettered. What could they do? Now go."

The guards saluted, and the chamber swiftly emptied. Vairaj lagged behind but grudgingly obeyed.

When Kamini didn't move, Ridhi realized she'd been manacled, too.

As soon as the doors had clanged shut, Queen Kauberi waved her hand, unshackling Ridhi and Nilesh. "Now, what is it you wish to relay that necessitated such secrecy?"

Ridhi felt strangely bare without the restraints. "My queen, I know Ishika didn't come up with this plan."

The maharani arched an eyebrow.

"You tried to negotiate with Lord Indra; if he wouldn't give you the Kalpavriksha outright, you said, a branch would do. But all he'd agree to was the ten-year ritual—which he could terminate whenever he felt like it. So you waited, and then, when you thought he'd become complacent, you enacted your plan to annex that branch."

"And why would I do this?" Queen Kauberi inquired, her face blank.

Ridhi was treading on dangerous ground. The shrewd thing

would be to retract her words and back down, like any sensible person would do.

But she never would have gotten here if she'd been sensible, so she plowed ahead. "You knew Ishika was sick of court politics and wanted to live free of the court. So you selected her for the ritual, coached her in private, and bade her hold her tongue while you awaited the outcome. If all went well, you'd get your Kalpavriksha. If not, she'd get the blame."

King Kubera's attitude transitioned from tolerant to baleful. "How dare you impugn my wife, mortal girl?"

Nilesh moved to screen Ridhi from the maharaja's ill temper. "She's just saying what the forest told us."

It was so still in the throne room—the trees themselves had checked their rustling—that Ridhi braced herself for a lashing of branches.

The maharani, however, smiled and stroked her husband's hand. "Continue, Ridhi. I find this narrative you contrive quite fascinating."

Nilesh stepped aside, and Ridhi took up her theory. "So you're in a pickle, Your Majesty. Ishika failed that day and hurt the Kalpavriksha, and everyone knew what she'd done. You had to punish her so no one would figure out your part in it."

"If this were so, why would I not simply demand the branch from her?"

Ridhi hesitated. "Because she'd hidden it from you. Except it was really Sulochana who did that."

A slight twitch around the maharani's left eye was the only inkling that Ridhi had startled her.

Sulochana made no effort to veil her smugness.

When the maharani didn't speak, Ridhi went on. "This time, they succeeded, but they did it through subterfuge and by flouting you. Which means you couldn't acknowledge them and set them free, even if the end result was exactly what you wanted. Everyone would always be suspicious of why."

"The mortal speaks verily," called Ishika. "You preserved your stature at all costs."

Ridhi saw how the maharaja leaned protectively toward his wife and hastened to intervene. "Pardon my impertinence, King Kubera, but I'm pretty sure you knew about this. The maharani would never have acted behind your back, any more than you would go behind hers."

For a few seconds, Ridhi feared he might strike her down. He was, after all, a mythic ruler accustomed to deference.

But he relaxed onto his throne. "All this rehashing of the past is well and good, yet you professed to have a solution for the current dilemma?"

"We're getting to that, Your Majesty. If I may beg your patience? The maharani asked what my reward would be, and I wish to answer her."

"Ah, so it *is* about your personal gratification." Queen Kauberi sounded oddly disappointed. "Well, go on. What would you have?"

It hurt to be dismissed by someone so powerful, but Ridhi cast that aside. "Sulochana would have won the parcel of land, right? For my performance?"

"Suppose she did," said the maharaja. "What of it?"

"Here's my solution. 'Exile' them there. Pardon them in absentia, as an act of your boundless mercy." The sentences tumbled out of Ridhi, as eager as she was to be done with this. "Then have your best musicians and composers write new ballads praising them. Start changing how you talk about them. By doing that, you'll overwrite the original story. As a bonus, you're ensuring yourself Sulochana and Ishika's silence."

The maharani seemed spellbound. "And then?"

"Once enough time has passed that the new stories have taken hold, let them come back if they want. Everyone wins!" Ridhi unclenched her palm. "The Kalpavriksha entreated me to pass its seed along to you—on those conditions."

Queen Kauberi's eyes narrowed. "You seek to extort me?"

But Ridhi sensed the exhaustion behind the irritation. It was the same exhaustion carved into Sulochana's and Ishika's cheeks. The maharani might be matchless in her beauty and mighty in her hold over the land, yet at her core, she, too, desired to move on from this mistake.

"Not at all," Ridhi said honestly. "I *want* to give you the seed. I want you to have a Kalpavriksha of your own."

"The tree wants to propagate itself," Nilesh put in, "as long as your realm is healthy." He bent his ear back for the monarchs' inspection. "I was its anchor, Your Majesty. Ridhi saved it. The Kalpavriksha is part of us, and it's tired of the fighting."

Ridhi could have hugged him. Later, she would.

"Lower your head," Queen Kauberi instructed her.

Ridhi did, and she felt the maharani's firm touch on her scalp. Agile fingers isolated a lock and brought it into the golden-green sunlight.

"Star jasmine. Yes. I should have seen it earlier; the forest has integrated you as its own."

Though Ridhi was dying to know what that referred to, she buttoned her lip.

"We would accede to this bargain," Sulochana abruptly declared. "I, for one, have had my fill of court intrigue."

"And I will never forget how speedily, how *thoroughly* I was condemned by those I held dear," Ishika said, sorrowing. "Alakapuri has long since ceased to be my home."

"I assume you wish my silence as well?" Prakash turned and wiggled his cuffed wrists. "Should you free us all, Kamini included, and name me sole proprietor of the elixir enterprise, Your Majesties, you will have it."

"Done." Another wave of the maharani's hand, and the last sets of golden shackles jangled on the floor. "With that, I pronounce the hostilities between us at an end. Lady Sulochana and Lady Ishika, my consort and I swear to send you off with a retinue and a subsequent pardon. Lord Prakash, you will also obtain a formal pardon and full control of your operation."

A beat of uncertainty ensued as her deathless eyes nearly gouged holes in each of them. "But that is not all. In exchange for my munificence, the six of you will maintain confidentiality on the matter forevermore."

Ridhi permitted herself an inward sigh of relief. She'd done it. She'd really done it.

"Thank you, Majesties," Sulochana said. "I appreciate your benevolence. Yet I would request one more favor."

Queen Kauberi waggled her head. "We will hear this request."

"It was Ridhi's intention to reside among our society; you would do worse than to change her into one of us."

"Is this, then, your truest wish, Ridhi?"

All the hunger, all the bottomless craving consolidated into one thing. A mekhala like the illusory one Ridhi had briefly crafted while dancing, opalescent with a spectrum of jewels, a symbol of all she was. All she would be. In her mind, the real mekhala manifested around her hips. It glittered with each movement.

But the words that spilled from her were ones she'd never imagined uttering. "One day, yes."

"As for Nilesh," Ishika said, "I also have a request. Lift the forest's claim on him. His was a miscalculation borne of emotion; he need not pay an eternal price for his rashness."

"What of his debt to Rakesh?" asked the maharaja. "I sense it on him, as much as he is also bound to our forest."

The maharani considered briefly. She rang the bell next to her throne, and the doors parted. As if he'd had his ear jammed against them, Vairaj stumbled into the chamber.

Queen Kauberi's lips thinned. "Vairaj, I would see the boy. Fetch him, if you would."

He gestured feverishly. Not long after, more guards led Malav forward.

His eyes flicked to Ridhi's, then away.

She'd thought she'd be furious, but she actually felt sad. They hadn't known each other, not really. For her, he'd stepped into the role of fairy-tale prince. For him, she'd been a mortal he could convert to his cause.

He'd planned that from the instant Sulochana assigned him to her, Ridhi recognized at last. If it hadn't been her, it would have been some other girl.

The maharaja gazed down at Malav with overt disapproval. "We have heard that you spearheaded a campaign to recoup mortal lands. Alas, you did so without soliciting the proper authorization first."

Malav's visage was volcanic. "You may be content to sit by while we are dispossessed of everything, Majesties, yet I am not. Nor am I alone in that sentiment."

Queen Kauberi cocked her head. "What was it you thought to achieve with your little rebellion?"

"Mortals have destroyed so much. They would reshape the world until it was uninhabitable. I would have won back what they stripped from nature."

The monarchs conferred in low voices.

He'd been planning to raze entire cities, Ridhi knew, but she was fresh out of righteous anger. Maybe there was a more benign way to help reintroduce nature on Prithvi. Maybe she could be part of it, whatever it was.

"Your Majesties," she blurted, "what if Malav served the rest of Nilesh's debt to the chaturanga players?"

"Ah, yes, mortal Nilesh." Queen Kauberi traded a knowing glance with her consort. Something about the gesture unnerved Ridhi. She wished she could hide Nilesh like he'd hidden her moments before.

"He was so very willing to be an anchor," mused the maharani. "Perhaps he will do so anew."

Ridhi coughed. "Your Majesties, please!"

"No!" Sulochana and Ishika said simultaneously. "You cannot do this," Ishika added. "It is mossbacked behavior!"

Queen Kauberi laughed. "You would presume to command us?"

"Mossbacked or not, we have arrived at our decision," said King Kubera. "You, Malav, are confined to the perimeter of Alakapuri until further notice. Should you be so bold as to attempt to depart, you will find that no tree will open to you."

With Malav impassively monitoring the marble floor, Ridhi couldn't tell whether she should feel sympathy or relief. Once more she thought that, while his means were questionable, his message wasn't.

She remembered her other promise to the wish tree. "Your Majesties, pardon the interruption, but the Kalpavriksha begs clemency for Malav. It is right and fitting that he takes over Rakesh's claim on Nilesh, yes. Absolutely. But—"

"Yes?" the maharani urged.

"Both the Kalpavriksha and I request a second chance for him after that. He's young and brash, and everyone deserves the opportunity to grow and improve."

"Sage counsel. We will abide by it." Queen Kauberi smiled. "And you, mortal Nilesh, may return home. Thus, the terms of the temporal debt will be paid. The claim of the forest, on the other hand . . ."

"What claim?" Ridhi asked, but she suspected the answer. From the way Nilesh's expression darkened, so did he.

He was bound to the forest, and the maharaja and maharani *were* the forest, its beating heart. They wouldn't let him slip away so readily.

"Your Majesties?" whispered Kamini timorously. Ridhi had almost forgotten she was there. "Surely not?"

King Kubera had regained his paternal air. "Every action has a consequence, dear Kamini, and this boy made his choice. Just as you must live with the consequences of your actions."

Kamini's mother. No one had to say it. Ridhi empathized, yet there was nothing she could do.

"Thank you, Your Majesties," Nilesh said. She hadn't seen him this stoic since before his parents separated. "Let's go, Ridhi."

"Yes, thank you," she hurried to say. "But . . ."

"But?" repeated the maharaja.

"You don't need Nilesh. I'll be your ambassador. Malav's not wrong. You need someone to bridge our worlds and help facilitate communication. Earth—Prithvi—can't keep going the way it is, and you can't stay cut off from us. I can do that."

"Oh, but I think we shall have both," purred the maharani. Her exquisite features had the quality of a self-satisfied panther. "You as our emissary and Nilesh as our anchor."

"Your Majesty!" Ridhi was no better than a bumbling child. Why had she imagined she could hold her own in a yaksha court?

"When you sacrificed parts of yourself to the Kalpavriksha, you became ours and were marked as such." The maharani consulted her consort. "Is that not so, my lotus flower?"

"It is," the maharaja confirmed, as implacable as Papa when he put his foot down.

Guards had reentered the chamber and were conducting everyone else through the doors. The monarchs weren't brooking any arguments, that much was evident.

"This is the mandate we hand down," said Queen Kauberi. "For one month each summer, from full moon to full moon, you, mortal Nilesh, shall journey here to live among us as a tree."

A muscle in Nilesh's jaw convulsed, but he was smart enough to keep his own counsel.

Ridhi touched his arm. Though she didn't yet know how, she swore she would find a way to help him.

"As for you, mortal Ridhi, the mekhala and all that it represents shall be waiting for you in exchange for the seed. In the interim, you will both find that your pledge binds you more strongly than you might have anticipated."

Bowing her head, Ridhi held out the seed. "Accept this as freely given, rather than stolen, Your Majesties. *That* is what caused the wish tree to sicken."

"So be it." The maharani plucked the seed from Ridhi's palm. "You may take your leave."

The audience was over, even if Ridhi still had questions. Which she definitely did.

"Come on," said Nilesh. "Let's go home."

Ridhi was certain her enchanted woods had never shone more brilliantly than they did that day. Nilesh and the others had gone ahead to the entrance so she'd have some privacy.

Her beloved trees rustled, heralding the coming of the yakshini sisterhood—all except Sulochana. They appeared as softly as falling leaves to surround Ridhi in a semicircle.

"You will always have a place among us, little sister," said Shatapratika. "Whether tonight or in fifty years, you need but call for us, and the path will show itself to you."

The old pining resurfaced, the vision of Ridhi as yakshini with her companion tree. Her body, her heart, hungered for it. But she thought of the Kalpavriksha and the bond that had formed between them. Even now, she bore its etheric energy. "One day."

She had work to do on Prithvi, as its covert ambassador to the yaksha kingdom. Mortals had neglected the old stories, their connection to the land, and through her perfumery, she would help them remember. In her bag were more of Malav's miniature forests for transplanting and a crown of lotuses Kamini had gifted her.

And whichever side of the portal she found herself on, the land was Ridhi's friend. Nothing could diminish that.

"One day, but not yet," she said staunchly, before she could backtrack.

Then she pivoted in the direction of home, where Nilesh and her family awaited her.

28

Nilesh kicked at his backpack. It was weird seeing Kamini outside his house. She didn't belong there any more than it felt like he did.

But Amar, Hetal, and Ridhi all stood there, too, and he *did* belong with them.

"We'll be inside," Hetal said. She jerked her head at Amar, then wheeled herself through the front door.

Amar chucked Nilesh on the chin. "Don't disappear on us again, buddy. I already had to go into the woods for you once. *The woods.* You owe me."

And then it was just the three of them. Well, and Ridhi's family waiting in their car at the end of the driveway, half hidden by the trees.

The world was so green. How had Nilesh never really noticed before?

Kamini held out her cupped hands, which were filled with a dozen bright purple strawberries that smelled like candy, but better.

"Moonberries," she said. "Eat all but one, and hold that one in reserve. Plant it when the moon stands at its highest, and you will be repaid ten times over with a bumper crop of this natural confection."

Nilesh didn't answer. The magic fruit reminded him too much of everything that had happened between them. He still wasn't sure how he felt about it.

"That sounds great to me," Ridhi said. She took half the berries and left the other six on the window ledge for him.

Nilesh didn't care about the moonberries, but with Kamini and Ridhi watching, he made himself eat three.

Even though he'd fought to get home, he was afraid to go in. He'd have to confront the fallout, not just of running away, but of his family. All the broken bits.

Ridhi watched him with obvious concern.

"I'm not going anywhere," he said, exasperated. Of course he wasn't. They were way past that.

"I shall tend to you during that month each year," Kamini promised. "And there is yet the quest for a solution to the forest's claim on the both of you. Such terms might be altered, if not annulled."

"Maybe something will turn up at the Night Market?" Ridhi suggested. "It's not like I won't have tons of chances to check."

"For your mom, too," Nilesh said to Kamini. "We'll find something to help."

He pointed to Ridhi's curl, the one that had transformed into a sprig of jasmine blossoms. More of the little white stars had bloomed since the maharani touched it. Nilesh wondered if Ridhi guessed how much it made her look like the yakshini she wished she were.

"But *you* always wanted that," he told her. "To be stuck there. Talk to the flowers, that kind of thing." He fingered the itchy patch behind his ear. "Not me. No offense, Kamini."

"You believed me unaware of that fact?" She pretended to bear down on him. "Moreover, you and I will be seeing quite a bit of each other even outside your term of bondage. I hope you are prepared for more pinball."

Nilesh tried to seem grossed out, but he wasn't fooling anyone, least of all Ridhi.

"We'll get through it together," she said. "One month at a time."

"If you come visit me, it won't be so bad. A couple of days here, a couple of days there . . ."

She nodded. "Of course I will. Amar and your sister, too."

Now that he'd had some time to think about it, Nilesh didn't mind the obligation as much. After all that running, it wouldn't hurt to be still once in a while. Find some of that peace Ishika had shown him.

A horn honked, and they both jumped. Only Kamini didn't react.

"Seems like Kartik's ready to go," Ridhi said. She slipped something into Nilesh's hand, then ran to her car.

And then there were two.

Nilesh opened his hand. It was the perfume he'd never given back, Damayanti and the Swan.

Kamini started to touch his cheek but tugged on his earlobe

instead. "It is time for you to go, too, mortal boy. Go and be with your family."

"What if I don't want to?" he challenged, to keep the conversation going. He wasn't ready to face Dad. He might never be.

Like always, she saw right through him. "But you do."

Nilesh broke her profile into parts, the defined cheekbones, the curve of her jaw, the slope of her nose. She was so hot, so mysterious. There was no denying that. What little he'd seen of her had been wild and intense, like a roller coaster full of twists and turns.

But he didn't actually know the person behind all that, just the person he'd needed her to be.

Maybe that could change. Maybe not. They had time to figure it out.

"Fine," he said. "I do."

Kamini fed him two more moonberries and stowed the last one in his backpack, next to his phone. "Delectable, are they not?"

Nilesh couldn't lie. The moonberries had gotten better with every bite. "Yeah."

She smiled, satisfied. "All will be to the good. Go and be brave."

And then an orange vixen bounded away from him and into the trees.

Nilesh shouldered the backpack. Then he turned the knob and went home.

"Don't ever do that again," Mom croaked, exhausted. She almost asphyxiated Nilesh in a hug. Then she rumpled his hair. "Dad's in there. I'll be in the kitchen if you need me."

His mouth dry, Nilesh continued into the den. Even knowing what it was, he still wished he had the dewdrop opal to hold on to. But he did have Ridhi's perfume, so he rolled that instead.

Dad stood from the recliner and cleared his throat. He'd become a guest in the house he'd bought and lived in since before Nilesh was born. "Beta. I'm glad you're home."

"Where's What's Her Name? The *girlfriend*?" Nilesh hadn't meant to come off so sullen, but he couldn't help it.

Dad winced. "She's gone. I ended things."

It took all his leftover willpower, but Nilesh curbed the million vindictive things he could've said. They wouldn't help anybody.

"When you ran away," Dad said, "it gave me time to think. Your sister told me I was being selfish, and at first, I didn't listen."

Hetal had said that? What a curveball.

"But then, when we didn't know what happened to you, I realized she was right. I was putting my own happiness ahead of your welfare. So I told Janaki now was the wrong time."

"What did she say?" Nilesh asked.

Dad chuckled sheepishly. "She told me I had wasted her time and she never wanted to see me again."

Nilesh folded his arms. "Sounds fair. What about the apartment?"

Mom reappeared behind Dad. "He's keeping it."

Hearing that triggered a landslide in Nilesh's stomach. He hadn't known he'd still been hoping. "But . . ."

His parents faced each other. They didn't look madly in love anymore, but they didn't look like they had after the gala, either, when he was sure they were about to inspire a true-crime documentary. They'd made peace with the situation—and with each other.

"We've been lying to ourselves for a long time, beta," Dad said. "Your running away forced us to confront that."

"So you're *not* getting back together?" But even as Nilesh asked the question, he didn't feel angry or crushed. A little demoralized, sure. That was it.

He remembered what Amar had said. Lots of people's parents got divorced. Hell, Kamini's mom was a tree, and not just for one month a year. Life still went on.

"No," Mom replied, while Dad shook his head.

"But you're still going to be our top priority," he said. "You and Hetal."

"We'd better be!" Hetal said, coming up next to Mom while Amar sidled up to Nilesh with a party-sized bag of chips.

"And now," said Mom, sounding more like her old self, "let's have a chat about how long you're going to be grounded. Because it's never okay to worry us like that. We were about to call the police!"

Nilesh didn't argue. He just glanced from his family to his best friend. For the first time, he thought maybe they really would get through this, after all.

29

It was a tight fit in Ridhi's bedroom, what with Mummy, Papa, and Kartik all huddled before the closet. But this was her chance to make things up to them.

She was taking her family to the Night Market, where she planned to treat them to the wares of their choosing.

Mummy seized her in a tight hug. It was as if she feared Ridhi might vanish again, this time for good. Ridhi returned the hug, pleased to prove that fear wrong.

But Kartik still wasn't talking to her, and that ripped her heart in two. She extricated herself from Mummy's grasp and touched his shoulder.

"I'm sorry," she said, hoping he would hear her this time. "I really am."

"You hurt me," he told the floor. His chin trembled.

Ridhi could hear how frightened he, too, had been of losing her. It might be a while before he forgave that.

She gulped hard. "I know. I'm so sorry."

"You'd better buy me something really nice," he said, trying to smile.

"I will." Ridhi's heart skipped with relief. "And I swear I'll bake all the cookies you want for the rest of the season."

Kartik sniffled but met her eyes. "You'd better! I want some more doughnuts, too. With lilacs."

She laughed. "I'll see what I can do."

Papa put his arms around both of them, then indicated the closet. "Remind me again why we're walking into a closet?"

Mummy had previously explained to Papa that magic was real, even if she had forgotten it until recently. But Ridhi knew he wouldn't believe anyone's testimony until he saw the evidence for himself.

"Someone had to take over Sulochana's stall," she pointed out. Praying that the portal wouldn't pick that moment to go rogue, she opened the double doors.

The coruscating expanse of the Night Market unspooled before her, ever-changing tents and stalls, ever-changing wares and vendors, ever-constant source of whimsy. Behind her, Ridhi heard Mummy's and Papa's joint intakes of breath. Since they couldn't see her face, she indulged in a smirk.

"That's so cool!" Kartik exclaimed. Before Ridhi could tell him to wait, he crashed through the closet.

Papa and Mummy barreled after him. "Slow down!" called Mummy.

Well, that took care of the incredulity issue. Ridhi grabbed her box of perfumes and gave chase.

The Market really must have been on its best behavior. Rather than sending her family all around its substantial breadth, it had permitted them to stay together. She found them assembled outside the stall Sulochana had vacated and bequeathed to her.

"This is my stall now," Ridhi said, holding out against the urge to do a little dance. She had to look professional for her clientele.

Yet she couldn't breathe freely until she had touched the swag of branches and witnessed its flowers fruit into berries. Red and gold and blue and purple, shining like the most precious jewels of the yaksha kingdom. Just as Sulochana had promised, the stall had accepted Ridhi as its owner and would protect her perfumes in her absence.

As if they'd been waiting for that signal, customers began lining up.

Mummy looked on with absolute euphoria. "Beti," she murmured, "this is amazing!"

"I know!" The joy of sharing this with her, the joy Ridhi had been certain she would never know again, was like the moment she'd first divined the leaves.

She set about unloading her latest scent, Bejeweled Branch. Papa, his hands clasped behind his back, observed while Ridhi haggled with all the style of the stall's previous owner. No matter what the customer's disposition—irascible, apprehensive, eager— she didn't miss a beat.

"We taught you well," said Papa after the fifth sale. "I'm so proud."

But Kartik's well of patience had run dry. "I wanna go explore!" he whined. "You said we could buy things."

Finishing up with her last customer, Ridhi closed her stall. "I did say that, and you can. Listen up."

She went through the rules of the Market again: be careful not to part with what truly mattered, do not be talked into a bad bargain, and think through the implications before purchasing.

Then she took her family shopping.

They saw, among other things, the breath of a dakini; the dream of a turtle; a kinnara's lullaby; lanterns that burned brightest when fueled by bliss and dimmest when fueled by despair; a bracelet strung with planets both familiar and strange; a spool of oil slick–colored thread for sewing up plot holes in a story; the loaded dice that had cost the Pandava brothers their freedom in the *Mahabharata*; a shard of Lord Ganesh's broken tusk; and an umbrella that shielded the wielder from the ravages of time, but only as long as it was in use.

Between stalls, they passed a beautiful girl with elegant features and starlight tresses that tumbled down her back. She grinned at a cute mortal boy with wavy black hair and a mischievous expression. He straightened the girl's starry circlet, and then, as one, they began to sing.

Ridhi hadn't heard anything like it. The music was an enchantment, a spell to drop the listener right into a wonder tale, just like her perfumes. The duo narrated the saga of the night sky, the history of the heavens, in voices like the cadence of the constellations. In response, the dark chambers of Ridhi's heart kindled with starshine, as though someone had lit a silver sparkler inside them.

When the song ended, she burst into boisterous applause and pleaded for an encore. The girl, who had laced her fingers through the boy's, declined. But before they could slip away, a nagini with a gold snake armband, a pair of twin sisters, and a second boy—this one with soulful eyes—cornered them.

"Sssssuch a marvelous song!" hissed the nagini, her stream of black hair undulating behind her like serpents. Beside her, one twin looked serious and wary, while the other clung contrarily to the second boy's arm. The boy himself held a glowing vial shaped from a sapphire, and Ridhi heard the word *dreams*. A dream seller?

She thought to ask, yet in the next instant, all six were gone, spirited elsewhere by the Market.

Still afloat on the memory of the melody, Ridhi and her family coasted into another tent.

Eventually, Mummy selected a sari made all of peacock feathers and half an ounce each of ground moonsilver and sungold flakes.

Papa picked out a kaleidoscope that, by turns, showed glimpses of disparate universes.

Kartik pounced on a set of literal shadow puppets, which kept slinking away from him.

And Ridhi, who could never say no to greenery of any kind, bought a padmamukhi plant in a minuscule pond. Its pink lotus petals sheathed a tiny, rose-skinned girl with waist-length violet locks, ovate silver eyes, and a lotus-shaped mouth that alternated between chanting mantras and telling random, inscrutable fortunes.

"Ridhi," Mummy said, looping an arm around her waist, "you

may go far. You may even leave us for the forest one day. But that day had better be far in the future, and until then, don't you dare forget you belong at home. With us."

"*And* you're my sister!" Kartik pointed out. "Don't forget that, either."

"And I'm your sister," Ridhi acknowledged with a chuckle. "There's a vendor here who sells crystallized flame candies. As hot as the heart of Lord Surya, he says. Want to see if we can find him?"

Everyone acquiesced enthusiastically, and as a family, they continued wandering the winding lanes of the Night Market.

A week later, another halcyon spring Saturday had dawned, flush with flowers and sunshine. Ridhi woke early and smuggled herself out for a stroll under the verdant canopy that covered the neighborhood. She tarried longer than she'd intended, attempting to personally greet each plant and laud each blossom she came across. As one, they embraced her, rooting her to the land.

When she returned home, Mummy opened the front door before Ridhi could. She was so blatantly trying to hide good news that Ridhi giggled.

"Remember the last boutique we went to?" Mummy burbled. "The one run by the auntie?"

That disaster of a day felt like a millennium ago, and since then, both Ridhi's online shop and her stall at the Night Market had garnered more sales. "Swati's Sweeties?"

The elation Mummy had been fighting to suppress rippled across her face, as bright as a field of buttercups. "The Night Market's not the only place you're in demand. Swati Auntie wants you to come back in. She was looking for you at the mandir, but you'd already left."

"Wait, what?" Ridhi replayed Mummy's words. "When?"

"How about now, my little nemophilist?"

Ever since Mummy had learned that term for someone who was fond of forests and haunted the woods, it had become her favorite endearment for Ridhi.

Ridhi hid her smile. "Now sounds good."

In her room, she pulled on a set of salwar kameez that conjured images of Alakapuri with its floral and leafy patterns. Then she made herself up and donned ample accessories to match, including the lotus crown from Kamini.

Ridhi inspected her reflection. If she said so herself, she looked fantastical, like a figure out of myth, with the sprig of jasmine barely peeping out of her curls. A purveyor of fine fragrances, the sought-after sort that swept her customers away to other lands and eras.

Speaking of, she had one final detail to tackle: a dab of Keeper of the Woodlands on both sides of her collarbone.

When at last she came down, Nilesh and Amar were waiting in the foyer. "We were in the neighborhood," Amar joked.

Nilesh elbowed him. "Your mom texted me. We'll take you."

Seeing them there, Ridhi felt safe. She wasn't alone. She had friends, both in Alakapuri and on Prithvi.

Mummy kissed her forehead, then shooed her out the door. "What are you waiting for? Go have fun. And good luck!"

Nilesh parked in front of Swati's Sweeties. "All right, everybody out."

Amar opened the door for Ridhi and scooped the box of perfumes off her lap. "You heard the man. Let's do this."

She reminded herself that it didn't matter how Swati Auntie had originally reacted to her. It didn't even matter whether the store stocked her perfumes after this visit or not. She was a success at the Night Market—she had her own stall, which she still couldn't quite fathom—*and* she'd wished upon the Kalpavriksha. Who else could say the same?

So really, there was no reason to be agitated.

Still, Ridhi's nerves refused to settle. What if Chetan Gopalkrishnan was there? Even after everything, the idea of him filled her with dread.

Yet flanked by Nilesh and Amar, who weren't about to let her turn around, she had no choice but to walk toward the boutique. If Chetan tried anything to spoil the moment, he'd have to contend with them. He had to know better than that.

Didn't he?

The three of them went inside.

The plants—more than there had been last time—spun out in welcome, vines creeping closer, buds blossoming, leaves unfurling. The previously bare shelves had been stocked with attractive ornaments for the home and fashionable Indian and nature-derived jewelry. Not only was it a store Ridhi would want to shop at, but her perfumes would fit right in.

Yet one thing tainted the scene. Just as she'd feared, Chetan leaned over the counter, hassling the girl from before. He cut off whatever crude joke he was in the middle of to goggle at Ridhi. "What're you *wearing*? Lotuses?"

Nilesh started to speak, but Ridhi didn't need him to. Her trepidation sharpened into bark-hard certainty. Chetan wasn't going to ruin this. She wouldn't let him.

She went up to the counter and greeted the girl. "Hi."

"You look like a dork—" Chetan went on.

"Shut up, Chetan," Ridhi and the girl said at the same time. They swapped amused glances, and Ridhi noticed how lovely the other girl's dark-brown eyes were. And, of course, that teal streak in her glossy hair.

"Don't you have anything better to do than stalk me?" the girl went on. "What, did your friends get sick of you or something?"

Chetan faltered. Without another word, he disappeared into the back.

Nilesh and Amar must have taken that as their cue, too, because they dropped off the box and moseyed over to an arrangement of handmade Indian elephant-and-parasol garlands.

The girl dusted off her hands, as if to be done with Chetan. Her gaze pierced through Ridhi. "Sorry about that. He's my cousin, so I can't just kick him out. I'm Jyoti, by the way."

"Hi." Ridhi felt an unaccountable rush of shyness. Dragonflies must have set up house in her belly, since they chose that moment to begin gamboling. "I'm looking for Swati Auntie. She asked me to come in?"

Jyoti burst into giggles. "Oh, Swati's my mom!" she rambled. "I tried your samples and made a whole big case about getting in on this before someone else does. She didn't have a chance. They're so good! They smell like magic. I felt like each one took me somewhere new, you know?"

Ridhi didn't trust herself to answer, not with the astonishment effervescing within her. She felt like a can of soda someone had shaken up.

To keep from exploding, she pulled out the packets of wildflower seeds she planned to bundle with the perfumes, blessed by the sisterhood and guaranteed to grow. Each flower would spread its own pollen—and with it, the wisdom of Alakapuri's trees. Not just rewilding, not just restoring, but re-storying.

Jyoti leaned closer. "I have to tell you, I love your look. That whole fusion fantasy aesthetic? Totally works for you."

Sitayana wafted from her, and the familiar notes of ginger lily and palmarosa went straight to Ridhi's head. She wouldn't have predicted her own perfume could do that to her.

She found herself reaching for her pendant of Aranyani Devi. "Thanks. I like it, too."

Jyoti produced the sample vials and tapped the top of each. "My mom will have to sign off on the order—she's in the back—but we'll start with three of each and go from there. If they sell, which I'm totally sure they will, we'll see about increasing the order." She shook her head. "My mom's still learning the ropes. We moved here a couple of months ago from Washington, and she's worried she'll do everything wrong. But it's always been her dream to own a store, so here we are!

"Anyway." She tucked a lock of hair behind her ear. "Here I am, talking your ear off. Sorry about that. I'll go get my mom, but first I wanted to ask if you're into tabletop role-playing games. I joined a campaign a few weeks ago, and you might like it. You know, if you want."

Jyoti was nervous! As nervous as Ridhi herself.

Did that mean . . . Jyoti was asking her out?

Jyoti pushed the vial of Sitayana toward her, and their fingers brushed. A current akin to static electricity yet far more compelling leaped between them. Ridhi went rigid, afraid to hope, but Jyoti left her hand where it was. "You should come," she said. "It'll be fun."

Ridhi had her initial order for the store, yet she couldn't focus on anything except the soft feel of Jyoti's skin and the vestige of interest in her pretty face.

A date with a girl who liked her perfumes!

Bubbles in her belly again, Ridhi smiled broadly. "I'd love to."

The flowers around them—amaryllis, daylilies, and begonias—bloomed even bigger, more aromatic. Maybe someday soon, she could point that out and demonstrate how it worked.

"Campaign? Sounds fun." Like a bat diving from the sky, Nilesh appeared out of the blue. "I'm in." He nudged her. "I'm *game* to try it with you. Get it?"

"Me, too," said Amar. "Sounds cool."

Where had they both come from? And why? Ridhi willed them to get lost.

Nilesh winked. Oh, he knew exactly what he was doing. As soon as they got outside, she was going to kill him.

Jyoti's nostrils flared with annoyance. "Great, I guess." She exchanged another private look with Ridhi, and they both grinned.

Ridhi decided she could live with that.

ACKNOWLEDGMENTS

This book had quite the challenging journey to publication, but we made it! Flower bouquets and thanks to:

Diana DeVault, my cottagecore girl, for being you. But also for the thoughtful suggestions and reassurance and shared love of typewriter teapots. You're as sweet as your lavender-marshmallow perfume.

Lindsey Márton O'Brien, my lotus-hearted yakshini, for everything. And specifically for Ridhi's fragrance formulations—you are magic!—and taking such joy in being read to. You're stuck with me, darling.

Michael P. Vuoncino, my eternal cheerleader, for your level-headed help and staunch yet practical faith whenever I need it. You're pretty much the best.

Leanna Renee Hieber, my sunshine Goth, for your commiseration, your fantastic ideas, and your love. All the bats and blueberry-rosemary scones for you.

Aryasura, for being the perfect life partner for me and never doubting that I could pull this off. Thank you for always supporting this dream of mine and nudging me whenever I need it.

Angela Shannon of Folk Owl, for Ridhi's flower-garden purse! I adore my real-life version.

Janet Chui and Jason Erik Lundberg, for originally publishing my field guide entry about Padmamukhi (my first story sale!). It was so fun to give her to Ridhi all these years later.

Christina Allen Page, for originally commissioning "Autumn Jewels" for your subscription box. I'm so happy it gets a second life as a tale the trees tell!

Grace Nuth, for our mutual love of faerie crowns and for Ridhi's love of the forest.

Jennifer Hubbard, for the suggestion of winter elixir and having the same thought I did about sunlit leaves resembling stained glass.

Sara Cleto, for telling me about Atlanta's protected trees and showing me around the city.

Vashti Bandy, for tossing out ideas with me, even if the book then spun off in its own unpredictable direction, as books so often do.

Renee Melton, for spending all that time on the phone with me to brainstorm a plot about phyllomancy and the forest.

Angie Richmond, for your delight at learning this book was happening and your encouragement through the various drafts.

Annaka Kalton, for reading and critiquing the manuscript at that incredibly critical stage. This book wouldn't be what it is now without you. A million hugs.

Lisa Eshkenazi of Steamberry Studio, for swooping in and reading when you saw I desperately needed help. A million hugs to you, too.

Kelsey Lecky and Meenoo Mishra, my wheelie girls, for generously vetting the portrayal of Hetal's disability. Any remaining mistakes are mine.

Jialu Bao, Nivair Gabriel, Charlotte Lily Gaspard, Kimberly Hatch Harrison, Jae Koyanagi, Claire Legrand, and Cassidy Ward for believing in me.

Laini Taylor and the delightful community of patrons you've curated around our collective love of fantasy. Thank you all for cheering me on.

Stephanie Stein, for snapping up the proposal for this book and then helping navigate my messy first few drafts. Sophie Schmidt, for your smart comments on those drafts. Elizabeth Agyemang, for meeting me at the finish line, and to Clare Vaughn, for picking up the torch from there. Thanks also to Gweneth Morton, Jessica Berg, Veronica Ambrose, and Vanessa Nuttry.

Beth Phelan, for all your work helping refine and then placing the proposal for this book.

Jane Putch, for your endless well of wisdom and savvy and your enthusiasm for my words. I appreciate you so very much.

Charlie Bowater and Corina Lupp, you two miracle workers, for this book's gorgeous illustration and title treatment! I am in absolute awe at my ongoing incredible fortune in regard to covers.

Barkha Patel and Shachi Phene of Aangan, for your lovely literature festival and your vetting of Ridhi's audition scene. I hope your students love the book.

Lunar Hine, for your kindness and support of my writing.

Terri Windling, both for first putting phyllomancy on my radar and then graciously allowing me to excerpt your poem, "The Night Journey," for an epigraph.

Kalidasa, for all your wonderful literature, particularly *Meghaduta*. What a gift to connect through your work despite the many centuries separating us.

Lord Indra and the yakshas and yakshinis—Sulochana, Kubera

Raja, and Kauberi Rani in particular—for permitting me to indulge in fan fiction of your lore. I hope I did you justice with my modern rendering.

Aranyani, divine patroness of forests, for letting me reference you and your dancing ways.

And Devi, as always, this book is my heart song to you. ॐ